THE BELGRADE CONSPIRACY

JASON KASPER

Severn River Publishing
SevernRiverBooks.com

ISBN: 978-1-64875-392-3 (Paperback)

ALSO BY JASON KASPER

American Mercenary Series
Greatest Enemy
Offer of Revenge
Dark Redemption
Vengeance Calling
The Suicide Cartel
Terminal Objective

Shadow Strike Series
The Enemies of My Country
Last Target Standing
Covert Kill
Narco Assassins
Beast Three Six
The Belgrade Conspiracy
Lethal Horizon

Spider Heist Thrillers
The Spider Heist
The Sky Thieves
The Manhattan Job
The Fifth Bandit

Standalone Thriller
Her Dark Silence

To find out more about Jason Kasper and his books, visit severnriverbooks.com/authors/jason-kasper

To Joshua Thoma

Inter Meos Fratres Et Mortem Sto

In difficult situations when hope seems feeble, the boldest plans are the safest.

-Titus Livius

Make no mistake, the hydra is still out there and waiting to strike again. And it's going to remain the only threat we need to concern ourselves with until Project Longwing locates it and finds a way to kill it for good.

-Duchess

1

Belgrade, Serbia

I pulled open the glass door and stepped inside, holding it ajar for Worthy to enter behind me. Given the frigid November temperatures, I was more than happy to enter a heated establishment.

Rubbing my gloved hands together, I appraised the store interior to find an elderly man carrying two bottles of wine toward a checkout counter, where a single clerk nodded toward me with the greeting, "*Popodne*."

"*Zdravo*," I replied, procuring a shopping basket from a stack beside the door and leading Worthy toward the aisles.

I was quite used to feeling like an outsider—even, and perhaps especially, in the peaceful civilian existence that was my life in America. Grocery stores, polite dinner parties, and my daughter's school events were all alien settings where I didn't belong.

Liquor stores, by contrast, were more or less a second home regardless of country.

I strode the aisles with a discerning eye, dismayed to note the *burbon* selection was limited to a few major brands without a drop of Woodford Reserve to be found. Scotch was far more abundant, exceeding the combined bottles of all the gin, rum, and tequila in the store. There was also a shockingly robust selection of cognac, but not until I rounded a corner was I met with this establishment's real specialty: a full wall of rakia, a fruit brandy that was wildly popular in the Balkans and nowhere else. Serbia alone had over ten thousand private producers, of which roughly one percent didn't consist of hangovers in a bottle.

So I kept to the top shelf, selecting three of the more expensive options to deposit in my basket.

Worthy tapped me on the shoulder, and I turned to see that the lone customer had completed his purchase and was making for the exit.

I unzipped my coat and took a circuitous route to the register, ostensibly perusing the shelves before giving a sidelong glance out the glass door to make sure no one else was approaching. With that confirmed, I set my basket beside the register and appraised the clerk.

He was probably in his twenties, with a barely-there goatee and an apron bearing the store logo and a name tag that read *BOJAN*.

"*Je li to sve?*" he asked.

"*Da, Bojan,*" I answered, reaching into my coat pocket as he scanned the first bottle. Once he set it down, I drew a taser and leveled it over the counter, firing twin probes that speared into his chest and abdomen.

He went completely rigid and fell backward, grimacing with the 50,000-volt pulse that surged through his system as I kept the trigger depressed and hoisted myself to a sitting position atop the counter. A switch somewhere was linked to a silent alarm, though not to summon police—at this point, they were the least of our concerns. If he managed to activate it, we were in for a hell of a ride.

Worthy vaulted the counter beside me, descending on the man and cocking back a fist. I let off the trigger, seeing the cashier's face go momentarily slack with relief before my partner delivered a vicious knockout strike.

"Go," he said.

Tossing the taser over the counter, I left Worthy to gag and restrain the man with flex cuffs while I moved swiftly to the front door and engaged the deadbolt. Then I flipped the hanging sign to indicate the store was officially closed for business, turned to face the service door on the back wall, and pulled aside my coat to access the weapon held against my side by a short elastic sling.

The H&K MP7 was marketed as a personal defense weapon, though its capabilities served equally well in an offensive capacity. Larger than a pistol but smaller than most submachine guns, the compact weapon in my hands packed a 20-round magazine loaded with armor-piercing 4.6mm ammunition, its total length almost doubled by the suppressor until I extended the buttstock.

I slipped alongside the checkout counter, seeing that Worthy was already rising and putting his identical weapon into operation. As I closed the distance to the service door leading to the back rooms, he retrieved a violet box from the most expensive rakia bottle and set it on the counter—a decidedly un-tactical move that I'd give him hell for later.

Pulling twin radio earpieces from beneath my coat collar, I inserted them in sequence and whispered a transmission.

"Front is clear, start the count."

"*Ten*," Cancer replied over the team net as I took up a position beside the door, angling my suppressor toward the handle. By the time he reached seven I heard Worthy fall in behind me, followed by a squeeze of my shoulder to let me know he was ready.

"*Five*," Cancer transmitted, and I leaned forward to check the door handle—if it was locked, Worthy would have to kick that fucker in.

My fingertips found purchase on the handle, and I gingerly tested it only to find it spin clockwise of its own accord. By then Cancer was at his three count, and I interrupted him to whisper a transmission.

"Target to your twelve—execute."

Cancer was poised outside the back door, prepared to enter as the first of his split team with Reilly serving as the number two man. He responded to David's transmission by giving a quick nod.

The act queued Ian to hoist his battering ram upward and outward, and Cancer had only the duration of its downward swing to consider the radio message. A target to his twelve meant he'd be engaging someone the moment he entered, which was of particular note given the two split teams would be assaulting toward each other from opposite sides of a short corridor. In between, if the intelligence reports were to be believed, were a couple small rooms, two relatively large rooms, and three mafia assassins who'd been dispatched from neighboring Bulgaria.

David must have heard one of those assassins at the service door, and rather than risk shooting toward the other split team in the opening moments of the raid, chose instead to initiate prematurely and let Cancer take the kill.

So much the better, he thought as Ian's battering ram impacted the door and sent it swinging inward.

Cancer moved through the breach with his MP7 at the high ready, his first sight of the building interior confirming his suspicions—a lone man with a pistol stood at the end of the short hall. The assassin whirled away from the door leading into the store's retail section to face the sound of the intrusion behind him.

That was all he had time to do, however, before being struck in the torso by three bullets that Cancer fired on the move. He spun right to face the nearest doorway, hearing a volley of suppressed shots as Reilly entered the building behind him. By then Cancer was already slipping inside the next room, stepping clear of the "fatal funnel" to visually clear the rightmost corner and sweep his barrel in the opposite direction. The room extended to his front as he proceeded forward, the first obstacle in his line of sight consisting of a round card table. Atop it he noticed, almost too late, the barrel of an assault rifle being aligned by a big bastard kneeling behind it.

Cancer knew without a doubt that he was dead, that being first through the door was finally going to cost him, but he fired anyway. His shots were reflexive, virtually unaimed as he continued moving along the wall.

He was aware of incoming bullets cracking through the air to his left and hitting the wall behind him when the impossible occurred: one of Cancer's 4.6mm rounds actually struck his opponent's rifle, visible as a spark of metal before the muzzle flash extinguished. And whether the man had stopped shooting due to malfunction, damage to his weapon, or shards of metal being flung into his face, Cancer didn't know and didn't much care.

Whatever the case, he exploited it by coming to full stop and shooting four rounds at a distance of just over three meters.

The effects were predictably catastrophic, with one bullet ripping off the side of his opponent's skull amid an ejection of pink mist and gray brain matter. His upper chest was then spattered by a loose grouping of bullet impacts courtesy of Reilly before the dead fighter fell out of view, his rifle clanking off the table and rattling a bottle and its surrounding glasses without knocking any of them over.

With the immediate threat vanquished, Cancer performed another sweep of his sector with an unsettling thought.

In the game of close-quarters combat, where life and death were often separated by fractions of a second and mere inches of bullet trajectories, he'd just prevailed by the hair on a gnat's ass. And while he visually confirmed the dead man was their only opponent in the room, the clearance wasn't over yet—they were now eight seconds into their raid with two Bulgarian mobsters down and a third still at large inside the building.

Cancer spun to lead his split team's clearance effort only to find that Reilly had beaten him to the punch—the hulking medic was already making a right turn out the door.

Reilly entered the corridor in time to see Worthy vanishing through a doorway on his right. He hastened to follow, having only a moment to observe the dead mobster sprawled before the threshold leading to an enormous selection of liquor in the retail area.

Then he was hooking right through the next doorway into a long storage area lined with tall shelves supporting neatly packaged cases of booze and wine. David was ahead of him and moving between the shelves, clearing with his MP7 as Worthy did the same. When the two men lowered their weapons in near unison, Reilly knew the room was a dry hole.

He reversed course to the corridor, taking up a position by the doorway to see the two remaining rooms on the far wall: to his left, an office where Cancer and Ian were completing their clearance, and to his right, a closed door.

Reilly knew from the floor plan that the latter was the building's lone bathroom and felt with growing certainty that the missing Bulgarian had picked the worst possible time to relieve himself. And while he'd very likely gone there unarmed, Reilly wasn't taking any chances—he'd barely taken aim at the door when a shotgun blast rang out and the wood panel was suddenly chipped by a cluster of small holes.

He dropped to a knee amid the hissing pings of buckshot pellets ricocheting in the corridor, squeezing off rapid trigger pulls as fast as he could.

Reilly heard a dull thud followed by a groan above the sound of his suppressed shots. Lowering his point of aim to account for a fallen target, he continued firing until his magazine emptied to the sound of a bloody gargle beyond the door.

Then Worthy was standing behind him, opening fire as Reilly reloaded. By the time his weapon was back in operation, all firing had ceased and Cancer moved beside the bathroom door, flinging it open to reveal a prostrate figure who'd fared far worse. The man was beyond dead, hit at least a dozen times even before Worthy administered a pair of headshots just to be sure and, presumably, for sport.

Then Reilly felt a hand on his coat collar as the pointman behind him said, "Come up."

He rose in time to hear David announce, "Clear—transition to search."

Ian plunged into the room that served as a staging area for the three-man hit team, now deceased.

He let his MP7 hang on its sling, freeing his hands to retrieve a folded satchel from his coat pocket and pull the strap over his shoulder.

The space was not unlike any number of safehouses that Ian's team had occupied over the years: luggage and sleeping bags were piled into a corner, while a small table ringed with chairs held playing cards, drinking glasses, and a half-depleted bottle of rakia. Between them was the dead mobster Ian passed now before dropping to his knees at the pile of luggage and casting aside the sleeping bags smeared with fresh blood and brain matter to begin his search.

Unzipping the first duffel, he upended it and shuffled through the contents—clothes, toiletries, a bottle of cologne—before moving on to a carry-on bag. In addition to personal effects, this one held a trio of 9mm pistols with suppressors, all of them intended for a hit that, absent his team's intervention just now, would have occurred the following evening. Promising, he thought, though still not what he was looking for.

Then David transmitted an unfortunate update that could have only come from the finest communication intercept efforts the CIA had to offer.

"*Someone got a call out—mafia shooters will be coming through the front door in three minutes. I want us gone in one.*"

Ian heard footsteps beside him, presumably Reilly as he carried out his assignment of photographing the dead men's bodies.

The assumption was confirmed a moment later when the medic cautioned him, "Better hurry this shit up. We can fabricate the intel if we need to."

"Not convincingly," Ian shot back, "and if they suspect we did, we're fucked."

He unzipped the next bag, where he found paydirt in the form of a manila folder that he extracted and, holding his breath, flipped open.

The first page was a map of New Belgrade, with three routes highlighted in various colors. So far, so good, Ian thought as he flipped through the subsequent pages to find a comprehensive list detailed by day, time, and location: a full surveillance-generated pattern of life for a single target.

Beyond the multi-page list was a photograph of Bridge Pub in Belgrade, along with its address, hours of operation, and a blueprint for the building's floor plan marked up by hand to indicate the locations of each table, one marked by a red *X*. The next page had photos of a group of men sitting at that table on various nights, judging by their changing wardrobes, and Ian flipped it over to see everything he'd hoped for.

The photograph was outdated, an old mugshot, but the man in it was unmistakable. Sunken cheeks and a trim beard marked his narrow face, together with almost eerily light blue eyes.

Beneath the photo was his name—*Branimir Gudelj*—and a host of personal information.

"Got it," Ian called, flipping the folder shut and stuffing it into his satchel.

Worthy was tucked behind the doorway leading into the retail portion of the liquor store, aiming his suppressed MP7 at the main entrance in anticipation of mafia hitmen bursting through it at any moment.

Instead he heard David transmit, "*Exfil, exfil, exfil.*"

Then the sound of running footsteps behind him as his teammates moved down the corridor on their way to the back door. Worthy held his position, standing as the only shooter covering the withdrawal until Cancer called out behind him, "Move."

Worthy hesitated a half-second, then yelled back, "Wait one."

Then he darted into the retail area, making for the item he'd staged on the way in and snatching it off the counter. The front of the violet box was cut away to reveal a round bottle of dark amber liquid, the glass emblazoned with the words *Slivova Rakia FAMILY RESERVE 1989*, and he stuffed the parcel into his satchel before racing back to the corridor.

Cancer had already replaced him in the doorway, now pulling security and dipping his barrel as Worthy ran past, careful to avoid the blood pooling beneath the first Bulgarian shot in the raid. Then he moved down the hall to the back door and took up a firing position before calling out, "Move."

His team's second-in-command did so at once, flowing past Worthy in a reversal of their planned assignments. As he moved, Cancer said, "Better be worth it," and then slipped out of view.

Worthy remained in place long enough for Cancer to close the distance with their retreating teammates. His last glimpse of the corridor revealed the battering ram that Ian had deposited just inside the doorway in the event its services were needed further inside the building—and there it would remain. There were precious few advantages to operating in a city with a full-blown mafia war in progress, but the element of plausible deniability couldn't have been much better. With weekly killings between various mob factions, the Belgrade Police Department would have little reason to suspect a covert CIA paramilitary team was operating within their jurisdiction. The survival of a young cashier with no real mafia affiliation was perhaps the only calling card that the Bulgarian assassins were dispatched by men with a conscience, but there were lines his team simply didn't cross when they could avoid it.

Then Worthy collapsed the buttstock of his MP7 and tucked the diminutive weapon beneath his coat before pulling the back door shut and exiting the building into the frigid air.

He moved left over a surface of crumbling asphalt, following Cancer toward an overgrown tangle of brush surrounding a cinderblock wall. The rest of his team had already moved past it, negotiating a trampled section of weeds that, judging by the discarded bottles and cigarette butts, was traversed by teenagers well after business hours.

Worthy tried to look casual as he moved. Vehicle traffic aside, several vantage points in the surrounding buildings overlooked the rear parking lot, and judging by the fact that police were yet to be notified, there was no reason to invoke further suspicion by sprinting away from the bloodbath. Instead he pushed aside the dried brambles of thicket and ducked underneath to find the gap in the cinderblock wall. Slipping through it and out the far side, he entered an alley between a church and a laundromat.

The Opel Vivaro parked there was like an American minivan but far uglier, generating misty clouds from its exhaust as Cancer ducked in the open passenger side. Worthy followed suit as the last man inside the vehicle, which was already pulling away by the time he managed to close the sliding door.

Fleeing the objective in a hideous minivan wasn't the most glamorous escape he'd ever been a part of, but some indignities were well worth it. He reached into his satchel to procure the box before setting it on the center console.

"Got your 1989," he said.

The driver gave a momentary glance toward the package, giving Worthy time to take in the profile of her face.

Jelena Bradić wasn't just beautiful but drop-dead gorgeous, as were all too many of the women he'd seen in Belgrade thus far. Between her high cheekbones and hazel eyes, to say nothing of her impossibly full lips,

Worthy had to take pains not to stare during their interactions. And here she was, driving a getaway car for a hit team with the possibility of police interdiction and/or attack by one or more vehicles filled with gun-toting mafia men, and her hair and makeup were nothing short of impeccable.

She turned her gaze back to the road, leaving him with a view of glossy brown hair descending in waves past her shoulders.

Then Jelena responded in a Serbian accent that was equal parts sultry and businesslike.

"I was joking about that. But *hvala* just the same."

No more words were spoken as she spirited them through the streets of the Savski Venac municipality of Belgrade. While not without its challenges, the daylight raid had accomplished its stated aim, and for the time being they were free of pursuit. Whether that status held firm remained to be seen, and Worthy scanned out his windows for any sign of police or mafia intervention as his team leader transmitted a situation report to Duchess.

2

CIA Headquarters
Special Activities Center, Operations Center F2

"*Raptor Nine One, this is Suicide Actual.*"

Duchess eagerly seized her hand mic—unlike the team's previous mission, no unmanned aerial vehicles kept her informed with real-time video feeds. "This is Raptor Nine One, send it."

David Rivers sounded far more self-assured than she felt at present.

"*Objective complete, exfilling now. Your intel was solid. Three EKIA, Gudelj target packet recovered, one civilian restrained and left on-site.*"

"Understood," she said. "Be advised, police response in progress, no vehicle description over the scanner and I'll let you know if that changes. We'll be standing by for a scan of the target packet. Nice work out there."

"*Good copy. Suicide Actual, out.*"

She hadn't finished setting down her mic before calling out, "Still clear?"

Duchess had spoken louder than she intended, her voice silencing the muted conversations inside the operations center.

Only one voice responded from the tiered workstations descending toward a wall of screens before her, the communications officer speaking while holding headphones over one ear.

"Yes, ma'am, first squad cars are still en route to the objective. No red flags yet."

She gave an approving nod, then leaned back in her seat as the dialogue resumed between various staff elements. Normally the OPCEN was dedicated to surveilling terrorist groups in the team's area of operations; this time, however, their efforts were split between Serbian mafia factions and local law enforcement. A first for Project Longwing, she thought, though her staff had thus far proven admirably up to the task.

"Seems that went well," she said with muted self-congratulation.

"For a kill mission," a woman to her right agreed, "but I would argue that is the least of the team's potential, to say nothing of this program as a whole."

Duchess turned to face her, considering her response carefully.

Meiling Chen was the daughter of Taiwanese immigrants yet spoke with a neutral American accent. Her workstation had previously been occupied by Project Longwing's military oversight in the form of one Navy Commander Jo Ann Brown serving as head DoD liaison. But her temporary assignment to the CIA had ended, and before a replacement was nominated Duchess had found herself managing a no-notice deployment to Libya. It was the first mission where she'd run the OPCEN without someone looking over her shoulder, a not-unwelcome change that was soon followed by one more.

In the wake of his daughter falling hostage and then being rescued, Senator Thomas Gossweiler, Chairman of the US Senate Select Committee on Intelligence and the very man who'd mandated military oversight in the first place, had decreed that Jo Ann's replacement be called off.

It should have been a good thing. But no good deed went unpunished, at least not in the intelligence community, and between the senator and the seventh floor, a decision was made to fill the vacant OPCEN seat with an entirely new billet, that of deputy chief for Project Longwing.

And that was how Meiling Chen had come to occupy the desk at Duchess's right hand.

Duchess sighed. As if juggling political approvals and running a ground team in and out of hotspots around the world wasn't enough, it was now her responsibility to mentor a former station chief whose history in the Agency, if one believed all accounts from those who worked with her, was checkered at best.

Duchess responded, "This program's successes speak for themselves, particularly considering that we wrote the playbook from scratch."

Chen looked at her with a blend of consternation and pity.

"That playbook," she said, "should be an evolving concept, not dogma. If Project Longwing remains nothing but a hammer, we'll come to see every problem set as a nail. But the political world is changing swiftly, and the days of lethal authorities being granted at every juncture are coming to an end. Particularly," she added with an ominous tone, "when a more agile organization that sees things differently adapts faster than we do."

With a slight shake of her head, Duchess replied, "We exist to execute lethal authorities, period, and in that regard, I think we've adapted remarkably well to what frequently amounts to near-impossible mission sets. When the nonlethal option is required, they certainly don't tap our people for the job."

"And they might stop tapping us entirely. The DEA's 960 Group has made quite a name for itself by capturing, not killing..."

Duchess unleashed a weary sigh, though it went unheard if Chen's tone was any indication as she continued, "...Monzer al-Kassar, Viktor Bout, Paul LeRoux."

"Each of whom," Duchess pointed out, "were lured to a US-allied country in an elaborate sting operation, because the relevant DEA authorities—which they didn't even possess prior to 9/11—are predicated on permission from the host government. Our current target isn't making the same mistake, and if we so much as tried to gain Serbian approval, he'd be the first to know. Maybe second, after the Kremlin."

Chen blinked, then spoke in an analytical tone. "Capturing a target and operating in semi-permissive or denied areas aren't mutually exclusive."

"Aren't they, though?"

"Not according to this team's successes in Montenegro and China."

Duchess felt her posture stiffen. She forced herself to take a breath, but few things were more irritating than a recent arrival casually referencing operations that transpired long ago, particularly with zero acknowledgment of the tremendous effort required.

"The Montenegro snatch occurred half an hour from the Albanian border. That was a rare exception."

"And China?" Chen asked.

It was all Duchess could do not to laugh in her face, though a grin crept across her features as she replied, "An unexpected development, Meiling, and I dare say you're underestimating the succession of miracles the ground team had to pull off to make that happen. China was the exception that proves the rule: to deliberately attempt a capture mission in the places we operate would *exponentially* elevate the risk to our team."

"Elevated or not, that risk is exactly what they're being paid and paid well to confront head-on."

Duchess eyed Chen warily, noting that the woman's expression was deadpan. Nor was there the slightest hint of irony in her voice, an indication that squared with every rumor and firsthand account of the woman's well-earned professional reputation.

Chen seemed to register the judgment against her, and pressed on regardless. "Mark my words, an operational pivot will be required sooner rather than later. If you don't like the idea of placing an easily replaceable ground team under further risk, you may well like irrelevance far less."

"I'm not so sure I would," Duchess said, feeling remarkably unsettled by the brazen assertions of a woman who'd barely had time to occupy a desk in the OPCEN, much less begin naysaying everything that had worked thus far in the program's existence.

Then she went on, "And I dare say that any notions about the future of this program are speculative until we deal with the current threat."

"This 'hydra' you speak of?" Chen asked rhetorically, incredulously.

Duchess felt her jaw settle. "Make no mistake, the hydra is still out there and waiting to strike again. And it's going to remain the only threat we need to concern ourselves with until Project Longwing locates it and finds a way to kill it for good."

3

Ian looked out the passenger window of the Audi A7, the sleek, leather-wrapped interior representing a considerably more luxurious setting than he'd enjoyed on his minivan exfil of the liquor store earlier that morning.

The car crossed onto a low bridge that spanned the tranquil waters of the Sava, its placid surface reflecting the glistening riverside buildings that lit the night beside moored boats. The Sava River was a tributary of the Danube, and the two shared a beautiful intersection at Belgrade's northern boundaries.

But they were well outside the city now, on their second and final crossing of the Sava as they traveled south, ever further into Serbia's less developed countryside.

As the river gave way to the far shore, Ian asked, "Gudelj has never had an issue dealing with a woman?"

Jelena chuckled softly from the driver's seat.

"Gudelj cares about one thing: money. He would gladly 'deal' with a chimpanzee if the price was right."

She sounded oddly calm about the upcoming transaction, and Ian looked over to see that Jelena's appearance matched her tone—her features were placid in the car's ambient LED interior lighting, which she'd configured to a shocking neon blue. Her hair was pulled into a loose ponytail over a flannel shirt and jeans that made him question the business casual attire he'd selected for the evening.

Ian cleared his throat. "So you've gotten used to this sort of thing?"

"As much as one can, I believe. After six years in NOC status, this was a fairly seamless transition. Why, are you nervous?"

"About tonight?" he asked rhetorically. "Not at all. About what happens if Gudelj doesn't extend an invitation to meet his boss in a week? Yes, I'm nervous in the extreme."

Jelena guided the Audi beneath a highway overpass before replying to that.

"May I give you some advice?"

"Please."

She sighed. "It is true that Gudelj has the authority to determine who meets the boss. But it is also true that we have set the conditions as much as we possibly could. Therefore, try not to worry about the future. Play your part tonight, and know that what is done, is done."

"But if he doesn't like something I say—"

"Gudelj made up his mind about whether to extend an invitation the moment I negotiated this deal. And as soon as he is paid, we will know what he has decided. It is that simple."

Nodding, Ian turned his gaze back out the passenger window. The surrounding countryside was largely dark, the periphery of the Audi's headlights falling on agricultural fields and patches of forest on either side of the road.

He said, "So I won't really affect the outcome one way or the other."

"Unless you come right out and tell him you work for the Company, no. He already believes us to be legitimate. My work over the last eight months has made that much certain."

"Should I be relieved about that, or concerned?"

"You should be relaxed, Ian."

Looking over at her again, he clarified, "What I mean to say is, do you think I'm going to get the invite or not?"

"I should hope so, because this is the largest purchase I have ever done for Affinity."

Affinity Gold was as secretive as it was effective—each buyer was a CIA officer of foreign descent who was sent back to their birth country to establish longstanding ties with black-market arms dealers under the guise of facilitating purchases for an ostensibly larger trafficking organization.

For the CIA, the benefits were threefold: access and placement in support of future operations such as this one, attaining unattributable weapons for America's covert lethal arming of select militaries and resistance forces, and removing major threat weapons from the global market. If all went according to plan, not only would the contents of tonight's purchase be denied to violent extremist organizations but they would also soon be in the hands of Ukrainian fighters.

For eight months now, Jelena had been moving up the totem pole of credibility with the Janjicari Mafia, whose leadership had been publicly photographed at various intervals with the Serbian president's son, a testament to their extensive state ties. In addition to funneling arms to the Special Activities Center, she'd worked her way ever closer to accessing a reclusive boss who rarely left Russian soil. When the Agency linked that boss to equipping the terrorist attack in Cairo four months earlier, his death became the purview of Project Longwing—and, with an Affinity Gold asset in place at the strategic crossroads of Belgrade, Ian's team was sent in to tip the scales toward a face-to-face meeting and all that would entail.

But first, they had to receive an invitation.

Jelena continued, "And due to the size of this transaction, I feel good about our prospects."

Ian released a grateful sigh, though it halted mid-exhale when she added, "However..."

"However what?" he asked.

"The Janjicari are very smart, but also very superstitious. I have put enough money in Gudelj's pocket to ensure he trusts me, or at least as much as he ever will. But if he happens to step on a cricket before our meeting, or see an owl or a black cat or a crow? Or if he simply has the wrong feeling, then who knows what he shall decide?"

He frowned.

"If you're trying to comfort me, you're doing a terrible job."

"I asked if I could give you advice. Not comfort."

"Yeah," he acknowledged, "I know. But what happens if he doesn't give us an invitation?"

"One step at a time, my dear Ian. One step at a time."

4

I unlocked the exterior door, pulling it open to let my team enter the farmhouse under cover of darkness.

Cancer was the first in, whisking past me with his sniper rifle case and gear bag while quietly transmitting, "*This is the only full dress rehearsal we're going to get—make it count.*"

Worthy was next through the door, wordlessly following while toting his own kit to serve as Cancer's spotter. Both men made for the stairs. That left Reilly, who approached with the motherlode of equipment, chief among which was the enormous cylindrical bag slung over his shoulder. I closed and locked the door once he'd passed, lowering my night vision to illuminate the farmhouse in a shadowscape of green hues.

Then I moved up the stairs behind my team, hauling a massive hiking pack, and reached the second floor in time to see Worthy slipping inside a doorway to the left. Reilly and I broke right to enter a master suite that represented the largest room in the house. Leaving the door open behind me, I moved to the two windows located on the back wall and swung them open on rusty hinges.

I turned to approach Reilly, who had already removed his HK417 from its carrying bag. He propped it barrel-down against the side of a small dresser we'd previously aligned with the single window overlooking our target area, set back just far enough that we could take aim without risk of our barrels protruding.

After opening that window as well, I moved to Reilly's right side and deposited my own kit in time to see him withdraw a long object from the largest bag he'd carried in: a Carl Gustaf 84mm recoilless rifle, affectionately referred to by its operators as the Goose, Carl G., or simply Gustaf.

Originally developed by a Swedish armament firm whose name became synonymous with the weapon itself, the Gustaf had long been the rocket launcher of choice for special operations forces and, more recently, standard issue to some conventional infantry units. It was more or less a modern bazooka, albeit equipped with a laser rangefinder and reloadable with an imaginative variety of rounds, one of which I prepared now.

Reilly mounted a short bipod to his Gustaf, then hoisted the launcher's bipod atop the dresser, cocking the enormous weapon before he took up a firing position with his hands on the twin grips.

"Load," he said.

I reached atop the Gustaf and grabbed the rearmost of two spherical knobs, pushing it forward and rotating the hinged breech counterclockwise. Then I retrieved a high-explosive, dual-purpose round that was set to detonate on impact and slid it into the launcher, closing the breech and confirming it was locked with a slight rearward pull on the knob.

"Ready."

Reilly took a moment to confirm his point of aim through the thermal sight. "All right, we're good."

"Gustaf set," I transmitted.

Cancer's response came a few seconds later. "*Sniper team set—one minute and forty-seven seconds. No movement on the objective. You remember to open all the windows, Denzel?*"

"Fuck yourself," I answered, although he wasn't necessarily wrong to ask the question.

Hollywood seemed confident that firing rocket launchers from confined spaces would leave the room in pristine condition. *Man on Fire* depicted Denzel Washington shooting a rocket-propelled grenade with no apparent effect to an apartment or its elderly senior citizens sitting beside him with their pet birds, all of which emerged unscathed without so much as using earplugs, but the reality was that if Reilly fired the Gustaf, whatever backblast wasn't channeled out the doorway or windows would fill the room with blazing smoke, debris, and the tooth-rattling blast of overpressure.

We'd done what we could to mitigate that, selecting projectiles that would launch with a minimum of backblast and fly clear of the house before their rocket motors fired to take them the remaining distance to their target.

Reilly let the Gustaf rest atop the bipod, then lowered his night vision to scan out the window. "This seems almost too easy, doesn't it?"

"For us, sure. But I wouldn't want to be Ian right now."

Other than the uncertainties inherent in any undercover role, this entire mission was shaping up to be a slam dunk. Of the acceptable firing positions we'd identified among the various structures surrounding our target area, the Agency had simply found one to buy—not just the farmhouse, but the five-acre lot it rested on. It had made the purchase through a front company long before we'd actually boarded a plane for Serbia.

We'd conducted a single dry run prior to this, getting eyes-on our target area and identifying the specific locations for each shooter. But there had been no reason to risk toting weapons inside until tonight, which was our only chance for a full-scale emplacement prior to returning for the actual hit. And while full on-site rehearsals such as this were an exceedingly rare luxury in our line of work, the hassle was justified by virtue of Ian and Jelena entering the target area. Ideally they'd conduct their transaction without issue, but if it turned out to be a trap of some kind, then those two would need every ounce of firepower we'd brought in with us.

Even that might not be enough to save them.

Worthy transmitted from his spotter position, "*All right, boys, let's buckle up for a long, cold, and boring night.*"

"Yeah," I agreed, "maybe we should have brought some rakia with us."

Worthy went silent at that, surely sensing the inevitable.

Cancer, however, gladly filled the void.

"*Maybe that nice bottle of 1989—or is that spoken for?*"

"Great question," I offered. "Where did that come from, anyway? I seem to remember Racegun setting it on the counter but not taking it."

No one had spoken a word about that little indiscretion since we'd departed the liquor store earlier that day, nor did we need to—at this point in our history together, Cancer and I could all but read each other's minds when it came to keeping our team in check.

Cancer replied innocently, "*That's because he didn't. Went back for it with mafia shooters closing in.*"

After a moment of silence, Worthy said, "*It was a spur-of-the-moment kind of thing.*"

"Oh," I began, "I'm sure it was. But you're too inexperienced to make good judgment calls yet—oh wait, you've been with Longwing since the beginning and been shot twice that I can think of off the top of my head. Man, you must *really* like the rakia here."

"*Or,*" Cancer replied, playing into my verbal trap, "*you took Jelena really seriously when she dropped us off with the words, 'Grab me a bottle of 1989 while you're in there.' I mean, I took it as a joke, but I guess she didn't specify either way, so why not risk getting shot in the face?*"

I spoke in a curious tone, as if I found the topic utterly fascinating. "Good point. Cancer, do you think it might have had something to do with Jelena?"

"*Dunno. She's hot, I guess, if you're into white chicks. Not really my thing, but I can't speak for everyone.*"

"I hadn't thought of that," I said. "You might be right, though—"

Worthy cut us off.

"*All right, it was dumb. I get it. Won't happen again.*"

I keyed my mic once more.

"See that it doesn't. You want to fly back here to see her, or ship her to the States for a little R&R, I'm all for it. Hell, I'm not going to ask any questions about what goes on after business hours while we're in Belgrade so long as the mission comes off without a hitch. But I've got to be honest, Racegun—when I heard we'd have to work with a female here, I thought it was Doc I'd have to worry about, not you."

"Meh," Reilly replied, transmitting for the benefit of the sniper/spotter team across the hall, "Jelena is all right, I guess. Nothing to write home about."

Worthy sounded incensed. "*'All right?' Christ, Doc, I watched you lose your mind over a Colombian prostitute a few missions back.*"

"Isabella was a sex worker," Reilly objected. "You're not supposed to call them prostitutes anymore."

"*Whatever.*"

I felt my phone buzz in my pocket and pulled out a radio earpiece to answer the call.

"We're all set here."

"Good," Ian replied, "we'll be there in forty minutes. See anything yet?"

I looked out the window, past the headlights crossing State Road 27 and out to the grassy field beyond.

"Nothing yet," I answered, then noticed a set of headlights break away from the traffic and turn down a side road toward the field. Another followed in short order.

"I stand corrected—looks like the first cars are pulling in now."

5

The Audi pulled to a stop, and Ian waited until Jelena killed the engine to steel himself with a final breath. Then he formally transitioned into the one among them who'd issue all further orders that evening.

"Let's go."

"Yes, sir," Jelena replied, and they exited the vehicle in unison, stepping into the frigid night air and retrieving their coats from the backseat.

Ian glanced about casually as he donned his outerwear—they stood on a swath of grass beside a small, closed hangar, the headlights of vehicle traffic crossing State Road 27 dimly visible through a strip of trees. He deliberately avoided looking northwest, where in the darkness beyond the road, his team surveilled him from a farmhouse acquired for the purpose. Instead, he looked south toward the grassy clearing extending over five hundred meters in either direction, almost paralleling the road from west to east.

Valjevo Airport was located an hour south of Belgrade, consisting of little more than a landing strip capable of supporting a plane of almost any size provided it was equipped to operate from unimproved runways. That alone made it an obvious choice for aerial smuggling, where goods could be transferred from vehicle to plane or vice versa far from the terminals and control towers of larger airports in Belgrade, Niš, and Kraljevo. As such, it had long served a key role for the Janjicari, who had meticulously taken over control of Serbia's lucrative status as a weapons hub connecting Europe to conflict zones in the Middle East, Africa, and beyond.

The airfield hosted plane and helicopter flight schools, and while it was overwhelmingly utilized during daylight hours, nighttime traffic attracted no attention from drivers on nearby State Road 27 or Route 150. Nor from the relatively few surrounding homes and businesses with a clear line of sight.

At present it was heavily secured—they'd just passed through a checkpoint of three vehicles at the main entrance, where the only two visible men checked their identities and inspected the trunk before allowing them to proceed. Ian knew from longstanding intelligence efforts that many more men were stationed in the shadows, both as an early warning network and to react in the event a competing mafia element like the New Zemun tried to intervene in the proceedings ahead.

But the only ones he could see at present were a trio of figures approaching from the hangar, none visibly armed.

"That's him, in the middle," Jelena said.

Ian quickly retrieved one more item from a pouch on the seatback—a manila envelope he folded lengthwise, then across its width, before tucking it into an interior pocket of his coat, followed by a letter-size envelope he slid beside it.

He was zipping up his coat when Jelena appeared at his side, then took the lead in advancing toward the group of men.

"Mr. Gudelj," she began, "allow me to introduce Mr. Cutler."

Ian extended his hand as the central man did the same; he was tall and lanky and spoke in a thick Serbian accent.

"Please, call me Branimir."

Ian had an entire cover legend mapped out for his undercover persona, but only select clues would be parceled out to Gudelj over the course of this exchange—starting with no attempt whatsoever to conceal his American accent.

"Jon. Pleasure to meet you."

When the exceptionally firm handshake ended, he continued, "How long do we have the airfield?"

Gudelj gestured for them to follow him toward the hangar. "Normal operations do not resume until eight. You have all night to inspect the load."

"I don't think I'll need that long, Branimir. The samples you provided to my associate last week have passed inspection and testing with flying colors, and we've already run a pilot load to test our route. And you don't seem like a man who'd be interested in sabotaging a mutually prosperous relationship, am I right?"

"Of course," Gudelj responded, his tone accommodating and polite. So far so good, Ian thought, noting that the two men were flanking himself and Jelena as they proceeded, an overt gesture of protection that was more ceremonial than anything else given the players involved.

Then Ian continued, "But since it's my neck on the chopping block here, I'll need to confirm the quantity prior to loading. Along with spot-checking the serial numbers."

"I would expect nothing less. And my people have conducted a full inspection at the point of departure and prior to your arrival, so I believe you will find everything in order."

Gudelj stopped before the hangar door, pulling it open for Ian and Jelena to enter.

The brightly lit structure wasn't much warmer inside than it was outside. Four small planes were parked against the far wall, along with a helicopter sitting atop a trailer. Of more interest to Ian, however, was the Renault box truck that had backed in prior to his arrival, now flanked by dozens of open crates in varying sizes.

Ian turned to see Gudelj entering behind him, and caught his first good look at the man's face—gaunt, lined with a well-groomed beard beneath icy blue eyes that crinkled into a forced smile.

"Here we are, Jon. Podnos, RG-60s, and Strelas, as requested. My men can help with anything you need."

"Just the loading, when the time comes." He looked at Jelena and nodded toward the crates, which they approached together.

The first set held five 2B14 Podnos mortars, each broken down into its 82mm barrel, baseplate, and bipod assemblies, with a separate case containing the sight units that a crew would need to adjust fire with precision. Together with the one that Jelena had previously obtained as a sample of the full load, they comprised a battalion's worth of indirect firepower originally intended for Soviet light infantry units.

With his eyes on the mortars, Ian said, "Model, part number, and year of manufacture for all barrels."

Jelena dutifully approached the mortars with her notepad, which contained the requisite specifications from the Nizni Novgorod Engineering Plant that had originally produced the weapons. While the provided sample had matched up and Ian was obligated to accept the full load if it satisfied the same, it was routine practice for less scrupulous black marketeers to mix in items of lesser provenance—Chinese-made knockoffs were a popular choice—and spot-checking various details before accepting delivery was simply a part of the buyer's due diligence that would cause no offense.

The mortars were being purchased below standard commercial value, a benefit to easy availability without any corresponding tax burden. But as Ian moved onto the next batch, he faced the bemused thought that this was where the savings ended.

He stopped before a single crate of fifty foam-lined packing cylinders lined up in five rows, the tops removed to permit easy visual confirmation of the contents.

Guns and mortars were one thing, plentiful as they were on the global market. But an item's price rose in direct proportion with its rarity and, therefore, the difficulty involved in acquiring it. Ian reached down to one of the cardboard packing cylinders, gently upending it to extract a single grenade of exceedingly unusual construction.

The rounded black cylinder felt cold in his hand, and was topped by a spike of metal with the safety pin and pull ring intact. It looked vastly different to the other grenades he'd wielded in training and combat, and that was largely a result of its function; in contrast to standard fragmentation devices, this was a thermobaric weapon.

Ian could feel the tension in the hangar rising with each second he examined the device— its safety clip was still in place from the factory as a shipping safeguard, and as such, Gudelj's men would have plenty of time to shoot him if he tried to put it into operation. Be that as it may, however, deploying it now would unleash a vast cloud of liquid fuel whose ensuing flame and blast wave would create a vacuum effect with far more destructive power than an equal weight of conventional explosives. The RG-60TB in his hand would kill anyone within its seven-meter blast radius and quite possibly beyond, particularly when the overpressure reached the identical grenades below.

He returned the item to its foam-lined packing tube and selected six others for Jelena to inspect.

That left Ian with the final three dozen crates, which were the real cornerstones of this exchange.

Any black marketeer worth his salt could procure firearms, and the exceptional ones could even manage to get exotic items like the thermobaric grenade Ian had just held.

But one category of weapon remained something of a unicorn in the murky depths of illegal military hardware exchanges, and for good reason.

State-run arms manufacturers like China's PolyTech would happily supply everything from grenades to land mines to Triad buyers who then distributed them on the international market, as would counterpart companies in Iran and North Korea. Precious little would be denied to someone with the proper contacts, motivation, and funding to obtain them—to such a buyer, the only uncertainties were the minor details of quantity, point of delivery, and perhaps end-user certificates if something so crude as a paper trail couldn't be avoided.

But none of those manufacturers would sell shoulder-fired surface-to-air missiles, no matter the price.

The reason was simple: when a Boeing Triple Seven or an Airbus A340 was blown out of the sky by a young terrorist who required no more effort or instruction than reading the operating manual of such a weapon, the international reaction would be swift and severe. The launcher system would be traced all the way back to its point of manufacture, and whichever country had built it would be at the receiving end of every possible recrimination from crippling sanctions to military action—a proposition that was not remotely worth the risk amid a thriving arms trafficking market that netted over a billion dollars each year.

The Serbian mafia, however, which operated extensively on multiple continents, had no such qualms.

Their biggest challenge was sourcing the missiles in the first place, which required ties to Russian organized crime with access to Soviet hardware and the means to move it. It wasn't often that product became available, and when it did, a Serbian gangster was usually brokering the sale.

Ian smiled as he confirmed the total count, the expression both genuine and unintended, and while Gudelj likely thought it was born out of financial satisfaction, in reality Ian was almost overcome with gratitude that these missiles would soon be off the market. They were as rare and exorbitantly expensive as they were deadly, and the fewer of them that remained in circulation, the better.

The NATO reporting name structure had distilled the weapons' Russian nomenclature—*9K34 Strela-3*—to a more palatable codename of SA-14. With an infrared homing seeker head, the 23-pound missile could take out a passenger jet at almost ten thousand feet anywhere within a three-mile radius of its takeoff or landing or, given the reduced susceptibility of its seeker head to flares and jammers, any number of military aircraft flying at a higher speed but lower altitude.

There were 36 crates in total, half of which held the three components of the weapons themselves, with the launch tube, gripstock, and battery coolant unit disassembled. The remaining boxes held a set of three missiles for each launcher unit. A single SA-14 with a trio of munitions was considered a "kit," and at 75,000 dollars per kit, Ian was looking at just over three million dollars' worth of nearly impossible-to-acquire surface-to-air firepower.

Ian looked over to see Jelena approach with a nod. The mortars and grenades had checked out, as he had no doubt they would.

He returned his gaze to the SA-14s, pointing to three of them in sequence.

As Jelena moved out to check the serial numbers, Gudelj came to a stop beside him and commented with satisfaction, "Your clients' helicopter problem will not remain a problem for long."

Ian nodded absently, thinking that the Serbian's assumption was sound —a minor number of terrorists had employed such missiles against passenger jets and cargo planes, mainly in Africa. The feat had been accomplished by the Zimbabwe People's Revolution Army, Polisario Front militants in the Sahara, Tutsi militia, and UNITA in Angola, among others.

But run-of-the-mill ideological extremists couldn't afford to purchase such weapons in the quantity on display here. A far more likely explanation as far as Gudelj was concerned was that a large organization wanted to defend their territory from police and military helicopters, just as the FARC had done for so long in Colombia.

Jelena knelt before the final SA-14 she was ordered to inspect, comparing its serial number with the information on her notepad.

It went without saying that there was a no-warranty, no-return policy: standard practice on the black market was for a sample size of the total request to be delivered in exchange for a down payment, and that sample—in this case, one mortar, two thermobaric grenades, and a single SA-14 kit that Jelena had procured two weeks ago—could be tested as exhaustively as the customer wished at a time and place of their choosing. Once the sale moved forward, the buyer was obligated to accept the remainder of the order and take possession at the earliest possible opportunity.

And that opportunity, Ian knew, was fast approaching.

He recovered the phone from his pocket, holding it in his palm until Jelena announced, "We are good."

Only then did he dial, waiting for the man to answer before speaking.

"I'm taking possession, send it."

The only response he heard was an ETA, which he relayed for Gudelj's benefit after hanging up.

"Five minutes."

Gudelj nodded approvingly and barked an order to his men. "*Spakuj ga*."

The meaning was apparent enough from the actions of the Serbian mobsters in the hangar—they converged on the merchandise and began assembling the loose weapons, replacing them in the crates as Gudelj made a phone call of his own.

Ian folded his hands and waited, marveling both at the efficiency of this exchange and the fact that it was possible not at the ignorance of the Serbian government but rather by its knowing consent. It was a fascinating arrangement that had its basis in history, back when Serbia, along with Croatia, Bosnia and Herzegovina, Macedonia, Slovenia, and Montenegro were not sovereign nations but constituent republics forming the Socialist Federal Republic of Yugoslavia.

Decades earlier, the greatest minds in Yugoslav intelligence made the arguably brilliant decision to outsource their foreign assassinations to mafia hitmen, and when those hitmen were arrested abroad, they were extradited right back to their homeland for future employment. In exchange, and often in tandem, the Yugoslav government allowed the mafia to establish operations across Europe. And while Yugoslavia had since fractured, the relationships had not.

Today, the top mobsters were longstanding family friends with senior officials in Serbian police, military, and intelligence organizations. They'd once served the same cause in their own way, all fully sanctioned by a state that no longer existed, and those ties hadn't evaporated with the establishment of new borders across an ancient land—nor even, Ian thought, with the mafia's assassination of Serbia's prime minister in 2003 and the subsequent government crackdowns.

Gudelj spoke into his phone in brief bursts of Serbian, ending with a single "*Da*" before informing Ian, "My people have received the payment in full."

"Excellent," Ian replied without enthusiasm. He watched Gudelj in silent anticipation of some further exchange, ideally an invitation to meet the yet-unacknowledged puppet master behind not only standard fare black market exchanges such as this, regardless of quantity, but also more insidious transfers to far worse people than the Janjicari and their associates.

But Gudelj instead spoke once more to his men, one of whom activated a switch on the wall to initiate the upward movement of a rolling hangar door.

"Shall we?" Gudelj asked, making for the grass outside without waiting for a response.

Ian shot a neutral glance to Jelena as they both slipped out of the hangar.

Gudelj came to a stop and looked skyward, searching for an

approaching aircraft that didn't appear until seconds later, its red and green position lights turning on the final leg of its landing pattern to the west. Shortly thereafter Ian could hear the thin hum of twin turboprops rising above the ambient traffic noise.

The An-24 was designed from the ground up for use at unprepared airstrips: even its wings were mounted atop the aircraft, keeping its enormous twin propellers high above the uneven terrain and loose rocks it was built to land on. Originally produced in the sixties, over a hundred were still in use by militaries and civil operators across Europe, Asia, and Africa. Owing both to the widespread distribution and ease with which they could be operated at remote airfields with nonexistent ground support, one such platform was owned by the CIA's Air Branch for use in covert operations.

That particular An-24 was descending toward its touchdown now, and Ian was minutes away from either receiving the invitation he'd orchestrated this entire event for or being dismissed without it. He had one more card to play, though he intended to play it as a measure of gratitude for the invite rather than a desperate last-ditch response to achieve credibility with Gudelj.

The aircraft finally made landfall at the far west edge of the strip, the hulking Soviet-era plane decelerating with astonishing speed across the smooth grass surface. Given its size, Ian had anticipated it would roar past them and have to turn around; but owing to the tremendous length of the airstrip, the skill of the pilots, or the aircraft's capabilities, it slowed to a gradual roll long before coming abreast of the hangar.

Once it did, the plane came to a complete stop, reducing the throttle until the propellers came to a muted idling status without shutting down completely. Then the rear door swung open, and two men within the fuselage lowered a stairway to the ground.

Now that Ian had seeded clues as to his cover legend—a turncoat intelligence official who'd leveraged his contacts to go into business for himself—the remaining question burning a hole through Gudelj's mind was related to the end user of all this equipment.

And that, Ian thought, would be settled by the Agency's selection of loading crew.

Every one of the five men who descended the ramp were members of the Special Activities Center's Air and Ground Departments, all of Latin descent and fluent in Spanish, a language they used to shout at one another as they advanced beyond the prop blast.

Ian glanced at Gudelj, who had clearly noticed this detail. He returned Ian's gaze and gave a nod of approval, though whether he'd suspected this would occur all along or hadn't given the matter enough thought remained a mystery.

The Mexican cartels were an obvious choice for the ghost buyers of all this weaponry: they had unlimited funding and a correspondingly endless need for further armament. Ian hoped to imply the future possibility of wholesale drug exchanges that cut out whatever middlemen were currently taking their pound of flesh out of Gudelj's profit margins. And while Ian wouldn't ultimately be able to deliver that, for the purposes of this mission it didn't matter—he only needed credibility as a VIP customer.

Credibility, he thought, and an invitation to meet with Gudelj's facilitator. Because until he got that invite, this entire ruse was one elaborate waste of time.

The ostensible Mexican cartel members met Gudelj's people halfway, the latter hauling out the crates with a man at each side. Since there was no tail ramp, they'd have to cross-load the weapons onto the aircraft one at a time, and the process began in a remarkably efficient manner.

Gudelj turned to Ian and offered his hand with the words, "It has been a pleasure doing business with you."

"Our business has not concluded yet," Ian replied, unzipping his coat halfway instead of returning the handshake. "I have one more matter to discuss."

"Oh?"

"Indeed. A gift, as it were."

Ian retrieved the folded manila envelope from his coat pocket, handing it to Gudelj and letting the man rifle through the contents. He turned away, proceeding two steps toward the building to scrutinize the pages in the ambient interior light, and Ian noted a look of growing concern before he explained.

"I employ extensive intelligence efforts ahead of a major transfer, and in this case they alerted me to a threat against you. The assassination was to occur tomorrow night, when you conducted a meeting at Bridge Pub. I suggest you change your pattern of life immediately."

Gudelj looked up from the papers, his eyes wide.

"Who was it?"

"The New Zemun Clan. They brought in a three-man hit team from Bulgaria to distance themselves if the effort was unsuccessful. The assassins were staged at Srecno Liquor, which is, as I believe you're fully aware, one of their money laundering sites."

"And the killers?"

Ian smiled politely, procuring the second envelope and handing it over. "My people took care of them this morning. I expect it will be in the papers tomorrow."

He watched Gudelj open the envelope and flip through the contents: photo printouts of the bullet-riddled corpses his team had left behind at the liquor store just twelve hours earlier.

Then the Serbian looked up and said, "I offer you my most sincere gratitude."

"Let's not get ahead of ourselves, Branimir. I removed the threat to safeguard this transaction, but in the future I should hope that such precautions are taken ahead of my arrival."

Gudelj blinked quickly.

"Of course. This war—this *fucking* war—has gotten out of hand."

"At any rate," Ian continued, "this will not be my last purchase. Once the delivery is made, I anticipate that my clients will request additional hardware. Potentially an order that will be extremely lucrative for both of us, and I intend to remain in Belgrade for at least two weeks to facilitate that order."

"Just let me know, when the time comes. I will see what I can do about fulfilling the request in the quickest possible fashion." He replaced the photographs in the envelope, then refolded the papers and tucked the sum total into his coat. "Now if you will excuse me, I must arrange some unfortunate fates for a few members of the New Zemun leadership."

And that was it, Ian thought—this massive purchase hadn't resulted in an invitation, which he knew full well that Gudelj had the power to issue at his discretion. To probe further would be to invoke suspicion, and if there was one thing Ian had learned from sustained relationships with foreign contacts, it was to end each interaction on a positive note.

He extended his hand to Gudelj.

"Thank you for the business, Branimir."

Gudelj shook his hand curtly, eyes smoldering with anger. Not toward Ian, fortunately, but rather because he'd been unknowingly reliant on a client to stop a threat against his life. No matter, Ian thought, as the action would be appreciated in due time—but not tonight.

The exchange was over, and in terms of his team's mission in Serbia, it had been a catastrophic failure.

6

"Looks like Cutler made it back," Reilly said.

Cancer rose from his seat and approached the small foldout table where the medic was surveying a ruggedized laptop.

The display was subdivided into four live feeds, each projecting a real-time view of a corresponding camera surreptitiously emplaced to provide surveillance across the street access points. Ian crossed beneath a street-lamp with his hands in his pockets, an all-clear signal that meant his surveillance detection route had come up clean and he intended to return for the night. That SDR had taken a considerable amount of time, Cancer thought; the rest of the team had time to break down their setup at the farmhouse, return to Belgrade and stash their vehicle with the weapons and gear, *and* make their way back here with time to spare.

Then again, if anyone was going to be followed after the arms buy at Valjevo Airfield, it was Ian and Jelena.

He turned to face the interior of this "safehouse," if such a word could even be applied with a straight face. Because Cancer had occupied many such establishments in his ever-growing Agency career, but nothing quite like this.

It was little more than an isolated basement with a single staircase providing street access, a holdover from some long-forgotten construction plans that had never reached fruition. That made it a grim prospect for any prospective business which was, Cancer assumed, the reason it had remained available for rent ahead of the team's arrival. Above it was a small food market on the ground level, plus an additional two stories of apartments from a neighboring structure amid the chaotic Belgrade architecture. All five hiking packs with sleeping bags were laid out on the floor against the opposite wall, an urban equivalent of a patrol base in the woods. The sum total of interior furniture consisted of foldout chairs and plastic tables, one of which supported a bottle of rakia between David and Worthy, both of whom watched the sniper for a response.

"He's clean," Cancer said. "Let him in."

Worthy moved to the door.

David checked his watch and sighed. "Well, at least we have a couple hours left to figure our shit out before the cafés open."

Reilly called over his shoulder, "If that SDR took any longer, we'd be at risk of dying from natural causes."

"Shouldn't you be watching for cops?" Cancer reprimanded him.

Broad shoulders sagging, Reilly turned back to the computer. The Agency was monitoring the feeds as well, along with the greater CCTV network in Belgrade, to say nothing of police transponders and tapped mafia phones, so ideally they'd have some early warning in the event of compromise—but Cancer knew better than to fully outsource security to anyone besides his teammates. Part of the issue was the operating environment itself: previously, his team had run missions in outright hostile terrain with no need for a safehouse, or in established Agency safehouses run with the complicity of the host nation government.

Serbia presented an interesting contradiction in that it was fully permissive to tourists, but US paramilitary efforts would be frowned upon, to say the least. The team needed a Belgrade location to stash its five members, and Jelena's house wasn't going to cut it due to neighborly observation. Nor would something so simple as a rental property do, mainly because a standard house or apartment would be far too easy for the police to isolate if the Americans were identified as a foreign intelligence element.

So they'd arranged a compromise, keeping the vast bulk of their weapons and equipment secured in a full-size cargo van at Jelena's residence while the team occupied this rented basement space in the Savamala neighborhood of Belgrade, just a half-mile removed from the Sava River waterfront. The exact location wasn't as important as the nuances of their surroundings; here in Serbia, a safehouse was only as good as the ability to escape it if cornered, and to that end the team had engineered a somewhat unorthodox exit plan down to the last detail.

And the end result, he knew with bitter resolution, was that exiting the premises while carrying all their worldly possessions was indeed possible; the downside, however, was that if a fight to the death was required to escape, they had very close to none of the resources required to do so. That contradiction was a neat summation of his experience as a warrior—for every advantage there was an equal or greater disadvantage, and the balance of power in the interim more often than not relied on either training or determination.

Or both, which would most likely be the case if this safehouse was compromised.

They heard a double knock at the door, and Worthy unlocked it before pulling it open to let Ian in from the cold.

The intelligence operative took two steps inside before halting in his tracks, appraising the room and waiting for Worthy to lock the door behind him before speaking. As was all too common with Ian, his first reaction was to judge everyone before him.

"Should we really be drinking right now?" he asked, unzipping his coat and stripping it off.

And to his credit, David sniffed and muttered a response that couldn't have possibly been more iconic if it was drafted into the final screenplay of *Casablanca*.

"That's a question of tolerance," the team leader began. "We all know what the getaway route requires. If anyone falls behind, they're on their own."

Cancer gave a solemn nod in support of his ground force commander.

"Which means," he added, "an all-expenses-paid trip to a Serbian prison. Because that's where any incarcerated members will live out their days in between trips to the interrogation room or worse."

David raised a provocative eyebrow, fixing Ian in his glare. "My liver was pounded into submission long ago, but I can't speak for anyone else. Choose your own level of involvement."

Ian rubbed his temples, shaking his head in resignation.

"One shot, then cut me off."

Cancer took his seat at the table, reaching for the bottle and a plastic cup from the inverted stack beside it. He made a small pour, repeating the process with two other cups as Ian and Worthy dropped into the remaining foldout chairs.

Ian lifted his cup and gave the customary Serbian toast, equivalent to "cheers" in English.

"*Živeli*, gentlemen."

A tap of plastic on plastic, and everyone but Reilly took a sip. Cancer wasn't particularly wowed by the strong nose and sticky-sweet plum finish, which in his mind left precious little room to consider why this particular beverage had spent the better part of centuries failing to expand beyond its Balkan origins.

David, bless his heart, downed the entire shot without so much as flinching.

Ian spoke over the sound of cups hitting the table.

"What did Duchess say?"

"Duchess?" David winced with offense at the inquiry rather than the rakia. "She said fucking 'copy all.' Which means she's having a panic session with her staff at Langley. Besides, it doesn't matter what she said. I'm running this operation on the ground, and as far as you're concerned, it matters what *I* say."

"Which is...what, exactly?"

David shrugged. "That it's time for us to have our own panic session. We need to go back to the drawing board."

Worthy scoffed, going on in his aw-shucks, good-natured drawl that Cancer, under the present circumstances, found supremely annoying.

"With all due respect, boss," the pointman drawled, "I think the Agency needs to unscrew themselves. If it weren't for their lawyers and their so-called 'threshold for positive identification,' this would be a piece of cake."

Cancer grunted for emphasis before leveling an index finger at the team's resident Southerner.

"Listen, you little slack-jawed hick, you're still on probation after that little stunt at the liquor store. If we need more rakia, we'll let you know. Until then, let the adults talk."

Worthy's gaze didn't falter, nor did it concede defeat. He knew he'd fucked up, and the fact that he was the last person on the team Cancer would anticipate making a tactical error in judgment over a woman didn't prevent him from wanting to save face.

David seemed to sense everything Cancer was thinking, and the team leader laid a palm flat on the table before intervening. "Here's what's about to happen. I'm going to go over everything we know—or think we know—and we're going to challenge any assumptions, because on the current glidepath we're dead in the water as far as this little Serbian jaunt is concerned. Ian, let me know if I'm missing anything here."

Ian nodded. "All right. Go ahead."

David responded by opening the laptop beside him, unlocking it, and flipping it around to expose the screen.

A black-and-white surveillance shot depicted a stern-looking man in a suit, the picture snapped as he crossed a Moscow sidewalk.

In stark contrast to all of the team's primary targets to date, Yuri Sidorov actually *looked* like a card-carrying sociopath: his beady eyes were as emotionless as a stripper's, Cancer thought, mouth set in a low jowl, close-cropped gray hair against a well-receded hairline.

The sniper almost grimaced at the sight. He'd never so badly wanted to personally kill one of his team's targets—perhaps it was due to his contempt for the man, or a desire to beat the odds after mission success had just become more or less impossible after Ian's failure to obtain a meeting with him.

Most likely, however, it was Sidorov's somewhat remarkable physical resemblance to Vladimir Putin.

Sidorov was, at present, filling the void of those who'd gone before him as international arms mega-merchants. That list was both exceedingly short and crowned by Viktor Bout, the so-called "Merchant of Death" who was arrested in Thailand, extradited to the US, and sentenced to 25 years in Marion.

Like Sidorov, Bout had enjoyed the support of the Kremlin, which had taken every possible step to proclaim his innocence and request his safe return, up to and including blacklisting the arresting officers and members of the prosecution from ever obtaining Russian entry visas.

Which was just as well, Cancer supposed, because they'd be crazy to try and enter the country after putting away a man with extensive connections to Russian intelligence services and political officials all the way to the deputy prime minister.

But none of that concerned Project Longwing so much as Sidorov's links to twin terrorist attacks during their last mission to Libya, one of which had been successful and one foiled by the narrowest possible margin. In the fallout, the Agency had determined that Sidorov was responsible for obtaining Iranian-supplied military hardware from Yemen, along with the former Quds Force advisors required to ensure its successful operation. That unquestionably made him the top weapons boss to a shadowy international terrorist syndicate headed by Erik Weisz, a pseudonym that Project Longwing had been chasing across the globe for two years and running.

David went on, "We kill Sidorov, we sever Weisz's access to considerable weaponry. And every attempt made by Weisz to establish a new supply chain will raise his signature for Western intelligence to locate him. So killing Sidorov is our top priority."

"Technically," Ian interrupted, "it's the second priority. Top prize would be getting intelligence from Sidorov. We know about the hardware he sent into Libya, but we have no idea what else he has previously supplied or is currently supplying to Weisz."

David threw back his head with a short, mocking laugh. "And getting that intel is fucking impossible because we're lucky enough to have a chance of killing Sidorov in the first place—otherwise this would be a capture mission, and let's all thank God that it's not. For our sake."

Ian, who didn't seem to find the humor in the situation, scratched his jaw and said, "Conceded. But still."

Then David continued, "DEA's 960 Group has been successful in arresting each of Sidorov's predecessors by luring them to countries who value America's favor more than they value Russia's. So Sidorov doesn't leave Russia—"

Cancer said, "Where we're forbidden from operating."

"—except for annual or biannual trips to Iran—"

"Where we're also forbidden from operating," Cancer noted once more, reaching for his pack of cigarettes.

"Right," David acknowledged. "A 'no-borders' charter is only as good as our ability to get mission approval, and that's not going to happen for Sidorov's point of origin or final destination. His only layover is in Serbia, and the DEA can't run their normal operations here. They'll never get host government approval because Serbia is basically an island of pro-Russian, pro-Slavic nationalism surrounded by an ocean of pro-European, pro-NATO countries. And courtesy of Sidorov's diplomatic passport, they can't force him to land in a NATO or EU country in order to arrest him. So Sidorov has been flying unhindered in a Pilatus PC-24, the only medium-light business jet that can operate on unpaved runways, which he presumably encounters quite a few of when he's doing God knows what in Iran. He makes the flight from Moscow to Valjevo Airport here in Serbia, and then flies from Belgrade to Urmia International in northeastern Iran."

Cancer fingered a cigarette out of the pack and waved it at the table. "And while he's refueling at Valjevo, he takes meetings aboard his plane."

"Which," Reilly noted, "he never sets foot outside of unless he's in Russia or Iran. Cancer, let me bum a smoke."

"Fuck off," Cancer replied, flicking his lighter and raising it to the tip of the cigarette now in his lips as he spoke around the filter. "Blowing up that plane should be, and frankly *is*, extremely simple."

Reilly frowned, sounding hurt. "Thanks to my skills with the Gustaf."

Cancer inhaled a drag and said, "You've had more time on the Goose than anyone. Teach a monkey to do anything for long enough, and eventually it'll become pretty damn good at it—"

He groaned at the sight of David meeting his eyes and waving toward himself. That bastard wasn't supposed to do this until a mission was either complete or deemed impossible, neither of which applied at present. But Cancer complied nonetheless.

Passing the cigarette to David, he found another and sparked it as his team leader continued addressing the group.

"Blowing up the plane would be extremely simple if we weren't saddled with the Agency's legal threshold for positive identification. They require us to obtain eyes-on Sidorov via a face-to-face meeting, which was a viable possibility until Ian—excuse me, *Mr. Jon Cutler*—didn't receive an invitation for the layover at Valjevo that we know for a fact will occur in seven days."

Reilly added, "And they're sticking to their guns on this because Sidorov sometimes remains in Moscow and sends one of his captains to Iran instead. When he does, it's usually a last-minute change that the Agency doesn't even know occurred until the plane has reached Urmia. Right?"

"Correct," Ian acknowledged, "and they're not wrong about that. We can complain all we want about their PID requirements, but even if blowing up a civilian aircraft in a sovereign nation wasn't a big deal, if we miss Sidorov, then we can scratch our chances of ever getting another shot at him. He'd never leave Russia again."

Cancer took a pull from his new cigarette, extracting it from his lips and examining the ember with idle curiosity as he added, "Where we're forbidden from operating."

David smirked.

"Right. But the Agency specifies positive identification; we've been pursuing a face-to-face meeting because we thought it was the only way to establish that."

"It is," Ian said forcefully.

"We're going back to the drawing board, remember?"

When Ian presented no viable counterpoint, David opened a regional map on the computer and went on, "Point of departure is a private terminal in Moscow, and there aren't sufficient assets there to either confirm or deny whether Sidorov boards his PC-24. Even if the CIA had assets in place, Sidorov is too careful to make his presence overtly known, either visually or over his encrypted communications. And he's got the KGB making sure of that."

"FSB," Ian corrected him, "but yes."

Reilly noted, "And now that the Agency is monitoring various Serbian mafias, we know that they never refer to Sidorov by name or code, only his plane whether he's onboard or not. So how do we meet the PID threshold without boarding the PC-24?"

Ian sighed. "We can't. Look, he never gets off the plane in Serbia and sometimes he's not on it at all. We've got zero chance of running long-distance voice recognition with all the ambient vehicle noise, and Duchess knows damn well that the windows on that plane are tinted so we can't claim positive identification through an optic. There's no way we're getting authorized to take the shot without getting me on the invite list."

Cancer looked to the ceiling and said thoughtfully, "Unless Duchess gets the legal restrictions altered, or we do our thing anyway and beg forgiveness."

David grimaced as he considered the thought and dismissed it in one fell swoop while flicking the filter of his cigarette to deposit ash in an empty cup.

"As long as we're discreet about it, I think Duchess is fine with us bending the rules in some areas. Legal restrictions aren't one of them, and if the lawyers were going to budge, it would have happened prior to a high-risk undercover op getting authorized. We can't just shovel problems her way—we have to come up with a possible solution."

"And I'm telling you," Ian insisted, "there's no way we can meet the threshold for positive identification without an invite to meet him. But we just bought a metric fuckton of weapons in a single order that was already a record-setter for Affinity Gold. If that didn't work, we can't expect that running a bigger order will achieve different results, and even if we tried, it's going to take Gudelj more time than we have available to find all the hardware."

Then Ian fell silent, as if in consideration of his own words.

The intelligence operative drew a breath, then held it. His eyelids flew opened, then narrowed, before he leaned forward to prop both elbows atop the table and steeple his fingertips.

"Unless," he said, "there's something sufficiently high value nearby that Gudelj could acquire quickly, that would move us up the priority roster for direct access to Sidorov."

Cancer waited a beat for Ian to follow up that thought with a viable comment, but he remained silent.

Finally the sniper lowered his cigarette and spoke in a near outburst. "Well, is there?"

Still, Ian didn't speak—he almost gasped at his own internal monologue, after which he spoke a single word.

"Maybe."

Reilly frowned. "What's that supposed to mean?"

Only then did Ian's gaze dart between each member of the team before him, and when he spoke, it was with a rapid-fire momentum that convinced Cancer the little bastard was onto something big.

"There's something that's suspected, but not confirmed. And even asking Gudelj about it brings a whole new set of variables into play, namely him suspecting we're affiliated with a Western government. But at this point, it just might be worth the risk."

Cancer took a drag and spoke amid the smoke streaming through both nostrils. "You gonna tell us what it is, asshole?"

Ian didn't respond.

Instead, he pulled the open laptop to himself, began typing rapidly, and then spun it around so his teammates could view the screen.

7

"This is lunacy, right?"

Meiling Chen looked distraught, her eyes imploring Duchess for a semblance of hope amid the seeming insanity of the team's request.

"Maybe," Duchess replied crisply. Then she added, "I almost hope it is."

"Then why are we even entertaining the notion?"

Duchess drew a breath, examining the OPCEN ceiling as she gathered her thoughts.

"Meiling, the men on that team are many things. I'd like to say that 'dumb' wasn't one of their defining characteristics, but they have a long and distinguished track record that valiantly disputes that notion. However, I will say that when they've generated a possible solution in the face of every tide of fate to the contrary—and there have been quite a few, to date—it's never been without merit."

Chen's visible discomfort pleased Duchess to no small end. It was a petty response, to be sure, but Duchess couldn't help herself from feeling it nonetheless.

The silence between them drew out another few seconds before Chen erupted.

"They're not analysts. That's our domain, and the fact that no one on the staff has so much as considered this option leads me to believe that it's not a good one."

"Ian is the closest they've got," Duchess said by way of concession. "And granted, most of their self-generated plans have been tactical, not tradecraft. They're well outside their comfort zone operating this close to outright espionage, but I can tell you for a fact that they take mission success as a very personal matter. We've an obligation to hear them out, if nothing else."

"Well," Chen replied, glancing at her watch, "it's time."

Duchess rose from her seat, setting her fingertips on her desk as she scanned the alert gazes of her OPCEN staff and settled on the J2, her intelligence officer.

Then Duchess began the meeting in a tone that was a half-step removed from outrage.

"What's this nonsense about asking for uranium?"

Lucios flinched, a momentary reaction that was quickly replaced by his sedate, Spanish-accented voice rattling off the analytical particulars.

"It's not exactly nonsense. There may be an active stockpile that's escaped detection thus far, and if so, their request isn't as ludicrous as it seems."

"A *stockpile*, now? If there's evidence for that, how is it still in the wild?"

Lucios consulted the screen beside him, likely more out of reflex than anything else; the man's brain was an encyclopedia unto itself.

He explained, "There have been twenty-plus arrests for the attempted sale of nuclear material since the collapse of the Soviet Union: beryllium, fuel rods, concentrated plutonium, and uranium. Only three of those arrests, however, are pertinent to the team's proposal. The first was in Bulgaria, 1999—a border guard searched a vehicle returning from Turkey and recovered four grams of highly enriched uranium. Officially, it was a lucky guess by border control. Unofficially, an asset in Istanbul reported the seller was on his way to Romania after failing to find a buyer in Turkey, and we alerted the Bulgarians."

"And the other two arrests?" Duchess asked.

"Paris, 2001. A five-gram sample was recovered in a police operation. And the most recent was Moldova in 2014, which was a sting operation using a police informant. That effort recovered 200 grams of highly enriched uranium."

Chen blurted, "If there have been over twenty arrests, then what makes these three so relevant?"

Duchess cut her eyes to her new deputy, silencing the woman in a half-second before she fixed Lucios in her gaze once more, waiting for a response to the not-invalid inquiry.

The intelligence officer went on, "All three samples were analyzed at the Lawrence Livermore National Laboratory and were found to share the same isotopic signature—they originated from a Russian nuclear facility in the closed city of Ozersk called the Mayak Production Association. Date of production for each sample was assessed as October 30, 1993, plus or minus one month of fidelity. All were being presented by the owners as samples of a much larger cache, ranging in size from 10 to 39 kilos depending on the source. It's possible, of course, that the samples are just that: small quantities smuggled out of Russia to facilitate a larger deal, upon which the buyers would be killed after making payment."

"I should think so," Duchess said. "It strains credulity that a sizeable cache of uranium wouldn't have been ferreted out by now."

Lucios cleared his throat uncomfortably.

"Unfortunately, ma'am, highly enriched uranium is not difficult to conceal. It requires very little shielding to block its radiation from sensors. All three samples were packaged in identical lead canisters that could have easily passed through 99 percent of standard radiation detectors without raising an alarm, which indicates the cache, if there is one, is similarly safeguarded."

Duchess was fully conscious that she should have been horrified by this news; instead, she was increasingly exhilarated as the discussion progressed. Granted, rogue nuclear material was a living nightmare for anyone with a conscience, much less a member of the intelligence community, but she was more concerned about Sidorov continuing his facilitation for the syndicate behind the largest terrorist efforts since 9/11. And if trying to purchase said material was what it took to put Ian aboard that plane to establish positive identification, then so be it.

She tried to keep the emotion out of her voice as she asked, "Any assessment on where such a cache would be located?"

To his credit, Lucios didn't hesitate.

"Moldova, ma'am. More specifically the Transnistria region. It's a hotbed for smuggling, with a sizeable community of Russian expats including the retired military colonel who brokered the attempted 2014 sale. And each of the three arrests involved Moldovans with links to internal and Russian organized crime."

"What about Affinity Gold, deep-cover black-market buys, that sort of thing?"

"Every Western government has been trying to scoop up rogue nuclear materials ever since the collapse of the Soviet Union, and that hasn't stopped since denuclearization of former member states was completed. When there's a deal to sell highly enriched uranium—and those negotiations happen several times each year, up to the modern day—it's usually between agents of various governments who've wandered into one another's sting operation."

Damn, she thought, that was bad news. She quipped, "I'm guessing that's well known to black marketeers by now."

Lucios nodded. "Absolutely, which is likely why the cache has gone unsold. Now, it's probably widely assumed that anyone trying to buy the cache is a government operative."

"So if our team requests it from Gudelj, he's likely to think the same."

She watched him closely, trying to gauge the response by his expression—a futile endeavor, Duchess knew, but one she couldn't stop herself from attempting nonetheless.

"Not necessarily," he said thoughtfully. "The nuclear acquisition efforts have thus far occurred under separate programs. No one from Affinity Gold has yet tried to purchase highly enriched uranium, mainly because it risks erasing months or years of funneling arms out of the black market and into the resistance movements we've been supporting. In those cases, the certainty of securing thousands of surface-to-air missiles outweighs the possibility of a single cache of degraded uranium."

Duchess tried without success to keep a smile from her face as she responded, "And if there was ever a time to test those waters, this is it."

"From the perspective of Project Longwing," Lucios said tentatively, "of course. Our mission is to positively identify and kill Sidorov. If that mission is already at a standstill, then we have precious little to lose. For Affinity Gold, it's another matter altogether. If Jelena gets burned trying to escalate her purchase history, then she's burned for good, and with it, the Agency's access and placement with the Janjicari for the foreseeable future."

"But if we were to proceed—"

"The first order of business would be to request a sample for testing. Enrichment of twenty percent is considered weapons-grade, and the previous samples were between eighty and ninety percent."

Duchess could sense Chen's gaze burning a hole through her, a nonverbal begging to side with the cons rather than the pros of this emerging proposal.

"Next question," Duchess said. "What's the transit time from Moldova to Serbia?"

"Fourteen hours by car."

She looked to Gregory Pharr. "Legal issues?"

The lawyer gave a helpless shrug.

"Ma'am, this would occur under Affinity Gold authorities, not Project Longwing's. If their department approves it, there's no issue from our end."

She nodded and, after a satisfied moment of self-congratulation, spoke again.

"I'm going to coordinate with Affinity to see if we can get this proposal pushed through."

That simple statement seemed to suck all the oxygen out of the room, and Duchess countered the momentous sense of crossing into uncharted territory by taking her seat in a casual and almost anticlimactic manner.

The OPCEN staff were slow to resume their normal tasks, and it only took a few seconds for Chen to lean in and speak with measured forcefulness.

"Forget the legal authorities. The very act of having our team make the request could end the entire Janjicari penetration."

Duchess swiftly responded, "We can't get a lethal operation approved for Russia or Iran, and the only other country Sidorov stops in is Serbia. If we don't take him down there, he'll continue to operate."

"For now, maybe—but that doesn't mean he won't alter his pattern in the future. Going forward with this doesn't just risk taking our team out of the fight in Serbia, it risks eradicating all the progress Affinity Gold has made there. We have to consider the bigger picture."

Duchess leaned toward her counterpart, whose expression didn't soften in the slightest amid a withering glare.

"And if Sidorov wasn't supplying Erik Weisz," she almost hissed, "there would be room for debate. But Weisz has killed five thousand in Cairo alone, and I don't want to consider how much higher that number would be if he'd pulled off either of the other two attacks we've stopped so far. We don't know where he is or what he's working on. What we *do* know is that he's getting the bulk of his hardware from Sidorov. That's the only link we can sever at present, and I'm not going to wait for it to slip through our fingers."

8

Ian was facing the wall, arms folded in thought, when a voice behind him drawled, "How confident are you feeling about this, buddy?"

Turning to face the pointman, Ian found that Worthy hadn't moved from his position on the floor, leaning against his hiking pack with his hands behind his head.

"Don't know," Ian admitted. "But the fact that we didn't get shot down upon asking has to count for something."

Reilly paused his current exercise—seemingly endless volleys of pushups, flutter kicks, and crunches followed by more pushups, completing a final grunted repetition before lowering his knees to the ground.

"I mean," he panted, "on one hand it's no different than all the other dumb ideas we've had when backed into a corner, and there have been a lot—all of them easy to judge, but not so easy to provide a better alternative."

Ian nodded. "Or any alternative at all. Yeah, I'd say that's about the size of it."

Cancer looked like he was on the world's shittiest vacation—he was leaning back in a folding chair, feet propped on the table beside the bottle of rakia. This was life in a safehouse: waiting and more waiting, a seemingly endless purgatory spent at the mercy of decision makers located on the far side of the world.

David was at the computer, tending to the encrypted chat with Duchess. One of the many detriments of occupying a basement safehouse within a pro-Russian "flawed democracy" was the inability to establish satellite communications via the attendant relays required to maintain the connection.

As a result, Ian was entirely reliant on either staring at the screen or implicitly trusting whatever David relayed, the latter of which occurred now.

"We just got approval to request a sample," the team leader said, turning in his chair to face them. "If it's legitimate, the Agency will pay for the entire load out of the black budget just to get it off the market—up to 200 million dollars, no questions asked, and anything beyond that will require additional approval. All we'd owe them in addition to the uranium is any intel related to the sale."

Reilly blinked.

"Did you say 200 *million?*"

Shrugging, David replied, "They've already spent billions denuclearizing post-Soviet states. What's a few million more?" Then he cut his eyes to Ian. "So when should we call Gudelj—does it make a difference to him?"

Ian considered that, then gave a slight shake of his head.

"Fuck it," David said. "Let's get this over with before anyone at Langley changes their mind."

Ian gauged his team's responsiveness after consuming varying degrees of rakia the previous night—Cancer had a deadpan stare, to be sure, while Worthy appeared to view the proceedings as a formality and nothing more.

And David, ever impatient, held up his wrist and tapped his watch for emphasis.

Uncertain what to make of the sum total of these observations, Ian turned his attention instead to the particulars of their getaway—all bags were packed and neatly aligned against the wall, an easy "out" if things went sideways and the safehouse was compromised. That sole factor remained his beacon of hope under the circumstances, and Ian found the encrypted cell phone he'd been using to maintain communications with Gudelj. Hitting the speed dial, he raised the phone to his ear.

When Gudelj responded, he sounded like he was annoyed at the unscheduled call. "Yes?" he asked.

Ian responded neutrally, calmly, affecting the voice of someone who'd transitioned to giving orders for far longer than he'd been relegated to receiving them.

"Do you have connections in Moldova?"

Gudelj hesitated, though only for a moment. "That depends on what you are looking for."

"The thing that only Moldova can provide," Ian said.

The silence that ensued was palpable, broken not by Gudelj but rather David, who snapped his fingers without breaking his gaze from a sudden fixation on his computer screen. Worthy and Cancer rose and joined the team leader, who was now making a slashing motion across his throat as he leapt up from his seat. Ian leaned in to see the surveillance feed of Sarajevska Street, just outside the stairs leading to their basement, where a full-size van was screeching to a halt behind a sedan whose doors were being flung open by the passengers.

By the time he processed the sight, David had slammed the laptop shut and yanked it off the table. The team scrambled into motion, recovering what little equipment remained in the open and stuffing it into bags before donning their packs in hasty succession. Their withdrawal procedure had progressed from a contingency plan held in reserve to a crisis execution phase in the span of two seconds; timing was everything, Ian realized, and his own couldn't have possibly been worse as it pertained to this call.

He tried to speed things up by continuing, "If you're not connected, I can go directly to the source—"

"I must warn you, Jon," Gudelj cautioned. "Asking for such a thing is a very serious matter. You must be very clear."

Ian didn't hesitate in responding; even before the need to abandon the safehouse, his team's mission in Serbia was as dead as JFK, and there was precious little to lose by delaying the obvious. By contrast, he thought, there was alarmingly little to risk by laying his cards on the table.

He tucked the phone against his shoulder and was reaching for his hiking pack as he replied, "Uranium-235. I know a cache is out there, and I want a five-gram minimum sample for my client to test. If it's authentic, and enriched to, say, seventy percent minimum, I'll buy the entire load at wholesale pricing based on total quantity up to my client's cap."

The pause that followed was tangible both in significance and length—Ian had slung his pack over both shoulders before Gudelj spoke at last.

"If I try to arrange what you ask, you must already be prepared to test a sample, and then remain available around the clock to receive it whenever and however I dictate. Any failure to comply will blacklist you forever, if such merchandise exists in the first place—"

"We've both followed the arrests, and uranium doesn't get better with time. Someone is sitting on a rapidly depreciating asset at great risk to themselves. I'm prepared to conduct enrichment testing right now, and if that checks out, I'll take all of it off the seller's hands and make you and me very wealthy in the process."

And that, Ian realized, was as far into the conversation as he'd ever get.

His team was already shouldering the final bags containing what little operational gear remained on the premises, with Worthy leading the way on his stomach as he slipped through the team's sole structural modification to the basement safehouse: a modest cutout in a non-load-bearing wall, beyond which was a utility room for the adjoining apartment building. Judging by the fact that David followed him through without the sound of any subsequent gunshots, it appeared their pursuers, whoever they were, hadn't anticipated such an alteration to the floorplan.

Ian was next, third in the order of movement as per both the plan and, annoyingly, the fact that Cancer was manhandling him toward the only viable exit.

The intelligence operative had only one sentence left before requiring both hands to negotiate the wall cutout, and he made it count the only way he knew how.

"Make a call to Transnistria and get back to me—or I will go there myself."

Reilly uncapped the twenty-liter can beside the basement's lone door, then hoisted it to his waist before upending it to spew gasoline on the concrete floor.

He started with an arc directly before the entrance and then began working his way backward while pouring a zigzagging pattern of fluid.

The goal wasn't to do any serious structural damage—the impending blaze would be short-lived and largely contained by the basement walls—but to present the incoming shooters with a temporarily impassable obstacle that would delay their discovery of the drywall cutout through which the rest of his team was now escaping.

Reilly's gas can ran out by the time he reached the improvised exit, and he tossed it aside before dipping a hand into his pocket.

He procured a double-jet lighter filled to the brim with liquid butane and pressed its switch to ignite the hissing dual sparks of conical flame. Without hesitation, he lowered the tip of the twin flames toward the splattered liquid before him in anticipation of a viable outcome.

The medic had barely begun the process when a blast of flame erupted and launched toward the room's sole entrance, the effect so explosive that he momentarily wondered if his eyebrows had survived. A wave of searing heat blasted across the exposed skin of his face, and by the time that occurred he'd released the lighter switch, its former flame now replaced by a lake of fire that stretched across the entire floor.

With his diversion accomplished, he pocketed the lighter and was in the process of moving himself and his ruck through the wall cutout amid voices shouting in Serbian on the other side of the door, a final barrier that wouldn't remain a barrier for long judging by the booming double blasts of a shotgun breach.

By then Reilly was slipping inside the dusty confines of an apartment building utility room on the far side, and a moment before his hearing was eclipsed by the noisy hum of an industrial HVAC unit, he detected an oddly familiar clattering of metal against the concrete floor below.

Looking back through the hatch, his last glimpse of the former basement safehouse revealed the familiar shape of a narrow metal cylinder rolling clear of the flames.

Reilly had exactly one second to move sideways and away from the cutout before the concussion grenade exploded in a dazzling flash of light, eradicating the sound of the HVAC as his sense of sound transformed into one continuous bell ringing at a uniformly high pitch in both ears.

Fighting through the effects of the flashbang—it felt like he'd just gotten slugged in the sternum, even on the other side of the wall—Reilly raced across the utility room toward the stairwell access, struggling to rejoin his team.

Worthy rounded the final stairwell landing on the apartment building's top level, making a momentary diversion to yank down on the fire alarm.

A shrill howl sounded at once, leaving the team sixty seconds or less before the stairs and street were flooded with evacuating civilians who would impede his team as much as their pursuers; the latter would be arriving in short order once the basement fire subsided and they discovered the wall cutout.

Worthy had no intentions of being around when that occurred, and he turned to advance up a final stretch of stairs that led to a short metal ladder rising the remaining distance to the ceiling. He pulled himself up the rungs until reaching a closed ceiling hatch emblazoned with a red sign and bold Serbian Cyrillic lettering.

And while he didn't speak the language, he knew well enough what it said—the same message existed on emergency exits the world over, some variation of *EMERGENCY EXIT ONLY, ALARM WILL SOUND*. Worthy muscled the bolt free from its locked position, then flung the hatch open as a metallic buzzing sounded its objection, the security alarm barely audible over the howling siren.

Then he climbed through it, or tried to, his hiking pack snagging twice on the edge of the hatch before he managed to force it clear and scramble onto the roof.

He rose to a standing position only to be buffeted by a blast of icy wind, the dull gray sky overhead allowing enough sunlight for him to see the glaze of wetness covering the rooftops before him.

The entire city block was lined by a perimeter of interconnected buildings that presented a unified front on all sides, ranging in height from one to seven stories and everything in between, interspersed with select cutouts to allow access from the street to internal parking lots and vice versa. One of those internal parking lots was in the courtyard to his left, dotted with trees that would at least provide a chance of breaking his three-story fall if he slipped. To his right was the sidewalk and street, all of it unforgiving asphalt and pavement in plain view of whoever had just tried to roll up his team.

Worthy took off along the apex of the roof, moving southeast toward a one-story rise of the next interconnected building on his egress route. They'd prepared for this, but what they hadn't counted on was a barrage of freezing rain that morning. While it had stopped an hour or so earlier, the damage was done—the roof tiles beneath his boot soles were as slick as oil, which turned an otherwise basic urban evasion route into a high-stakes obstacle course. The price of falling was imprisonment if not death, and at present he wasn't sure which would be preferable.

He didn't so much as look backward until he'd reached the next exterior wall and, with it, a maintenance ladder leading twelve feet to another rooftop. Only when he was halfway up the rungs did he cast a rearward glance that revealed David arriving at the base of the ladder, Ian and Cancer carefully threading their way across the apex, and Reilly emerging from the hatch before slamming it shut behind him.

Then Worthy continued to climb, mounting the next roof and resuming his movement as the fire alarm faded to the sound of wind, traffic, and car horns. This apex provided worse footing than the last, its shingles made of unforgiving corrugated steel. He had another forty feet to cover before reaching the ladder leading to the next and final roof—a flattop, thank God, provided he stayed upright long enough to see it.

He placed his footfalls carefully, taking short and calculated steps as he led the way for his team while scanning the path ahead for icy patches. The weight of his hiking pack didn't help: the slightest shift in his center of gravity threatened to send him barreling to one side of the apex or the other.

But Worthy covered the stretch without incident, closing within a few feet from the next ladder. He was almost close enough to reach out and grab the nearest rung, and was extending his arm to do just that when the threat of a misplaced footfall came into play in spectacular fashion.

Worthy's boot sole scraped the left edge of the roof before he lost his footing altogether, tilting violently to the point of no return before he fell.

I saw Worthy vanish from my sight in a flash of movement, my blood running cold as I leapt forward in an attempt to grab him.

Too late. His ass struck the apex and he corkscrewed down the left slope of the roof, helplessly flinging an arm upward as I knelt and shot a hand toward it.

Our palms slapped together as I shifted my weight in the opposite direction to arrest his fall, very nearly going down with him myself. Ian grabbed my hiking pack from behind, stabilizing my position as we established an uneasy three-way standoff on the pinnacle of the roof. I heard Worthy gasping for breath as he came to a complete stop, after which I began hoisting him back up while Ian held me in place.

Worthy clambered up the steeply angled steel shingles, feet struggling for purchase as he threw his free arm over the apex. It landed alongside the source of his fall, a transparent patch of ice that would've been completely invisible save the scrape his boot sole had made when sliding on it.

Finally he managed to regain his footing and rise in a crouch, gingerly stepping over the ice and securing a grip on the ladder before proceeding forward as a good pointman should. His only concession to the fact that I'd just saved his life congealed into a single word whispered over his shoulder.

"Thanks."

After Ian helped me rise to standing height, I gripped the bottom rung and extended a hand out to him. He accepted the offering as I assisted him over the ice, and then Ian vanished up the ladder as I remained in place to repeat the process with Cancer and finally Reilly, whose normally ruddy face was now pale with the strain of moving his considerable weight across the potentially fatal stretch of rooftop.

Once the medic began climbing, I followed suit, now making out the sound of police or fire sirens approaching from the street beside me. I didn't bother checking which it was, knowing full well that while our pursuers couldn't see us from ground level, any number of possible observers watching from the surrounding windows might be calling the authorities to report five daredevils threading their way across the rooftops.

That fear subsided as I reached the top of the ladder and clambered atop a mercifully flat surface. Worthy had already reached the fire escape on the far side, with the rest of the team following suit, trailed by me as the last man.

From here, our escape was a piece of cake: we descended the fire escape stairs to an interior courtyard where our Toyota Land Cruiser was staged amid rows of similarly parked vehicles. Worthy was at the wheel and firing the engine by the time I made landfall.

I deposited my hiking pack alongside the others, then closed the rear hatch and slid into the passenger seat.

Worthy pulled forward and turned toward a vehicle path between buildings, taking a left on Durmitorska Street after braking for a fire truck to scream past with its sirens blaring.

Having departed a basement at the western corner of the block, now we were making a vehicle egress on the south side—a clever getaway plan that had been executed with textbook precision, which would've been a considerable victory if not for the overwhelming indicators that pointed to our team being totally fucked.

We were now down one of two possible safehouse options in Belgrade, had no idea who had come to arrest or kill us and why, and had only Cancer's adamant insistence on round-the-clock camera monitoring to thank for our current freedom. My encrypted chat with our Agency operations center had only flashed an evacuation order a moment before I flipped the laptop shut in response to a SWAT-grade team of fully equipped shooters pouring out of the van beside our basement stairwell.

I withdrew my phone and dialed. At some point in the near future I'd have to reach out to Duchess to confirm that we'd made it out okay, but first I had a far more pressing call to make.

Jelena answered promptly.

"Go ahead."

"Safehouse just got compromised, we're headed to the alternate. Can you clear it ahead of our arrival?"

"*Jebati*," she cursed. "I can be there in ten minutes."

9

Worthy had his MP7 in hand as he entered the house.

Intellectually, he knew this was an unnecessary precaution. Jelena had unlocked the residence and done a full walk-through ahead of their arrival—an ostensibly unarmed civilian female native backstopped by a full cover story drew a lot less attention than five clean-cut men of military bearing that didn't even speak Serbian. But whether he was still jumpy after nearly falling off a roof or genuinely concerned about imminent compromise, he couldn't relax until he'd personally entered and checked every room. He offered no apologies for doing so with a suppressed automatic weapon held at the low ready, and his team asked for none.

The spartan interior had a funky smell to it, maybe not mold but definitely mildew. The odor reflected what it was: a structure that remained unoccupied for long periods of time, maintained under the assumption that it may eventually be required in case of a blowout from a better location.

Which wasn't to say this was a step down in terms of available space—it was a 1,300-square-foot residential home. Not exactly posh accommodations, but better than squatting in a basement hovel.

But it was the alternate location for good reason.

The current location in eastern Belgrade placed the team significantly farther from any time-sensitive transactions in the downtown area, which meant less time to reconnoiter meeting sites and establish security. And if that wasn't a dealbreaker, then the lack of a viable escape route certainly was. They'd emerged from the basement location unscathed for good reason, namely that no opposers could feasibly isolate the entire block. Particularly, Worthy thought, when they had no way of anticipating the team tunneling through an interior wall to an entirely separate structure like sewer rats.

But in the suburbs, it would be all too easy for any opponents—mafia, police, didn't matter—to surround a single home, particularly one as small as this. If the team was lucky enough to escape an initial assault, they'd be relegated to running on foot through backyards and side streets, with the largest building in the area a pet supply store. Not exactly ideal territory to evade detection while running for their lives, nor was shooting it out a viable option with the bulk of their non-concealable weapons stashed at Jelena's residence. Unless their opponents came at them with slingshots, Worthy thought, the team's present MP7s and Glock 26 pistols wouldn't keep a determined enemy force at bay for very long.

That reality seemed to have occurred to the other members of his team as well. By the time he'd finished checking each room and consolidated in the kitchen, where Jelena was waiting with a degree of patience that said she knew the score with Agency paramilitary types, Worthy noticed that not only had no one else taken off their hiking pack until he did, but that to a man everyone either had their MP7 in hand or easily accessible on its sling.

Finally, amid the muted thumps of hiking packs hitting the cheap laminate floor, David spoke.

"What the fuck just happened? Those guys were law enforcement, right?"

Worthy nodded. "Definitely. Way too organized for a mob hit."

David threw up his hands.

"Then how did Duchess not pick up any radio intercepts?"

Jelena interceded, leaning against a Formica countertop and folding her arms. "Speaking from long experience in Belgrade, I can assure you that the Agency is monitoring what they can, mainly the Belgrade Police Department and communications between mafia segments."

"So?"

"So that means the raid was probably conducted by the BIA."

Cancer frowned. "Serbian intelligence?"

"Yes," Jelena clarified. "The Security Intelligence Agency. They have sufficient encryption to evade detection."

Ian's eyes narrowed. "You think Gudelj ratted us out?"

Jelena shook her head. "Gudelj did not know about the safehouse, nor would he have any reason to disrupt a profitable relationship. Quite the opposite, in fact. If anything caused the compromise, it was someone reporting unusual activity and the state figuring out it was not sanctioned—which is to say, they were not profiting. Protection in Serbia comes from money or personal connections, nothing else."

Reilly ran both hands through his hair, speaking with an air of grave finality. "I'm starting to wish we were back in Libya—the government may have been virtually nonexistent and corrupt as fuck, but at least they weren't trying to actively kill us."

Jelena smiled politely.

"What can I say, this is Serbia. If you are looking for stability, you came to the wrong place. My grandfather has lived in six countries without ever moving from his childhood home in Belgrade."

Worthy asked, "I didn't think we'd ever need to broach this topic, but any chance you have any other backup safehouses we don't know about?"

"Not in Belgrade," she conceded. "If you get compromised here, we must transition to Kovačica, one hour north."

"Maybe we should go there anyway, as a precautionary measure."

Ian finally spoke, dismissing the notion in one fell swoop.

"Except I'm on call 24/7 for a zero-notice meeting to accept a uranium sample. If we miss that, our 'in' with Gudelj is as good as dead." Then he lifted his gaze to the team, eyes ticking across the other members. "I mean, you guys could go, but Jelena and I have to remain in Belgrade."

David said adamantly, "We all have to remain, because there's no way I'm letting you two head into a meeting without backup. Look, bouncing safehouses this early isn't ideal, but it's nothing we can't handle. We didn't lose any equipment and we should count ourselves lucky that Worthy came out of that rooftop slip without shattering both legs and his pelvis to boot. Jelena, can you get us a new surveillance kit so we can post cameras?"

She considered the question for a moment.

"Within six hours or so, yes."

"Good," David continued, "because we're going to need it. Until then, it's going to be Worthy, Reilly, and Ian on guard. Cancer, you and I have some planning to do for this next meet."

10

Duchess had never thought she'd see the day when she had to explain both herself and Project Longwing to someone with zero covert experience beyond the standard Agency case officer career pipeline, but that day had apparently arrived.

She was seated at the desk in her personal office, squared off with one Meiling Chen, who'd finally broken and requested a private audience.

Chen began, "I've got some concerns about Project Longwing that I'd like to discuss."

"Then you're in good company," Duchess swiftly replied, already sensing where this conversation was headed and why, "because concerns are all I've got, especially at the moment. And if you've got any viable suggestions on how to make the clock tick more smoothly around here after two weeks on the job, then you've got my undivided attention."

"Actually, I was bothered within the first three or four days. I've spent the last week and a half waiting to see if I was missing something, and I don't believe I am."

Into battle, Duchess thought.

"Let's hear it."

"First is Erik Weisz."

Duchess grinned. "My favorite topic of discussion."

"The capture mission in China resulted in a living captive who met the man, which gave us a composite sketch, along with behavioral cues, linguistic analysis—I mean, David Rivers actually *spoke* with him over the satphone. We know he's either Italian or speaking very convincingly and consistently with an Italian accent, and yet haven't been able to determine his identity."

"Everything you just said is correct."

"I've looked over the Weisz file, and believe me, I'm not trying to call your judgment on his threat level into question."

"And yet," Duchess said with a trace of a smile, "you're about to, somehow. Go ahead and speak freely. I'm afraid we don't have the luxury of standard office politics here."

Chen drew a breath and continued, "Weisz has to be running complex security protocols to have evaded Western intelligence thus far. We should go public with that information. The FBI's Ten Most Wanted Fugitives posters exist for a reason. It takes a village to bring down Billy the Kid, but step one is telling the village about Billy the Kid in the first place. We'd instantly have every country in the world looking for this guy and his network."

Duchess felt herself continuing to smile despite her best efforts. "That is an extremely valid point."

"And?"

"And I've been considering the same thing for some time now. That decision point rests far over my head, but the seventh floor has thus far decided to limit the scope of dissemination—"

"To the Five Eyes, I know. Which leaves a vast majority of the globe uncovered."

Duchess nodded. The Five Eyes was an intelligence alliance abbreviated as FVEY on official documents: the US, UK, Canada, New Zealand, and Australia.

Then she explained, "Geographically, it's a small portion of the globe, as you said. In terms of intelligence reach, it's a great deal larger. That gap, regrettably, is covered by Russia and China, neither of which are keen on sharing information with us. That being said, I agree with you: we cannot discount the possibility of someone with knowledge about Weisz who may come forward if we go public."

"And yet we haven't. Why?"

Duchess held up a hand with her index and middle fingers extended.

"Two reasons, mainly. The first is the likely impenetrability of his circle, which we've verified includes foreign politicians who are bribed to either participate in or protect the operation. And the only one we have identified by name tried to flee Nigeria as soon as he failed to uphold his end of the bargain, and was assassinated almost immediately."

"Chukwuma Malu. I know."

What Chen didn't know, Duchess thought, was that the politician was captured by David's team and briefly interrogated under the guise that they were acting on behalf of Weisz—that particular off-the-books operation was known only to Duchess and Chen's predecessor, the latter of whom had helped to orchestrate the entire thing. And it had ended not in an assassination per se, but a covert kill.

She nodded. "But the main reason is one of recruitment. If we publicly brand Weisz as the figurehead behind Cairo, then we instantly funnel every disenfranchised individual looking to join an extremist organization toward any number of terrorist recruiters, all of whom will instantly claim to be connected to Weisz. We have ISIS to thank for that precedent—a worldwide recruitment phenomenon that sent 30,000 willing men and women from eighty-plus countries into their ranks. And Weisz isn't raping and murdering his way across the Middle East. His operations have been extremely sophisticated, so the average IQ of those willing to join his cause —and the technical and cyber capabilities they bring with them—will be substantially higher."

"That makes sense, I suppose."

"Good," Duchess went on, "and make no mistake, there will come a day when Erik Weisz's true identity becomes a household name. The sole purpose of Project Longwing at this point is to ensure that particular event occurs after he's dead."

Chen summoned an audible breath.

"Be that as it may, I have concerns about half-stepping to achieve that goal."

"I'm sorry, did you—did you just say *half-stepping*?"

"Our mission in Serbia barely achieved liftoff before being shot from the sky. We don't even have an invitation to meet with Sidorov, and the entire team was nearly rolled up by the secret police a few hours ago."

"Escape plans exist for a reason."

"I understand that," Chen clarified, tucking her hair behind one ear, "but now we're trying to bridge the gap by bringing highly enriched uranium into play."

"Your point?"

"Project Longwing has had its successes to date, but if my understanding of the mission debriefs is correct, most if not all occurred by the narrowest of margins. I attribute that in large part to an under-resourced and insufficiently staffed team of five men, which restricts their effectiveness to lethal authorities at best when a majority of the targets would be far more useful if captured alive."

"Snatch missions typically require a whole lot more than five individuals, but at the moment that's all we've got."

"Which is why in the long-term, Project Longwing should be expanded, not expected to produce results on the same play. Sidorov could be apprehended with appropriate units from Ground Branch or JSOC."

Duchess raised her eyebrows. "That's your solution—to punt our mission?"

"If your concern really is Erik Weisz, and capturing Sidorov alive would be instrumental in achieving that, then yes, in this case I would. But if you're asking how I would influence the mission as it currently exists in Serbia, my answer would be to send more officers under various pretenses—enough for the government to detect, but not to prove. Base them in geographically disparate parts of the country to create a smokescreen that depletes secret police surveillance resources and draws attention away from our team."

"Smokescreens have a nasty habit of becoming a marker for paramilitary operations more than a genuine diversion, and I dare say we've received all the Agency support we're going to get at this point."

Chen frowned. "Then you should concede that other elements are more suited to capturing Sidorov."

"You're conflating Sidorov's capture with tracking down Weisz, but the key to finding Weisz is in maintaining his pursuit in the hands of Project Longwing, no matter the cost."

"I fail to see how that should be true."

Duchess shrugged.

"And until you have proved yourself, you'll just have to take my word for it."

In truth, Chen wasn't wrong; from a tactical perspective, the five-man ground team could easily be swapped out with a larger element from Ground Branch or a Tier One unit.

But the cornerstones of both were oversight and accountability, either of which would be a death knell to Project Longwing as it had existed thus far. The uneasy truth was that to date, combating Weisz had required men who could never pass a military, much less Agency, polygraph. David Rivers had lied in his reporting on multiple occasions *that she knew about*, and after speaking with him afterward, all were for damn good reasons. She had no doubt his team would continue to bend the rules as needed to achieve results, and frankly, that's exactly what Project Longwing needed right now. Erik Weisz operated in the gray area, if not the black—killing him would require the same.

Duchess could say none of that to Meiling Chen, whose cheeks were reddening, her gaze growing colder by the second.

"You don't trust me because you've heard the rumors."

"I prefer," Duchess said noncommittally, "to hear both sides of the story before making a judgment one way or the other."

Chen shook her head slowly, gravely.

"And I prefer not to explain myself. I was internally cleared by the Agency, and that's all you need to know."

Duchess leaned forward and set her hands on the desk, assuming a more dominant position in preparation for a tirade she'd been waiting to deliver.

"You were internally cleared, yes," she began. "And you did your follow-on assignment at a hinterlands desk before being assigned to a highly compartmentalized program that could as easily or not be a death sentence to your career. So my educated assumption based on long years of experience in an often-cutthroat bureaucracy is that you're making the Hail Mary play of bringing up 'concerns' and 'suggestions' that run counter to everything that's currently in progress. I'm guessing you're going to leave this meeting and make some record of the date and contents of our discussion, so if I drive the ship aground you can claim to have seen a better way and advised me to pursue it with no result. But if I get the ship to port, all your suggestions—which you bear no responsibility for implementing—will mysteriously evaporate. Do I have that right?"

Chen's sudden ramrod posture assured Duchess that she was a hundred percent correct, and the guilty woman sputtered, "I resent the implication that—"

"Don't patronize me, Meiling," Duchess said with a wave of her hand that indicated all of this was too obvious to warrant mention. "I understand where you're coming from, but you've got it the wrong way around. You want to insulate yourself from any fallout, but the way to do that isn't in opposition to me, it's in working through me. I didn't ask for you, and to be blunt, I'd far prefer to run this alone, because after two years on the job, I know what's required. Considering the inherent fallout if Project Longwing becomes public, and because Senator Gossweiler is fully on board now that his daughter was kidnapped, I suspect my career will die in the saddle in that OPCEN. No one is going to replace me until Erik Weisz is defeated, and that's a very, very good thing—for you as much as anyone else."

"Provided you succeed," Chen pointed out, now regaining her bearings. She was no longer disputing Duchess's assessment; instead, the woman was retreating to safety, looking for some confirmation that she could remain professionally secure by playing ball.

To that end, Duchess responded, "If I don't succeed, then I'm out of your way and I take all responsibility with me—while potentially leaving you with a glowing assessment. But if I pull off defeating Weisz in the long run—which I will—then your star gets all the redemption it needs to continue rising in the Agency."

Then, upon seeing Chen relax, Duchess decided to drop the bomb.

Without breaking eye contact, she said, "Let's not mince words. You've been internally cleared, sure, but people aren't lining up to work for you. This assignment can change that, provided you stay out of my way. If you don't, I will leverage any and all connections I've made in decades of service to ensure that this is your final assignment for the government, after which I will personally contact every intelligence consultant company with which you could ever find commensurate employment to ensure you're black-listed long before the Agency notifies you of termination."

Chen looked horrified, her cheeks no longer reddened—quite the opposite, Duchess noted with pleasure, the expression indicating that both women now understood there was no bluff involved in either the extent of Duchess's connections nor her willingness to exercise the nuclear option if so inclined.

Duchess let her expression fade to a deliberately neutral set of her jaw and asked, "Do we have an understanding?"

Chen nodded, reaching for the arms of her chair as if about to leave.

"One more thing," Duchess said, causing the woman to freeze.

"Yes?"

"I appreciate your progressive notions of one day expanding Project Longwing and pivoting to a focus on capturing, rather than killing, our targets. That may well come to pass in the future. But this is the present, and with the five men we've got, we must never, *ever* deliberately increase their degree of risk. We can't allow ourselves to be any more reckless with that team, because they're already reckless. To shift the scales by an ounce would be to annihilate them entirely."

Chen considered the words before her lips parted to reply—and, Duchess realized with a burst of anger, she'd never have the chance.

The door to her office flung open to reveal Wes Jamieson, her operations officer.

There was very little in life she detested more than an unannounced intrusion to her office, and when she spoke, it was with a degree of anger she didn't bother to conceal.

"Better be a damn good reason, Wes."

Jamieson gave a curt nod. "Gudelj just called Ian—he has less than an hour to reach Kalemegdan to accept a sample of highly enriched uranium. If he misses the meeting, he'll never hear from Gudelj again."

11

Cancer walked uphill in the sun's waning light, threading his way past scattered tourists as he headed to the observation point he'd selected for the upcoming exchange.

He tried to make sense of why Gudelj had selected this particular site for the handoff—of all the unique locations in Belgrade and the surrounding area, this was one of the last Cancer would have anticipated. As an avid student of military history, he'd studied up on this area with great interest and was particularly keen on visiting under less urgent circumstances; it was a rare circumstance where his interests were in line with those of the masses, given that this was the most popular tourist attraction in Belgrade.

Serbian locals, Jelena included, referred to the entire fort as Kalemegdan due to its placement in the larger park by the same name. Its formal title, however, was the Belgrade Fortress, and it represented the city's historical core; for centuries, the entire population existed within its walls, which had been the site of over a hundred battles, conquests, and sieges dating back to the third century BC when a Celtic tribe took it by force. The Romans had later sacked it as a strategic location in their fight against the barbarians, after which it was invaded by the Goths and Huns, then rebuilt by the Byzantine Empire before alternating ownership with

Bulgaria. It had since been claimed by the Ottomans, Hungary, medieval Serbia, and Austria, sustained damage in both World Wars, and was finally designated a cultural monument and opened to the public—the kind of landmark that a military history buff like Cancer would give his left nut to visit.

So why the hell had Gudelj chosen a fortress for the handoff?

Cancer had come up with a few possible explanations, none of them convincing. There were far more discreet locations to either hand off a sample of uranium or try and kill both Ian and Jelena, and given the current site's popularity as well as the timing just prior to sunset, when views from the elevated terrain were at their most breathtaking, it seemed like Gudelj wanted to ensure the presence of the highest possible number of civilian bystanders.

For his part, Cancer had already made a substantial climb up stone staircases and cobbled walkways, and could now make out a tall fortress wall topped by a minaret, all lit by the orange glow of floodlights preceding the arrival of nightfall. To the left of the defensive fortifications was a stone building that he came abreast of now—Ružica Church, he knew from the map, which meant he was getting close to his destination. He followed a walkway toward the front entrance to get a better look at the guardians stationed on either side of the thick wooden doors.

According to the local lore, both statues were cast from molten cannonballs. One was a medieval soldier in full chainmail and armor grasping a halberd-like polearm, some type of lance rarely seen since the sixteenth century outside of museums, reenactor troupes, and the Papal Swiss Guard. The other was a Serbian infantryman from the early 1900s with a bolt-action Mauser 98 dutifully slung over one shoulder. Cancer momentarily considered what he'd look like beside them as a continuation of this military lineage in Belgrade updated to the modern day.

He envisioned himself as a third statue with a cigarette dangling between his lips, holding a Glock 26 in one hand and a suppressed MP7 in the other. Both weapons were concealed on his person, the latter in a backpack, and while amusing, he dismissed the mental image with the thought that he wasn't fit to serve as a symbolic guardian of Ružica Church—particularly not in his current civilian attire. It was undignified.

Cancer turned right and followed the walkway toward a drop-off ahead, where he identified a series of park benches that would serve his purposes well. They were, after all, intended for gawking tourists, and he was currently playing the part himself; more importantly, it was the most strategic vantage point from which he could overlook the specific meeting site that Ian had been ordered to.

As he approached, he felt a sense of relief that he'd almost arrived at his destination after the long uphill journey to get there. That wasn't to say he was thrilled about the current assignment—if there was going to be gunplay, he wanted to be smashing heads on the playing field rather than watching from the sidelines.

But David had demanded an experienced eye playing God in what was about to occur, and when it came to experience, if nothing else beyond moral latitude and sniping ability, Cancer was the undisputed team champion. His role as scout required him to get to the meeting site as quickly as possible, by any means available, and serve as the all-seeing eyes for his team to identify any staged or inbound threats in the general vicinity: loitering enemy observers, indications of concealed weapons, signs of ostensible civilians waiting to close in for the kill.

Upon reaching the nearest unoccupied bench, he was pleased to find that the overlook afforded all the tremendous advantage of elevation that he'd been hoping for. The view was unparalleled, the horizon marked by the intersection of the Danube and Sava Rivers, both speckled with boats making sunset cruises and topped by a darkening sky scattered with the first twinkling stars.

He was now on the fortress's eastern outer bailey, looking over the roof of Saint Petka Church down the hill to his front. It was backed by a stone fortress wall, and beyond that was the small, dome-topped structure of a Turkish bathhouse that had since been repurposed to a planetarium. The paved walkways just north of it formed a Y-shaped intersection, the specified location for Ian and Jelena to wait for a container that allegedly contained a sample of highly enriched uranium. He could see all this clearly, as well as the surrounding area and any potential threats.

But that was where the good news ended. Admission to the Kalemegdan Park was free, and it showed.

The entire clearing was teeming with visitors, a churning mess of civilians ranging from groups of teenagers, to families with young children in tow, to duos and singletons snapping pictures. There was precious little to distinguish tourists from mafia representatives, simply because he was now witnessing the full gamut of possible behavior among the crowd, all or none of which could be considered suspicious.

He found his phone, confirming it was still dialed into the team conference call.

"I just got here," he began. "Currently at the overlook just west of Ružica Church."

David replied, "See anything?"

"Yes and no. It's a madhouse down there, packed with people. There might not be any bad guys or there might be an army of them—Gudelj is sending us into a shitshow."

Reilly was listening to the team conference call over a Bluetooth earpiece that he wore out of necessity—his hands were occupied by directing the bicycle he'd been maneuvering between pedestrians for a few hundred meters now.

"Wonderful," David replied without enthusiasm, "never a dull moment. Me and Lance Armstrong are about a minute out."

Looking over his shoulder, he saw David following on his own bike, likewise wearing a backpack that contained a suppressed MP7 and its requisite ammunition. Which would be immeasurably helpful if things went sideways, at least provided they had time to recover the weapons in the first place. Otherwise they'd be limited to the Glock 26 pistols in their waistbands, and while neither weapon was a fitting substitute for a proper assault rifle, the combination was far more preferable to rolling into this debacle unarmed.

"Splitting off," Reilly said over the conference call, veering right, "taking the Barutana side path."

David said, "I'm still trailing the Sava, one minute out from cutting east toward Donji Grad. Ian, how are you guys looking?"

The intelligence operative replied, "We're parking the van now, about to proceed on foot."

Ian and Jelena had deposited the two-man security element along with their bikes, and now it was a matter of getting everyone into position prior to their approach. If this thing was a setup, a crowded tourist attraction would be a fine place for it—identifying enemy shooters would be next to impossible right up until they drew weapons, by which time mere fractions of a second would remain to put them down without hitting any civilians in the process. The slightest error in judgment could result in innocent deaths, to say nothing of Ian, Jelena, or both getting their fucking heads blown off.

And while Cancer had never been particularly melodramatic—which was, Reilly thought, the most polite way he could frame the sniper's somewhat unbridled sociopathy—he certainly hadn't been lying about Kalemegdan Park being a shitshow at sunset. The crowds were out in force, bundled in their coats against the November chill, and Reilly had to maneuver his bike with considerable effort to avoid the many distracted civilians crisscrossing the walkway as they took in the sights, checked their phones, or did both at the same time.

Ahead he saw his destination: a brick-and-stone outbuilding with a steepled roof and ornate carving above an arched porthole. It wasn't attached to any fortress walls beyond waist-height barriers, and therefore offered no more tactical use than a freestanding gate surrounded by manicured lawn; any given vehicle could simply drive around it with ease. Nor, as Reilly knew from his fleeting research prior to setting off for the handoff, had it ever been intended as a defensive fortification.

The Gate of Charles VI was a triumphal arc, an entirely ceremonial structure whose only relevance to Reilly at present was its proximity to the graffiti-covered building that now served as a planetarium.

Reilly pulled his bike to the side of the walkway, then found his phone and pretended to be replying to a text.

"I'm in position," he said.

David replied, "Turning toward Donji Grad now. Ian, you're clear to make the approach."

Ian slipped through the crowd, moving in a loose formation that was probably imperceptible to all but an elevated observer—hopefully Cancer was the only one of those at present.

Jelena was staggered a few meters behind him and to the right, keeping enough spacing that a single shooter couldn't take them both out before the team's security elements reacted.

Worthy moved behind both of them, straight down the middle, toting his MP7 in a leather satchel for quick access. Given his experience as a bodyguard, he was the obvious choice to directly accompany them to the transfer site, if a transfer was going to occur at all.

Gudelj had been remarkably vague beyond the particulars needed to facilitate a handoff: *Kalemegdan, one hour from now. Meet at the walkway junction just north of the Belgrade Planetarium. Bring your friend.* He'd obviously meant Jelena, and Ian knew that could have spelled one of two possibilities. If there was a genuine sample for transfer, then having a pair of known contacts present doubled the chances for one of Gudelj's men to pass a sample without drawing attention.

But if the request for uranium was interpreted as proof of government complicity, then Gudelj could just as easily have been arranging an easy hit far from the Valjevo Airport and indeed any known mafia stronghold.

And with every step he took on his march toward the designated meeting site, Ian became slightly more convinced that he was walking into a trap.

He'd asked for a sample of highly enriched uranium the previous morning, and given the fourteen-hour minimum trip to drive it from the Transnistria region of Moldova all the way to Belgrade, one of two things had occurred. Either Gudelj had ensured its delivery as quickly as possible, or he'd taken the request to signify the presence of government agents ferreting into his organization and sought to remedy that at the earliest possible opportunity.

Either way, Gudelj himself wouldn't be present—he'd simply arranged the time and place, and had one or more expendable killers among the crowd, scanning faces for any sign of Ian and Jelena.

Knowing from overhead imagery that the Y-intersection was in the clearing ahead, he scrutinized the clusters of trees on either side of the path: they'd be the closest source of cover in the event of a melee. If that happened, Worthy would prioritize protecting Jelena as Ian defended himself with his Glock 26 until the cavalry arrived in the form of David and Reilly, whose bicycles represented the best mobility they could achieve in a setting blocked to vehicle access. But the bikes wouldn't help Ian or Jelena escape, so once fire superiority was achieved, they'd hand off their pistols before any police intervention and escape with the civilians who would, by then, be fleeing in every direction.

Checking his watch, Ian saw that less than a minute remained before the designated meeting time. He'd been scrutinizing the visitors around him since arriving at the park and nearly jumped out of his skin when a young girl shrieked at her mother behind him. No sooner had he directed his gaze forward than the crowd parted and he could see the walkway intersection. After he stepped past the final trees, the dome-topped planetarium building whose chipped and faded exterior was covered in spray-painted graffiti came into view.

Ian's senses were on fire now, a level of hypervigilance exceeding anything he'd experienced prior to shots being fired. He had to remind himself to limit his path to the left side of the walkway to provide Worthy the greatest possible field of fire between himself and Jelena, and he maintained that path right up until he reached the intersection, when he came to a complete stop.

And then—nothing happened.

Annoyed tourists swerved to avoid him, and by the time he completed a 360 visual sweep Jelena had stopped a few meters away. To his right, he would see the fortress walls and a towering minaret behind the steeple of Ružica Church, where Cancer intended to provide early warning. *Good luck with that*, Ian thought as he watched people traversing the walkways. Most were on their way uphill, presumably to get a better view of the sun setting over the Danube and Sava Rivers, though a few—mostly families with children—were heading past Ian on their way out of the park.

Ian kept his focus on the adults moving alone or in pairs, watching for the shooters among them as he mentally rehearsed drawing his handgun from beneath his coat. That focus caused him to entirely ignore a boy who brushed past his shoulder, then turned to apologize.

"*Izvini*," the boy said, and Ian replied with little more than a distracted nod until realizing that the kid had stopped behind him.

Ian spun to face him, finding a fifteen-year-old in a blue coat and black jeans, hair concealed beneath a stocking cap.

He held out a plastic shopping bag to Ian with the words, "You have 24 hours to test it. He will call you after that to negotiate."

Ian had barely taken hold of the bag before the boy turned and walked off, heading northwest toward the waterfront with his hands stuffed in his coat pockets.

After a stunned moment of disbelief that a sample of highly enriched uranium was casually handed over by a kid who wasn't yet capable of growing a mustache, Ian looked inside the bag. It contained a cellophane-wrapped sandwich, an apple, and a bag of chips, all of them intended to support the seemingly innocuous presence of the final item, which was the heaviest of all.

The thermos was a dull silver affair, fully capped and probably wiped for fingerprints prior to its transfer.

Turning to depart the way he'd come, Ian gave a sidelong glance to Jelena and said, "We've got it."

12

I pedaled my bike along the sidewalk south of Pariska Street, heading eastbound amid the glare of headlights.

The exchange had gone as well as could be expected, I thought. Ian now possessed a sample that could contain baking soda for all I knew, but everyone had made it in and out with no shots fired. Far from our team's usual arrangements, and yet under the circumstances the best outcome by far.

Now the follow-up work began. We had six people on the ground, with Reilly and me on bicycles. Our ultimate goal was to consolidate everyone into the two vehicles we'd staged outside Kalemegdan Park and return to our suburban safehouse. Before we could do that, however, we first had to assure ourselves that we weren't being followed.

Enter the SDR.

It was perhaps my least favorite part of low-visibility work, namely because it spanned long hours of generally boring effort. A combat patrol in austere terrain made short work of the task: all we had to do was head in one direction, then pull a buttonhook maneuver to set up an ambush on our backtrail. If any pursuing enemy stumbled past, their number would determine whether we hit them or not before initiating evasive maneuvers.

It was a profoundly simple process that allowed us to continue our mission in the quickest possible fashion.

But Belgrade was, well, Belgrade, and the sheer number of civilians demanded we run individual surveillance detection routes, or SDRs, before we risked returning to a safehouse established less than 48 hours ago.

The basic principle was to drag out the distance traveled over a significant length of time with numerous changes in direction, drastically reducing an opponent's ability to rotate unnoticed pursuers by swapping out vehicles or clothes. At the outset, potential tails were everywhere, but hours of seemingly nonsensical progress through the city would make any real surveillance team stand out in time.

And since I was on a bicycle pedaling my way alongside a major vehicle thoroughfare, step one was to lose any drivers trying to keep eyes-on my progress.

I veered right onto a side street that diverged from Pariska Street, noting that no cars diverted from the main road to follow me.

Proceeding alongside a row of parked cars, I gradually identified a pole-mounted clock at the brightly lit intersection ahead. This was my first visual landmark of Knez Mihailova Street, a one-kilometer stretch through one of the oldest and most celebrated areas of Belgrade. As a result it was heavily trafficked at all hours, which wouldn't help me identify surveillance with one notable exception that became evident as soon as I completed a right turn and began biking southbound across its tiled expanse: it was completely blocked to vehicles.

Widely regarded as one of the most beautiful streets in Southeast Europe, the Kneza Mihaila lived up to its reputation. While a low wall to my left was plastered with advertisements spray-painted over with graffiti, a gallery of beautifully elaborate architecture stretched to my right, its facade reminiscent of Rodeo Drive more than anything I'd yet seen in Belgrade.

I needed only to travel a block before there were buildings on either side, all of them finished in the Balkan style that spanned renaissance to romanticism. I saw gilded balconies and sidewalk cafes before slipping beneath a fine mesh of tiny lights strung overhead, creating a manmade starscape in the idyllic and upscale pedestrian area. Using my bike mirrors as well as the reflections of surrounding windows, I identified a fellow cyclist gliding urgently down the walkway behind me.

Slowing my bicycle, I pulled to a stop beside the entrance to a Turkish steakhouse and examined the menu with feigned interest. Within seconds, the biker I'd spotted cruised past without so much as glancing in my direction.

Abandoning the menu, I prepared to resume my southward progress toward another turn a few blocks down. Using the opportunity to look left and right across the lit storefronts, I saw only milling pedestrians with shopping and takeout bags, happy couples holding gloved hands, and children darting in circles around their parents. At that moment I knew I wasn't being followed, could feel it in my gut, and yet I'd have to dedicate the next two hours to reconfirming that fact before declaring myself free of surveillance and moving to link up with my team.

And that was why I hated SDRs, I thought as I began pedaling again. How or why anyone wanted to join the CIA's Clandestine Service and commit themselves to a career of doing this, often several times a day and with next-to-zero chance of employing a firearm, I could only imagine.

I'd barely resumed riding when my Bluetooth earpiece chirped to life.

Tapping it to return to the team conference call, I heard Ian say, "We've got a tail."

"Shit," I said. "Secret police?"

"No, Jelena says these guys are too overt for that. Two military-age males, both white and wearing ball caps. One's in a bomber jacket, the other in a puffy vest, neither realize they've been made. Either one of Gudelj's people dragged a tail into Kalemegdan and it transferred to us, or Gudelj assigned a tail to see where we're bedding down."

I scanned my surroundings, looking for a place to get off my bike and into my phone's digital map overlay. Absent the time required to plan for various contingencies in the wake of our time-sensitive meeting to receive the uranium, I'd have to sketch out our response on the fly.

A solution presented itself across the side street to my front, where a raucous crowd of smokers had assembled beneath a glowing green sign that read *Harat's*.

Good enough, I thought as I pedaled for the entrance while Ian continued speaking. "We might be able to lose them—"

"They're not getting off that easy," I cut him off, dismounting my bike and leaning it against a wall. "If they're New Zemun, I don't want them to be able to positively identify any of you. And if they're Janjicari, it means Gudelj is trying to play us and we need to send a message. What's your location?"

"Čubrina southbound, approaching Park Vojvode Vuka."

"All right, knock off the SDR for the time being. We don't want to spook these guys or cue them that Worthy is with you and Jelena. Start heading north-northeast, make for the Central Park Residence Hotel, and take your time getting there. Cancer, Reilly, start making your way toward the mosque. Give me a few minutes to figure this out."

I proceeded on foot through a congealed mist of cigarette smoke, bypassing the laughter outside the bar to pull open the door.

The interior was an archetypal setting that could be found in most parts of the developed world.

It was an Irish pub in name and form, complete with a live band merrily blaring away in the corner and Guinness murals painted across brick walls. If I wanted peace and quiet I wasn't going to find it here, but at least I was off the street, and besides, settings rich in alcohol had a way of focusing my thoughts far more than a silent library ever could.

I ordered a beer and paid in cash, retreating to an unoccupied table and setting the pilsner glass aside.

Taking my phone in hand, I panned across map imagery of Belgrade to locate the park where Ian and Jelena were currently being tailed along with Worthy, their assigned security for the SDR.

Killing a few pursuers would be easy; we had Glocks and suppressed MP7s. But doing so without getting seen—and more importantly, while having time to search the bodies and figure out who in the fuck these people were—would be far more difficult, particularly in Belgrade's densely inhabited tourist center.

I told myself not to overthink the problem set. Time wasn't on our side, particularly if our opponents' intent went beyond passive surveillance and into the realm of vectoring a kill squad. Besides, combat tactics in their most fundamental form had survived the test of time for a reason. What we needed was an L-shaped ambush applied to an urban setting, which would require similar principles to any other environment with the notable exception that our support-by-fire element would have to serve its noble purpose while on the move. All we needed was a suitably isolated location, and another thirty seconds of weighing available options on the city map provided the best spot we were going to find.

"All right," I said, returning to the conference call, "here's what I want everyone to do."

13

Worthy strode along the sidewalk, resisting the urge to look behind him as he trailed his two protectees.

Ian was walking arm-in-arm with Jelena, the lucky bastard. Worthy consoled himself with the thought that the intelligence operative's balls were very possibly getting zapped by radiation from the highly enriched uranium, if indeed it was actually handed off at Kalemegdan. Whatever was inside the plastic bag Ian had inherited at the exchange now resided in a large Faraday pouch that he carried for the purpose of blocking any location-transmitting devices embedded inside it—otherwise, there wasn't much point in conducting an SDR in the first place.

And while Worthy was responsible for guarding them from the rear, Ian and Jelena had proved remarkably adept at whatever spy bullshit they both seemed to have mastered by now—how they'd managed to identify the two men following amid the crowded sidewalks, much less relay the details of their attire, was beyond him. He'd barely even seen either Ian or Jelena look back in his direction, and even then only in nonchalant glances before crossing a street.

Worthy heard a voice in his Bluetooth earpiece.

"In position."

The speaker was whispering, making his voice difficult to distinguish, but the next message made it clear enough that it was David.

"Reilly, where are you?"

A moment later the medic issued his reply.

"Should be there in one mike."

Worthy sidestepped to give clearance to the group headed his way, a chattering trio of girls who appeared to be in their teens or early twenties, dressed to the nines despite the evening chill.

Belgrade was famous for its nightlife, no part of the city more so than the historical Stari Grad area they'd been traversing for close to an hour now. The vehicle and foot traffic around them was only now beginning to subside as they continued northeast along Kralja Petra Street, passing between a women's clothing store and a hotel.

Then Ian's voice came over the conference call. "Passing the museum now, approaching the intersection at Gospodar-Jevremova."

David replied, "Got it, I just linked up with Reilly. Cancer, what's your location?"

"Almost to the mosque."

Finding a suitable ambush location was difficult. Many of the city blocks were entirely lined with interconnected buildings that had, at best, narrow channels for vehicles to access central parking between the structures. When it came to evacuating a safehouse as the team had done the day before, that architecture was a very good thing; but it was somewhat damning now that they wanted to eliminate pursuers without drawing attention.

Ian continued, "Crossing the street now."

"Confirm visual," Cancer said.

Worthy arrived at the intersection a moment later, pausing a beat for a car to pass before committing himself to the crosswalk and glancing left.

The team had studied notable landmarks across the city for the purposes of navigation and easy reference when conveying their own location, and it had already paid off with the ability to ambiguously reference a mosque with no further explanation required.

Though as he caught his first sight of the dome and minaret rising over trees in the sidewalk, Worthy considered that precious little detail was required for this particular landmark.

Like everything else in the Balkans, the mosque had undergone considerable metamorphosis. It was built as a place of Islamic worship under the Ottomans, survived Austrian rule only by being converted to a Roman Catholic church, and was abandoned before being restored to its original function only to be set ablaze during the 2004 unrest in Kosovo. In that regard, its biggest distinguishing factor was the fact that it existed at all—there were close to 300 mosques in Belgrade when it was ruled by the Ottoman Empire, and Bajrakli was the only one that hadn't been destroyed in the centuries to follow.

As Worthy reached the other side of the street, he saw another pedestrian coming his way from up the block, a shadowy figure whose only distinguishing feature was a glowing cigarette ember.

"Clearing the intersection," Worthy said. "Next people you see should be the targets."

"Got it," Cancer replied, and then he was gone from view. Worthy passed storefronts and restaurants, continuing to follow Ian and Jelena as the seconds ticked down to an inevitable confrontation.

As the foot traffic dissipated, Worthy strained to listen for footsteps approaching behind him. He faced a delicate balance of protecting Ian and Jelena to his front while remaining exposed to a threat at his rear that he couldn't confront without exposing himself, although his fear of getting shot in the back subsided considerably after Cancer's message over the conference call.

"Targets in sight, I'm thirty meters behind them and closing the gap."

"Better close it fast," Ian responded. "We're crossing Jovanova now."

Worthy's pulse quickened as he approached the next intersection and saw that Ian and Jelena had arrived at the far sidewalk and cut left to proceed northwest past a student dormitory. He strode across the street and followed suit, barely clearing the building's edge before he noticed two bicycles leaning against the wall ahead beside a fenced break in the structures.

The small gate was ajar, and Ian held it open for Jelena before both vanished through the gap.

Worthy followed them, now keenly aware that the men behind him were picking up the pace to maintain visual contact. The path led into a central courtyard shared by the occupants of the dorm and surrounding apartment buildings, all of which contained pedestrian entrances that their quarry could disappear inside at any moment.

Slipping through the gate, Worthy trotted down a flight of stairs and set foot onto a paved path that snaked between buildings and clusters of trees toward a central courtyard.

Unable to restrain himself, he asked, "Boss, sure you don't want me to back you up at the ambush?"

"No," David replied over the conference call, "I don't. Just because Ian and Jelena are out of sight from these two shitheads doesn't mean they're in the clear—you need to safeguard them until this is over. No telling what's around the corner."

The final sentence of the team leader's message was audible not just over Worthy's earpiece but as a muted whisper from the trees that he bypassed now. Then he broke into a jog to catch up with Ian and Jelena.

Reilly watched Worthy slip past along the walkway and into the central courtyard, noting a particular edge to the pointman's step—as the team's top close-range shooter, he was arguably the last person who should be exempt from what was about to occur.

But Ian and Jelena needed safeguarding more than anyone, and never more so than now, when a chance event as simple as being mugged could result in the loss of everything they'd risked traveling to Kalemegdan to obtain.

At present, Reilly was poised in the shadows behind one of the larger tree trunks in the courtyard, his MP7 in hand with buttstock extended. David was similarly positioned two meters to his left, and together they formed the assault element of an ambush that would unfold any second now—at least provided the surveillance element was foolish enough to proceed through the channelized courtyard entrance in pursuit of the three team members they'd been tracking across Stari Grad.

Which, apparently, they were.

Cancer spoke quickly over the phone connection. "They're going for it—we're on."

Equally important was what the sniper didn't say: any mention of civilians entering the courtyard from the street.

Reilly glanced right, confirming no foot traffic in the opposite direction. "Right side is clear."

Then he brought his MP7 to bear on an apartment building a short distance to his front, his point of aim a word spray-painted across the surface in Cyrillic letters. He had no idea what it said, but by the time he arrived David had selected it as the center of their kill zone; the next person to cross it would fall in a hail of suppressed gunfire.

The men shouldn't have stood a chance, not with him and David engaging from their flank and Cancer spewing 4.6 x 30mm rounds into their spines.

But this wasn't a video game; it was the real world, in a tight alley with limited ambient light, no night vision, and Murphy's Law working against them as it always had.

How the first man detected their presence, Reilly had no idea—even Worthy would have slipped past unaware if he hadn't been informed of the ambush position's ultimate location.

Maybe it was a preternatural sixth sense of impending doom, or maybe he'd simply been in too many urban scenarios where a predator lay in wait, but the lead man suddenly darted forward and out of view no sooner than he'd appeared, leaving a stunned comrade in his wake as Reilly and David opened fire.

The remaining man's body jolted with the bullet impacts amid suppressors muting the gunfire to a low woofing sound, not just from Reilly and David but Cancer as well—perpendicular fields of fire had converged to drop him in place as suddenly as a brain aneurysm.

But the remaining man was out of sight, and if Reilly exposed himself he'd be stepping into the sights of the one man who had a chance to terminate the threat before it reached the most vulnerable members of his team.

Goddammit, Cancer thought as the lead man darted out of the kill zone.

There was always something.

He lowered his MP7 and leapt down the stairs, speaking as he made landfall.

"Cease fire, squirter moving into the courtyard. He's mine."

Then he ran.

This should have been the easiest job of his career: floating support by fire, trailing a pair of unsuspecting targets before shooting them in the back. Fucking child's play, especially when two of his teammates had a supporting field of fire.

Instead he'd scarcely fired his first shot when the lead man bolted and was now barreling into a courtyard where Ian, Jelena, and Worthy were supposed to wait out a fail-proof engagement. At present, however, they were the least of his worries.

Far worse were the 360-degree surroundings of dormitory and apartment windows, any one of which could hold a civilian bystander unknowingly waiting to receive an errant bullet. When you'd seen a human life snuffed out by something as absurd as a ricochet puncturing glass and negotiating a statistically impossible series of interior wall angles before lodging in the trachea of an eight-year-old boy, as Cancer had in Iraq, the so-called "big sky, little bullet" theory of leaving such shots to chance held no sway over your willingness to leave even a single factor to the tides of fate.

He vaulted the slain opponent, now face down in a spreading pool of blood, amid the sounds of David and Reilly extricating themselves from the microcosm of urban forest in which they'd hidden for the ambush. As he did so, Cancer knew that he was right in his instinctive call to take sole ownership over the fleeing adversary. By the time either teammate was in a position to begin pursuit, he intended to have terminated this now-rogue threat.

Cancer rounded a building corner to gain a vantage point into the greater courtyard, his mind making another intuitive calculation. With no other street access, Worthy would have sequestered Ian and Jelena in the position offering the greatest cover and concealment. He was a former bodyguard, after all, and would leave nothing to chance any more than

Cancer would. That meant anyone standing would be either the lone target or an innocent civilian.

And to his immeasurable horror at the sight past the corner, he identified both in the same split second.

The innocents were easy enough to distinguish, a group of men milling around park benches with beer bottles in hand and a cooler at their feet. More concerning was a single figure not only fleeing but swinging one hand with a pistol back the way he'd come.

Cancer was taking aim when the pistol sounded three times in rapid succession, each shot corresponding with a flaming spark from the barrel. The MP7 was aligned by the time all three bullets cracked harmlessly past Cancer's left side, by which time he returned fire with three shots of his own. His weapon was aimed not for a kill shot, which would place it in line with the first-floor windows surrounding him on all sides, but rather at waist height, seeking impact with pelvis or thighs.

The effort was rewarded when a 4.6mm round struck the target's buttocks and he collapsed mid-stride.

By the time he impacted the paved courtyard, Cancer had assumed a stable shooting position and delivered five more bullets, each intended to finish off the man who convulsed once, then twice, before giving a spasmodic leg twitch and finally going still.

Cancer swung his aim toward the loitering civilians, prepared to deliver a warning shot if they tried to intervene—an unnecessary measure, as it turned out.

All five had dropped their bottles and were darting toward the nearest building entrance, a sight that he barely registered before hearing footsteps behind him and wheeling to face whoever was approaching.

"Friendlies," Worthy drawled, emerging from a row of trash bins, behind which Ian and Jelena were rising to follow.

Jelena took the lead and ran to the fallen opponent; Cancer and Worthy followed, seeking to protect her search of the body against the multi-level buildings around them. Whatever windows hadn't been lit before were now, with the silhouettes of civilian occupants appearing to investigate the sound of gunshots.

But at least one thing was going according to plan, Cancer realized as Jelena lifted the right wrist of the still-warm corpse below her.

"New Zemun," she said, indicating the tattoo of a crescent moon emblazoned on the man's hand in the webbing between his thumb and index finger.

"Go," Cancer said, watching the trio move toward the street access as he provided backside security while speaking over the phone earpiece.

"Clear, four friendlies moving back out."

Then he turned to run.

14

Ian donned a pair of nitrile gloves, then took a seat at the kitchen table in the residential safehouse.

His work equipment was arrayed before him, and he paused briefly to go over the sequence of events in his mind. While there was certainly a sense of urgency to this situation, it was up to Ian to document formal contents as the first person in the formal chain of custody.

“Ready?” he asked.

Jelena stood beside him, likewise wearing a pair of nitrile gloves and holding a digital camera. “Born ready.”

She leaned over the table and took a top-down photograph of the large Faraday pouch. Once the flash subsided, Ian unzipped it and used a handheld scanner to sweep the plastic bag within—no wireless transmissions whatsoever.

Setting his scanner down, he held the pouch open for Jelena to take a snapshot of the contents. With that complete, he withdrew the plastic shopping bag and pushed the Faraday pouch aside, repeating the process for a third photograph.

Then he arranged the bag’s items in a single row, a ridiculous formality given the circumstances but nonetheless one the Agency demanded. Jelena took a picture first of the sandwich, then the apple and bag of chips, before

Ian moved them away from his workspace and centered the only object that mattered: a heavy silver thermos that was slightly larger in height and diameter than a pint glass.

Jelena photographed the thermos from above, then waited for Ian to hold it lengthwise and rotate it at quarter turns for the subsequent shots. Finally he upended it to allow her a snap of the underside, waiting for her to check the camera display before he touched it again.

"Okay," she said quietly, "go ahead."

Ian turned the thermos upright, took a breath, and delicately began to unscrew the lid.

A voice boomed from behind him.

"What if it's a boobytrap?"

Ian froze, an unwanted pang of adrenaline shooting into his bloodstream.

Then, placing both hands on the table to recenter his thoughts, he said, "David, you can either wait outside or sit down and shut the fuck up. Pick one."

The team leader chose the latter, sauntering around the table and pulling out a chair on the far side before dropping into it. He eyed the food items arrayed before him, fixating on the sandwich as if he were struggling mightily to decide whether to try it or not. Finally, he folded his arms and asked, "Should we be worried about radiation?"

Jelena responded before Ian could.

"In enriched form, it's only mildly radioactive."

David shrugged. "What if it's not enriched?"

Ian returned his gloved fingertips to the thermos lid, carefully twisting it counterclockwise as he replied, "All three samples from the Mayak batch were transported in lead thermoses, just like this. Which means the ampoule is inside."

"What the fuck is an ampoule?"

Ian set the lid down, looked inside, and then tilted the thermos to deposit a six-inch-long, harpoon-shaped glass vial into his palm.

Holding it up to the light, he said, "This is."

David leaned forward to squint at the object—inside the sealed glass container was a shifting mass of black powder that looked no different than coal dust.

"That's it?" he asked.

"That's it," Jelena confirmed, taking snapshots as Ian held the ampoule for her to see.

Ian explained, "This is how the Soviets kept samples of specific production runs at their nuclear facilities—there might be hundreds just like this in storage at the Mayak Production Association. The real question is, are there solid masses from the corresponding batch buried somewhere in Moldova right now?"

David looked like he was at once both highly skeptical and supremely frightened by the possibility.

"Well," he asked, "do you think there are?"

"I don't know," Ian said helplessly, then replaced the glass object in its cylinder before screwing on the lid. "At this point, I'm more concerned about whether this nets us an invitation to meet Sidorov or not."

Jelena seemed disinterested in the debate, focusing instead on returning each item to the plastic shopping bag, the thermos last of all. Then she placed the bag into the foam-lined interior of a Pelican case that sat open on the counter beside the sink. The case was considerably larger than what the paltry bag and its contents required, and with a pressure equalization valve and rigid watertight construction complete with O-ring seal, it was certainly overkill from the standpoint of structural integrity.

But not until she closed the lid, clasped the double-throw latches into place, and lifted it by its carrying handle did the real suitability for such a transport vessel become visible from Ian's vantage point at the table: a circular logo of an eagle clutching an olive branch and a cluster of arrows in its talons, wings outstretched and ringed by the text *DEPARTMENT OF STATE, UNITED STATES OF AMERICA.*

Beneath America's great seal were the words *DIPLOMATIC POUCH, PROPERTY OF U.S. EMBASSY, ONLY TO BE OPENED BY AUTHORIZED PERSONS*, with the message repeated in an imaginative range of languages, Serbian and Russian among them. Jelena routed a pair of cable ties through the two pre-drilled holes in the container's front corners, connecting the ends in serial-numbered lead seals to serve as anti-tamper devices. Combined with the official document she carried identifying her as a diplomatic courier, the contents had just become immune to legal search or detention in accordance with Article 27.3 of the Vienna Convention on Diplomatic Relations. Ian hoped that would maintain the package's legitimacy for its five-mile trip to the US Embassy, where it would be transferred to a CIA officer with similar credentials.

Then the case would proceed another thirteen miles to Belgrade Nikolov Tesla Airport to be spirited aboard a soon-to-arrive Dassault Falcon business jet containing a so-called "light lab" and its associated eight-person team from the Army's 20th Support Command, and more specifically CARA.

The "C" in CARA combined the standard chemical, biological, radiological, nuclear and high-yield explosives acronym into a single letter, with the remainder of the title designating the unit as an Analytical and Remediation Activity. Their purpose was to diagnose suspected WMD samples with the help of a mobile expeditionary lab, and Ian suspected that they'd be doing just that for the entirety of their multi-leg flight to the federal research facility in Livermore, California. There, the sample would be analyzed at more robust facilities that had processed the previous three samples proven to be from Russia's Mayak Production Association.

Without rising, David looked at Jelena and said, "Worthy will ride shotgun with you. We'll have Reilly and Cancer in a trail car. I'll get those photos over to the Agency."

"Very well," Jelena replied, still holding the case as she cut her eyes to Ian. "Are you coming?"

Ian stripped off his nitrile gloves.

"No. I've got to call Gudelj."

David recoiled. "What for? We know he didn't send that tail to follow us."

But Jelena gave a knowing nod. "Which is exactly why he should leverage this. Trust him."

David sighed, pushing back his chair and snatching the digital camera before he stood at last, then gave a deferential bow to Ian.

"Whatever you say, Mr. Cutler."

Then he and Jelena departed the room, leaving Ian to recover the phone he used to communicate with one man and one man only.

After toying with the device in silent consideration of how to best make his accusation, he dialed and waited for the call to connect.

Gudelj answered with the words, “You cannot be done testing already.”

“You know I’m not,” Ian shot back. “We have other business to discuss.”

“What business? I delivered exactly what you asked—”

“I told you not to have me followed,” Ian cut him off, speaking in a low, threatening tone.

“I did not.”

“Two men pursued me out of the exchange point. My people took care of them near the corner of Gospodar Jovanova and Kralja Petra.”

“I will look into it,” Gudelj said uneasily, “and communicate what I find back to you. In the meantime, check the sample. The seller is quite eager to unload his merchandise.”

Ian hung up the phone.

15

Duchess retrieved her keys as she hurried to the front door of her house, trying to get out of the cold. She shuffled the keyring in the glow of her security lights, identifying the house key and securing it by the time she ascended the steps to her front porch with an exhausted sigh.

It had been a long, drawn-out afternoon and evening: monitoring a high-stakes exchange for an alleged uranium sample, her team's confrontation with a hostile surveillance element now known to be New Zemun, and finally transferring the sample to a courier for transport to the CARA team's mobile lab aboard a plane that was, by now, surely airborne.

Duchess didn't know for sure, and didn't particularly care; she'd left work the moment her team was consolidated at their new safehouse and bedding down for the remainder of the evening.

Not that she was any stranger to long hours and even run-on days spent living out of the OPCEN and her office: that type of thing was far too common during Project Longwing missions, which was precisely why such reprieves at home tended to be exceedingly rare while her team was deployed. Her various staff capacities had primary and assistant members who could rotate shifts, but she did not—unless she was willing to count Meiling Chen as a suitable replacement, which was, as yet, certainly not the case. And given what she'd seen from the newcomer so far, it probably never would be.

But the fact remained that regardless of what the CARA team determined about the sample, Gudelj had set a very definitive 24-hour deadline for testing. Barring another safehouse compromise—and she sincerely hoped that particular bolt of lightning wouldn't hit a second time—her team wasn't going anywhere. In the meantime, Duchess could spend the evening at home with a glass of white wine before heading back to work in the morning, somewhat refreshed and rejuvenated.

Duchess unlocked the door and stepped inside to the echoing chime of her security alert, then flipped the deadbolt behind her before entering her code into the keypad beside her.

The chimes went silent, and Duchess stripped off her coat and hung it on a hook by feel.

Then she flipped on the light.

An initial glance at the foyer would lead an unsuspecting observer to conclude that this was a happy family home; the truth was, Duchess thought bitterly, that a closer inspection of the many photographs would reveal that every one of them depicted her son and grandchildren. None of her ex-husband and, with few exceptions, not even her.

Duchess swept past the photos without so much as a sideward glance—as she'd learned long ago, they were too hard to look at when returning to her empty home late at night. Now she restricted herself to scrutinizing them only during daylight hours when fond recollections were even a remote possibility.

She went to the kitchen instead, turning on a light over the sink before retrieving a wine glass and a bottle from the fridge. Her pour was a small one, as it was and always had to be when the team was on the ground in some foreign nation, and she replaced the bottle before taking her first sip.

Duchess set down the glass and reached beneath her collar to retrieve the lanyard around her neck that held the dangling blue government employee badge that she tucked out of sight before leaving the Agency parking lot every day. After depositing it in a drawer, she let her gaze linger on the badge and, before her thoughts drifted to everything it represented in the wake of what she had to do now, slammed it shut with more force than she intended.

The sound boomed in her kitchen as she retrieved the wine glass, took another sip, and turned to lean against the counter as she recovered her cell phone.

She first checked the date to confirm her remaining time for procrastination had dwindled to 72 hours, then tapped the Amazon app with her thumb.

For most women of her age, the occasion of a grandchild's birthday was one of eager anticipation, including an invitation to the actual party. But that wasn't the case for her, nor had it ever been, and she instead typed *gifts for 11-year-old boys*.

The results were a veritable yard sale of sponsored ad placements, and she scrolled past them to find an ever-deeper rabbit hole of junk. How the hell was she supposed to choose?

By the time she'd gotten him Legos and board games, he was into drawing and comic books. When she sent him art supplies and graphic novels, her son chastised her with the revelation that the boy was now an athlete, concerned only with baseballs and cleats for Little League. And now that he was turning eleven—God help her, only two years removed from becoming a teenager—she was once again confronted with the biannual reminder that she had no idea what either of her grandsons were interested in, nor what material items they already possessed.

Then Duchess committed the ultimate act of surrender, and resorted to Google.

Entering the same search string raised more questions than answers: there were bikes, board games, hoverboards, and video games for a variety of consoles she'd never heard of.

Duchess considered texting her son, was prevented from doing so out of pride as much as the fact that she would likely receive some curt and ambiguous response, and gave a weary sigh of resignation instead.

She'd begun her Agency career as a newly married woman, recently graduated from George Mason. Duchess was well into her pregnancy before the first red flags emerged that her husband didn't appreciate her lengthy and frequent absences as a case officer, culminating in full-blown affairs by the time their son had reached middle school. And when she'd finally received the kingmaker assignment as station chief in Yemen, the unaccompanied tour was no hardship—she was already living alone. Her role as an intelligence officer had eclipsed all others, particularly wife and mother.

Now her biggest victories outside the professional realm consisted of visiting her grandchildren, those glorious reprieves that her son allowed at infrequent intervals. He'd once even clarified to her, as if to quell any hopes that she could make up for lost time, "I'm not doing this for you, I'm doing it for them."

Duchess set her phone on the counter, exchanging it for the glass, and took another sip of wine with the single thought, *had any of this been worth it?*

She asked herself that question often, and the answer seemed to be a moving target. There were times she'd been exceptionally assured of the importance of her work, with the establishment of Project Longwing chief among them. But no sooner had that occurred than her newly-formed staff and ground team picked up on various threads that all led back to Erik Weisz. Until he was stopped, the many framed photos would serve as reminders of the cost rather than the spoils.

Duchess thought she detected a noise down the hall leading to her bedroom, and swung her gaze in that direction. If so, there was no innocent explanation—pets weren't an option for someone in her line of work who lived alone—and she set down her glass of wine with great care to do so silently. In the movies, this was the moment where even the lowliest CIA recruit would retrieve a suppressed handgun from some cereal box in the cabinet and proceed into the shadows.

Instead, she quietly slipped off her heels, grabbed her phone, and proceeded toward the front door while dialing 911 and hitting the call button.

She didn't begin running until she heard a second noise, this one indisputably from a human presence in her home, by which time Duchess had already rounded the corner and was well on her way to the door. A second's delay could serve to press the panic alarm on her security system, but she didn't bother—if someone was inside, they'd already trumped it. Instead, she reached for the deadbolt and threw it open.

Her hand alighted on the doorknob, and Duchess twisted it halfway before realizing she was too late.

16

I burst awake when someone touched my shoulder, sitting upright to the sound of Ian's voice.

"It's all right, David. We're good."

While my conscious mind understood that we weren't under attack or otherwise facing some imminent crisis, my body hadn't yet processed the message: a jolt of adrenaline brought me to my senses far quicker than caffeine could manage, my pulse hammering as I fought to keep my eyes open against the daylight streaming in between closed blinds.

I appraised my surroundings, making out a dingy bedroom in our alternate safehouse and Ian now standing a few steps back to avoid getting hit in the wake of one of my characteristically violent wakeups.

Cancer stood beside him, which meant that we had a major development.

"All right," I allowed, "I'm guessing that sample tested positive?"

Ian replied, "The CARA team confirmed 6.2 grams of uranium-235. It had the same isotopic signature as the other three samples from Mayak, date of production October 1993. Enriched to 87.8 percent."

"Meaning?" I asked, swinging my legs off the rickety twin-sized mattress to set my boots on the shabby carpet. I'd slept fully clothed, and all that remained was to recover my Glock from the nightstand, slide it into the concealed holster, and sling my MP7.

Ian continued, "The Hiroshima bomb was only 80 percent, so our sample is more than suitable for use in a standard nuke. But it only takes a quarter of that enrichment for a primitive weapon, whether nuclear or a dirty bomb. What Gudelj provided wasn't just legit, it was the fourth known sample from a confirmed production run. We just became nuclear material traffickers, and so did he."

"Holy shit. So this just went from a ploy to get an invitation to a full-blown uranium deal."

"Pretty much, yeah."

Something about the ease with which this was playing out gave me pause. "I want to get a verbal from Duchess before we proceed—once Gudelj calls to set up the buy, there's no going back. Let's establish a satellite connection through a window and give the OPCEN a heads-up on chat that I'll be coming up on voice comms. Notify Jelena and have her bring the battle wagon with our full combat load. I want us rolling in heavy in case this thing goes sideways."

Cancer didn't so much as nod, just slipped out the doorway to execute.

That left Ian and me alone, and I took the opportunity for a last-minute private counsel before this became a topic of team discussion with all the banter and bullshit that would entail.

After looking past his shoulder to make sure no one was approaching, I met his gaze and said, "I want to be happy about this. But all we know for sure is that Gudelj doesn't think we're government agents. He could still be trying to kill us for the full payment."

Ian looked conflicted.

"No," he began, then corrected himself. "I mean, yeah. Sure. It's possible. But if this whole thing is a ploy to lure us into a trap, Gudelj might not even know it; he's brokering this deal, and if there's a legitimate seller they're not letting the cargo out of their sight until they're paid. Either way, the seller would have a lot more motivation to wipe us out than the Janjicari would."

"Why, because Gudelj is expecting continued business?"

"Exactly. But whoever's been trying to hawk that uranium for decades now, if there's a real cache at all? For them, it's an easy payday. Trying to move that load is a play they can only run one time, and prior to this all the arrests have been made at the sample exchange itself. No one's made it this far—not Al Qaeda, not ISIS. We're in uncharted territory now."

Pausing to consider that, I gave him a nod and said, "All right, let's go."

We moved to the kitchen, where Worthy was manning the computer.

He looked up to see us enter, focusing on me as he asked, "You believe this shit?"

"You sign up to be an assassin," I began, "you end up slumming to buy half a nuke."

Reilly appeared before he could respond, rolling out a radio cable connected to the mobile satellite antenna.

"My high school guidance counselor said I should take a hard look at skilled trades. Check me out now."

Cancer was the last to enter, pocketing his cell phone.

"Jelena's on her way with the van."

"Good," I replied, watching Reilly attach the cable to the radio and its corresponding hand mic before checking the signal strength.

"Should be hot to trot," he said, stepping back from the table.

I became aware of everyone watching me expectantly, and glanced across the collective formation of my team—a motley bunch, under the circumstances, all attired in civilian clothes with their handguns and MP7s just as I was. This mission had begun about as far outside our comfort zone as we'd ever been asked to operate: undercover black market involvement, sneaking weapons and people across a major industrialized city rather than the backwater terrorist haunts that we'd grown accustomed to.

No point delaying this any further, I thought as I checked my watch. Gudelj could call at any moment to set up the full exchange, and I first needed to clear the air with our Agency handler.

I moved toward the hand mic, then lifted it and pressed the transmit switch.

"Raptor Nine One, Suicide Actual."

No response, and that queued Reilly to dart off toward the satellite antenna to check his connections.

I repeated, "Raptor Nine One, Suicide Actual."

Finally a woman responded, "*Suicide Actual, Raptor Nine One.*"

The only problem with the response was that it wasn't Duchess speaking; not a dealbreaker in and of itself, as there were times I'd had to communicate with an intermediary when she wasn't present at her workstation.

But those times were precious few, and in the wake of such a monumental development in our mission here in Belgrade, it struck me as highly suspicious that Duchess would outsource direct contact with us for the foreseeable future. My mind immediately turned to the possibility that our satellite comms had been hacked; the odds of that occurring were extremely slim, but if anyone could pull it off, it was Russia. And no country in all of Europe enjoyed more support from them than Serbia.

"Identify yourself," I said, eyeing the packed rucksacks lined up along a row of cabinets. If I didn't receive a suitable response in the next ten seconds, we'd be executing our second blowout procedure in three days.

The woman responded, "*My callsign is Mayfly.*"

Nothing suspicious there, I thought. My team used radio callsigns just as any military unit would, but for members of the CIA, the monikers served a far more vital purpose. Station chiefs and the like would be referred to by such nicknames in any correspondence that could be read outside strict Agency channels. When they were proficient enough to warrant a legacy within their respective branch, as Duchess had, the callsigns became their de facto names even in person, as a matter of respect. I was vaguely aware that Duchess's real name was Kimberly Bannister, but I'd never once called her that to her face.

The woman continued, "*I'm the deputy chief for Project Longwing, newly assigned. As of five minutes ago, I've been assigned responsibility as the primary.*"

I looked at Ian, who was shaking his head grimly—clearly he was as skeeved out by this proclamation as I was.

Keying the hand mic, I responded, "No dice. I want to hear a familiar voice, and you're not it."

"*Suicide, I have some unfortunate news to deliver. Duchess dialed 911 after returning home last night, and the call ended in seconds. As per protocol, we dispatched an IA team to her home to interface with the first responders. I'm very sorry to report that she was killed.*"

The silence that ensued was broken by the crisp flick of Cancer's lighter, and he was exhaling his first cloud of smoke by the time I could muster a response.

"Killed...how, exactly?"

"Gunshot wound to the back of the head. Her house was ransacked, and the initial indications are that she returned home during a robbery."

I shook my head, my suspicions taking a new course. "Did you ever see Duchess flashing jewelry? Because I sure as hell didn't. And I'm certain that her security system was on point, so whoever bypassed it knew what they were doing."

"Of course," the woman replied, *"and according to law enforcement, the robbery was consistent with a string of highline residential burglaries in the northern Virginia area over the past three weeks—McLean, Bethesda, D.C. A half dozen in total, all targeting upper-income homes while the residents were gone. Duchess had been pulling all-nighters for the previous few days, so it's possible they didn't anticipate her returning when she did."*

"Or," I suggested, "the robberies were intended to build a cover legend to make her death look like an accident. And if that's the case, we're burned."

I looked at Ian to see if he had any objection to that assessment. He watched me levelly, his lack of response indicating that I wasn't being overly paranoid.

And whoever she was, Mayfly seemed to think the same.

"We agree, but our internal investigation is just getting started. Until it's complete with a full report concluding beyond a shadow of a doubt that this was a random incident, we cannot discount the possibility that Duchess provided information under duress before the first police unit arrived. But all I can definitively provide are the facts, and until I have a full autopsy report to tell me otherwise, the coroner's initial assessment is that there were no overt signs of torture. In the absence of any other information, I have no choice but to defer to your judgment as ground force commander as to the extent of risk you're willing to undertake."

"Stand by."

I set the radio mic down, and had barely looked up before Worthy asked, "Who would have hit her?"

Ian rubbed his temples.

"If it wasn't random, we can safely assume it to be the work of Erik Weisz. Particularly," he added, glaring at me, "after David talked shit to him on the captured satphone in Libya."

Reilly offered, "Let's say her death was targeted—they knew we'd find out. That means Duchess didn't give up our safehouse, or someone would have hit us already."

"True," I agreed. "What are the odds she could even recall the address off the top of her head? I'd say they're low to nonexistent."

Cancer took another drag off his cigarette.

"But she didn't forget that we're in Belgrade, so if it was a setup, Weisz's people know we're here. David?"

Frowning, I asked, "How far out is Jelena?"

"Ten, fifteen minutes."

I swallowed against a dry throat.

"We load up the main van, cut our losses here, and move to the tertiary safehouse—where was it?"

"Kovačica," Ian said, "an hour north."

"Right. So we might be late to a time-sensitive meeting, but I'd rather make excuses for that than hang around Belgrade any longer."

And before anyone could either agree with my assessment or present any dissenting views, a cell phone rang.

Ian pulled the phone from his pocket, holding it aloft for me to see.

"It's Gudelj."

I muted the SATCOM volume and said, "Put it on speaker."

Ian pressed a button and said, "Yes?"

Gudelj replied promptly, "I have investigated the men who followed you. They were indisputably members of New Zemun, as confirmed by their tattoos and known associates. I have the crime scene photos as well as their criminal records, which I am happy to send if you do not believe me."

"I believe you," Ian said. "Send them anyway, to my colleague's Proton-Mail address."

"Done. Shall we move on to more important matters?"

"Absolutely."

"The deadline for testing your sample has elapsed—I need an answer right now."

Ian hesitated, knowing that to delay now was to kill the deal altogether. Then he said, "My client is quite pleased with the quality."

"Good," Gudelj went on. "Here are the remaining terms: you and your friend—no one else—will meet me in two hours."

"That's barely enough time for me to reach the airfield, much less line up a plane for transport."

"The meeting will occur here, in Belgrade."

"Nonetheless, I'm afraid I still need an aircraft to move this—"

"And I am afraid," Gudelj cut him off, "that this will not be that kind of party. The cargo I am sitting on is in a secure location, but too hot for a standard transfer. I want it off my hands immediately. You come, you verify the package, and I leave with my people. Then you have it moved on your time, not mine. One hundred eighty million USD for twelve and one half kilograms, and if the transaction goes smoothly, then my boss would like to meet with you in person. Do we have a deal?"

Ian's eyes were wide and locked on mine as he withheld a response.

This was the crux of being a ground force commander—making the difficult decisions using whatever information happened to be available. Which, in this case, was that the sale could be a trap; if so, we'd have one hell of a fight ahead. If we survived at all—a big "if," in my mind—then it would not be without its cost. Gudelj's men wouldn't fuck around; some of the Janjicari were former members of Yugoslav special forces units, and the rest had cut their teeth with the wanton slaughter of criminal competition. Regardless of whether this was a setup, I had the sinking gut feeling that at least one of us would die in Serbia.

But if it was a legit transfer, we'd not only secure a stockpile of highly enriched uranium, but do so before leaving the city for yet another safehouse, all while gaining an invitation for Ian to meet our ultimate target, Sidorov.

This would be either a strikeout or a grand slam, with no possibility for any other outcome.

I gave Ian a nod, and he spoke into the phone.

"Done. What's the address?"

17

Jelena wheeled the Audi A7 through a right turn, proceeding with the flow of afternoon traffic onto a six-lane road flanked by wide sidewalks lined with hardwoods and teeming with civilians. Ian appraised the view from the passenger seat: to his left were storefronts and apartment buildings, but to his right was a sweeping manicured park.

He asked, “This is King Alexander Boulevard?”

Jelena smiled slightly, apparently undaunted by their measured procession into a possible ambush. Ian had seen the expression before, when he’d used the wrong local slang or misunderstood some nuance of the Serbian language.

She responded kindly, “To tourists, yes. But of all the boulevards in Belgrade, we call this one the *Bulevar*—where the Yugoslav Partisans and the Red Army assaulted to reclaim Belgrade from the Nazis.”

Ian considered that those ties between Yugoslavs-turned-Serbians and Mother Russia did not fade easily, though it was a far more recent incarnation that concerned him at present.

He asked, “Do you think the location for this exchange is significant?”

“In terms of what?”

“1999,” Ian clarified, trying to keep the emotion of what was very likely a bad hunch out of his voice. “In terms of NATO, a supposedly defensive organization, bombing Serbia without approval from the UN Security Council. In terms of a few strikes turning into 78 days' worth of nonstop sorties, killing hundreds of civilians. And in terms," he concluded, "of Russia going apoplectic, and being unable to send troops because of overwhelming Western support in the surrounding countries. Milošević resigning, the eventual end of Yugoslavia, all of it."

By then she was turning left through an enormous intersection, reorienting the Audi southwest on a collision course with their destination.

"Perhaps," Jelena allowed. "But if Gudelj simply wanted to eliminate us, why tip his hand with such symbolism? Whether this is a trap or not, I believe the location was selected for its usefulness. And if you wanted to store a stockpile of highly enriched uranium in plain sight somewhere in Belgrade, you must admit it would be difficult to choose a better site."

Ian admitted, "I can't argue with that. But if they're going for poetic justice in removing known US government operatives, to say nothing of getting revenge on behalf of our Russian target, it's the perfect spot for it."

"We will soon find out, one way or the other. In the meantime, we trust the plan."

Ian shot her a skeptical glance and pointed out the obvious.

"It's not much of a plan, though."

As if to confirm his assessment, David transmitted a moment later.

"*We made it inside*," he began. "*Trying to find a way up, but it's a shitshow. Be ready to hold your own until we can make it to you.*"

"Super," Ian replied. "Just the vote of confidence we needed."

"*If I had better news, I'd give it to you. We're going as fast as we can without getting compromised.*"

Being up on the team frequency provided some measure of familiarity, and therefore comfort—given the tremendous risk in the upcoming meeting, they'd decided not to forego radio earpieces. Between the bloodbath at the liquor store and wiping out a couple New Zemun members on a surveillance tasking, Gudelj already knew they had a security element in Belgrade. This was no time to try and build additional confidence beyond taking possession of the uranium stockpile, if it existed at all.

And just like that, Ian's time for consideration was over. Jelena steered through a gap in oncoming traffic to pull through an archway leading to a parking lot. Pulling into an open spot, she killed the engine and pointed to the time display on the car's touchscreen.

"Shall we?" she asked.

Ian sighed. "Six minutes left. We've stalled as long as we can."

He gave a final pat to confirm the placement of his concealed Glock 26, opened the passenger door, and stepped out onto the pavement. With a slight roll of his shoulders, Ian adjusted the placement of his soft armor vest—it was a low-profile variant designed to fit unobtrusively beneath clothes, still capable of stopping the average handgun bullet, though not the higher calibers that his tactical armored plates could. Better than nothing, he thought, when the alternative consisted of signaling the presence of armor in a close-quarters undercover scenario, and thus notifying your potential attackers that shots to the head or pelvis were highly encouraged.

Then Ian turned to survey the meeting site.

The building had a roofline that began nine stories up, with an additional three partial floors rising in a stepped progression to its summit. Its red brick and concrete exterior was certainly more industrial in appearance than most Belgrade structures of that size, most of which were beautiful to the point of being distracting; but that spartan exterior was far from its most notable distinction.

Seen from ground level, it was a monument to destruction: crumbling facade revealing swaths of barren floors, collapsed stairwells, glimpses of sky visible through tangled wreckage within. The closest Ian had ever come to personally witnessing such structural carnage was amid one of the worst-hit cities in Syria, where artillery and mortar barrages had reduced a massive apartment building to a spectacle of horror. Yet here he was, viewing a similar degree of chaos amid the bustling population center of a major industrialized European city, all of it being more or less ignored by passersby as they carried on with their peaceful existences. The jarring inconsistency was almost incomprehensible to an outsider like Ian, all the more so because of its selection as Gudelj's meeting place for an exchange of highly enriched uranium.

Why the current Serbian government had chosen to leave the Yugoslav Ministry of Defence headquarters in the same shattered state that it had assumed upon being hit by a NATO airstrike on May 7, 1999, remained unclear—no officials had ever released a formal statement on why the ensuing decades had resulted in neither repair nor demolition. And yet the exterior was eerily free of the spray-painted graffiti Ian had witnessed across other parts of the city, the result of police officers who patrolled the building until the time of Gudelj's phone call.

That was when the guard was abandoned to allow Ian and Jelena to enter, Gudelj had explained, without clarifying whether that was the result of a personal favor or a simple bribe. Or both, Ian wondered as he eyed an unmanned gate in the chain link fence surrounding the gutted structure, one of several around the perimeter.

Jelena took up a position alongside him, maintaining the facade of deference before whispering, "The clock is ticking, Mr. Cutler."

"Moving to the northern entrance on foot," Ian transmitted to his team, and without another word, he strode toward the gate.

Cancer was in the process of sweeping his suppressed HK417 barrel across an empty swath of the dusty building interior when Ian transmitted over his earpiece.

David radioed back in a whisper.

"*Copy, we're on the second floor, moving north, still looking for stairs.*"

Lowering his barrel, Cancer turned to follow Worthy, David, and Reilly, the small formation moving in a loose diamond when the sections of intact walls permitted and collapsing into a file as needed to negotiate doorways. He wondered if Ian would bother asking the obvious—how was the team on the second floor if they hadn't found stairs?—but the radio frequency remained silent for the time being.

Gudelj specified that Ian and Jelena meet him at the abandoned building's northern entrance, so the rest of the team had entered from the south in a hodgepodge of civilian clothes and equipment bags. Once they'd made it inside, it had been a matter of kitting up quickly and quietly to penetrate deeper inside the structure in an effort to locate a viable stairway. Without it, they were severely hamstrung in their ability to flex as required if this turned into a meet-gone-bad.

And that simple task had proved a fool's errand so far: they'd located a stairway all right, or what was left of one, in the form of a car-sized chunk of concrete that had fallen down a shaft from God knew how high and crushed every step in its path. They'd been able to climb atop the bomb-crafted boulder and then hoist themselves onto a second-floor landing, but that was the extent of their vertical progress thus far.

Still, getting in the building was no small accomplishment and greatly facilitated by Gudelj calling off the usual guard force. Their only alternative would have been to wait in the parked van, then shoot their way in if and when the situation demanded. And the monumental size of this structure was both a blessing and a curse, allowing them to slip inside without being detected but equally forcing them to cover a great deal of ground in the search for a yet-elusive intact stairwell.

Ian transmitted, "*Eyes-on Gudelj, stand by.*"

"*Copy,*" David replied.

Cancer saw the three men to his front sweep sideways ahead of a doorway, forming a stack before slipping through. He performed another security sweep of their rear, rotating back to cross over into the next room as the last man.

A blast of cold air hit him then, the result of a fractured section of wall exposing the cavernous room to the elements. And while an initial glance showed it to be empty, Cancer heard chattering cries along with a fluttering, whooshing sound—a dozen birds were taking flight, sparrows maybe, scattering through the missing wall on their way outside. The building had been devoid of people so far, but apparently the birds had found it a fitting refuge: the floor was peppered with their dried shit, a pile of rubble beside him forming innumerable crevices amid which tiny nests were stuffed. A damned aviary, he thought, continuing forward as Ian transmitted.

"*—the third floor is no problem. What about the building guards?*"

"*Copy third floor,*" David replied, leaving Cancer to take a glance out the missing wall to his left.

He was, in truth, pissed about almost everything about this so-called exchange, from the short timeline to his own team's inability to provide a modicum of security beyond the half-assed effort in which they were currently engaged. But most of all, he was pissed that he was here at all—

his role should have been as a sniper, where he could provide the greatest early warning and inflict the greatest damage in the event things went wrong.

Rarely was any building so suitable for distant observation. Its shattered facade left most of the floors open to outside view for a marksman in an elevated vantage point, a luxury afforded in exceedingly few war-torn countries. Why Serbia's government had chosen to leave this monument of NATO destruction virtually untouched since the bombing campaign, he had no idea. There was no doubt in his mind, however, that he could have exploited that fact to devastating effect. The building across the street couldn't have provided a better host of sniper positions if Cancer had designed it himself.

Just one small detail foiled his plan, having revealed itself within seconds of his initial map assessment: the structure in question was the Serbian Government headquarters, and therefore ringed by enough security cameras and armed guards to make any attempt at infiltration an absolute fantasy. Particularly, he thought, due to the fact that its staff were no strangers to a sniper threat. In 2003, Serbia's sixth prime minister—the first to declare that he'd put an end to the rampant organized crime—was shot and killed when exiting his motorcade on the building's north side. The assassination was planned and carried out by members of a Serbian mafia not unlike the one Ian and Jelena were currently en route to meet; history, Cancer decided, had an oddly twisted sense of irony.

It wasn't until he proceeded another few meters, however, that he caught sight of his would-be sniper perch in the form of a sloping red-tile roof atop four stories of stunning architecture covered in elaborately crafted stonework.

When he did, the view caused him to freeze in his tracks.

He darted to a pile of rubble, flipping down the bipod legs of his HK417 and resting them atop a slab of concrete to take aim through his scope.

His teammates must have heard his diversion, because a moment later David rushed to his side and whispered, "What is it?"

By then Cancer was confirming his worst fears: two men that he could see, a sniper/spotter team set up at the roof's apex, their view aligned southeast toward the meeting site. To an observer watching from an elevated vantage point, they would elicit no more suspicion than Secret Service agents positioned atop the White House, but to someone who knew what was about to transpire in the otherwise abandoned building across the street, the situation was painfully clear. Nor were they the only marksmen perched atop the government building; a cursory scan revealed a second duo fifty meters to the right.

Aligning his optic on the more distant pair, Cancer transmitted, "Snipers. Abort."

Then he fired, sending a subsonic 7.62mm round over the traffic on Kneza Miloša Street and into the shoulder of the man behind a Zastava sniper rifle. By the time the bullet impacted, he was shifting his aim to the spotter as Worthy, Reilly, and David took off at a sprint, the team leader transmitting as they ran.

"*Abort, abort, abort—it's a setup.*"

Cancer fired a second round, wounding but not killing the spotter. Good enough, he thought, transitioning to the rightmost sniper team as David continued, "*Snipers to your north, abort, how copy?*"

The fate of the first sniper/spotter team wasn't lost on their comrades; Cancer had scarcely realigned his sights when he caught the remaining men as little more than flashes of movement, the sniper ducking behind the apex and dragging his rifle with him.

His spotter wasn't so quick to remove himself from the line of fire, and Cancer had just enough time to crack off a round intended as a clean headshot but broke low instead, ripping through his throat before he fell out of view.

This was no time to revel in the hollow victory, however. Cancer was sweeping the rooftop for additional targets amid David's increasingly urgent transmissions when he heard the first unsuppressed gunshots ring out from the floor overhead.

Ian saw Branimir Gudelj stationed exactly where he specified, outside a hollow doorway at the building's northern corner.

He was flanked by two security men in jeans and jackets, and as Ian approached he scanned the group for any disparities at odds with their last meeting—any indications, however subtle, that Gudelj had foul play in mind. The scan came up empty: posture, attire, countenance all as they had been at the airfield, if not more relaxed and personable given this was their second face-to-face encounter.

Ian called out, "Good afternoon, Branimir."

"Jon," Gudelj said curtly, shaking hands with a momentary glance to the radio earpieces he and Jelena wore. If Gudelj disapproved, he gave no indication whatsoever, instead casually gesturing to a stairwell just inside the hollow doorway. "Shall we?"

"Absolutely. Which floor are we headed to?"

Gudelj was already leading the way up the dusty stairs as he replied, "The third. I apologize for the climb, but the upper floors were more secure to protect the cargo. But I trust you will have sufficient manpower to carry it down?"

"Yes," Ian replied, surreptitiously keying his radio mic before continuing, "the third floor is no problem. What about the building guards?"

His earpiece crackled with David transmitting, "*Copy third floor.*"

Gudelj called back over his shoulder, "You tell me when they should resume their posts, and they will. Until then, no one will interfere with your transport of the material."

They crossed onto the second-floor landing, then continued upward amid the echoes of footsteps—Gudelj to his front, Jelena and the two security men behind her—as Ian considered how truly fucked they were. The remainder of his team was on the floor he'd just passed, looking for vertical access that had yet to be found, to say nothing of their lateral separation of God knew how far. He and Jelena were on their own, and couldn't count on any backup beyond their pair of subcompact pistols and a few spare magazines. Children's slingshots, he thought, compared to what awaited if this was a trap.

His team had considered the particulars of how that contingency would unfold, and as Ian proceeded up the final flight, he knew that he was looking at the path of his final executioners if any were inside the building.

What would happen, his teammates concluded with somewhat casual flair, was that the uranium and/or kill zone wouldn't be on the ground level.

Far too accessible from the street, they'd reasoned. Instead, it would be higher in the building, but not *too* high; after all, whether an ambush or a legitimate exchange, Gudelj would want himself and his men outside the building and into a car asap in the aftermath. The third or fourth floor, perhaps.

Regardless, the floor *above* that would be where the real threat was: six men minimum, probably more, all well-armed and waiting just out of sight until the quarry was ushered to the designated site. Gudelj wouldn't even have to summon them; they could simply listen for footsteps below and wait for the procession to reach the appointed floor before quietly slipping down the stairs. Their task would be twofold: killing the exposed duo of government agents, then securing Gudelj and getting him out of the building, likely through an alternate staircase in the event Ian had some rescue force following at a distance. Game, set, match.

He forced his mind back to the present moment as Gudelj stepped onto the third-floor landing and, as promised, moved through a door there. Ian gave a quick glance at the stairs leading upward before following, directing his gaze to the open floor where a set of three crates were lined end to end beside a missing chunk of wall through which the government building was visible across the street.

At that moment David transmitted, "*Abort, abort, abort—it's a setup.*"

Gudelj glided left before coming to a stop, sweeping a hand toward the crates as if introducing his guests to a museum gallery. He was also, Ian noted, clearing a field of fire not only for his bodyguards but whoever was going to come down the stairway.

"*Snipers to your north, abort, how copy?*"

Ian felt a deep, unrelenting pressure in his chest, his body's response to his greatest fears manifesting in the worst possible way as his perception of time slowed to a millisecond-by-millisecond progression.

This location for the meet, he now understood, was less about its symbolism as a target for NATO bombing and more about creating an isolated trap with the possibility of sniper overwatch to reinforce the imminent ground assault. Gudelj could easily have arranged for Ian and Jelena to be killed at any time, and had instead chosen to lure not just them but their entire team into an elegant urban kill zone. No minor setup, this, but an ironclad gambit to eliminate the entire Agency paramilitary unit in Belgrade in one fell swoop that was seconds away from initiation.

And placing the cargo before a partially missing section of wall, Ian realized, was the masterstroke that would force his hand.

Gudelj intended on waiting until he and Jelena went to inspect the crates, at which point his men would slay them both. Even if they reacted in time to defend themselves, an unlikely if not impossible proposition under the circumstances, the snipers would easily pick them off. Their bodies would then serve as the bait to direct the team's response, sending them barreling into the view of snipers, to say nothing of a superior assault force that had yet to appear.

It was up to Ian to disrupt the enemy's momentum before it reached the point of no return.

Clearing the remaining exterior wall would be the equivalent of signing his and Jelena's death warrant. Several meters beyond the crates was a corner forming an L-shaped juncture in the floor plan, but they wouldn't make it that far.

Jelena moved to his side in preparation—she had also received David's transmissions and was waiting for him to initiate the only hope of their survival. The pair of bodyguards behind them were the priority—for all his mafia status, Gudelj would undoubtedly be slower to react. With the edge of the intact wall approaching, Ian took a final breath, blinked, and, while mid-stride, asked Gudelj, "What about the radiation?"

On the last word he drew his Glock 26 while spinning in place, queuing Jelena to do the same. Ian opened fire even as he extended his arms, saw the bodyguard he aimed at lurch with a trio of bullet impacts while pulling his own pistol free of its holster.

Ian swung his Glock right, but not before Jelena squeezed off a double tap against the second bodyguard. She achieved a perfect kill—the man tipped forward in an oblique fall that would be his last.

Gudelj was gone in a flash, darting through a side door as footsteps thundered down the stairs. Ian's mind raced through an instinctive play-by-play: the stairway was out for obvious reasons, and to run through the side door would be to get shot by Gudelj, who was surely hunkered down and waiting to be rescued. The only answer was to race past the open section of wall, either outpacing the snipers' aim or outright risking their fire, to put distance and cover between them and the stairs while moving south through the building, closer to the four teammates who now represented his and Jelena's lone chance of escape.

Ian fired his fourth shot mere seconds after his first, this one into his initial target who had since dropped to his knees, wounded but still trying to take aim. That bullet punched into the space almost directly between the man's collarbones, and then Ian spun in a lunging sprint toward the crates, a known kill zone that nonetheless represented the only available protection.

Jelena was already a full step ahead of him, rounding the crates and dropping into the prone to take aim at the stairwell door. Ian scrambled to the opposite side and followed suit, hitting the ground while half-expecting to be hit by a sniper's bullet at any moment. But the stairwell was, at present, an even greater threat.

He'd barely managed to point his barrel at the door before it was darkened by a human form, and both he and Jelena began firing immediately. Their only chance of buying time was to hit the lead man and hopefully stall the assault, and they emptied the remainder of their ten-round magazines in record time.

Out of those collective bullets, Ian saw the impacts via puffs of concrete and plaster around both the doorway and the floor leading up to it, a testament to the challenges of employing subcompact weapons at any meaningful distance.

But incredibly, at least one round struck the lead responding shooter, hitting him in the thigh and dropping him in place.

By then both Ian's and Jelena's pistol slides were locked to the rear, and they moved behind the crates to reload with the first of their respective 17-round spare magazines—too long for a pistol to remain concealable when inserted, but if the initial ten rounds didn't solve a problem, you'd damn well better be able to reload with something more substantial.

Ian thumbed his slide release to chamber a bullet with the word, "Go," before he angled out from behind the crates, still on his belly, and processed the sight beyond.

Now fifteen seconds into the fight, they'd achieved almost inconceivable results. The lead man from the assault force was on the ground and partially blocking the stairwell doorway, screaming as one of his teammates tried to step over him while taking in the sight of two downed bodyguards, one of whom was twitching spasmodically.

Ian opened fire at the doorway again, and after three shots, he registered Jelena rising to a crouch and turning to dart deeper into the building.

Only then did he notice a flash of movement to his front—one of the assaulters had already made it inside and was now firing at Jelena's retreating figure. Ian shifted out further from behind his cover, emptying the remaining rounds in a last-ditch effort to save her life. He succeeded in eliminating the threat, but only at a cost that he was surely about to discover in gruesome fashion.

He was now overexposed as the result of trying to save a partner who was probably dead already, to say nothing of holding an empty pistol once more. Ian valiantly attempted to scramble behind the crate to reload again when he took a panicked glance at the stairwell doorway—if he was going to be killed, he may as well look his shooter in the face. Instead he saw a seemingly impossible flurry of new bullet impacts.

At first Ian thought that his team had arrived, but he distinguished the pops of an unsuppressed pistol behind him. He pushed himself to his feet, turning to run as his view revealed the impossible: Jelena was still alive. She had somehow made it to the corner and was now providing suppressing fire from a relatively covered position.

Ian dropped his empty magazine on the run, and by the time he slammed a new magazine into place, Jelena's pistol went silent, her slide locked to the rear.

Then she abandoned her position to sprint further, now on a perpendicular path away from the stairs, leaving Ian to occupy the corner and judiciously expend his ammunition as they continued this rolling break contact drill long enough for the rest of the team to arrive.

Things were moving faster now—Ian saw shooters advancing to either side of the crates; he couldn't tell how many. He discharged his pistol with frantic, blazing speed, prioritizing volume of fire over accuracy. He and Jelena were running out of ammo fast, entirely reliant on the four teammates who had yet to show, and every second in the bank represented a victory, however fleeting.

His pistol went empty, and he darted behind the corner to run.

Four meters ahead was a pile of rubble from a shattered interior wall, and Ian was beside himself with relief at the sight of Jelena taking a position behind it, setting up to engage anyone who followed him around the corner.

Ian suddenly realized that they might actually pull this thing off. They'd managed not only to get the drop on their immediate ambushers but to also successfully evade a dedicated assault force while moving ever closer toward four teammates who would stop at nothing to reach them.

He swung his sprint wide right, making space for Jelena to fire as he reloaded his final magazine, noting the sudden appearance of a man through a side door to his left.

Gudelj.

Ian spun to fire but his body wouldn't comply; Gudelj vanished anyway, driven back by a flurry of gunshots from Jelena.

Only then did Ian feel a sledgehammer of pain pummeling into the right side of his gut. He went down hard on his opposite side, hitting the ground with the abstract realization that he'd been shot and intuiting from the subsequent head rush that he only had seconds remaining before passing out or worse. Unable to summon any control over his limbs, he used his final moments to glance down at his stomach.

Exactly where the bullet had penetrated his soft armor to enter his flesh, he had no idea; his entire shirtfront was bathed in hot crimson fluid that continued to pour out of him, bearing with it the horrifying sight of bright arterial blood weaving its way into the ever-spreading pool.

Ian fought to maintain consciousness, to apply pressure to the wound, now knowing that to fall asleep now was to never wake up.

It was no use. His head tilted until it was resting against the concrete floor, eyelids suddenly impossibly heavy and closing against his will. His final sensation was all pain vanishing amid an overwhelming wave of peace and tranquility, and then he blacked out entirely.

Worthy rounded the corner in a state of near-panic.

Engagements with enemy fighters, no matter how chaotic, imbued him with a certain orchestrated control: a seamless chain of considerations on how to best shoot, move, communicate, and manage sectors of fire across an ever-shifting landscape. Even when outnumbered, even when things were looking grim, his weapon and his willpower enabled him to direct his focus until the last second.

But never before had he felt so utterly helpless. He was leading his team, still on the second floor, while Ian and Jelena were trapped somewhere overhead, the sustained crashes of unsuppressed gunfire his only indication that one or both were still alive.

Now as ever serving in his capacity as pointman, Worthy still hadn't found a way *up*.

But when he cleared the next corner, darting forward while scanning for a stairwell instead of another empty elevator shaft, he finally saw what he was looking for: a collapsed section of ceiling that formed a ramp of sorts to a gap overhead, through which he caught his first glimpse of the third floor.

David saw it too, calling out from behind him.

"You're off the leash—*go!*"

The tactical implications were clear enough. Most of the team could run just as fast as Worthy, but no one could run *and shoot* with anywhere near the capacity that he'd honed over years of training and competition. And the team's internal ethos was that there was one, and only one, scenario when they'd willingly sacrifice security for speed: when required to save lives. They'd done just that on several previous occasions, when faced with a downed pilot, a village massacre, and exactly one hostage rescue, but never with members of their team isolated and facing certain death.

It was uncertain territory that Worthy barreled into with all the speed he could, flinging his HK416 back on its sling to scramble atop the sloping tangle of concrete fragments and metal beams until he'd reached the near-pinnacle. Then he stood and leapt to grab the exposed floor of the next level up, swinging his legs one way and then the other to smear a boot across the wall and assist an adrenaline-charged upper body pull that culminated in hooking one leg over the edge and pressing himself up against the weight of his armored plates and equipment.

Then he was on the third floor at last, shifting his weight over solid ground and bringing his suppressed rifle into a seated shooting position for a momentary scan. Nothing.

Rising to his feet, Worthy ran toward the sound of guns.

It was a surreal battlefield—amid the rubble of a decimated building were slips of bright blue sky and elaborate buildings on the surrounding streets, an unsettling blend of order and despair that shifted with each racing step he took.

Amid this bizarre kaleidoscope of combat unlike anything he'd ever experienced, Worthy finally slowed as he approached a corner that, judging by the sound of automatic fire beyond, would be the last thing he saw before identifying his first enemy combatant of the day. Skidding to a stop, he angled his HK416 around the corner and put every shred of his hard-won shooting experience to use in dealing himself into the fray.

It was a fucking shooting gallery.

He'd somehow run directly into the flank of a half-dozen mafia shooters wielding assault rifles and submachine guns, firing as they marched almost on-line with one another down a wide corridor. Worthy had a perpendicular angle of fire, and he dropped three shooters with six suppressed shots before the first survivor so much as looked sideways—and then he got it too, a pair of subsonic bullets to the chest.

And then the party was over.

Two weapons were being leveled in his direction, and unwilling to relinquish this hard-won fighting position, Worthy dropped to a knee as he continued to fire from behind the corner.

He managed to land a gut shot, then a sternum hit, against the leftmost of the two men. Transitioning his aim right, he saw the remaining mafia shooter convulse and fall as if by magic, a quartet of entry wounds dotted across his torso.

Then Worthy felt the squeeze of a hand against his shoulder—David, he surmised, signaling that the pointman was now operating with backup and could adjust his tactics accordingly.

For Worthy that meant rising without bothering to reload and advancing toward the corridor, secure in the knowledge that when his weapon went empty, the man behind him could pick up the slack. He tilted his barrel progressively further to the side as the corridor came into view, assuming from the wild gunfire of the slain men that they were the first wave and therefore unconcerned about hitting one of their own.

His judgment paid off a moment later when the next enemy took a tentative sidestep with his rifle raised only to be lit up by Worthy and David in the same moment.

"On your right," Reilly called. Worthy glanced over to see the medic sweeping down the wall beside him with Cancer to his rear, both bringing their HK417s toward the leading edge of the fight.

David transmitted, "Friendlies approaching, hold fire."

Jelena breathlessly replied, "*Out of ammo. Hurry.*"

That prompted Worthy and Reilly to advance their pace toward the T-intersection ahead, both men aiming ahead of the other in a cross-clearance as they gained increasing visibility across the corridor beyond. They came to a stop ahead of their respective corners and gave each other a brief nod, then conducted simultaneous high-low maneuvers, dropping to a knee and rotating 180 degrees to aim around the corner. Their backup simultaneously assumed standing shooting positions with a hand on the carrying handle of their tactical vests, prepared to drag them to safety in the event of overwhelming enemy gunfire.

Worthy's knee hit the ground as he scanned for targets and found none, just a pile of rubble ahead. From the sound of suppressed gunfire to his rear, however, he could tell that Reilly and Cancer were getting it on.

Then he saw movement from the rubble and took aim only to see Jelena's face peeking around the side.

Her eyes were wide, hair in disarray, but she was alive. Despite the sound of unsuppressed weapons sporadically returning fire against his teammates, Worthy's instincts as a bodyguard took over.

He rose to a crouch and sprinted to the rubble, dropping to his ass and sliding the remaining few feet before rolling behind cover and reaching for Jelena to throw her down.

But she was facing away from him, on her knees and hunched over as if racked with sobs, and it wasn't until Worthy looked to the floor that he saw why.

Ian's body was sprawled there, his placid face now gray to an extent that Worthy had never seen outside of a dead enemy combatant. Jelena had stripped her jacket and was pressing the wadded fabric against his abdomen with all the pressure she could. Worthy vaguely registered the cessation of incoming fire in one fell swoop—a radio order, most likely, as they withdrew to allow the Americans to be interdicted by some other element, mafia or police, it didn't much matter. If his team didn't make their way out of this massive structure as fast as they could move, that was exactly what would occur.

Worthy shuddered upon seeing the amount of blood ringing Ian, meaning he was most likely dead already. Then he noticed a bloody smear that indicated Jelena had dragged his body to safety, mingled with the bright liquid contents of one or more arteries. Worthy's final thought before crying out was that his team was down to four.

Against a soul-crushing feeling of loss, he shouted at the top of his lungs.

"*MEDIC!*"

Reilly wasn't fazed in the least by Worthy's cry, despite the somewhat panicked tone from a man who usually delivered anything but.

The truth was, no matter how much cross-training he did with his team, non-medics reacted in odd ways when faced with a real-world casualty. He'd seen this during his time with the Rangers as well—an infantryman would often come across someone wounded, see the blood, see that the patient was unconscious, and instinctively overestimate the extent of the injury. A good medic would arrive and, even before beginning treatment, think something along the lines of *gunshot wound to extremity, passed out from pain and shock rather than blood loss, easy day*. And nine times out of ten, that medic would conclude their full treatment and sweep for further injuries only to find they'd been right.

But his reaction was the same regardless: he bolted toward Worthy's call, secure in the knowledge that not only had the mafia shooters retreated but that every teammate in earshot would immediately cover down on his sector of fire.

His running path led him toward a heap of rubble behind which Worthy was waving urgently. Owing to both the discretion required in infiltrating this objective as well as the stealth needed once inside, Reilly hadn't brought a full aid bag. Instead he unzipped his plussed-up medical kit as he moved, less glamorously known as a "med fanny." Ordinarily he'd exhaust the patient's individual first aid kit before tapping his own supplies, but the only candidates for patient at present were Ian and Jelena, neither of whom carried anything more than soft armor and subcompact weapons.

And upon rounding the mass of fallen brick and concrete, he saw that Worthy hadn't overreacted.

Jelena was applying pressure to Ian's wound, which regrettably was in "the box," an area defined by medics as nose to hose—in other words, between face and dick—where so many vital organs were packed that the odds of a wound proving fatal were exponentially higher than a run-of-the-mill extremity injury. Ian had probably passed out almost immediately from not only shock but blood loss as well, and judging by the quantity of the latter soaking into the floor, if he wasn't dead already he would be soon without medical intervention that far exceeded Reilly's capabilities.

"Cut it," he said to Worthy, dropping to his knees beside Jelena with the word, "Move," pushing her away for good measure as he tossed her blood-soaked jacket aside and slid a hand under Ian's shirt and soft armor. He moved his fingers against a hot, greasy slick of blood to apply manual pressure against the point of injury. With his other hand, he removed a plastic package from his med fanny and ripped it open at the tear point with his teeth, spitting out the excess.

Worthy was already kneeling next to him, pulling Ian's coat back and using medical scissors to cut the body armor at its elastic connection points before slicing open his shirt. By the time that occurred, Reilly had withdrawn the contents of his package and lifted his opposite hand from the wound, momentarily assessing that a bullet had passed through Ian's soft armor and appeared to have either nicked or completely punctured his liver—the medic had only a moment to look before stuffing the entry wound with XGAUZE.

He started with the first flap of the Z-folded material, now wadded into a "powerball" between his fingers, driving it as far into the bullet cavity as he could and then threading the remaining length of the fabric into the wound with both hands.

XGAUZE had a significant advantage over regular gauze when it came to wounds that were surrounded by space and soft tissue: namely, it contained embedded discs that looked like Altoids, actually rows of compressed cellulose microsponges. A single dressing could soak up close to a half-liter of blood before reaching the saturation point, after which the expanded sponges would apply pressure internally and free up Reilly for other tasks, like getting Ian the fuck out of this building.

Reilly glanced over to see Worthy kneeling with another XGAUZE prepped before redirecting his focus to Ian.

He heard footsteps come to a stop beside him, and then David spoke.

"What do you need?"

Replying as he continued stuffing the wound, Reilly said, "We get him to the van, you and Worthy drop a bag on the way to an OR."

"You can't stabilize him?"

Reilly hissed a frustrated sigh, then spoke the unenviable truth of the matter.

"If he's not going into surgery within the next hour, he's dead."

18

We loaded Ian's body into the van floor, scrambling inside as Cancer fired the engine.

Any sense of physical fatigue was overcome only by adrenaline: winning a gunfight was exhausting enough, much less when it was immediately followed by carrying, dragging, lowering, hoisting, and otherwise manhandling a gut-shot casualty across and down three vertical levels of bombed-out building interior as fast as we possibly could.

By the time we slammed the van's rear doors shut, it was time to go to work. Jelena rode shotgun to navigate for Cancer, and Reilly recovered his full aid bag to tend to his patient while Worthy and I tore open the Velcro seams at the bottom of our armored plate carriers.

Reilly made each of us carry a blood transfusion bag underneath our front plates, but we'd never needed it on an actual operation. All of us had practiced this many times, and no one took it more seriously than me as an O negative bearer, making me the only universal donor on the team. Worthy was a close second with O positive, and now the two of us were in a race to fill our respective bags.

Jelena asked, "Where should we go?"

"Back toward the safehouse," Reilly replied.

I'd just finished rolling up my right sleeve, and was in the process of applying a latex tourniquet to the bicep, when I said, "I thought he needed an OR."

"He does," the medic shot back, recovering a vial of tranexamic acid. "The vet clinic by our safehouse has the right equipment. We better hope the surgeon is in."

I pumped my fist, slapping the AC in the crevice of my elbow and asking, "You want to let an animal doc work on him?"

"Most of the hospitals in Belgrade are a stone's throw from the building we just shot our way out of, and police will be canvassing all of them. Even if we dumped Ian at an ER, he'd die of natural causes in a Serbian prison. Agency will cut him loose and we're not pulling off a jailbreak with four guys."

No fault with his logic there, I thought as I pinched the end of the clear tubing attached to my donor bag, which I lifted to distribute its clear fluid along the length of the line. That liquid was citrate, an anti-coagulation agent that would prevent our blood from clotting before it reached the patient.

I asked, "What if we take him to a hospital outside of Belgrade—"

Reilly cut me off.

"He won't make it that far."

Shaking my head in frustration, I extended my arm and administered an 18-gauge needle, driving it into my vein and seeing a splash of blood before sliding the catheter all the way in. Then I withdrew the needle and dropped it—sharps hazards were the least of our worries at present—and recovered a strip of tape applied to the bag with a folded quick release tab. Peeling it off, I secured the port to my arm before grabbing the end of the bag's line and uncapping the attached needle. Driving its tip into the catheter port with the bevel facing down, I set the donor bag between my boots and let my latex tourniquet and gravity do the rest.

My blood began pouring down the line, assisted by me pumping my fist as fast and hard as I could. Worthy was doing the same across from me, his eyes meeting mine as he said, "Race you."

"You're on," I said, marveling at how the competitive drive remained alive and well despite the circumstances. We tapped our respective bags with our boots, keeping the citrate in circulation for the duration of the filling process.

By now Reilly had injected the tranexamic acid into Ian and was preparing a needle with a solution I'd never seen him use.

Worthy nodded toward it. "What's that for?"

"Injectable calcium," Reilly explained. "Transfusion will take the existing calcium out of his blood because we're adding citrate. If I don't offset that, he'll get hypocalcemia."

Cancer waited until he reached a straightaway to call back, "Need me to fill a bag? You can stick me while I drive."

"Nope," Reilly said dismissively.

"My blood isn't good enough?"

"You've got too much nicotine coursing through your veins, and besides, you're one of those B negative weirdos."

"Yeah," I added, still pumping my fist to speed up the blood flow. "Shut up and drive, freak."

Worthy's thoughts turned to more pragmatic matters.

"How long will the surgery take?"

"If it was a regular surgeon," Reilly answered, preparing the rest of his equipment for a blood transfusion, "thirty minutes, tops. Given he'll be treated by someone who specializes in dogs, maybe more."

My thoughts turned to another piece of team equipment that we'd all tucked away for the nightmare scenario that would require them—silk balaclavas.

I said loud enough for Cancer and Jelena to hear, "We do it with masks. Roll in heavy and treat it like a takeover bank robbery. Lock all doors, everyone inside becomes a hostage. Reilly supervises the surgeon. Everyone else stands guard and we kill anyone who tries to force their way in. The clinic will be our stronghold until he's patched up."

There were no objections or additions to my order, nor did I anticipate any—with Ian's life hanging in the balance, what choice did we have?

Instead an unsettling silence fell over the van now lurching through traffic on an eastbound course through Belgrade.

How quickly had I agreed to this disastrous meeting? I replayed Ian taking the call from Gudelj, looking to me for the order. And I'd nodded as casually as if it were my daughter asking if she could get a popsicle out of the freezer. What was I thinking? Duchess was in a morgue, which was not yet definitively an accident of fate, and the closest I'd come to risk mitigation was to order a safehouse rotation before blundering into a carefully laid snare that seemed more obvious with every second I thought about it.

Then there were Ian's words: *If it wasn't random, we can safely assume it to be the work of Erik Weisz. Particularly after David talked shit to him on the captured satphone in Libya.*

I snapped out of my thoughts when Reilly said, "David, you win. Hurry up."

After a moment of confusion I followed his gaze to my donor bag, now bulging with blood and creased by two dimples that indicated it possessed a full unit.

Stripping the latex tourniquet from my bicep, I said, "Suck it, Worthy," and yanked the needle and catheter from my arm. Lifting the bag, I let the blood drain down the line before making three loops in the tubing, pulling it taut to form knots as Worthy voiced his objection.

"How's the team alcoholic more hydrated than I am?"

I ignored him, using my knife to sever the line between the second and third knots before handing it to Reilly.

The medic accepted it eagerly, wrapping it with a pressure infuser that looked like a blood pressure cuff. Then he hung it on a ceiling handle from which he'd already suspended and spiked a bag of saline. The latter was connected to a Y-port from which a single line ran down to a saline lock in Ian's arm. The line was already primed, and all Reilly had to do was bleed the unlinked infusion line from the Y-port with saline to remove air bubbles before spiking the blood bag.

Worthy's bag was full by that point, and as he tied off his line I watched my own blood flowing, along with saline, down the long tubing that led to Ian's body. But pressure infuser or no pressure infuser, my donor bag was depleting with uncanny speed.

I asked, "Is it supposed to be going that fast?"

"He's hemodynamically unstable," Reilly said, accepting Worthy's bag. "His body is soaking this shit up as fast as it can."

Jelena turned from the passenger seat, her gaze darting from Ian's pale face to the transfusion in progress before fixing on me.

"We are twelve minutes from the clinic."

19

Cancer pulled the van to a stop at the vet clinic, retrieved his HK417 from the seat beside him, and exited the vehicle to follow Reilly as he approached the front door.

They'd already dropped Jelena off to infiltrate the lobby as a customer, and within a minute she called back with the particulars: one receptionist at the desk and a pair of customers in the waiting area, both just to the right of the main entrance. A closed door led to the exam rooms and treatment areas.

By the time she provided this update, Cancer was stopping the van at the clinic's only back door to deposit Worthy and David, faces hidden behind black balaclavas. They would await his order before making entry unless some vet tech emerged to smoke a cigarette or take out the trash, in which case they'd accelerate the assault.

Now that Cancer was on foot and approaching the main entrance of a civilian facility with the intention of taking it over in record time, the contingencies raced through his mind as they always did in the moments before he initiated a raid. The possibility of a seemingly routine customer packing a concealed weapon was a very real one, but as in all things, the devil was in the details.

An experienced off-duty cop, seasoned military veteran, or logical civilian gun owner wasn't the problem—none of the above would try to take on multiple men with assault rifles and body armor executing a nonlethal raid to achieve a singular aim, after which they'd be gone as soon as possible. So much as drawing a pistol against those circumstances would be to invite a hail of gunfire that would potentially result in dead civilians, and anyone with sufficient experience would know well enough that the fastest means of alleviating the threat was to swallow their pride and comply.

But guns attracted whackos like flies to shit, Cancer thought, and it was the outliers who gave him cause for concern.

A mafia man, for one, could assume himself to be a target and respond as if he had nothing to lose. Then there were the paranoid and overconfident civilian types who fell into a godawful trifecta: one, they'd never fired a weapon outside a shooting range or hunting expedition; two, they'd seen far too many movies; and three, therefore envisioned themselves as capable of downing multiple assaulters in a split-second series of headshots if the slightest opportunity presented itself. If Serbia was anything like America, then there was a better-than-passing chance that someone exactly like that was picking up their dog from an annual health exam and would react to the team's sudden presence with eager if misguided enthusiasm.

As Reilly pulled open the door, Cancer transmitted for the benefit of Worthy and David at the clinic's back entrance.

"Execute, execute, execute."

Then he slipped through the threshold and into the clinic.

The first person he sighted was a friendly—Jelena, who'd drawn her Glock 26 and was using it to intimidate the lone receptionist into submission. He cut right to find Reilly directing his HK416 at the two customers, both of whom had thrown their hands up and averted their gaze downward, one with an almost instantaneous fit of sobbing.

Reilly directed both of them to lie on the ground so he could frisk them for weapons and phones, while Jelena clambered over the desk to do the same to the receptionist.

That left Cancer to lock the main entrance, then pivot toward the closed door leading to the clinic's working area. Only as he was slipping toward it did he register the excited barking of dogs and Worthy and David shouting orders.

The door flung open and a rail-thin man in powder-blue medical scrubs came racing out, his sudden appearance leaving Cancer only time to raise his barrel a few inches and torque his right shoulder into the buttstock. But that combination of actions had the desired effect, aligning his HK417 with the man's chest and allowing his sternum to impact the business end of the suppressor at maximum velocity.

Cancer winced at a flash of pain in his right shoulder—how ironic, he thought, if their frantic scramble for a veterinary surgeon would require him to go under the knife to fix his rotator cuff. The skinny man in the scrubs dropped to the ground with the wind knocked out of him, clearing a line of sight down a door-lined hallway leading into the treatment area where Worthy's masked figure was aiming back at him.

They lowered their barrels in unison, and after giving a cursory glance toward Reilly applying flex cuffs to the two customers now lying flat on their stomachs, Cancer knelt to do the same to the man now gasping in the fetal position at his feet.

20

Reilly situated Ian's body on the operating table, speaking quickly.

"Gunshot wound to the right abdomen, suspected liver penetration, hemorrhage controlled by hemostatic dressings, no exit wound."

The air stank of dog fur and antiseptic, a nauseating mix tinged with the coppery scent of the blood covering both Reilly and his kit. Stopping an arterial bleed and running a field blood transfusion didn't make for a pretty sight in the aftermath, particularly when the latter part of that exchange was conducted in the back of a moving vehicle.

Ordinarily he'd have full team support in the event of a casualty, but with the manpower required to herd the flex-cuffed civilian detainees into exam rooms while pulling security on a surgeon and his attending technician, who'd been interrupted seconds before making an incision on an unconscious tabby, of all fucking things, Reilly had to exit the building solo, pull the van around to the back, and situate his still-unconscious casualty onto a poleless litter before finally receiving assistance to transport him into the OR.

Reilly continued, "He's had two grams of TXA plus calcium, two bags of donor blood. He needs the round taken out, bleeders stapled, and prep for transport. Once that's done, we're out of here."

Then he stepped back from the table, cutting his gaze to the two people in the room. Both had been relieved of their cell phones but were otherwise unrestrained, awaiting their orders.

The surgical technician was a mousy-looking woman in her late twenties, her hands clasped tightly at her waist as she avoided eye contact.

But it was the surgeon who responded, and he bore no such modesty—he was six feet tall, solidly built, with a wide face and unflinching blue irises that stared back hollowly as he said simply, "I do not have that equipment."

Reilly looked from the surgeon to his technician and back again, wondering if they were in a relationship and he was somehow inconceivably trying to save face.

"Yes, you do," Reilly said gravely. "Don't fuck with me, Doctor."

"Not vessel staples," the man insisted.

Reilly considered his options.

It was his job to assess the levels of care afforded at all possible medical facilities, veterinary included, and he'd conducted that assessment a second time after his team had to move safehouses. Vascular surgery was no picnic as it applied to human patients; this clinic advertised abdominal surgical procedures for small animals, and Reilly was acquainted well enough with veterinary medicine to know that such procedures required the use of Surgiclip devices if not thoracoabdominal or ligate-divide staplers.

The surgeon was lying and they both knew it; and since Reilly had to remain in the OR to supervise the procedure, he couldn't afford to play bad cop.

So he didn't.

Instead he took a step toward the door and called out, "I need a pipe hitter."

He wasn't surprised when a teammate came bursting in the door within seconds of the request being issued—he was, however, shocked that it was not Cancer, but David. The team leader's expression was rendered indecipherable by virtue of the balaclava with the exception of his eyes, which were wide with apparent bloodlust at the delay.

Reilly cocked his head toward the surgeon, redirecting David's gaze to the deserving party and regretting it a moment later.

David advanced with three rapid steps and delivered an open-palmed blow to the sternum, knocking the man backward. By the time he crashed into the operating table and attempted to push himself upright, his progress was halted by the tip of a Winkler knife now being pressed against the bottom edge of his right rib with enough force to draw blood.

"English?" David asked.

"Yes," the man gasped, shakily lifting his hands in surrender.

"Good. Then listen carefully: either you stop the bleeding in my friend's liver, or I carve yours out right here in this fucking room. Questions?"

"No."

Still, David kept the blade in place, using his free hand to pat down the surgeon's pockets until he recovered a leather wallet that he held in front of his face.

"If there are any complications, if he dies after you work on him, I'm coming for you and your family. *Razumeti*?"

The man blinked, nodding quickly.

Only then did David step back and sheath his knife, his expression momentarily calming before he flew into a rage when the surgeon didn't immediately leap into action.

"Well *move*, goddammit!"

That was all the motivation the surgeon needed to direct his technician, and together they pulled open drawers to produce the very equipment Reilly knew they'd had all along.

But now he had a new problem on his hands—David made no move to depart, instead taking up a position beside the medic.

Reilly put a hand on his shoulder and whispered, "I need you to wait outside."

"I'm staying," he replied, his voice resolute.

"This dude can't operate if he's looking over his shoulder. You made your point, now get out. I'll handle it."

The team leader seemed to deflate at the order, finally realizing he'd fucked up. There was no second-guessing Reilly in matters of medical care, and every second David let his ego prevail was a detriment to the odds that Ian would survive.

Without a word, he turned and left the room.

21

I paced the corridor of the veterinary clinic, approaching Worthy as he stood vigil at the back door.

Six civilians who'd been inside the building were now separated between the three exam rooms, a dental treatment area, and an X-ray radiology room.

I came to a stop before that final room now, glancing in at the occupants—two men, both attired in scrubs, sitting back to back on the floor. Their ankles and wrists were flex-cuffed together, with a separate flex cuff joining their wrist restraints and binding them together. Any unified movement would require intense coordination between them, further complicated by the fact that both were gagged and blindfolded along with the rest of our hostages. Traumatized for life, I thought, and facing an uncertain future that was going to get worse before it actually got worse: if we did make it out of here, they were going to remain right where they were until some janitor, cop, or concerned family member finally broke down a door to get in.

The surgeon and his technician would join them prior to our departure; or maybe, I corrected myself, just the tech. Because if Ian died during this procedure, I was going to execute the surgeon no matter what Reilly said or did to stop me.

Turning back the way I'd come, I sidestepped a row of dog kennels to find that most of the occupants had grown accustomed to my presence—a few slept, most eyed me warily, and a particularly irate Schnauzer gave a low growl just as he had every time I'd passed.

To my left was the locked operating room door, and I paused to hear silence interspersed with a few low murmurs, though whether in English or Serbian, I couldn't tell.

I cleared another exam room to check in on the next pair of hostages, both bound and blindfolded in the same fashion as the last.

The man had pissed himself, whether from fear or how badly he'd needed to go before being detained for the past—I checked my watch—42 minutes and 31 seconds. Behind him was a woman, one of the customers, her gag lowered as she accepted a sip of water from the bottle offered by Jelena, who'd been tending to our captives with the whispered assurances that we'd do them no harm, and this would all be over soon.

How much that did or didn't help, I had no idea.

Everyone on my team had a fair share of posttraumatic stress—hell, in our line of work it was difficult if not impossible to find someone who didn't, whether they admitted it or not—but the last thing we wanted to do was spread that malaise to undeserving civilians. If that was what it took to save Ian, so be it, although I didn't exactly feel like the warrior I'd set out to become when enlisting in the Army at the tender age of 17. There were idealistic notions of warfare and then there was the reality of warfare, I thought, and never the twain shall meet.

I passed between another pair of exam rooms and gave the hostages a once-over to ensure there were no escape attempts in progress, but so far the clinic's staff and patrons had proven remarkably docile, without so much as one would-be hero in the mix.

My final steps took me toward Cancer. His masked face looked at me and then away; normally we could communicate via eye contact almost as effectively as with the spoken word, but for once I found his gaze inscrutable, devoid of either anger or empathy.

Cancer stood at the door leading to the lobby, whose locked entrance now bore a sign in Jelena's neat handwriting declaring that the clinic was temporarily closed due to an emergency surgery, thank you very much, and that all routine appointments would occur at the same time the following day.

That hadn't stopped at least two people from knocking, one of them forcefully, before finally abandoning their attempts. We'd unplugged the receptionist's phone when it began ringing within sixty seconds of Reilly locking me out of the OR, a personal slight that I would gladly bear were it not for the fact that I'd gotten my team into this mess.

I heard a chiming sound and came to a stop, finding the source: a cardboard box atop a shelf, where a pile of cell phones and one pocket knife were consolidated to eventually be reclaimed by their owners, hopefully long after we'd departed the building.

But for the time being we were stuck here, relegated to being surrounded by police at any moment. If that occurred, it would be either a hostage standoff at best or a barricaded shootout at worst, at least until Ian's treatment was complete: Reilly had assured us in no uncertain terms that even if we surrendered our casualty to an ambulance crew, he'd die before reaching a hospital. With a teammate facing certain death, I'd ordered my entire team to risk a lifetime of incarceration in a Serbian prison—no one had objected, nor was any objection conceivable. Any of them would have made the same choice in my position, Jelena included. Grim as it was, the situation reminded me of the meme that showed five mice all pinned by the same mousetrap, dead in a semicircle around a single piece of cheese, underscored by a one-word caption.

TEAMWORK.

One of the hostage phones beside me chittered and vibrated with an incoming call, and I flung the box off the counter to send the devices skittering across the floor that reeked of disinfectant.

Suddenly the operating room door swung open. I steeled myself for the inevitable reprimand from Reilly—he'd requested silence or as close to it as we could manage, and whichever hostages hadn't pissed themselves yet probably were doing so now thanks to the racket I'd just made out of nothing more than sheer frustration.

And sure enough, Reilly stepped into the hall and met my eyes, though he looked more elated than upset.

"Let's move."

"He's alive?" I asked.

Reilly gave an odd shrug, as if to convey that he was less than impressed with the veterinary surgical expertise as it pertained to a human patient.

"For now."

22

After a seeming eternity with no transmissions from the ground team, Meiling Chen was surprised when the speaker box finally crackled to life—and even more so to hear that the man transmitting sounded calm, even disinterested.

"*Raptor Nine One, Suicide Actual.*"

The OPCEN went silent in the time it took her to grab the hand mic and transmit back, "Suicide Actual, this is Raptor Nine One, send SITREP."

"*Surgery was a success,*" David said, "*if you can call it that. Angel's vital signs are stable for the time being, and until that changes we will not attempt an emergency cross-border movement.*"

"Copy," she said, feeling her tension abate with the confirmation that the wounded team member remained just that—wounded, not dead.

"*Currently en route to our tertiary safehouse at Kovačica.*"

Chen glanced at the world time zone clock on the OPCEN wall, then to Duchess's computer—her *own* computer, she quickly corrected herself, now that she occupied the late Kimberly Bannister's workstation—and consulted the digital map of Serbia as David continued.

"*I need you to stay up on law enforcement comms for early warning on a vehicle BOLO. We're moving with the Audi and the cargo van. All weapons and equipment accounted for, but we left the rest of our vehicles behind in Belgrade for now. Second priority is any mafia traffic that indicates how thoroughly they're searching for us, and in what parts of the country. Advise you come up with a deception plan to leak information that we've fled Serbia already."*

She felt a flashpoint of anger at what was, to put it lightly, a team leader issuing orders after all but going completely rogue, and felt the eyes of her OPCEN staff upon her as they awaited a response.

Keying the mic, she replied, "I did not, I repeat *not*, approve your seizure of a civilian facility."

A long moment of silence.

"*Was there a question in there?*"

"I am clarifying this matter for the mission transcript."

"*Clarify away,*" the team leader said breezily. "*You didn't approve it, and I didn't ask permission. If we didn't take that clinic, my team would be down a man right now. But there were zero civilian injuries, and everyone we found there is currently restrained and awaiting discovery.*"

There was an edge to her voice when she replied, "Your orders are to travel to Kovačica and await further guidance."

"*We're doing that. I just told you.*"

Chen felt herself shaking her head in genuine disbelief. She knew David Rivers by little more than name, voice, and service record, none of which suggested this jaw-dropping level of arrogance.

Duchess's yet-unresolved death had saddled her with the sole responsibility of managing the fallout of what amounted to a nightmare scenario: a failed meet resulting in a wounded contractor, followed by the unlawful takeover of a civilian veterinary facility by a ground team whose commander had not only barely notified her of the event, but had done so seemingly only to benefit from the OPCEN's ability to monitor communications from the far side of the world.

She considered exerting her newfound authority and decided against it. Doing so would merely showcase her impotence, trying to win an ego battle from the opposite side of the world, and at this point she was far better off conserving what little power she may have had at present.

Chen tried to keep her voice level as she transmitted back, "We'll keep you posted on any relevant police or mafia traffic that comes over the net. Send a location update every fifteen minutes until you arrive, then check in once you reach the safehouse so we can discuss the way ahead."

She let that comment hang, considering whether it had its intended effect of a double edge that applied to his future as ground force commander as much as the status of their mission in Serbia.

Whether it did or not, David's response was amicable.

"*Much appreciated and will comply. Suicide Actual, out.*"

The exchange had gone from combative to an uneasy truce, she thought, setting the hand mic down and preparing to update her chain of command in the Special Activities Center.

She reached for the phone and paused, considering how her career could survive at this point.

Chen hadn't been thrilled with her assignment to the Special Activities Center, and less so when she found out her destination was within the newly-relabeled Ground Department, still mostly referred to by its long-running designation of Ground Branch. In an Agency whose specialty was clandestine human intelligence, paramilitary operators weren't exactly considered second-class citizens.

But they weren't far from it, either.

CIA officers who either sought assignment or willingly remained there were typically comfortable with the fixed paygrade of a career plateau, a sacrifice they willingly made because they enjoyed the work. Chen, by contrast, had struggled across the finish line of her tenure as station chief only to wind up here, in a niche program that was a lateral career move at best, her supervisor and mentor murdered not after imparting the sum total of her wisdom but instead scarcely after Chen's arrival.

Now she occupied the seat of a dead woman whose role she had no idea how to fill, facing an entire OPCEN full of primary staff members whose names she'd only recently committed to memory, along with the members of their respective shop who she was still struggling to identify beyond recognizing their faces, much less duty descriptions.

Lifting the phone from its cradle, Chen considered that this was like being assigned to ride shotgun in a racecar to learn the trade and, when the vehicle was speeding around the track at 150mph, the driver had a heart attack. Chen didn't put the car in motion, and she damn sure wouldn't have selected the track in the first place, and now all eyes were on her to resolve an impossible situation that was arguably fated to disaster no matter what she did or didn't do.

23

Reilly was in the back of the van, completing a round of vital checks on his unconscious patient when David finally signed off his radio exchange from the passenger seat.

"Much appreciated and will comply. Suicide Actual, out."

Shaking his head, Reilly took his seat and completed Ian's casualty card and vital charts. Now he was in the holding pattern of care for an unconscious patient—checking that vitals remained stable and bandages didn't suddenly become soaked with fresh blood, and standing by with everything he'd need if either took a turn for the worse.

Cancer, who was driving the van-turned-casualty evacuation vehicle northeast along European Route E70, casually asked, "So what did Mayflower say?"

"Mayfly," David corrected him.

"Whatever."

"She sounded pissed."

"Oh, so she's filling Duchess's shoes already."

Reilly leaned forward in his seat and ventured, "Just a guess here, but it might have had something to do with the fact that you sounded like a raging asshole."

David protested, "I did no such thing."

"Really?" the medic asked, committing to his best impersonation of David as he continued, "'I didn't ask permission...we're doing that. I just told you.'"

Cancer looked over from behind the wheel. "You did say that."

The team leader exploded.

"So what? We're doing what we have to in order to stay alive. And I don't need someone trying to call the shots from Virginia, especially when her main concern is avoiding accountability for this mess."

Rolling his neck in an attempt to clear the muscle tension that had been building since the discovery of Ian bleeding out on the floor of a bombed-out building, Reilly pointed out, "You need her if you want to stay employed. Remember when we got split up last mission, and Cancer was in charge? It was a disaster."

Cancer muttered, "That's true."

"And that was part of our plan," Reilly continued. "Now imagine how bad it would be if you got killed and Cancer had to take over in the middle of an op."

"Your point?" David asked.

"My point is, that's exactly what Mayflower is dealing with right now. A dead boss and being thrust into the hot seat at the worst possible time. Try and have a little empathy."

The team leader was unapologetic. "Empathy is your specialty, not mine. And it's not Mayflower, it's Mayfly."

"Whatever." Reilly was about to press the issue when a raspy voice caught him off guard.

"Jelena?"

Reilly looked down to see Ian's eyelids fluttering open.

He knelt beside his casualty, taking Ian's hand and peering into his pupils to assess dilation. "Hey, buddy, glad you're with us. How are you feeling?"

"Jelena," Ian repeated.

"She's fine, totally fine. Driving the point car with Worthy."

"Everyone else?"

"Bro," Reilly said incredulously, noting that Ian wasn't slurring his words in the least, "somehow you were the only one to get hit."

Ian tried to raise his head, grunting with exertion before abandoning the effort.

"Where are we going?"

David answered, "North of Belgrade, en route to safehouse number three. Next stop Kovačica."

"Meet went bad," Ian said with a grimace.

Reilly nodded, eager to keep him talking. "Yeah. Yeah, it did. Crates were empty. But you're going to be fine, I've got enough narcotics on hand to keep you going. At least until Cancer finds my stash."

Ian pinched his eyes shut, frowning as if he couldn't make sense of the situation. "There was...arterial blood."

"Small branch of the hepatic artery."

"How am I not dead?"

"Hemostatic dressings kept you alive until we got you to the car, then you took two bags of blood, one from Worthy and one from David. That got you to the OR for vessel repair."

Ian's eyelids flew open.

"What OR?"

"Vet office," Reilly continued, "by the safehouse. You've got some staples that'll never come out, internal suturing in your oblique, external sutures, and a diaper bandage that I'll have to switch out. Bottom line is you're going to be sore as shit but functional in a few days. Back on your feet in a week or two, and you can forget about drinking rakia or anything else with alcohol for a few months."

"Our mission?"

"Fucked," David blurted, "is my guess. I doubt that Sidorov is going to show up after an Agency team got outed trying to hit him. But you're alive, and that's what matters right now. There's always going to be another shit-head to kill, but where are we going to find another geeky Jewish intel dude?"

"Don't say that," Ian croaked. "We practically grow on trees."

"Yeah, well, hopefully the fucker who shot you is dead right now. Most of those guys are, I assure you—Worthy came in blazing, and the rest of us weren't far behind."

Ian swallowed hard.

"Did you get Gudelj?"

Cancer shot back, "No, we never even saw him. Why?"

"He's the one who shot me."

David turned around from the passenger seat, eyes smoldering.

"*Gudelj?*" he asked. "You're sure?"

"Yeah."

The team leader fixed his gaze on Cancer. "We're going to kill him."

Reilly winced.

"The Janjicari might have something to say about that—"

"I don't give a shit what they have to say," David insisted. "I'm in the most badass mafia on earth, the only Project Longwing ground team. We might not get Sidorov this time around, but you don't nearly kill one of our guys and get away with it. We've got mercenary experience and Agency resources. I don't know how we're going to do it, but before we leave Serbia, Gudelj will get what's coming to him. He will die by our hand, and it's going to be in spectacularly horrific fashion."

This comment intrigued Cancer, who glanced over with an enticed look that would, under any other circumstances, indicate sexual arousal.

"Such as?" he asked.

"I don't know," David said with exasperation. "You're the sadist here. Start brainstorming."

Cancer responded with an eerily ill-timed Biblical reference.

"Ask," he said with dramatic flair, "and ye shall receive."

24

Chen was startled when her intelligence officer called out, "Quiet in the OPCEN."

She looked at him for explanation, but Andolin Lucios didn't turn to face her; instead, he spoke in his normal monotone while facing his computer.

"Ma'am, I've just received an intercepted communication with Sidorov."

Chen's eyes narrowed. "I thought our Moscow station was at gridlock with his comms."

"They are," he explained. "It was picked up by Triton flying over the Caspian Sea. Point of origin for the call was Tehran."

At that moment, the speaker box on her desk came to life.

"*Raptor Nine One, Suicide Actual.*"

She snatched the hand mic and transmitted "Stand by" before addressing Lucios once more.

"Contents of the intercept?"

"Call begins at—"

"Give me the summary."

Lucios cleared his throat and went on, "Unidentified middleman requesting confirmation of Sidorov's arrival in Urmia in three days' time. Sidorov declining on the grounds of recent kinetic activity in Belgrade.

Caller states that Sidorov's presence is no longer optional, that the, quote, 'big boss' will be waiting for him. Assessment: Erik Weisz is or will be on the ground in Iran, and Sidorov will be making the trip to meet him."

"So we're back on," Chen said in disbelief.

"Not quite—the caller confirmed that Valjevo is out of the question, and specified an alternate airfield for Sidorov's meetings and refuel."

She gave a curt nod toward the front of the OPCEN. "Pull that location up on the main screen, please. Ops, I want a recommended scheme of maneuver."

The burly red-haired former Marine at the operations desk nodded as Lucios relayed his monitor display to the central screens at the front of the OPCEN.

Raising her hand mic once more, Chen transmitted, "Suicide Actual, go ahead."

David replied, "*Safehouse occupied, standing by for guidance.*"

"Do you have your mission planning suite up and running?"

"*Negative, we just completed clearance.*"

"I need you to establish full connectivity asap; call me back as soon as you're online. We've had a development."

"*Good to hear, give us a few mikes. Suicide Actual, out.*"

Chen set the mic down, her pulse quickening. Could this really be happening? She momentarily considered whether to let Sidorov reach his destination unscathed in order to track his linkup with a far more strategic target in Iran.

But almost as soon as the thought occurred to her, she dismissed it out of hand.

Aside from North Korea, Iran was perhaps the single most difficult country in which to establish and maintain the access required to track an individual. Sidorov would disappear almost as soon as he arrived, and even if they somehow managed to follow him to Weisz, so what? An airstrike within Iranian borders, much less a capture mission, would never be approved, particularly against a man they knew by little more than a pseudonym. Weisz would drift out of surveillance coverage long before leaving the country, if he left at all.

No, she resolved, they couldn't risk letting Sidorov reach his ultimate destination. Particularly when his presence aboard the plane had just been confirmed for them by a somewhat miraculous signals intelligence intercept that they were lucky to have in the first place.

Chen was suddenly aware that her operations officer had turned to face her, his expression inexplicably dour in stark contrast to her own wave of optimism.

She looked over his head to see the new airfield that Sidorov's Pilatus PC-24 would be landing at in three days' time. Lucios had pulled up not only an overhead view but a three-dimensional model of the surrounding topography.

Jamieson spoke without prompting. "It's a suicide mission."

He looked back at the screen to narrate a devastating play-by-play that drained every shred of her hope.

"Our team's packing a Gustaf rocket launcher. Maximum effective range against a stationary target is 500 meters. From one tip of the runway to the other, it's completely open ground within that entire radius. So let's say we push it all the way to 1,000 meters. They've still only got a small area of possible concealment in the woods to the northwest, and I can guarantee that area will be crawling with roving patrols. Zero chance they remain undetected before the plane arrives. And even if they had rocket-boosted, laser-guided ammunition—which they don't—to range a full 2,000 meters for a Hail Mary shot, there's still no direct line of sight where they won't be spotted in the open. Now if they could acquire a mortar system ahead of time, 82mm at a minimum, they could drop rounds from a few kilometers out. However—"

"However," interrupted Gregory Pharr, the OPCEN's lawyer, "we are restricted to line-of-sight engagements using direct-fire weapons systems. Mortars are out of the question."

Jamieson continued, "As are sniper rifles, by virtue of the fact that Sidorov won't step off the bird until it's wheels down in Iran. That leaves us with the Gustaf, and even if they somehow got close enough to the airfield *and* went undetected—which again, isn't going to happen—they'd get rolled up within thirty seconds of shooting it."

The OPCEN fell deathly silent then, dashing Chen's hopes that a dissenting voice would rise from the ether to contradict what was seemingly obvious to everyone seeing what she did now. Sidorov would land there, then refuel and proceed unmolested to Urmia, Iran, to meet with Erik Weisz, all while the collective brains and brawn behind Project Longwing stood by, powerless to stop it.

As if to mock this grim reality at the worst possible time, an upbeat voice eagerly shattered the quiet.

"*Raptor Nine One*," David Rivers transmitted, "*be advised, we're fully online and ready to start planning. Ready to receive your update.*"

25

My brow furrowed at the response from the woman I knew only as Mayfly.

"*Copy,*" she began, "*we'll be sending it momentarily, just collecting some more information. But I may have spoken too soon—stand by.*"

I lowered the hand mic and scanned the figures beside me: Cancer and Ian, our trio seated at a grimy dining table where we'd arrayed a pair of ruggedized laptops with recently established satellite connectivity. Cancer turned his palms upward, giving me a *who the fuck knows what that means* gesture, and then Ian offered a more logical assessment.

"Some new intel," he surmised, "but I can't imagine why she thought it would be good news. There's no way Sidorov will risk the trip after everything that just went down in Belgrade."

Then we waited, watching the radio speaker box; there was no one left to comment.

Jelena was assisting Worthy and Reilly as they set up security cameras that would ultimately allow us to pull 360-guard with one team member sitting in front of a computer. Cancer had initially supervised the effort, but that went out the window as soon as Mayfly advised us to get our mission planning equipment up and running. A good sign if ever there was one, at least until her latest transmission.

Our current safehouse on the outskirts of Kovačica stood amid agricultural fields that stretched in all directions. It bore an almost uncanny resemblance to the farmhouse outside Valjevo Airport where we'd planned to hit Sidorov in the first place, an unfortunate reminder, since we couldn't have been any further from our goal.

Two from my team had escaped certain death by the narrowest margin, with Ian's survival credited only to Reilly's quick action, compatible blood donors in our ranks, and the coerced services of a Serbian veterinary surgeon, all on what was supposed to be our simplest mission to date. Operating in the Balkans where we could blend in with the populace for once, with a simple one-rocket shot to kill our primary target.

What had gone wrong in the interim?

In short, I concluded, everything.

Someone had gotten to Duchess, and while she'd probably made every effort to resist and keep her information ambiguous, clearly they persuaded her. I idly wondered if she had family members threatened during the transaction. At this point we'd likely never know, and it didn't matter much to the immediate situation: Sidorov tipped off to our presence, Gudelj alive and well after wounding Ian, and our mission presumably scrapped.

Finally the woman transmitted, "*Suicide Actual, Raptor Nine One.*"

"Go ahead," I replied.

"*Data shot in progress. Here's a brief rundown: we've just had a SIGINT hit out of Iran, and the message seems to be from one of Weisz's middlemen directing Sidorov to make the trip as planned.*"

"If he's dumb enough to do that, we've got him dead to rights. What's the catch?"

"*The catch,*" she said, "*is that he won't be stopping in Valjevo. Instead he'll be flying into Ponikve Airport in western Serbia, near the border of Bosnia and Herzegovina.*"

Ian's fingertips alighted on his laptop keyboard but halted abruptly when Mayfly added, "*Be advised, it's under renovation and you'll need the most current imagery to get an accurate picture. I'm afraid it won't matter much either way.*"

By then our data shot upload was complete, and Ian opened the file to reveal overhead and topographic imagery of the airfield and its surrounding area.

The three of us leaned forward to scrutinize the images and, perhaps more significantly, the distances between the runway and any semblance of a covered and concealed position, as Mayfly continued speaking.

"*A strike appears tactically unfeasible due to terrain, as does the status of the objective—it's a mountain airport located near a few major ski resorts. But it was heavily damaged during the NATO bombing campaign. So the state took it over, installed a perimeter fence, and it's been in varying phases of reconstruction ever since. The airfield is closed to civilian traffic, with just over half of its runway resurfaced to date—more than enough for Sidorov's PC-24, and landings are permitted by the Serbian government on a case-by-case basis for which he apparently qualifies.*"

"Wait one, let us take a look."

By the time I set the mic down, Cancer was already shaking his head.

"Gustaf is out—look at that open terrain. Way too exposed, and no buildings for us to hide in."

Ian asked, "What about those woods on the northwest side?"

"Still pushing the max effective range for a stationary target, and that area is gonna be crawling with security. That means compromise for sure, and even if we had invisibility cloaks they'd kill us as soon as we took the shot. We need mortars."

Now it was my turn to shake my head.

"Not going to happen."

That wasn't good enough for Ian, who shot me a quizzical glance. "Did you ask?"

Heaving a sigh, I keyed the mic and spoke in a droll tone.

"Mortars?"

Mayfly responded, "*Hard no. Legal won't sign off on it.*"

"Legal," Cancer muttered. "Super."

Ian pointed at the roads crossing the open ground surrounding the airport. "What if we dismounted from a vehicle, then did a 'shoot-and-scoot?'"

Cancer responded before I could. "Roads will be covered in checkpoints at a minimum, if not blocked. Mobile op is out."

Then the three of us fell silent, and when a solution didn't arise despite our eyes scrutinizing the screen for some shred of hope, I leaned back in my chair and groaned.

"The fucking irony. It's killing me."

"What irony?" Ian asked.

Running both hands through my hair, I replied with exasperation.

"Four days ago we bought a bunch of surface-to-air missiles from Gudelj. Don't you wish we held one back instead of shipping them all out right away? It'd come in really handy right about now."

Then we fell silent again, though it was clear that Cancer had caught something I didn't. His eyes flashed with excitement, then fixed on mine as he waited for recognition that I didn't provide.

Ian was next, annoyingly, emitting a slight gasp before he said, "Right. I'll check the weather."

He set to work on an adjacent laptop, leaving me to stare at the airfield imagery for a full five seconds before I snapped my fingers.

"Shit," I cried, staring at the screen, "that might work. Ian, check the forecast—"

He interrupted, "Prevailing winds this time of year are strong, and consistently from the east."

I grabbed the radio mic and transmitted, "Mayfly, we might be able to take him."

Her response was far less enthusiastic, bordering on defeat.

"*My operations officer says it would be a suicide mission.*"

"Your operations officer," I pointed out, "is still looking at this like it's a shot against a stationary target on the runway. It's not. We'll have to hit the bird on its final approach."

"*While it's airborne?*"

"While it's coming in for landing, flying low and slow. According to Angel, the prevailing winds are from the east and fairly strong. Sidorov's pilot won't risk a downwind approach—he'll have to land into the wind like any other pilot, *especially* if the runway's only partially resurfaced."

"*So?*"

Analyzing the screen, I continued, "So take a look at the west side of the runway—about a kilometer of open ground, then a whole lot of forested hills that Sidorov's plane will have to fly right over. We'll have to work out some math on the trajectory of a PC-24 relative to its touchdown point, but the approach azimuth is a sure thing—there's only one runway. The maximum effective range of the Gustaf is only a dealbreaker if we look at this as a horizontal shot once the bird is on the ground; but if we engage while it's flying right overhead with its flaps and landing gear down, then all we need is one elevated shot to bring it down."

I looked at Ian, then Cancer, to see if I'd left anything unsaid. Both remained silent.

Mayfly, however, was considerably less enthusiastic.

"*Even if you made that shot, you'd be overrun by security forces responding from the airfield.*"

"They'll try," I conceded. "And I'll be the first to admit these are somewhat long odds. But it's not a suicide mission, either. Not anymore."

"*You're down to four men now that Angel is injured.*"

Cancer cupped his hands over his chest in a pantomime of female breasts.

I transmitted back, "Our Affinity Gold representative has proven herself capable thus far." Making eye contact with Ian, I continued, "And don't worry about Angel, he's got Jew powers."

"*Say again?*"

"Never mind," I said dismissively. "Point is, this entire mission has been a train wreck from the start. Neither of us wants to get fired, and my team certainly doesn't want to come home empty-handed. Nothing would be better for Weisz than if we packed our bags, and that's not going to bode well for the citizens of whatever country he strikes next. All we need is approval."

When she didn't immediately respond, I cut my eyes to Cancer and whispered, "Get Worthy in here, now."

Cancer departed before Mayfly finally came back on the air.

"*That's a tall order, and I'm afraid all I can do is ask. At this point the decision is out of my hands.*"

"Then be persuasive," I quipped. Unable to restrain myself, I added, "Duchess would find a way."

This time she didn't hesitate. "*Are you always this insubordinate?*"

"Pretty much. Your predecessor should have warned you. But I'm right about this and you know it."

Cancer returned with Worthy in tow as Mayfly reluctantly conceded, "*I'll see what I can do. But let me be very clear: your team is in a holding pattern until I tell you otherwise.*"

"Copy," I said, then unkeyed the mic and pointed at Worthy. "We've got planning to do. Take Jelena and don't come back without a bottle of rakia."

Mayfly went on, "*You will remain at the safehouse, period. No exceptions.*"

"Make that two bottles," I said to Worthy.

Cancer added, "And some smokes. I'm running out of smokes."

Then I transmitted, "Copy all, we'll remain at the safehouse to conduct refit and mission planning until we receive further guidance."

Ian looked thoughtful as he commented, "Some food, too. Reilly flips out when he's hungry."

"Jesus Christ," Worthy snapped, speaking for the first time. "Rakia, cigarettes, food. Anything else?"

Cancer folded his arms and, raising his eyebrows at the pointman, said, "You're still here?"

26

"You're headed west," Worthy said, completing a scan out the Audi's windshield and focusing on the side-view mirror to see a set of headlights turning onto the road behind them. "We need to make a left to get back to the safehouse."

Jelena made no effort to alter course, steering with a single hand as she replied, "I know where I am going."

The vehicle behind them suddenly accelerated, its headlights bearing down on them between a row of houses on either side of the road.

By now Worthy's MP7 was in both hands, his grip tightening. "Six o'clock, coming up fast."

"It's fine," she said, the dismissal striking Worthy as the first gross error in her tactical judgment he'd witnessed thus far. Worse still, he was completely at her mercy, with every possible response and field of fire subject to the restrictions of how she piloted the Audi on a second-by-second basis.

But with a vehicle speeding toward them at twenty meters and closing, there was no time to argue the point; he unbuckled his seatbelt and rolled down the passenger window to a freezing blast of wind, shifting his weight in preparation to serve as the one and only gunman defending them against an unconfirmed threat.

Jelena didn't accelerate or brake, much less change course down a side street.

Instead she continued cruising with barely a glance toward her rearview, and Worthy watched in disbelief as the vehicle behind them swerved into the opposite lane and roared forward in an aggressive passing maneuver that exposed the threat—or, he realized, lack thereof.

The hulking pickup had people in its bed, all right, all of them clad in winter attire and clutching not guns, but bottles.

He relaxed his grip on the MP7 as the truck pulled in front of them and sped forward, the Audi's headlights glaring against the teenage passengers as they continued their late-night joyride.

Worthy rolled up his window, feeling embarrassed as he clicked his seatbelt back into place.

Jelena, however, dismissed the incident outright.

"Kovačica nightlife. We are not in Belgrade anymore."

"No," he acknowledged, "we are most definitely not."

The route toward Kovačica earlier that day had reminded him more of rural Indiana than anything else: endlessly flat expanses of farm fields dotted by low buildings and country houses, with a few rows of wind turbines serving as the only visual landmark to speak of. He was hesitant to leave the safehouse for anything so trivial as groceries—they'd recently fled their siege of the vet clinic, both Ian and Jelena were surely the subjects of police composite sketches by now, and the entire team had the Janjicari looking for them—but his concerns of being discovered eased considerably once they actually made it into town.

Kovačica had exactly one main road that was bisected by a single-digit number of side streets, each of them fanning out into a town with a few thousand people united in an island of civilization amidst the sea of crops. To his surprise there wasn't a bar in sight, but there was no shortage of restaurants, grocery stores, and even a few hotels open for business despite the late hour. The town was home to an art gallery, Jelena explained, that drew a steady trickle of tourists from Belgrade. As a result, they'd been able to procure everything on their shopping list without the Audi drawing so much as a sideways glance.

Jelena abruptly spoke. "You guys are a pretty tight team."

He looked over at her, the soft blue glow of interior lighting illuminating a half-smile on her face. Still, Worthy thought, her eyes were glinting with a kind of energy he hadn't seen out of her before. Maybe it was the near-death experience she'd had earlier that day, a jarring close-combat encounter that her background as a non-official cover operative would have in no way prepared her to deal with.

Then he looked away, committing to another scan across the windows and mirrors before finally resting the tip of his MP7 suppressor against the floorboard between his legs.

He responded, "We've been running together for a couple years now. Longer, even, if you want to count the mercenary time."

"Are Longwing missions always this disastrous?"

Worthy blinked and shook his head.

"More often than we'd like to admit, yeah. Name of the game is generally to make a plan, watch everything go to hell, and try to scrap together some way to make it happen regardless."

"It sounds," she noted, "like a good way to get killed."

"So far, it's a miracle we're all still here. Ian more than anyone."

Jelena was still inexplicably driving west, he observed with dismay, and there wasn't much town left to drive before they reached the fields again. Worthy considered whether to push the issue of navigating back to their safehouse, then decided to hell with it. Jelena hadn't exactly been a liability so far, and he decided that whatever her intentions now, he'd trust her.

Those intentions were soon clarified as she asked, "You were going to ask me out, weren't you?"

Worthy swallowed. "Was it that obvious?"

"The puppy dog eyes. Yes, it was that obvious."

She turned left at the next intersection, where neatly trimmed grass was dominated by what appeared to be a medical practice that was closed for the evening.

Drawing a breath, he replied, "If it's any consolation, I was going to wait until after the mission. But the way things are headed, we might not make it that far."

"I was thinking the same thing. Shall we consider this a first date, then?"

"Works for me," he said.

Jelena pulled the car off the road and into the parking lot, steering behind an adjoining building before stopping the Audi and cutting the engine.

"Then let's make it official."

27

"I'm telling you," Cancer said, nodding toward the imagery on the laptop screen, "any terrain that works against us, works against them threefold. But we'll have an escape route planned, and that's going to make all the difference."

Ian wasn't convinced.

"You're talking about this like all the bad guys are going to be on foot. They're not. The roads aren't the only consideration because the Janjicari security element is going to have vehicles, ATVs, maybe even snowmobiles. And the roads allow them to be deployed from here—" He leaned forward to point, his sentence seizing up along with his lungs, by the sound of it.

Reilly was on his feet in a split second, hands on Ian's shoulders as he guided him upright.

"Nice and easy," the medic said, "just breathe."

Ian's face was rigid with pain, breath coming in gasps as he sputtered, "I can't...it fucking hurts..."

"I got you, bro," Reilly replied, sweeping out of the room without further explanation.

Cancer sighed, looking over at David beside him. The team leader gave a slight shake of his head—Ian wouldn't be fit for duty, not on this tight timeline—and Cancer mirrored the expression, albeit with an entirely different nonverbal message conveyed in his glare.

He'll be ready, because he has to be.

Then Cancer cut his eyes to Ian and said, "You're going to have to pick your vagina off the floor sometime in the next two and a half days. We're going to need every teammate we can get."

"I'll be fine," Ian said with a grimace.

David replied, "You don't look fine."

"Yeah, well, I got shot earlier today. Yesterday. Whatever."

With a weary sigh, David checked his watch. "What's taking those two so long?"

Cancer could take a fairly well-educated guess, but Reilly entered the room before he'd decided whether or not to voice his assumption.

"Lose the shirt," Reilly ordered, clutching an ACE bandage in one hand.

The intelligence operative complied, though it took considerable effort for him to do so. David stood and assisted the process, exposing a fresh diaper bandage taped around Ian's side.

Cancer watched Reilly wrap the ACE bandage tight around Ian's abdomen like a girdle, knowing that its greatest contribution beyond holding the medical dressing in place would be for the placebo effect. If Ian concluded the same, he gave no indication of it; instead, the intelligence operative appeared supremely relieved at the addition, looking oddly vulnerable in his wounded, pale, half-naked state. He was probably the least suited among them to psychologically recover from a near-fatal gunshot wound, and yet had demonstrated remarkable grit in joining if not leading the planning process over the past hour.

Once Reilly had fixed the ACE bandage in place and David helped him slip back into his garment, however, Ian was done.

"I'm going to get some sleep," he said, easing himself upright from the chair.

David asked, "You sure? Food should be here any minute."

"I'm sure," he said without further explanation, shuffling out of the dining room.

Cancer fired a cigarette and said ominously, "And then there were three."

"Five," Reilly corrected him, pointing to a computer screen where, in one of the camera feeds, Jelena's Audi was reversing into its parking position.

They leaned forward to watch, surely all wondering the same thing as Reilly spoke once more.

"Think anything happened out there? Worthy's got a little spring in his step."

Cancer exhaled a cloud of smoke.

"And Jelena looks disappointed. Yeah, I'd say something happened."

David grunted softly. "At least one of us got laid. Is that like a case of beer, or—"

"No way," Cancer objected. "Sets a bad precedent."

The team leader's shoulders sagged. "You're right."

They went quiet then, listening for the sound of the door unlocking and hearing it a few moments later, followed by footsteps in the entryway.

Jelena led the way into the kitchen with a bulging paper bag under each arm. Worthy followed in short order, avoiding his teammates' eyes as they pushed the laptops aside to make room for the groceries.

"Traditional Serbian cuisine," Jelena announced as she set her bags down without taking a seat.

Reilly immediately began removing Styrofoam containers from the bags. "You're not joining us?"

"And listen to you argue about the plan for the next three hours? No, thank you—I'm off to bed."

She left the room then, leaving Worthy to absorb the collective gaze of his teammates as he uneasily set his own bags down and procured two bottles of rakia.

David snatched one from him, stripping the seal and uncorking it as he looked to make sure Jelena was out of earshot.

"Took your sweet time out there, didn't you?"

Worthy shrugged. "The first couple stores were closed—"

"Yeah," Cancer said, grabbing the remaining bottle out of his hand and speaking around the cigarette pinched between his lips, "and it's easy to get lost in the bustling metropolis of Kovačica. Fuckin' urban maze out there, isn't it? Let's skip the excuses and half-truths, because no one here gives a shit. You ready to contribute to planning, or what?"

Worthy cleared his throat.

"I'm ready."

"Good," Cancer said, opening the bottle, "because here's the bottom line: the runway is 3,200 meters long, but they've only resurfaced 1,900 meters of it. A PC-24 can land on half that distance, provided it's at sea level. But performance decreases with air density, and since this is in the mountains, the pilot is going to have to fly low over the hills to the west."

Setting the bottle cap down, he plucked the cigarette from his mouth and set it in the saucer-turned-ashtray to slide one of the laptops in front of Worthy.

Pointing at the screen, he went on, "These hills, right here. Then the pilot will descend further into that clearing for the final kilometer of open ground, to make touchdown on the western side of the runway and have enough time to stop without giving Sidorov a neck injury. Flight path will follow this line"—he traced with his finger—"over the woods and between the roads, but closer to the northern one. Seeing as we have to install a tree-stand and wait for the bird to arrive without getting seen, we're looking at a slightly oblique firing angle to land an unguided rocket on a moving target with a few seconds of visibility."

David took a swig from his bottle of rakia and winced. "So the question becomes, who should take the shot?"

Worthy considered the question and then nodded to Reilly, who was procuring a plate-sized rolled pie from a food container and lifting it toward his mouth with both hands.

"I thought Reilly was on the Gustaf."

Cancer rolled the rakia cap sideways and off the table.

It cleared the edge at a 45-degree angle, freefalling toward the dining room floor until Worthy snatched it mid-air.

"Reilly was," Cancer said, recovering his cigarette, "because any roid monkey could make a few-hundred-meter shot against a fixed target at Valjevo. This is a different ballgame, and you've got the quickest reflexes on the team."

He looked at David, who promptly slid his own rakia cap in the opposite direction.

It flew off the table next to Reilly, who didn't so much as attempt to catch it; instead, he bit into the rolled pie, closing his eyes to nod in approval as he chewed.

"See?" David asked. "And he knew that was coming."

Worthy frowned. "I mean, shit. My reaction time's great in a run-and-gun, especially at close range. But this distance is what again?"

"Five hundred meters, give or take—right at the max effective range for a moving target."

"Seems to me that's more of a sniper operation, that's all."

Cancer took a drag and replied, "And a trained sniper is going to be in remarkably high demand when the Mongolian horde comes racing off that airfield to find us. If I come off the long gun to plant a rocket up Sidorov's ass, it's going to be hell on the ground."

David leaned forward and added, "We need to be realistic about this. The situation has changed, so we need to be flexible with our plan. Split-second shot on a moving target from an elevated position using a weapon that was in no way designed to be fired that way means there's a certain magic that's needed, that killer reaction time that's...what's the word I'm looking for..."

"Ineffable," Cancer said, tapping his ash into the saucer.

"Fucking ineffable," David agreed. "Exactly."

Then he pointed the neck of his rakia bottle toward Worthy. "That's where you come in."

Reilly swallowed and paused his next bite to whistle the opening notes of Elton John's "Rocket Man."

"Knock it off, fatass," Cancer snapped. Reilly shrugged and continued eating.

Worthy tilted his chair back on two legs, then let it settle forward with a soft thunk.

He said, "Well all right then. Guess I'm on the Gustaf. I'll try not to let you guys down."

"You won't let us down," Cancer replied, "because you're going to nail that shot."

Worthy gave a slight nod at the compliment but froze when Reilly commented with his mouth half-full.

“And probably get crushed under the wreckage.”

28

Ian had a gut feeling this mission was going to be a shitshow.

He rolled to his side in the snow, scanning the trees for any sign of a threat before checking behind him—all quiet save an icy wind from the east that swept through the pine boughs in gusts.

Then he lay back on the foam mat that provided some meager amount of insulation from the cold, resuming his grip on the suppressed HK416. He surveyed the low ground before him that served as a streambed in the warmer months, judging by the lack of trees in the wide strip snaking its way downhill. Now, however, it was simply blanketed in white. Snow had yet to fall at sea-level Belgrade, but the elevated border region of western Serbia was dotted with ski resorts for good reason, and at three thousand feet elevation, he was breathing crisp mountain air at the cost of freezing his ass off.

Cancer broke his firing position before the sniper rifle, reaching into a pocket on his kit and whispering, "Want a nicotine tablet?"

Ian took in the sniper for a moment—the usual combat gear worn over puffy white cold-weather top and bottom, a marshmallow man awaiting battle—and shook his head.

"I always preferred nasal snuff. Quit that a while back, though."

Popping a tablet into his cheek, Cancer said, "You're worried about Worthy missing the shot."

"No," Ian began. "It's more a matter of..."

He went quiet as a gust of wind coursed through the trees, rattling brambles and causing a pine cone to crash through the branches to make landfall in the snow. The sound of moving air faded to a thin whistle before ebbing into near-silence; both men listened intently, knowing by now that such interludes were not only rare but allowed sound to travel great distances through the forest.

When the eastern breeze picked back up again, this time at a moderate speed, Ian continued, "I'm not concerned about Worthy making the shot—he will."

"Then what's the problem?" Cancer asked.

"Based on the intercepted radio traffic alone, there's at least two dozen mobsters at the airstrip right now. So if there's one thing that bothers me, it's making it out of here in one piece after the plane blows up mid-air."

"Hell," Cancer scoffed, "getting out is the easy part. We've got a plan."

"Combat doesn't honor plans."

A quiet chuckle.

"But she seems to hold luck in high regard, and that's pulled us through so far, hasn't it?"

Ian said nothing. What was there to say?

There was certainly a time when he considered Cancer as brave, maybe even valorous. He'd since learned that the sniper's battlefield actions, however audacious, had nothing to do with heroism.

Cancer would put everything on the line to save a teammate or an innocent civilian, sure. But Ian knew beyond a shadow of a doubt at this point in his involvement with Project Longwing that the sniper simply didn't care whether he survived or not. The lives of those around him were to be protected at all costs—Cancer's own life, however, was a commodity with which he gambled freely because losing it would mean nothing.

If the man were some fresh recruit, that attitude would make him a severe liability. Given his vast experience, he became the one who would bring the others home. The odds would catch up with him one day, Ian sensed, and when that occurred, the least concerned person among them would be Cancer himself.

Reilly transmitted then, his voice dramatic over Ian's earpiece.

"*Cold as fuck out here. We might have to pull a Luke Skywalker.*"

Cancer keyed his radio and responded, "What's that supposed to mean?"

"*You know,* The Empire Strikes Back."

"I don't get it."

After an exasperated sigh over the net, Reilly clarified, "*Where he kills and disembowels his Tauntaun, then crawls inside it to survive the night.*"

Now frustrated, Cancer asked, "What the *fuck* is a Tauntaun?"

"*Snow lizard,*" Reilly said.

Ian quickly corrected him over the team frequency. "Actually, they're a species of semi-sentient reptomammal."

"Whatever," Cancer muttered, "you're both children."

That comment served to pause the conversation between members of a team who were presently arrayed in a somewhat bizarre fashion.

Worthy was in his treestand with the rocket launcher, just as planned. David and Reilly were serving as his personal security detail, guarding the area surrounding the tree—the pointman needed all the help he could get if a roving patrol came along. Slim odds of that happening given how deep in the woods they were, and how prohibitive the steep terrain was to foot movement, but more importantly, the second he fired that shot everyone in a one-mile radius would know *exactly* where the rocket had originated. Nor could he simply run immediately after the fact: first he had to climb down the ladder pegs installed during the previous nightfall, a time-consuming process that would occur while the considerable security forces at the airfield closed in from the east.

And that was where Ian and Cancer came in.

Anyone else on the team would be a more fitting choice to serve as Cancer's spotter, which was just as well: given the mission ahead, he didn't need a spotter so much as local security. Ian had been the obvious choice not because of any tactical bonafides but because he simply couldn't move as far or as fast given the injury that racked his entire upper body with tense, crippling pain at any sudden movement. Reilly had given him just enough meds to dull the effect, but not nearly enough to induce the narcotic-laced stupor that would make the wound bearable.

But once the exfil commenced, pain or no pain, he'd need to run like hell.

He and Cancer were situated 350 meters west of the rocket team, manning the high ground overlooking a ravine through which Worthy, David, and Reilly would come sprinting minutes after the shot was fired. The snowy gulch ahead represented a linear danger area separating otherwise dense swaths of evergreens, which was why Cancer had selected it for his shooting position. He'd hold the line as his teammates retreated past him, gunning down any pursuers to cover the withdrawal until the other three set up their own firing position to the rear. Then it would become a standard break-contact drill all the way to the road a half-kilometer to their west where, if their luck held out, Jelena would be arriving with the cargo van to spirit them out of the area.

A simple plan requiring an unorthodox execution, Ian thought, and perhaps that was what bothered him so much.

David abruptly transmitted, "*Hey, Doc—since you're such a big Star Wars fan, do you know the internal temperature of a Tauntaun?*"

"*No,*" the medic replied. "*What?*"

"*Lukewarm.*"

Ian shook his head slightly, unamused and assuming from the radio silence that Reilly felt the same.

But when the medic replied, it was with a deep belly chuckle that reduced his response to staggered sentence fragments as he transmitted.

"*Dude...that joke...so good...so many, many...layers—*"

Cancer finally had enough, transmitting back, "Doc, ever wonder why you're still a virgin? Maybe you should talk to Racegun, get some advice. Even though Jelena told me she's had better."

Worthy responded immediately.

"*No, she didn't.*"

"She was thinking it, though. Doc, you jealous or what?"

Reilly's return transmission was nonchalant. "*I'll survive.*"

The comment was oddly genuine and self-secure for Reilly, a man who was typically far more interested in, and obsessed with, the affection of women than anyone else on the team. Ian felt a pang of curiosity and then brushed it aside; the last thing he needed to worry about this close to enemy contact, particularly in his wounded state, was Reilly's love life.

Worthy, however, had no such inhibitions.

"*Doc*," he asked, "*are you seeing someone or what?*"

Reilly responded, "*No. I mean, yeah. Sort of.*"

"*Who?*"

"*What does it matter?*"

The ensuing pause assured Ian that Worthy was choosing his words carefully.

"*Doc, I love you, but I've seen you strike out with every female we've ever come across. And between our training and deployments, you're never home long enough to reverse that track record.*"

Undaunted, Reilly said, "*Maybe you're just underestimating me.*"

David followed that up with an absurd order.

"*Angel, I've got your next intel job—explain how Doc has a girlfriend.*"

Ian rolled his eyes, frustrated with his team's constant attempts to pervert his specialty in intelligence into an assumed ability to know absolutely everything they didn't.

He transmitted back, "I'm not a mind reader. How should I know, and why would anyone care—"

But before he could complete his rant, his mind clicked into action.

"Wait," he said, taking a moment to think. "No game, super awkward around women, and no time to meet anyone..."

He looked up abruptly, locking eyes with Cancer before transmitting his conclusion. "He's seeing that hostage from our last mission."

Cancer gave an audible snort, as if the very notion was too ridiculous to speak aloud.

But Reilly didn't reply, and after a few seconds of silence, Cancer transmitted.

"Holy shit, it's true, isn't it?"

Reilly shot back defensively, "*She's not 'that hostage.' Her name is Olivia.*"

"*Yeah*," David readily agreed, "*Olivia Gossweiler. As in, daughter of* Senator *Gossweiler.*"

"*I know who her dad is.*"

David continued, "*Well, does* he *know who* you *are? Because that dude could shut down Project Longwing in a heartbeat if he wanted to. Getting rid of you would be child's play, and then we'd have to find a new medic—*"

"*He knows,*" Reilly interrupted.

Cancer asked, "You sure about that?"

A brief pause before the medic replied, "*How do you think she found me after we got back to the States?*"

That served to shut everyone up, and Ian was checking the surrounding area for movement when another breeze roared in from the east, cresting over him and Cancer with a low whooshing noise.

The sound was punctuated by David's next transmission.

"*Net call, we're still in business. Sidorov's plane is five minutes out.*"

"Copy five mikes," Worthy transmitted back. "Clear the backblast area, I'll be in receive mode only from here on out."

"*Backblast area clear,*" David confirmed. "*Happy hunting.*"

Worthy was a hundred feet off the ground, sitting in a treestand mounted on the trunk of an enormous Norway spruce. The tree was probably two centuries old at least, and he'd felt worse with every bough he sawed off to establish visibility, the effort beginning just after sunset and continuing into the early morning hours. But with a lot of elbow grease and some triangulation work with compass and GPS against known hilltops in the distance, he'd established a hard-earned window to the sky beyond, a conical view through which Sidorov's plane would have to fly along its 110-degree final approach heading for Ponikve Airport's one and only runway.

In retrospect, everything about this seemingly ludicrous plan had come off without the slightest hitch. Serbia held some of the most famous hunting grounds in Europe, with abundant deer, boar, and goat-like mountain animals called chamois. The team had been able to acquire all the snow-white cold-weather gear they hadn't anticipated needing when they departed the States, along with a pair of treestands.

Only one of them supported Worthy in his current cross-legged shooting position; the other was mounted two feet above it and at a perpendicular angle on the tree trunk, supporting the weight of the Carl Gustaf 84mm recoilless rifle atop its bipod.

He stripped his cold-weather gloves, stuffing them in a pocket so his hands were clad only in his usual tactical shooting gloves. Patting the olive drab cylinder before him, he whispered, "All right, girl, let's do this."

Assuming a firing position at this point required little more than adjusting the angle of the rocket launcher, placing his hands on the dual pistol grips, and leaning forward into the shoulder pad. He'd already manipulated every aspect of this one-time rocket site to remove as many variables to accuracy as possible, and his first glance through the telescopic sight revealed the dead center of his limited field of fire at thirty degrees of elevation. Worthy shifted the weapon up, down, left, and right from center, re-orienting himself to how far he could move his aim and in what direction before taking what was hopefully the only shot he'd have to take today.

"*Four minutes out,*" David transmitted. "*Airspeed three hundred knots, altitude 4,300 feet above sea level, turning onto final now. Lining up at 110 degrees, just got clearance to land.*"

Worthy registered the words but didn't react, focusing instead on testing his ability to stabilize his aim at various points in the distance, switching between them to test his reaction time and harmonize himself with the weapon one last time. With the rocket launcher supported between his shoulder and the bipod, it was surprisingly easy; the Gustaf was a somewhat unwieldy beast, but it could have been worse—this was the latest variant, which, at 15 pounds, was only half the weight of the original export version from the 1960s. Even with the addition of a seven-plus-pound high-explosive anti-tank round, set to detonate on impact rather than the usual one-tenth of a second delay required for armored targets, Worthy could maintain this shooting position for hours if necessary, much less the few minutes he'd be required to do so here.

Nor would he have to do anything so unbecoming as haul the rocket launcher off the objective.

There was an honest-to-God standing US Congressional directive mandating certain deniability protocols for covert action, and as a result all team weapons were covertly procured by the CIA's Armor and Special

Programs Department. The Gustaf and its round were no exception, bearing serial numbers that would trace back to the Czech Republic.

The biggest obstacle to him now wasn't experience—he'd undergone considerable training with the Gustaf, along with the rest of his team. They'd even fired it at moving targets—flat wood tank and vehicle silhouettes gliding on motorized tracks that crisscrossed a training range at Harvey Point—using practice rounds with identical ballistics but no warhead.

Regrettably, most of his expertise with the Gustaf was of absolutely no use in the current scenario: there would be no target spotting by an outside observer, no chance to reload, not even time to correct a simple misfire.

Instead he was waiting for a plane to appear in the gap before him and vanish just as quickly.

"*Three minutes out*," David said.

Worthy considered his target: with a length of 55 feet and an almost identical wingspan, the Pilatus PC-24 wasn't a miniscule bird but it wasn't exactly a 747, either. Even with flaps and landing gear down, it would be flying above the stall speed of 94 miles per hour. His current role would require the equivalent of hitting a semi-truck speeding past a narrow gap, and given the fact that his fin-stabilized HEAT round would take 1.6 seconds to travel the presumed 500 meters to the target, Worthy had to fire the instant he saw the damn thing in the sky.

On the plus side, the showdown here was between an anti-tank round and an unarmored medium-light jet flying as slow as it possibly could: any hit was a good one.

If he missed by so much as an inch, however, the rocket would go sailing off into the winter sky as nothing more than a visual beacon for every security guard and law enforcement agent within a mile radius as they looked toward the sound of the blast.

No pressure, Worthy thought as his team leader sent the next transmission.

"*Two minutes, airspeed reduced to approximately two hundred knots, altitude four thousand ASL and dropping fast. Still on course for the airstrip. Racegun, you're cleared hot, weapons free.*"

That served as the team leader's final radio message, though not the last transmission before the PC-24 came into view. That privilege was reserved for Jelena, who, in addition to her duties as exfil driver, was currently serving as the only external observer.

When her voice came over his earpiece, it was with breathless urgency.

"It just crossed over my position on the road, less than 200 meters over the trees."

Christ, Worthy thought—he knew the bird would be flying low, but not *that* low. It wouldn't affect his rocket, which would arm itself forty meters after clearing the muzzle. But while the round's shorter flight distance would narrow the flight time to a second or less, the close proximity also meant less time to take the shot.

He shifted his aim until the edge of his view through the telescopic sight was aligned with the evergreen boughs nearest the plane's approach. Next, he flipped the catch of the Gustaf's firing mechanism from safe to fire and heard the PC-24 approaching, its twin turbofan engines drowning out the gusts of mountain wind. Worthy let his index finger hover over the trigger.

Then he let all the thoughts and analyses evaporate from his mind as he would at a competitive shooting match, when he entered an almost Zenlike state of hypervigilance in the moments between an official calling out "Stand by" and the beep of the shot timer. No thoughts, just raw awareness, a focused state of consciousness that he could place himself in at will but only maintain for a matter of seconds—which, at this point, was the only time he had left.

In one instant, he was intensely staring at clouds drifting beyond his ballistic reticle, and the next, at a royal blue fuselage.

Worthy fired immediately, the Gustaf shuddering as the high-explosive anti-tank round blasted out of the muzzle with a deafening shockwave of sound. His view was gone as the weapon's backblast against the spruce boughs turned smoke and snow particles into a depthless cloud that swirled around him, marred only by a dull flash of light overhead that was followed by a second explosion, one that could only have resulted from the warhead's impact with the plane.

It was done. He'd hit the bird and now it was time to get the hell out.

Worthy shifted the Gustaf off his shoulder, slinging his HK417 by feel and then grabbing his treestand with both hands as he probed for the first ladder peg beneath him to begin climbing down. As he moved, he heard a groaning shriek of splintering tree trunks and metallic pops in the forest to his east.

His boots soon found purchase and he was working his way further downward in severely limited visibility when a radio transmission shattered his wave of self-congratulatory euphoria.

"*Rocket only clipped it,*" David began. "*The bird crash-landed 200 meters east of our position. Transitioning to assault.*"

Reilly was on his feet by the time he heard David's message. He had been fully prepared to run into the protection afforded by the overwatch position and a waiting exfil vehicle, and it took him a full second to process the new reality and begin moving in the opposite direction. He lumbered into motion on stiff limbs before achieving momentum against the bulk of cold-weather gear that had been a godsend over a long night in the woods, but would quickly turn into a smothering shell of heat retention now that he was moving. David had spoken the word "assault" as if it would be a team endeavor, but the reality was that Reilly would be the team leader's only backup. Cancer and Ian were no help: the latter couldn't run, and the former had better be standing by to pick off any pursuers as the rocket team came sprinting past. Worthy, meanwhile, would have his hands full climbing down a hundred-foot tree without falling to his death.

"Plan?" Reilly transmitted.

David replied, "*I'm flanking east to cut them off from the airfield. I want you to post on the north side; don't let anyone reach the road.*"

"Copy," the medic replied. As he raced between the trees, boots hammering across a blanket of snow covering the forest floor and every rock, tree root, and hole that could sprain or break an ankle at any given moment, he wondered if this unplanned maneuver was necessary in the first place.

David had been positioned east of the treestand, and had the best line of sight to determine the plane's fate following the shootdown. From Reilly's vantage point to the north, he'd only heard the shot, subsequent explosion, and the somewhat gruesome noises of the PC-24 plunging into the woods. It certainly didn't sound as if anyone could have survived, and he was now going off his team leader's assessment out of little more than blind faith: how such a small plane could've outlasted a round designed to take out a tank, much less crash into the mountains immediately afterward with survivors aboard, he had no idea.

He saw a flash of movement then, a white-clad figure darting through the trees ahead. David had a fifty-meter head start and was gone from view a moment later, obscured by a wall of blue metal that crashed down through the treetops between them. The object sheared off pine boughs as it fell and slammed into the ground to propel a blast of snow in all directions.

Reilly jolted at the sudden disturbance, altering his course around the object and registering that it was a wing that had ripped off and been temporarily entangled in the canopy before gravity prevailed. No way there was anyone alive on whatever was left of the plane, he thought, and held out hope that David would soon confirm that so they could reverse course with nothing more than a three-to-five-minute time penalty on their exfil.

His first indication that may not be the case was a cratered gash extending in a straight line downhill to his right, exposing fresh earth. At least part of the plane had remained intact, and after a few seconds of running, Reilly saw that God himself had apparently been on Sidorov's side.

The aircraft fuselage was in remarkable shape, no doubt the result of it crashing at an angle that almost exactly matched that of the terrain sloping toward the airfield. Now it was a battered and bent cylinder, partially aflame, while the remaining turbofan engine belched black smoke as it continued to churn with an eerie high-pitched whine. Worthy's rocket had only destroyed the plane's tail, which meant that anyone else would have missed entirely, and what had begun as an aerial shootdown had just turned into a ground fight.

That was about the last thing the team had planned on, but nonetheless a contingency they weren't about to shy away from. If Sidorov wouldn't die by the rocket, then it would have to be by the bullet instead, and the sooner the better. This wasn't their mission fucked, per se, but it was tilting perilously close to that, and it was now up to medic and team leader to race in and dispatch their ultimate target before the cavalry arrived from the airfield.

David transmitted, "*I'm on the east side, just off the nose. Hold fire until his bodyguards leave the bird.*"

Reilly said nothing until he'd scrambled behind a tree trunk and taken a kneeling position twenty meters off the plane's left side. The fuselage was angled left, toward him, and every pane of tinted glass from the six visible porthole windows was either scorched black or reflecting snow.

He spoke over the team frequency. "In position, north side, no movement."

If Worthy's rocket had landed just a few meters forward of the tail section, there would be a considerable hole in the rear of the cabin through which a hand grenade or three would easily slaughter every passenger aboard. The fact that it hadn't done that made the view all the more maddening: something as simple as a medium machinegun could eviscerate the remaining hulk from a distance, and even Reilly's HK417 could do some damage if he'd loaded armor-piercing bullets. But trying to shoot through the aircraft with subsonic 7.62mm rounds would be a waste of ammunition they may well need, particularly if the standoff was drawn out any longer.

"They're not coming out," Reilly transmitted. "We have to make entry."

David's infuriating response came a second later.

"*Wait for it.*"

There were precious few choices available to them now, and waiting simply wasn't one of them. Anyone moving on foot from the airfield faced a steep uphill climb to reach the crash site, sure, but as Ian had quite accurately pointed out, the objective was flanked by roads to the north and south by which Janjicari reinforcements could *and would* be deposited at any moment. Those men weren't going to stand idly by after watching the VIP they were sworn to protect get shot down; and for that matter, David was a solid if totally instinctive team leader, but no psychic. Who was to say whether the bodyguards aboard the plane would defend in place to await rescue, or try to spirit their primary east toward the security of the airfield?

No sooner had the thought occurred to him than a clamshell door just behind the cockpit lowered, striking the ground before it was fully extended as a result of the angle at which the fuselage had tilted. A figure appeared, scrambling down the airstairs with a submachine gun in hand. Reilly held his fire, not wanting to betray his presence until Sidorov was visible.

The good news was that, in stark contrast to most of their targets who would've been difficult to pick out of a lineup composed of similar ethnicities, Yuri Sidorov presented no obstacles to positive identification. In his case, no studying a photograph was required—just shoot the guy who looked like Vladimir Putin, Reilly thought, and their mission here was a success.

But the man who leapt off the airstair was a short, fat fuck, and he'd barely made landfall when his eyes locked onto Reilly and he swung his weapon into a firing position.

Reilly shot three times, scoring at least two hits before the first bodyguard fell and a second appeared in the open doorway, this one's presence evidenced by the spark of a muzzle flash before the medic returned fire at a furious pace.

He downed the emerging threat, causing a bearded man to careen sideways down the stairs and lose grip of a Vityaz submachine gun just as a new slab of metal slid into view—a cargo door at the rear of the fuselage, flipping open on the opposite side of the aircraft remains.

I'd barely registered the cargo door swinging open when Sidorov appeared.

My first shot missed entirely—the slippery bastard had already leapt toward the ground. I chased him with two more bullets, one traveling to parts unknown before the other snapped into a tree trunk that he vanished behind, visible only in a fleeting glimpse as he took off running in the opposite direction.

I rose from my kneeling position and took off after him, and then the race was on.

"Sidorov heading west," I transmitted, wondering if Reilly would be able to take the shot from his current position. Visibility in the mostly evergreen forest was limited at best, and I used that to my advantage as I flanked left around the wreckage, keeping trees between myself and the bird lest some enterprising bodyguard was covering his boss's withdrawal from the threshold of the cargo door.

But I cleared the missing tail section and left the whining engine noise behind me without incident—I'd succeeded in fleeing the objective.

Judging by Reilly's return transmission, however, so had Sidorov.

"*Didn't see him*," the medic said. "*I'll head west, see if I can pick up his trail.*"

I replied from a full-on run, gasping for breath in the thin mountain air. "In pursuit, cover my six. Racegun, see if you can cut him off."

The guidance to Worthy was made out of rational judgment alone: I located Sidorov's tracks in the snow, and now that I'd latched onto his path, I fully intended to finish him off myself. I needed only a few seconds with a clear line of sight, and I was going to get it one way or another.

Worthy replied, "*Copy*," without any further explanation on his status, though I had to assume he'd made it down the tree by now. Even if he hadn't, the situation couldn't have been any more in our favor at this point. We'd flushed Sidorov from the remains of his bird in record time, and he was now unknowingly headed in the same direction we needed to travel for exfil. If I didn't pick him off, Worthy would; if not Worthy, then Cancer or Ian would nail him from the overwatch position. Not the easiest day for us, but far from the hardest.

Provided one of us was able to see the son of a bitch in the first place.

Sidorov was ballsy, I had to give him that; once his security men began falling dead on the airstair, he'd exited the opposite side to take his chances alone. That was a move of desperation but not panic, a calculated choice that had very nearly paid off as far as he was concerned.

It wasn't until I rounded one of the countless spruce trees that I caught my next glance of my target, still headed almost due west on a downhill slope and about to pass out of view. I blasted through the majority of a magazine in fully automatic bursts to compensate, though none of my bullets found their mark. I'd seen all I needed to, however—Sidorov appeared unarmed, running across the snow in slacks and a dress shirt with a checkered satchel slung over his shoulder. This was going to be fun,

I thought, then cautioned myself at the thought of his satchel. It could very easily contain a pistol or submachine gun, either of which were more than sufficient to wreck my world if I got complacent.

"He's still moving west," I transmitted, reloading on the move and veering left to prevent him from drifting south and away from Worthy. Surely Sidorov could hear me between his own footfalls, I thought, considering he was only twenty meters ahead and the forest was almost silent aside from periodic gusts of frigid wind. I could already detect someone running behind me and to my right, which could only be Reilly. I picked up the pace, determined to close the distance and finish off Sidorov to exploit our hard-earned gains thus far.

Then I wondered, how had I known the bodyguards would flee the wreckage rather than defend in place?

There was certainly no guarantee, but the crux of my instinct came down to the fact that it was what I'd do in their position. Armed with the knowledge that they'd just survived a shootdown, they had no reason to assume they only faced five dickheads who had already fired their one and only rocket. It was far more reasonable to conclude that to wait would be certain death, and while we would have ensured that via grenades through the windows if not a forced entry into the fuselage, given our limited manpower the effort was likely to result in one or more casualties to our already minimal force.

My next glimpse of Sidorov revealed that he was cutting south in what seemed to be a very deliberate move. I fired again on full auto, hoping for a lucky hit that would slow him down and not getting it before he vanished. I pivoted left to cut him off, reloading again as I gradually made out a cliff ahead. Judging by the treetops beyond, it stood before a twenty-meter drop. Apparently Sidorov hadn't noticed it yet—he continued veering toward the precipice rather than away, which might make this the easiest kill of my entire career. If he fell over the edge, I'd need only put a few rounds into his already lifeless body as cheap insurance before moving the remaining distance to our exfil vehicle.

But nothing came that easy, and I knew he'd reverse course at any moment. There was no way he didn't see the cliff now; was he intending to take his chances with a blind leap? Please, I thought, let that be the case—

I'd get a clear shot if nothing else. Then I saw him in the gap between trees, stripping the satchel off his shoulder before he went out of view behind a spruce, still headed toward the edge.

I instinctively came to a full halt, raising my rifle to pick him off before he could return the favor. When he emerged out the other side of that tree, I knew it would be with a gun in hand if not a grenade. Perhaps his bag contained a demolition charge, a ready-made self-destruct mechanism that he'd detonate if capture was imminent.

To my immeasurable disbelief, Sidorov didn't appear on the other side of the tree at all.

Instead, the flash of movement I saw was his checkered satchel sailing through the air, over the cliff edge and into the ravine, before I heard Sidorov moving westward once more.

I faced a crisis decision, and had exactly half a second to decide before acting one way or the other. What was more important in this moment, the target or his possible intelligence?

If Sidorov escaped, he still maintained the connections and credibility required to supply the terrorist underworld with uncanny effectiveness. No one expected us to come back with any intel on his network's inner workings; we could kill him now and probably escape, and on paper it would be mission success for Project Longwing. It was that alone that we'd come here to accomplish, and that victory was almost within our grasp.

But the flip side of that coin was the simple question, *what the fuck was in that satchel?*

I had no idea, but two distinct factors assured me of its importance. First and foremost was that in the aftermath of a plane crash, he'd actually had the composure to recover the bag and take it with him; and second, even amid pursuit and the inevitability of his own death, Sidorov had just incurred a self-imposed delay to prevent it from being captured. I was the only person on my team who'd seen him toss the satchel and therefore stood any chance of recovering it, but to attempt that would be to force my team to hold ground for the time it took me to make it down the ravine and back up, putting their lives at risk as much as my own.

In the end it wasn't Sidorov, or Project Longwing, or even my team's safety that drove my ultimate decision.

It was Erik Weisz.

As long as he remained in the shadows, there would continue to be catastrophic terror attacks with seemingly no rhyme or reason other than sewing chaos. Certainly he had a strategic agenda, but no one could make any sense of it. Opportunities to gain insight in that regard were exceedingly rare, and if we passed up on this one it could be months or years before another lead emerged. How many civilians would die in the meantime?

I broke left, transmitting as I moved.

"He tossed his bag into a ravine, I'm going in after it. Doc, Racegun, I'll need covering fire to make it back to the high ground. Sidorov is still heading west. Cancer and Angel, he's all yours."

Worthy raced southward with his HK416.

He hadn't seen Sidorov yet, or even David for that matter; instead, he'd barely spotted Reilly running west before losing sight of him and receiving his team leader's transmission containing yet another questionable judgment call. The mission was to kill Sidorov, and David had just pulled half his team away from that to incur a massive time penalty they couldn't afford. In the meantime, maybe Sidorov would cross directly into Cancer's sights, or maybe he'd alter course and vanish for good.

Or maybe, Worthy thought, he and Reilly would get pinned down and killed here while David went tromping through the ravine in search of a bag that may well have disappeared into a snowbank.

He transmitted, "Doc, I'm inbound from the north, give me a visual."

Reilly darted out from behind an evergreen tree, locking eyes with him for a split second before moving back to his firing position and transmitting, "*Suicide climbed down the cliff right next to me. This is our strongpoint.*"

"Got it," Worthy replied, scanning his surroundings for the best location from which to establish a defense. "You take east, I'll cover the north."

"*Yeah*," Reilly replied, and that was it.

What more needed to be said?

Worthy found the best available position in the form of an old spruce to his right. The tree was growing from a slightly elevated mound, its trunk was wide enough to absorb 7.62mm rounds, and its lowest branches were elevated just enough for him to surveil a field of fire while remaining in the shadows.

He didn't approach it directly, instead continuing forward to circle a different evergreen and identifying a pair of potential fallback sites before approaching his ultimate destination from behind. Then Worthy crawled beneath the boughs on his stomach, moving up the mound and angling his HK416 beside the trunk amid the thick scent of pine needles and sap that reminded him of Christmas back home in Georgia.

Shifting his body slightly, he attained what he sought: an oblique view of his own backtrail, an appetizing spread of tracks in the snow that should serve to draw in the least experienced and most overeager members of the responding security forces. Now it was a game of remaining concealed while trying to pick off intruders from the greatest distances possible—which, in the current terrain and its exceedingly limited visibility, wasn't much. The enemy had an overwhelming advantage in numbers and likely firepower. By contrast, the only thing he and Reilly had in their favor was occupation of modest high ground and use of suppressed weapons.

Worthy procured a trio of magazines from the three least accessible pouches on his kit, arraying them with the bullets pointed left on the ground before sending his next transmission.

"We're sitting ducks up here, Suicide. How long are you going to be?"

David's voice sounded strained.

"*Going as fast as I can, terrain down here is a nightmare. But Sidorov wouldn't have tossed the bag if it wasn't important.*"

To this, Cancer pointed out, "*Unless it was a diversion, you stupid shit. You better be on your way topside within thirty seconds, bag or no bag.*"

No mention of Sidorov passing the sniper position, Worthy noted, which may well mean he was already gone.

Then Reilly transmitted a single whispered word.

"*Contact.*"

The frequency went silent then, and so did the wind. Worthy heard no chatter of a suppressed weapon, no shouts or incoming gunfire, meaning the medic must have spotted the first incoming fighter or a group of them, and either lost sight or chosen to wait for the best shot he could take.

And before he could gauge how the situation was progressing one way or the other, he had his own targets to worry about.

The first man to advance into view was carrying his FN SCAR rifle in what could charitably be described as the gangster low ready—no hardened mafia operator but rather the baby-faced cannon fodder sent in while the former Yugoslav special forces and the like stayed back to assess the situation and respond accordingly. This youngster was also, Worthy noted, moving with far too much confidence to be alone.

He held his fire accordingly, and was rewarded with a second target advancing into the open ground ahead, this one older and more vigilant, sweeping what appeared to be a SIG assault rifle across the trees. He was unlikely to spot Worthy until it was too late, but there was no sense testing Lady Luck at this point in the game.

Instead, he let them proceed only a few meters along the path formed by his footprints before opening fire.

The first man went down hard, dead before he hit the ground, but as usual with such engagements, his partner backpedaled wildly on the snow in an attempt to reverse course that was nearly successful. He made it exactly four steps back the way he'd come, taking subsonic bullets all the way, before finally tumbling and splaying out like a scarecrow with his eyes facing skyward.

Now both bodies were draining blood, the effect of crimson on white a visually jarring landmark that would serve as a warning to the others. Worthy intuitively knew that he'd just had the only easy kills he'd get in the unfolding engagement—setting up an ambush on his own backtrail was a handy trick but it was useful exactly once, and the next enemies he saw would be flanking his position rather than racing into the open.

He lifted one of his full magazines, then pressed it alongside the one in his rifle at an angle before executing a tactical reload. He placed the partially spent mag at the end of the row containing his spares, hearing unsuppressed gunfire ring out to his right, a brief burst that went quiet as Reilly finally found his mark. A good development under normal circumstances, but at present it signaled to every bad guy in earshot that the men responsible for the shootdown had been located and were ripe for the taking.

Worthy scanned every pine needle and snowdrift in his field of view, eyes wide and ears straining for any clue that would give him a moment's advantage over an incoming threat. Any second now, he thought, there would be no shortage of new targets.

And regrettably, his assumption proved accurate.

The next wave of shooters were little more experienced than the two men he'd just killed, appearing to his left and quickly driven back by Worthy's reflexive fire. Maybe he'd wounded one, maybe not. They hadn't been looking low enough to identify him, but that wouldn't last long as they searched for the source of the suppressed shots.

Worthy almost ignored the next round of automatic gunfire on his right flank, assuming it to be targeted at Reilly; he was proven wrong as bullet impacts whipped a flurry of snow across his eyes, forcing him to blink his vision clear as he shifted to the opposite side of the tree trunk that was currently popping and cracking with rounds meant for him.

His position held long enough for him to identify the shooter and put him down with a five-shot volley—the man had been kneeling beside a tree, knowing exactly where to look for an opponent maintaining a hasty defense. Probably a former military type, one who could have easily prevailed if Worthy were slower on the draw or equipped with an inferior optic.

More gunshots rang in from the left, and he pivoted to see that the young pups he'd scared off were back, this time knowing well enough to aim under the pine branches.

Worthy returned fire mercilessly, expending the rest of his magazine in rapid single shots that dropped one mafia gunman screaming to the ground and sent another limping behind cover. Rolling to his side to keep the tree trunk to his front, Worthy conducted an emergency reload and sent his bolt forward before transmitting.

"Suicide, it's getting bad up here. How much longer do you need?"

"*Almost there*," the team leader replied, "*but I still have to make it back up*."

That was the last thing Worthy wanted to hear—until a moment later, when he detected thin buzzing noises approaching from the north.

It was his first indication that in addition to their superior numbers and firepower, the security forces responding now had finally employed a third advantage: that of mobility, just as Ian had predicted.

"Fuck," Worthy said under his breath, keying his radio to transmit. "Vehicles inbound—or snowmobiles, I can't tell. We're about to be overrun. QRF, QRF, QRF."

Ian balked at the transmission.

QRF stood for quick reaction force, which meant something in the military: an entire element standing with means of air or ground transport for the on-call reinforcement of a decisively engaged unit. The acronym was a *break glass in case of emergency* term that was only slightly less desperate than "SOS," and Ian knew from his background with Worthy as well as the tone in the man's voice that it wasn't being used lightly here.

But there was one major discrepancy, namely that the team didn't have a designated QRF at all; Ian's ability to move was severely hindered by his injury and David was apparently running around in a ditch looking for Sidorov's bag. With Jelena restricted to the exfil vehicle, that left exactly one person capable of responding in time, and he leapt up now with the words, "Stay put."

Then Cancer was gone, racing down the slope and into the streambed, punching boot marks into the pristine belt of snow that represented their last chance of killing Sidorov. And if the Russian was on course with this kill zone, he'd quickly change his mind upon finding the surface marred with evidence of a passing hunter—the rocket team had skirted the cliff on their way in for just that reason, and now it couldn't have mattered less. The mission had already pivoted from downing the PC-24 to trying to catch a fleeing survivor, then to recovering intelligence, and finally to its current state: trying not to get wiped out in the mountains of Serbia.

Ian brushed the thought aside, struggling to his feet by the time Cancer cleared the streambed and vanished into the trees on the far slope.

Then came the pain, a now-sickeningly familiar sensation of tenderness in his right abdomen that was like the soreness of a brutal full-body workout concentrated into the space around his wound, mingled with nausea and lightheadedness whenever Ian forced himself into sudden motion. He fought through the unease, beginning his movement northward to parallel the streambed, the only remaining course of action to pursue an ever-dwindling chance of interdicting Sidorov.

His team's transmissions were becoming increasingly more frantic amid the distant thunder of automatic weapons echoing over the hills. Ian pulled out his radio earpieces, knowing they now represented nothing more than a distraction: there was nothing he could do to help his teammates, nor they him.

In the lull between wind gusts, he thought he heard a branch snapping on the far side of the streambed.

Ian froze, holding his breath to see if he could detect any other sounds. There it was again, he thought, a rustle of brush farther north, somewhere along the opposite bank. Before he could further pinpoint the source, the wind picked up again, revoking the possibility once and for all.

It had to be Sidorov, though—didn't it? Ian was left with the choice of closing the distance amid the risk of his quarry spotting the movement, or setting up for the best possible shot on the streambed and remaining in place.

He chose the latter, taking up a standing firing position and waiting for Sidorov to appear on the strip of snow. Three seconds passed, then five, and Ian suddenly became aware that he'd chosen wrong: Sidorov must have seen either him or Cancer's tracks and chosen to continue further north before he risked a crossing of this linear danger area.

Ian lowered his rifle and started to move once more, only to stop a moment later as a man emerged from the woods on the far bank and looked both ways before jogging downhill.

Definitely Sidorov, Ian thought as he took aim and tracked the man as he moved at an oblique angle perhaps thirty meters away. The trees and saplings between them obscured the view at points, and Ian resisted the urge to fire. One missed shot now would send the target scurrying back to the far side, where he'd likely flush north.

So Ian waited until Sidorov crossed the center of the streambed before resolving to shoot at the next available opportunity. When the man's form flashed between trees, Ian fired five times in rapid succession.

Sidorov dropped out of view immediately, though the churning wind masked any possible grunt or scream that would indicate a hit.

But at least one bullet had found its mark, Ian sensed, and he reloaded while loping northward to confirm his kill with all the speed he could manage in his injured state. The pain was so formidable that he couldn't tell how long it took him to reach a vantage point overlooking Sidorov's crossing in the streambed. A trail of footprints crossed the strip, ending in a mottled swath of disturbed snow marred with blood.

Then the footprints resumed, albeit at an irregular gait and flanked by splatters of blood, all the way up to Ian's side of the hill.

It only took him a fraction of a second to process the sight, after which he brought his rifle up to search for threats—too late, as he learned a moment later.

A single gunshot rang out, and Ian sensed the crack of a bullet zipping past his head.

He ducked out of instinct, then scrambled for cover as he squared off for a one-on-one showdown with Yuri Sidorov.

Regrettably, Cancer thought as he ran, his highly accurized HK417 was only as good as the lines of sight to use it at a distance.

That meant a great deal from his previous overwatch position, surveilling an exposed stretch of snow covering a streambed; here in the forest, however, he held the worst possible weapon and optic combination of anyone on the team.

But an SOS was an SOS, and Worthy wouldn't have called for his services unless they were desperately needed. David had just dragged them all waist deep into shit, and now it was up to the team to keep him alive long enough to be reunited for exfil. To that end Cancer had a single cause for gratitude at present: there was no need to navigate the mountainous terrain, because the sound of automatic gunfire made his destination readily apparent.

There was an intermittent lull in the raging battle ahead, during which Cancer heard a single gunshot to his rear. The blast echoed all the way to his position, and he knew without a doubt that Sidorov had fired it. When no radio transmission arrived, it was clear enough that Ian was either dead or decisively engaged; worse still, Cancer couldn't do a single thing about it. The rest of his team was ahead, the lives of three men versus one, and that simple math meant the intelligence operative was on his own.

Continuing his charge, Cancer had to marvel at the absurdity of this situation.

Here he was, racing in to reinforce Worthy and Reilly, who were themselves mired in a hopeless defense of David, who'd decided to throw their entire operation off the rails in pursuit of a bag that could be filled with Silly String for all he knew.

It wasn't until he'd cleared a small rise that he spotted his first enemy fighters of the day, and in supremely comical fashion—a snowmobile careened between trees less than twenty meters ahead, its operator laser-focused on piloting the machine.

The passenger, however, looked over at Cancer and actually locked eyes for a full second before looking away without the slightest interest.

A fatal mistake to be sure, but an understandable one nonetheless.

The two men were attired in remarkably similar fashion to Cancer and the rest of his team, with tactical gear worn atop white parkas and snow pants. He was looking, he knew, at members of some mobile response force that apparently had sufficient members to warrant the assumption that Cancer was in their ranks. A bank error in his favor, and as the snowmobile turned away, he took aim at the passenger's spine and fired a 7.62mm round that he idly hoped would serve as a twofer by killing the driver as well.

No such luck. Whether slowed by parka or halted by bone, the bullet toppled the passenger and left the driver to skid sideways to a halt, looking over his shoulder and becoming a momentarily stationary target that Cancer engaged with three carefully aimed shots.

That did the trick; the man jolted and slumped over the handlebars, and Cancer pumped another bullet into the fallen passenger before scanning his surroundings and conducting a reload.

So far, so good, though judging by the volume of gunfire ahead, his besieged teammates continued to face one hell of a fight.

Cancer transmitted, "Two down, I'm coming in hot from the west," as he threaded his way toward the battle in progress and heard Worthy's reply.

"*I've already fallen back once, have Doc in sight. We're both hunkered down, so kill anyone you see standing.*"

"Got it," Cancer said, rounding a spruce to see the first such candidates for his attention.

There were three of them, arrayed in a skirmish line between two stationary snowmobiles. All were facing away, blasting automatic weapons in a generally southeast orientation with not a whit of concern for their rear security—as far as they were concerned, the only threats were to their front. Cancer engaged them "family style" from left to right and back again as their bodies fell.

Each man received a final round in preparation for Cancer's next move, a hard sprint with a reload on the move, his fresh magazine slamming into place by the time he came to a stop beside the snowmobile to his left and used it as cover for a crouched firing position.

His first thought upon seeing the view beyond was that there were more muzzle flashes than clearly identifiable targets, all to his north and directing their fire southward while completely unaware that the western flank had just been breached.

But that would all change in the next few seconds, and before opening fire, Cancer sent a final transmission.

"Suicide, if we don't fall back now, we're dead. Where the fuck are you?"

Ian circled with careful steps, maneuvering in an orbit around the evergreen with the knowledge that somewhere on the other side, Yuri Sidorov was doing the same.

Between the echoes of a gunfight to his east and the wind crashing over the mountains in waves, he wasn't about to divine his target's location from the sound of footsteps on snow. Nor would the victor of this engagement be determined by anything so trite as following tracks, which, if anything, would lead only to an ambush. Ian paid careful attention to his own back-trail, knowing from Sidorov's actions thus far that he understood this was a playing field that melded offense and defense into one liquid truth.

The entire situation was ludicrous: Ian had a loaded thirty-round magazine and a suppressed assault rifle to convert that currency into a dead arms dealer while saving his own life in the process. If there was ever a time for split-second, instinctive heroics, then this was it—and yet here he was, facing the very real possibility of being outmaneuvered by his own target, who, while dealing in such exotics as surface-to-air missiles in his professional capacity, was currently equipped with nothing more than a pistol.

Both Ian and his opponent were wounded, one more recently than the other. Neither had backup coming soon enough to affect the outcome, nor did either have anything to lose. Yuri Sidorov wasn't trying to flee because he couldn't outrun his tracks in the snow any more than the trail of blood beside them. He'd thus decided to make a last stand and take out as many attackers as possible. Upon finding that they numbered but one, he decided to turn the tables, and in the next ten seconds, the situation was going to be resolved one way or another.

Ian had completed perhaps a quarter-rotation around the massive evergreen when a surge of wind buffeted the trees. In what would either be an act of lunacy or genius depending on how it played out, he exploited this momentary distraction to reverse course and run back the way he'd come.

The sudden movement was jarringly painful, more so when conducted in a crouch and with his HK416 at the high ready. He felt like he was moving underwater, pulse hammering in his ears and drowning out even the wind as he crossed over his own tracks on what he hoped would be a collision course.

Instead he found a new set of tracks making a beeline away from the tree. Ian froze and swept his barrel across them to find that Sidorov had wisely distanced himself to take cover behind a snow-covered slab of rock, where he was crouched with his handgun pointed in the wrong direction. He'd been expecting Ian to complete his circle instead of reversing course, though that proved only a momentary delay as both men simultaneously took aim at each other.

Ultimately it wasn't tactical judgments or even response time that made the difference between life and death as Ian and Sidorov opened fire simultaneously, but instead a matter of weaponry. It was a hell of lot more difficult to stabilize a pistol than an assault rifle, and at a range of ten meters, Sidorov's rounds flew high and wide while Ian's made a tighter grouping, landing in a spread that covered thin air, then the rock slab, and finally Sidorov's pelvis.

He was already kneeling, and the thwack of a subsonic 5.56mm round beside his groin was sufficient to make Sidorov fall forward, splaying out in the snow and losing his grasp on the handgun. Ian raced toward him even as the man struggled to locate his weapon, the clear loser in this engagement but certainly no coward.

And sure enough, he managed to find his pistol, though by the time that occurred, Ian had arrived and kicked it away. Then he stepped backward and aimed down at an incapacitated Yuri Sidorov.

He rolled onto his side, then his back, to glare up at Ian.

Then he let his head fall back on the snow and muttered two incredulous words.

"A Jew."

There was no malice in the statement. Sidorov wasn't hurling insults, he was trying to assign responsibility.

"Jewish," Ian agreed. "Not Israeli."

Sidorov winced and said with a distinct Russian accent, "Fucking Americans."

Ian gave him a nod, considering how to play this. The man was mortally wounded, no doubt, but between the hypovolemic shock of blood loss and the psychological shock of being blasted from the sky and then captured, it was entirely possible that Sidorov had yet to either realize or accept his fate.

"*Da*, I am an American. And if you want to live long enough to see a plea bargain in my country, then you need to tell me about Erik Weisz."

Sidorov lifted his right hand, showed it to Ian—from palm to fingertips, it was covered in so much blood that it looked like he was wearing a glove.

"This is my plea bargain," he said with a trace of a smile. "Consider it signed."

Ian swallowed, his throat parched. "Tell me anyway."

Closing his eyes, Sidorov gave a slight shake of his head. He probably had a minute or less to live; there was nothing Ian could threaten him with.

So instead, he bluffed.

"We recovered your bag."

The comment had the same effect on Sidorov's features that physical torture would arouse, possibly worse—his eyelids flew open, gaze panicked, breathing suddenly sharp and ragged.

"If this is true," he replied, eyes locked onto Ian's in a desperate attempt to ascertain whether it was a lie or not, "then it is better I die out here."

"You will. Now tell me what you know about Erik Weisz."

Sidorov grew adamant, speaking with an almost military gravitas. "Listen to me...you must make it known that I did not cooperate. That I did not hand over the bag, that it was...taken from me."

"Why does that matter?"

The slurred response was weak, spoken so quietly that Ian could barely hear it.

"Because I have a family in Moscow. My wife, my daughters. You understand?"

"I understand," Ian assured him, and Sidorov finally relented with a final request.

"The bullet, please."

Ian lifted his rifle for a headshot, a move that sent Sidorov into a fury.

"Not the face," he gasped with what breath he had left. "He must see. He must know that I am dead, *mudak*."

Lowering his weapon, Ian gave a slight nod, struggling to grasp the scope of this man's fear of Erik Weisz. Apparently, the simple fact that a plane had been blown out of the sky was insufficient for assurance that Sidorov hadn't somehow faked his own death and defected.

"Quickly," Sidorov said. "The pain is growing greater."

Then he made a sharp, hissing inhale and gasped, "*Mnye para.*"

I have to go.

"*Da vstryechee,*" Ian replied, taking careful aim as the wounded man closed his eyes for the last time.

Ian thumbed the HK416's selector lever from safe to semi-automatic. His next action was rapid, almost rushed. Ian had previously killed people only in the heat of combat; he'd never been forced to do so as a matter of euthanasia, much less after a one-on-one discussion that involved mention of his victim's wife and children. To hesitate now would be to dwell on these thoughts.

He fired twice into Sidorov's heart, then forced himself through the machinations that his training demanded. Weapon on safe, conduct a hasty clearance of his surroundings to confirm no incoming threats, then a tactical reload.

Before searching the body for intelligence, however, he had to update his team. Ian re-inserted his earpieces, and was preparing to transmit when he heard the first radio traffic since beginning his mobile hunt for Sidorov.

But Cancer was already speaking on the net, and his words sent chills up Ian's spine.

"*...if we don't fall back now, we're dead...*"

"*...where the fuck are you?*"

I didn't immediately respond to Cancer's message.

The delay would infuriate him, particularly given the contents of his transmission, but if I keyed my radio mic now, I'd plummet down the snow- and ice-covered slope to my death on the boulders some ten meters below.

My current situation was only marginally better, clinging to the cliff face with both hands, my weapon slung across my back. I was completely vulnerable, and if not for my team's defenses overhead, I would have been sighted and killed by now.

But Sidorov's bag was almost within my grasp, and provided I could make the short leap to a narrow outcropping on my left, I'd have it in my possession at last.

How the satchel had reached its present location was clear enough: once Sidorov tossed it, the bag had struck a pine tree before shearing off a neat strip of snow on its way down the angled boughs. That snow disturbance was the only way I'd been able to locate the satchel dangling from its strap, which had gotten tangled on a patch of dead branches extending from a crack in the cliff. Even then, the bag had been difficult to spot. If its pattern was camouflage instead of checkered, I may have missed it completely—which, frankly, would've been preferable to the harrowing climb up the slick rock slope to get as far as I had.

Under any other circumstances I would've abandoned the effort long before now.

But the satchel exerted an almost magnetic force that drew me ever closer against any possible counterpoint of logic or, considering my height off the ground, even physics. After all, it represented a direct link to Weisz, an uncensored glimpse into what he was planning next. Whatever the contents, Sidorov only transported them from Russia to Iran with a Serbian layover in between; no stops in Western-aligned countries ever, and therefore no chance for the Agency to obtain, much less scrutinize them.

Until now.

Cancer's transmission had barely receded in my earpiece when I took three quick breaths in an attempt to pump myself up. Holding the final inhale, I leapt sideways toward the outcropping I'd spent the better part of five minutes trying to access.

Then I was airborne between rock ledges, a fatal fall unfolding below me as I reached for either the satchel or the tangle of mountain scrub suspending it from the cliff face. Both feet struck the outcropping, though my boot soles immediately skidded sideways across the icy surface; only Sidorov's bag saved me, arresting my slide as I clutched its strap with both hands.

I exhaled with delirious gratitude, then quickly untangled the strap from the thorny brambles before slinging it over my shoulder. The satchel was heavier than I expected, adding four or five pounds to an already heavy equipment load. I looked down, trying to ascertain a route back to the ravine floor.

My salvation lay in a heap of rockfall that had accumulated at the base of the cliff to my left. If I could reach that, I'd cut an insanely dangerous, near-vertical descent in half. With both hands grasping the cliff, I shuffled sideways and down, lowering myself to the next outcropping and doing my best to proceed efficiently as gunfire continued to ebb and flow overhead. Risk to my teammates aside, if I didn't return their radio calls soon they'd assume I was dead; and if I botched any part of my ad hoc mountaineering effort, they'd be quite correct.

I succeeded in reaching the rockfall, however, and now faced only a steep scramble between me and the relative safety of the ravine below. Still, the process was not without its dangers. I did my best to maintain three points of contact while resisting the urge to provide my team an update until successfully reaching the ground.

And while my willpower held fast, my balance did not.

One of my carefully placed footfalls managed to dislodge a watermelon-sized rock, causing a chain reaction of loose gravel and stone chunks that moved beneath the crumbling snow.

I tried to leap to an area of stationary footing and, when that failed, to at least remain semi-upright and surf the mini-avalanche down the slope. The effort worked as well as I could've hoped, at least for the few seconds it took to reach a fallen tree branch blocking the path ahead. To strike that would be to flip forward and smash my head into the rocks, knocking me unconscious or worse.

So I leapt over it instead, a frantic, split-second act of despair that ended when my right foot plunged through the snow on the other side. I felt my shin descending and vaguely registered that it was doing so between two stones when my momentum carried me forward despite my best efforts to stop.

And stop I did, though not as intended—instead I heard a sickening, snapping crunch from my lower leg, felt an instant barrage of blinding pain, and then I collapsed in place with a hissing intake of breath.

"*Suicide*," Cancer transmitted, "*goddammit, give me something to work with here*."

By then I was fighting to sit up, using both hands to extract my right leg from the hole and confirming by white-hot flashes of pain that I'd broken my tibia.

Finally I keyed my mic and said, "Start withdrawing." Panting another breath, I continued, "Good news is I got the bag. Bad news is I just broke my leg."

"*Fuck. We're coming for you—*"

"Negative," I shot back, "keep heading west, pull them out of here. Make the exfil—I'm starting my E&E."

I cringed at the acronym for evasion and escape, close to the last term I ever wanted to speak on a real-world operation and, in particular, while I was incapable of a normal walking stride much less breaking into a run. But we had contingencies for one or more team members becoming separated from the main element, and hopefully that planning would pay off now.

It only took a quick mental recollection of our operational map to determine the nearest alternate pickup point, which we'd plotted in advance by way of identifying major landmarks that would be simple to navigate to with or without a compass—road intersections, hilltops, and the like. We'd also plotted what we called "Go To Hell" points at five-hundred-meter offsets in whatever cardinal direction would offer the greatest concealment and avenues of escape.

In the event we lost comms, they'd search for me at the point nearest my last known position, but I had no intentions of testing that assumption and clarified, "Pick me up at Go To Hell Point 2."

"*You won't make it that far with a broken leg.*"

"Then look for me on the way, but do it later," I shot back, knowing that he wasn't wrong—it was close to two kilometers distant, just east of a major Y-intersection, and the mountainous terrain wasn't going to help. To that end I was already scanning my surroundings for appropriate branches to fashion a makeshift splint as I concluded, "Pull everyone out, now—I'm not asking."

Cancer seemed to reach acceptance just then, realizing that the course of action I proposed was the only feasible one to execute. He could either abandon me out here now, or get the entire team killed.

He quickly replied, "*Copy, godspeed. We're out of here.*"

Reilly bounded away from his previous defensive position, heading west under the protective fire of Cancer and, to a lesser extent, Worthy. And while he'd begun his retreat—in military parlance, *breaking contact*—with a prevailing emotion of fear, he now felt an overwhelming sense of relief at what waited around a spruce tree.

Cancer was there, alive and well as he engaged targets, though his choice of cover was of far greater interest: a snowmobile, one of two that flanked a fallen skirmish line of enemy combatants.

Reilly darted to the nearest snowmobile, feverishly checking it for bullet holes and finding none. He located the ignition and found the key inserted, with a long, coiled emergency tether dangling as if beckoning to be attached to a rider.

Now he just had to make sure the machine worked.

He found the red kill switch and yanked it out to the running position, then pulled the choke lever out and turned the key. It locked after a quarter turn, his first indication that he was dealing with a manual snowmobile rather than an electric sled. Reilly located a pull starter handle, pulled it out until he felt resistance on the cord, and then yanked it to extension like he was starting a lawnmower.

The engine growled to life on the first attempt, maintaining an immeasurably comforting idle as Reilly slung his HK417 and straddled the front seat before positioning his boots on the foot rails. He released the choke and transmitted, "Racegun, I've got a sled—get on."

To his surprise, Worthy didn't transmit back at all. Instead he appeared beside him, taking in the scene in a single hasty glance and shaking his head.

"No fucking way," he shouted, moving to the other snowmobile and going through the startup process as Cancer moved to an alternate firing position to cover the withdrawal.

"Cancer," Reilly transmitted, "I've got a seat open."

By then the second snowmobile had roared to life, and Cancer took that as his cue not to approach Reilly but rather saddle up behind Worthy as he transmitted back.

"*You're on point*," he ordered. "*I'll take my chances with Racegun*."

Those fuckers, Reilly thought, thumbing the accelerator and twisting the handlebars right to guide the snowmobile away from their defensive position. When the dash-mounted compass indicated a westerly heading, he straightened out and began his escape with an iron grip on the handlebars, relaxing the rest of his body to absorb the bumps ahead.

Then he was off, piloting 500 pounds of metal through the snow and assisting his turns by shifting his weight to either side as he charted a course between the trees. Driving a snowmobile on flat ground was a piece of cake; here in the mountains, however, a very particular set of backcountry skills was required to avoid getting stuck, riding into a dead end between clusters of trees, or simply becoming physically exhausted trying to muscle the machine into submission when the terrain was "steep and deep."

He kept his gaze forward, directed not at the many trees but rather the spaces between them, looking five seconds ahead of the snowmobile while anticipating the lay of the land with his left index finger resting over the brake as a precaution for sudden obstacles.

"*Angel,*" Cancer transmitted, "*we're moving along the ravine, headed due west on two snowmobiles. What's your status?*"

Ian replied, "*I'm okay. Sidorov's dead.*"

"*No shit?*"

"*No shit,*" Ian clarified. "*Pick me up in the streambed by our overwatch position. Is there room for a third on Racegun's sled?*"

"*Negative. You're stuck with Doc.*"

Those fuckers, Reilly thought again, rounding a tree to find an uphill slope just beyond it. He accelerated almost as a panic instinct, knowing that if he did so too late he'd risk the snowmobile trenching its track and sending the front end skyward.

His burst of speed resulted in sufficient momentum for the sled to begin its movement uphill, and now he worked to maintain it by applying throttle throughout the climb while rising from his seat, positioning his boots farther back on the foot rails, and leaning forward on the handlebars.

The snowmobile made it up and over, and Reilly resumed a neutral body position as he wondered if he'd be able to pull this off without incident.

He had minimal snowmobile experience, all of it confined to northern and winter training courses in Colorado and Alaska. Reilly was prepared to be underwhelmed the first time he operated one of the machines, but exactly three seconds into his first acceleration, he'd become intoxicated by the speed and more or less convinced that he was a snow god.

It had taken several days and one rollover in which he was nearly crushed by his own chariot to cure him of that illusion; by then, he'd earned a team reputation as the absolute last person who should be in charge of such a vehicle. The recent verbal exchanges confirmed that the others hadn't forgotten, and now Reilly intended to prove them wrong as he led the way on their exfil.

He carved a turn to find the slope falling away steeply to his right. With no alternate route available through the trees, he assumed a sidehill position.

Rising from his seat, he made a small leap to swing his right leg over the seat and onto the left foot rail, planting the knee against the console. With this accomplished, he counter-steered the skis downhill and tilted the snowmobile in the opposite direction at a 45-degree angle while blipping the throttle, using his left leg to remain upright by marching through the snow in single-leg steps. It was a precarious maneuver, and if he lost control he could either send the sled into a roll on top of him or rocketing downhill.

But he made it past the drop-off, returning the snowmobile to relatively flat ground before hopping back into his normal riding stance.

Then he checked his compass and continued forward, carving his steering line between trees and fallen logs, occasionally being whipped by the edges of pine boughs as he shifted his body position to assist the steering inputs and working to maintain momentum to avoid getting stuck. His view was a constantly shifting perspective of between two and five possible routes, and he erred on the high side whenever possible—going low risked ending up in a depression too tight to climb out of, and above all he didn't have time to overthink this.

Cancer transmitted, "*Suicide, how are you looking?*"

David's response was full of static—they were quickly moving out of range.

"*...haven't been spotted yet...worry about Doc...*"

Then he cut out completely, replaced by a crystal-clear voice as Ian transmitted.

"I can hear you. Sounds like you're south of my location, you should be hitting the streambed any second now."

It was then Reilly realized he was piloting the snowmobile effortlessly, partly as a result of the terrain becoming less technical and partly because he'd unknowingly entered a zone of focus while tree riding.

As that thought occurred to him, he cleared a crest to see a blanket of pure snow in the low ground, completely free of trees, with Ian visible to his right.

Reilly steered toward him and downhill, determined to come to a precise stop just beside Ian. If his teammates were going to talk shit about his snowmobiling abilities in training, he'd show them exactly how precisely he could ride in combat.

He glided down into the streambed, then braked in what turned out to be a jarring stop that overshot Ian by two car lengths, spraying him with enough snow to make him look like he'd been rolling around in it.

If the intelligence operative was angry about that, he didn't show it. Instead, he raced to the snowmobile, clambering aboard on the rear seat and shouting, "Go, I'm good—"

That was as far as he got. Reilly throttled forward, glancing left to see Worthy and Cancer speeding past as he carved a turn to follow them up the far hill.

29

Cancer dismounted the snowmobile the moment Worthy brought it to a complete stop.

Bringing his HK417 to the high ready, he moved a few meters to the north before taking a knee and swinging his barrel in a 180-degree arc across their previous direction of movement as the pointman covered the opposite side. The forest appeared still, the only discernible movement a slight swaying of the treetops with wind and snowflakes that had recently begun drifting down.

He transmitted, "Point sled on foot, staged about thirty seconds from linkup, how are you looking?"

"*Road is clear,*" Jelena replied. "*All traffic has been going the opposite direction—some first responders, no one has paid me any attention yet. Ready to move when you are.*"

Her final words were interrupted by a second engine approaching, and Cancer cut his gaze right to catch a glimpse of Reilly's snowmobile gliding into view and then past him.

Keying his mic, he said, "Copy, stand by."

In the time it took him to perform another security scan, the engine noise had grown louder and then cut out entirely. He looked behind him to see Reilly and a snow-covered Ian abandoning the vehicle to take up hasty firing positions in the small perimeter.

"Racegun," Cancer transmitted, "take us out."

No further words were spoken. Worthy rose and led the way forward as pointman, with Ian falling in behind him, followed by Reilly. All appeared to be moving well, Cancer thought as he assessed their condition, aside from a slight hitch in Ian's gait. Confident that no one was bearing any major unreported injuries, the sniper turned his attention to the backtrail left by the snowmobiles. If any enemy fighters were going to try their hand at stopping the exfil-in-progress, that was where they'd appear; but the forest was silent, and the snowmobile theft had apparently succeeded in allowing them to outpace any meaningful pursuit for the time being.

He took a position at the rear of the file, turning frequently to maintain rear security but confident that if there was a threat, it would come from the road ahead. The small formation threaded downhill, and feeling doubtful about an uneventful exfil after the myriad complications to what should have been a relatively straightforward mission, Cancer heard his earpiece crackle and experienced the full expectation of a contact report to follow.

Instead, Worthy drawled, "*Road in sight thirty meters ahead, looks totally clear.*"

"Copy," Cancer replied, "break. Move to pick-up, move to pick-up."

Jelena transmitted, "*On my way.*"

Cancer performed another check to his rear, now completely unwilling to accept that the task ahead would be anything as simple as strolling into a van for a speedy getaway.

But he saw Jelena's vehicle come to a stop in the road, followed by Worthy, Ian, and Reilly darting into the cargo space.

Then Cancer was sliding into the passenger seat and slamming the door as Jelena accelerated away from the trainwreck of an operation. He stared hollowly forward as windshield wipers swept away the flakes at precisely timed intervals, clearing visibility of a paved road winding through the hills that was soon flanked by open fields.

There was a loud metallic *thump* in the cargo area. No one in the back was undisciplined enough to slam a weapon down, and he took the noise to indicate one of their fists striking the side of the van.

Which man had done it, Cancer didn't know and didn't bother looking back to check. His eyes were beginning to sting with tears, the collective weight of his suppressed emotions hitting him full force.

Psychologists called it survivor guilt, once considered an independent diagnosis and more recently categorized as a subset of posttraumatic stress. Cancer knew this because he'd studied the topic enough both in examining how to help ailing teammates over the years as much as addressing his own ideation; it was heavy stuff, requiring one to look no further than the vastly elevated rate of suicide among Holocaust survivors, much less veterans, compared to the general population. If killing didn't bother you, he'd long since learned, then the prospect of emerging unscathed while better men and women were lost may well do the trick. Every combat vet he'd personally met who'd claimed to have emerged completely unscathed psychologically was later revealed to be in severe denial, with the sole exception of those who'd turned out to have such limited experience in actual fighting as to not warrant discussing the topic.

Cancer had more mental scars than anyone on his team, and he was already considering whether this particular event would cause him to swallow a barrel in due time—though what troubled him far more was the fact that whatever he was feeling right now, it was also occurring to the trio of men sitting in the back.

But in this case, he alone retained the unspeakable pain of full responsibility.

The cardinal sin of all things related to military operations was leaving a man behind, and now his team had not just done it in spectacularly expedient fashion, but executed the feat as a result of his order. David had resigned himself from calling the strategic shots the moment he went into that ravine after a bag that may or may not be worth the cost of the material it was made out of; Cancer had ordered the exfil, and if David died as a result, then that decision would follow him to a tremendously early grave.

Cancer blinked his tears away, reaching for the satellite hand mic and forcing his attention to the road ahead and any threats it may contain before sending his first transmission to headquarters with a single thought burning a hole in his mind.

David was alone out there, and now they had to figure out a way to get him back.

30

Chen flinched upon hearing the transmission.

"Raptor Nine One, this is Cancer."

In that moment, she wasn't sure what bothered her more: the past twenty minutes without radio contact from her ground team, all the while intercepting a massive amount of radio and cellular chatter related to a plane crash and subsequent firefight in the hills surrounding the objective, or the fact that her first official reporting was occurring from the team's second-in-command rather than David Rivers.

Keying her mic, she replied, "Cancer, this is Raptor Nine One. We're flying blind here, send me what you've got."

"Have you received any comms from Suicide?"

"Negative," she replied, first incredulous at the inquiry and then in awe of the competence of her staff, who had begun accessing data and projecting it to the screens in the time it took her to process the query—a weather report, she saw, as well as David's CIA personnel record. Neither boded well for the status of the mission in Serbia, though both provided her with assumptions that were soon confirmed when Cancer continued his transmission.

"Bird was crippled but not destroyed. Sidorov escaped the crash site and we pursued. He tossed some kind of bag into a ravine, and Suicide Actual went in

after it and broke his leg in the process. We couldn't reach him. Bottom line: Sidorov is dead, all members of my team are conducting vehicle exfil except Suicide. Stand by for his last known location."

"Go ahead," she replied, sounding calm amid the frantic concern welling up in her gut.

He transmitted the grid and then said, "*I say again*," before repeating it verbatim and adding, "*Read that back to me.*"

Chen complied, more to put Cancer's mind at ease than confirm she'd gotten it right—Lucios was already in the process of projecting the satellite map onto the main OPCEN screen with an icon marking the location.

But her attention was focused on David's personnel record, and in particular what had been highlighted by her personnel officer: the portion dedicated to SERE training.

There were a dizzying array of military and intelligence courses on Survival, Evasion, Resistance, and Escape. The Level C course was mandatory training for anyone at high risk of both capture and exploitation, namely those who were in the training pipeline for assignment to a special operations unit. The school tested its students from survival to capture and time in a mock prison camp complete with interrogations, earning it the moniker "Camp Slappy" in military circles.

But that was only the starting point for the paramilitary officers and contractors of the Special Activities Center, who would over time attend advanced SERE courses as well.

Some of those schools were dedicated to specific operational environments ranging from jungle to arctic, while others comprised a deep dive on the finer points of evading enemy pursuit or escaping from a prisoner detention facility. The records of course graduates were meticulously updated for situations like this: when someone went missing behind enemy lines, it allowed a recovery force to anticipate their actions based on the level of training received.

In the present scenario, Chen found herself satisfied with the listing: David Rivers had attended four SERE courses over the years, all branded with three-digit numbers that would surely be explained to her shortly after she finished dealing with Cancer.

By then he'd finished confirming her recitation of the specified grid, to which he added, "*He's headed for Go To Hell Point 2. We're going back to intercept him because he's not making it all the way there with his injury. Requesting any and all assets to assist our recovery operation.*"

"There are no assets," she shot back, quite truthfully. "We've got a handful of people scattered throughout the country, exactly zero of whom are paramilitary case officers."

"*Then get some Ground Branch people on a bird and fly them out here. Tier One guys, something.*"

The universe had a truly sick sense of humor, Chen thought. Less than a week ago she'd done her best to make a case for those two elements to support if not take over the Serbia mission in its entirety, and Duchess had twisted the suggestion into a case of outright career blackmail.

Chen tried desperately to keep emotion out of her voice, a discipline that Cancer seemed yet to have learned.

"We don't have unassigned shooters to deploy, and even if we did I couldn't marshal them at the drop of a hat. Tier One is out of the question. There is no response force and this very program is, by definition, unattributable. That much was explained to me in no uncertain terms by my predecessor, so I'm certain you're quite aware of it by now."

"*It's not just about him,*" Cancer pointed out, as if there was some fault with her assessment of the current reality, "*it's about the intelligence he recovered. Think about that.*"

Chen could empathize with the man's attempt, though that did nothing to change the ground truth at Agency headquarters. She carefully explained the obvious.

"It doesn't matter if he has intel or not—if there was someone I could send to grab a missing contractor, I would. But there isn't and you know it. There's just you. Now I will gladly use all resources at my disposal to inform your recovery effort, but I will not, I say again *not*, let you go running in half-cocked to an area that's covered by heavily armed criminal elements and Serbian first responders. You need a plan, and you know the ground situation better than I do. So aside from asking me to send in shooters that I don't have, let me know how I can help."

This admonition seemed to restore some sense of composure to Cancer's voice.

For the first time in the entire radio exchange, he responded coolly. "*Running in half-cocked isn't our style, and frankly we don't have the ammo to pull it off even if we wanted to. We're headed back to the safehouse to refit and come up with a viable plan.*"

"Outstanding," she said. "What do you need from us?"

It was a genuine inquiry; while Chen was sure that her staff would inform her of the particulars in due time, not one among them save her operations officer had served in a Ground Branch tactical capacity.

Cancer replied, "*Here's what you can do now: provide a complete situational template of all known forces between Suicide's last known location and Go To Hell Point 2, and update that information in real time. Along with continuous monitoring of all possible comms to anticipate who's coming into or leaving that area, in particular law enforcement checkpoints to interdict suspects on the surrounding roads. I doubt Sidorov would have a tracker broadcasting from his bag, but if you find a signal that looks like it's co-located with Suicide, I need you to kill it asap. If you pick up any radio or cellular communications that indicate responders are looking for a missing shooter, I need you to jam all police and mafia radio frequencies, and shut down every cell phone tower in the area.*"

She took a deliberate breath, wondering how much of that request her OPCEN staff could fulfill given the entire situation was unfolding almost five thousand miles away.

"Stand by," she replied, nodding toward Brian Sutherland, who was urgently waving at her.

He said, "Ground measures won't cover all that—we'll need an aerial platform as well."

"We have no authorities to penetrate Serbian airspace—"

"No need," Sutherland cut her off. "The Navy has six EA-18G Growlers forward staged in Spangdahlem, Germany, as part of NATO deterrence in support of Ukraine. Given mission requirements and crew rest, we might be able to get one or two of those aircraft to support. There's a spur of Bosnian territory that comes within ten miles of Suicide's location outside Ponikve Airport. Flying there and back from Germany will chew up over half of a Growler's range, but it'd still give them some station time to orbit."

Chen frowned skeptically.

"They can jam comms from *ten miles* away?"

"Standoff jamming is their bread and butter, ma'am. They'll be able to conduct electronic isolation on a tactical bubble inside Serbia without ever violating the airspace—the only question is for how long."

"Start coordinating," she replied, then keyed her hand mic and transmitted, "We'll see what we can do. What else?"

Cancer continued, "*Last thing. It just started to snow here, and I think Suicide will cover some ground before holing up to let his backtrail get covered. I can tell you for a fact that he's got more balls than brains. You haven't heard from him yet because of the terrain, but at some point he's going to risk moving to a line-of-sight location for a satellite shot. I need to know as soon as you hear from him, because we're looking at a whole lot of ground to cover and only four guys to do it with. Every second counts here.*"

Chen looked to the communications officer giving her a thumbs up, then toward the level gaze of her intelligence officer, then to the screen displaying the weather broadcast, before issuing her response.

"Copy all. So far we've intercepted zero communications that reference Suicide's evasion, and given the amount of SERE training he's received, I feel confident he'll make the best decisions possible under the circumstances. Weather reports indicate four to six of steady snowfall, and that works in his favor. We'll stay on top of monitoring everything from our end, jam frequencies as necessary, and keep you informed. In the meantime I want you to focus on getting your team reset and coming up with the best possible plan. Once you have it, we'll bounce it off our operations staff and any late-breaking developments to finalize the best possible course of action."

"*Good copy. Cancer, out.*"

Then he was gone. In the span of five minutes, she'd gone from close to zero information to more than she could possibly process alone, and the sight of her staff members watching her closely for their chance to provide input served as a source of unfathomable comfort.

31

"We've got this," Cancer said to Ian. "Have a seat."

Ian stripped off his tactical gear, setting it against the wall where the rest of his team was doing the same. He momentarily protested, "I'm fine," before being swiftly rebuked by the acting team leader.

"Park your thirty-pound brain in front of that computer and shut the fuck up."

No arguing that, Ian thought, and lowered himself into the chair with a grunt. The low dose of painkillers he'd taken before the mission was wildly insufficient for the physical exertion he'd undergone in the process of dueling Sidorov, and if Reilly hadn't arrived on a snowmobile, Ian wasn't sure that he would have had the strength to make it to the exfil point.

He needed more Percocet and he needed it now; but there were more immediate priorities to attend to, and he opened the laptop before him to access his planning imagery.

This was no Agency safehouse but a cabin rental procured after learning of Sidorov's new airfield destination, and what would normally be a concentrated sit-down planning session was instead conducted amid a flurry of activity as Cancer issued his orders.

"Worthy, ammo. Reilly, radios. Jelena, water."

Once the assembly line refit began, Cancer addressed the group.

"This ain't a time to pat ourselves on the back, but let's not forget the fact that we fucked up a lot of people out there. Shot down a plane and stacked some bodies in those hills. Sidorov's dead thanks to Ian, and we managed to make exfil without Reilly killing himself on a snowmobile, which is probably the biggest miracle of all. None of us could control what David did, so I don't want anyone blaming themselves for his shitty decision to go after a bag."

"The bag was important," Ian said without breaking his focus on the screen, where he plotted on the top two points of significance: David's last known location, and his destination at Go To Hell Point 2. Then he added, "Important enough for Sidorov to be grateful he was killed rather than be held accountable for losing it."

Cancer was dismissive.

"Whatever. David made his choice and he paid the price. Now we've got to get his ass—the only question is how."

Reilly was in the process of swapping out everyone's radio batteries and placing the depleted units on a charger when he replied, "What's to decide? We know where he went into the ravine, and we know where he's headed. What's the distance?"

"1.8 kilometers straight line," Ian shot back. "With the elevation change and terrain features, we're looking at closer to three and a half."

"So we infil at Go To Hell Point 2, start at his destination, and work our way back to his point of injury. It's a basic Ranger School patrol, movement to contact until we find him. Then we throw him on a poleless litter and carry him back out."

"I disagree," Worthy said bluntly. He went on to explain his logic while clicking bullets into rifle magazines, tapping a reserve of ammunition that was brought into the country as a purely theoretical consideration. "If we all go out there dressed up like storm troopers, then anyone who sees us knows what we're there for. I think the situation calls for me to run as a low-vis pointman, dressed up as a hiker or a hunter. Everyone else trails, ready to react if I get into trouble or divert around any mafia or police I spot out there—seeing that a plane got blown out of the sky today, there's probably going to be both."

Cancer asked, "Ian?"

"Yeah," Ian replied, "I'd say that's about right."

"Fine. So Worthy's on point, and the rest of us trail him."

Jelena turned from the kitchen sink, scoffing as she capped a water bladder.

"None of you speak Serbian, and being American is a death sentence if Janjicari finds you."

Cancer shook his head. "You'll have to drive. Ian may be injured, but we're going to need his gun in the fight. No disrespect to your training at the Farm, but—"

Ian cut him off.

"If she couldn't fight, both of us would've been dead at the uranium exchange long before you guys showed up."

"It is not about marksmanship," Jelena declared, waving a hand at Cancer's mention of the Agency's most well-known training facility for clandestine service officers. "What matters here is the ability to buy time as a local, a task that none of you can accomplish. I can go on point with Worthy, and we can stage a vehicle somewhere."

Ian frowned, staring at the screen.

"We could stage a vehicle, but it wouldn't do us much good."

He hesitated to explain further; to do so would be to place himself in the least enviable position of anyone save perhaps David himself. The very suggestion could easily be construed as an act of cowardice, but that didn't change the fact that it was not only the best, but the *only* way they could feasibly proceed while mitigating risk to the would-be recovery force.

Looking up from the computer, he explained, "We're forgetting about the comms piece. If satellite communications were easy out there, the Agency would've heard from David by now. That means to commit our entire team to the woods is to sever our link to Mayfly and all the real-time updates she affords us. The exfil vehicle can't be sitting unoccupied; we're going to need it as a long-range communications relay between SATCOM and FM frequencies."

Cancer was the first to respond, setting a hand atop Ian's shoulder.

"Sorry, brother," he began. "You're right, and it has to be you."

32

I was freezing in the dark.

Not freezing to death in the literal sense, though that may well have been the case had I not packed sufficient cold-weather gear for the previous night's staging effort as we awaited Sidorov's flight. Be that as it may, my sweat-soaked undergarments made a second night in the mountains a far more brutal experience, and that was before taking a mid-tibial fracture into account.

But I was still alive, a fact that was attributable to blind luck more than anything else.

In a sense, breaking my leg had been the only *un*lucky thing that had happened since abandoning my team to enter the ravine. At that point Reilly's medical cross-training had come into play, and while my personal aid kit contained exactly one item that would be useful for splinting—a flattened roll of duct tape—nature provided the rest.

Locating appropriately sized sticks was easy enough, and I'd placed one on the inside and one on the outside of my broken leg before wrapping both in place with the tape. Then I'd removed the corresponding boot and taped around my foot and ankle in a figure-eight configuration to stabilize it for the journey ahead, which was a lot more painful than snapping my tibia in the first place.

I'd ended up stiff-legging my way to safety for less than five minutes before searching desperately for a walking stick, which, once found, provided a degree of comfort that was probably more psychological than physical.

Still, I'd managed to put some distance between myself and the ravine, and while I'd planned on gaining as much ground as possible, the shifting weather changed everything. In an evasion scenario, the primary rule for moving during snowfall was *don't*, and I directed my efforts to finding a bed-down site. I wasn't outrunning anyone in my current state, and the best I could hope for was hiding and letting my tracks fill in. My lack of a collapsible shovel removed most of my options for making a shelter, and the obvious inability to establish and conceal an above-ground structure took care of the rest. As with the makeshift splint, I was entirely reliant on my surroundings.

In the end it wasn't my survival skills that saved me, but the landscape.

The crevice in which I'd been hiding for the past five hours was a narrow, triangular space formed between the roots and trunk of a fallen tree that had long since come to rest atop a waist-high boulder. It provided just enough room for me to crawl inside and block the entryway with my poncho, then I'd pawed a depression in the snow to allow cold air to pool somewhat. A far cry from the snow caves we'd constructed in training, I thought, but the best I'd manage under the circumstances. After sunrise, I'd have to determine when and how to risk leaving my shelter to establish satellite communications through a gap in the trees, and transmit my location to what I imagined would be a recovery element consisting of my team blazing a path toward my point of injury and killing everyone who tried to stop them.

Or at least, I hoped.

I had no way of knowing whether they'd made their exfil successfully, or taken additional casualties if not been wiped out altogether. And yet there was a certain irony to the fact that I was out here worrying about them; if they had made it out, they were most definitely concerned about my ability to survive the night, for reasons that went far beyond the risk of enemy apprehension.

My team and I had attended basic and advanced SERE courses, which would have been a confidence-inspiring reason for hope save the fact that they were all well aware that I was undeniably the worst survivalist among them.

In my Level C course, I'd completely zoned out mere minutes into our four-hour class on edible plants. When an instructor later explained that the sassafras leaves I'd been ravenously consuming on a multi-day field exercise were nontoxic but entirely devoid of nutritious value, it was news to me.

Nor were my evasion skills anything to write home about: after a nine-hour ground movement through torrential downpours during my initial evaluation, the same instructor had complimented my uncanny ability to remain uncaptured, with my changes in direction being so frequent as to evade ground teams trying their best to close in on my student beacon. I had, of course, humbly accepted the praise as a credit to the training I'd received.

In truth, I was lost as fuck, haphazardly trying to close with various creeks on my map only to find that I was nowhere near them before selecting another landmark to move out toward in an attempt to gain my bearings.

There was no fooling my men, however, with Cancer making a half-joking remark that if our team ever would end up in a survival or evasion scenario, he'd have to take command before I ran the entire team into the ground. Reilly was the undisputed last resort in matters of operating a snowmobile—I'd been shocked to overhear radio traffic that indicated he was allowed to operate one of them during the escape, and wondered if he managed to survive that oversight. And the remaining team members were suitably incompetent at various facets among the countless tasks we were expected to master as a five-man team operating anywhere in the world with minimal support.

No one had to face their inadequacy with quite so much finality as I did at present, out here alone, and yet I was alive with roughly three quarts of water and a half-dozen magazines of ammunition remaining. In crippling pain, sure. With my uninjured leg so fatigued from supporting a foot movement that it hurt almost as much as the broken one, absolutely. But every minute I remained undetected and safely wedged between a rock and the root structure of a tree was one more for the snowfall to fill in my tracks, and above all I had a pillow to provide some degree of comfort: Sidorov's bag, a hard-earned prize that I couldn't resist examining any longer.

I delicately rolled onto my stomach, shifting the satchel to the rear of my shelter and, after a moment of hesitation, turning on my red-lens headlamp at its lowest setting.

The bag's canvas exterior was topped by carrying handles and a shoulder strap of soft, rich leather. I examined the checkered pattern to find three words printed at irregular intervals across the sides: *LOUIS VUITTON, PARIS*. Yuri Sidorov was a douchebag, I thought, confirming my long-held suspicion as I lifted the bag to gauge its weight. Four, maybe five pounds. I'd previously wondered if it had a tracking device, and assured myself that if so, the Agency would be blocking the signal somehow at Cancer's insistence. By now I knew it was either that or there wasn't a tracker at all—otherwise I'd be dead by now.

As it stood, I'd nearly died to recover this thing and still might; I desperately wanted to open it, and if it contained nothing more than porn mags and snack food the odds of me crying or having a nervous breakdown or both were perilously high.

The polished zippers were held together by a gold key lock, which was a charming bit of flair for a bag that could easily be cut open. Still, I couldn't rule out the possibility of an anti-tamper switch or self-destructive measure. Its owner didn't have time to prepare anything as crude as a grenade boobytrap, and if he had, the satchel would've exploded by now. But a man who'd survived as long as Sidorov had surely possessed some level of sophistication in his operational security measures. The CIA sure as hell wouldn't open this thing without first sending it through multiple scanners under the supervision of EOD-trained personnel, and I certainly shouldn't either.

I killed my headlamp and set the satchel back in its position as a pillow, resolving to leave it unopened until it arrived in the hands of trained professionals, if it made it that far at all.

Then I turned off my headlamp, taking a long breath that ended in closing my eyes, centering myself for the wait ahead, and mentally preparing for the pain of rolling onto my back. What I needed now was calm focus, cool restraint, and a calculated mind to make my way back to the team however I could.

My eyelids flew open and I reactivated my headlamp with the single thought: *fuck it*. My career had begun as a Ranger private, and beneath the do-or-die mindset and cool equipment, all Rangers were infantry grunts at heart. That meant any novel object was to be immediately investigated, messed with, and if at all possible, broken, and not necessarily in that order.

I drew my Winkler knife and sliced along the zipper line, then reached inside to feel a familiar shape greet my hand. Withdrawing it, I saw a leather-wrapped flask bearing Sidorov's initials and quickly unscrewed it to sniff the contents—vodka, which, like all clear spirits, I avoided whenever possible.

But as a bit of a boozer, I knew that I had little chance of resisting its allure until daybreak. Furthermore, I was well aware that the feeling of warmth imparted by consuming alcohol was actually an effect of vasodilation that directed heat away from vital organs. That was of particular consideration in a cold-weather environment such as this, and both factors led me to immediately swing my arm to pour it out.

But I was possessed by a sudden impulse to bring it right back to my mouth instead, and I took a sip of the foul liquid while simultaneously blaming the shock imparted by my physical pain as the case for this otherwise heinous indiscretion.

I regretted the action immediately, and remedied that with a second sip. Injured and isolated in the freezing cold with an extremely high chance of being captured or killed, I knew that the vodka was going to hit me hard. So be it.

Then I reached back in the satchel to recover a slim plastic case with a half-dozen clasps sealing it shut. I undid them, then opened the case to see a foam-lined interior with cutouts to accommodate rows of small black objects, each bearing a tiny label printed in Russian Cyrillic. Other than the text on the labels themselves, every item was identical to the next—the question remained, what were they?

I plucked one from the case and examined it. Smooth ivory plastic formed a semicircle cap around a beveled grip that I yanked on. It came free easily, though the only thing attached to it was a USB port connector. A flash drive, I realized, though at this tiny size it couldn't have held much information.

Then I flipped it over to see factory print reading *2TB*.

The scope of this recovery hit me in full, and I performed a quick count: five rows of eight, forty flash drives in total, equaling a staggering eighty *terabytes* of data storage for the Agency to scrutinize provided I could get it to them in the first place.

I put the cap back on the drive in my hand and replaced it in the case, closing the lid and clasping it shut. No wonder Sidorov had chosen to ditch his satchel: the contents of these devices were too valuable to risk transmitting even through the dark web. Instead, Sidorov was personally spiriting the drives aboard a plane that only touched down in Russia, Serbia, and Iran, all places where the word "Interpol" was a punch line and the governments wouldn't permit Western agents to enter their borders, much less enable a sting operation.

My heart was beating quicker now, whether due to the flash drives or the flask, and I spread the bag open and shined my light inside to see that both items were perhaps the least significant of its contents.

33

Worthy scanned the forest through his night vision, pulling security until Jelena donned her hiking pack, lifted her Winchester Model 70 from its resting place against a tree, and rose to whisper, "Go ahead."

He laid his primary weapon barrel-up against a stone and unslung his hiking pack, setting it down before kneeling to open the top flap. He removed his night vision device and corresponding head mount, stashing both in the flap pocket and catching a glimpse of his HK416 inside the back, broken down into upper and lower receivers arrayed side by side for later assembly if time and circumstance allowed.

Cinching the flap shut, Worthy re-slung his pack and recovered his primary weapon, blinking to adjust his eyes to the view. Formal sunrise had yet to arrive, though its onset was sufficient to illuminate the snow-blanketed forest just enough to continue movement. Ordinarily he'd have worn his night vision a bit longer, but the chance of being spotted with decidedly non-civilian equipment was simply too great to risk.

"Ready?" Jelena whispered.

"Whatever you say," Worthy answered. "You're the guide."

And with that, they continued their trek northeast, where, as of the last intercepted transmissions before the jamming effort went into full swing, there was no shortage of Janjicari mobsters combing the woods. They'd located Sidorov's body but not his bag, nor was it in the downed aircraft; they were now under orders whose point of origin remained unclear to search for the missing item until told otherwise.

As such, Worthy's initial assessment that a fully-kitted point element wouldn't do at all proved to be solid. Along with Jelena, their current choice of disguise was informed by a thriving hunting tourism industry in Serbia, which worked in their favor, as did the fact that every type of game was currently in season except for roe buck. As a result, they'd chosen their game based on the weapon that Worthy selected to open-carry into the operation—rifle hunting was by far the most popular in Serbia, and foreign clients brought everything from .270 Winchesters all the way up to 300 Win Mags depending on the intended quarry and anticipated shooting range.

But Worthy had no time to sight and zero a new optic or even iron sights on a locally procured rifle; furthermore, aside from his stashed HK416, he carried a suppressed MP7 concealed beneath his coat. With those ends of the shooting spectrum covered, he'd selected a somewhat niche weapon that the team possessed in their arsenal but had yet to use operationally. Most importantly, it wouldn't appear out of place when hunting wild boar in thick brush.

The Benelli M4 in his hands was a semi-automatic shotgun with an 18.5-inch barrel and tritium sights, with a carrying capacity of seven shells plus one in the chamber. Worthy made full use of that with double-aught buckshot and could, if needed, send nine tightly grouped lead pellets flying at over a thousand feet per second with every squeeze of his trigger. It was a formidable weapon, more so in his own capable hands—by now he'd done countless 3-gun competitions that required as much proficiency with a Benelli as any handgun or rifle.

But the shotgun came with one very critical drawback: noise. If he was forced to use it, a single shot would be as good as putting out an APB on his entire team sans David, and even he would most certainly hear the blast echoing over the hills.

And that risk, considerable though it was, was far from the only disadvantage they faced. They were presently negotiating public land, several kilometers removed from the nearest commercial or club-owned hunting grounds, and their disguises would only hold up for so long if confronted.

So far they hadn't glimpsed any movement during their ground infiltration toward David's point of injury, and now that the sun had risen, Worthy identified a few tracks from rabbit and deer as he and Jelena crossed the snowscape. No boot prints, which boded well for today's mission.

He keyed his radio to relay the same message he'd been repeating every few minutes since dismounting.

"Suicide, Racegun. Radio check."

A long pause before he got a response, which came not from David but Cancer.

"*You hear anything?*"

"Negative," Worthy replied.

Nothing more needed to be said. Cancer, along with Reilly, was in full tactical kit while trailing the point element by roughly a hundred meters, and that range disparity meant they could potentially miss a return transmission from the absent team leader.

More likely, however, David was still hunkered down wherever he'd hidden overnight; it was only six in the morning, after all, and their battery conservation protocol for evasion was to power up radios the first ten minutes of every hour for the first 24 hours after being separated from the main element. Then it would drop to even-numbered hours on the second day, noon and midnight on the third, before extending to noon each day into perpetuity or until all available batteries were exhausted.

David should've had some radio life remaining, and he'd damn well know the team was coming for him today. But he'd be equally restricted from leaving his hide site until well after first light, when he could evaluate the surrounding terrain and gauge how worthwhile it was to leave footprints now that the snowfall had ended completely.

And that was if the evading team leader didn't hear any possible aggressors moving in proximity to his location. If he did, they could be in for one hell of a wait before they heard from him.

Worthy caught an incoming transmission then, whispered and filled with static, but intelligible nonetheless.

"*Any station this net, Suicide. Radio check.*"

Momentarily freezing in his tracks, Worthy felt his heart leap and he locked eyes with Jelena, giving a quick nod before they increased their walking pace. He kept silent, however, waiting for the senior man in their ranks to respond.

When Cancer didn't transmit within the next few seconds, Worthy realized that he and Jelena were the only ones who had heard David's message —he must have just entered the fringes of his FM radio range.

Then he transmitted, "Cancer, I've got him on comms, break. Suicide, be advised we're inbound now, just over a klick northeast of Go To Hell Point 2, what's your status?"

David may have broken a bone, but his sense of humor remained intact. "*My leg didn't heal overnight. Other than that I'm fine. Stand by for my grid.*"

No sooner had Worthy received that message than he heard another one—this one audible through the trees to his left, a man shouting a single word.

"*Zaustaviti!*"

It took considerable restraint not to wheel toward the threat with his shotgun raised; instead Worthy followed Jelena's lead, coming to a stop and turning toward the noise to see a man approaching down the hillside to their left. He was flanked by two more, all in civilian hunter's camouflage and fanning out with assault rifles at the ready.

Worthy keyed his radio and spoke quickly. "Cancer, three armed men inbound from our ten o'clock, need immediate support. Suicide, you need to push your location over SATCOM."

"*On our way,*" Cancer replied.

Worthy discreetly pulled out his radio earpieces, tucking them inside his collar—the Navy had an EA-18G Growler orbiting across the border in Bosnia, and its full-spectrum electronic warfare suite was currently running interference cancellation that blocked almost all radio communications with the exception of the low end of VHF range that the team used. Getting spotted with radio equipment at the moment would be as good as pulling out an American flag and announcing he was here on behalf of the CIA.

And to her credit, Jelena looked for all the world to be undaunted by the sudden interruption.

She took a few steps toward the men and spoke a string of Serbian in an inconvenienced tone, as if the trio was guilty of scaring the game away. If this went bad, all three would *become* the game, although he was suddenly reminded of the greatest issue in having Jelena accompany him.

He didn't disagree that her presence was necessary from the standpoint of having a native speaker who could navigate personal and cultural terrain with anyone who spotted them. But while the Janjicari was a large and sprawling organization, it would only take one member who'd been present on security during her black-market arms deals on behalf of Affinity Gold to recognize her, and if that happened, there was no stopping a shootout now.

With his shotgun held barrel-down in one hand to prevent any misunderstanding that he was a threat rather than a tourist hunter, Worthy watched the three men advance down the slope toward them. One pair held Zastava assault rifles, moving on-line with a couple meters' spacing between them, and the third was dead center with a bullpup Steyr as he trailed out of a probable instinct for self-preservation—the guy in charge, he surmised. From their weapons and wardrobe as much as their reaction, it was clear these three were combing the area for intruders, which meant there would be other teams.

That assumption was confirmed when the central man responded to Jelena with what sounded like a rebuke, while his security men took up stationary positions. Neither was aiming at them outright, though it would only take them a moment to do so.

The back-and-forth continued with Jelena, who would soon be approaching the end of her cover story's feasibility. Worthy desperately hoped that the three men would fall dead any second now in a hail of suppressed gunfire from Cancer and Reilly, but it didn't happen—the two must've been trying to get a viable firing position, if they weren't still closing the distance.

Worthy struggled mightily with his limited options at present: he could employ the shotgun in time, but it would completely compromise the rescue effort. To abandon the shotgun in favor of the suppressed MP7 would add precious seconds to an already strained reaction time, particularly given the numerical disadvantage.

In the end, the decision was made for him.

The man in charge barked a very definitive order at Jelena, who responded in English with the word she was told to speak if it was go-time to open fire—Project Longwing standard operating procedure at its finest.

"This is *bullshit*—"

Worthy whipped his Benelli upward, steadying it with his left hand and pulling off a shot on the leftmost man in a fraction of a second.

Without his radio earpieces and their attendant decibel cutoff limit, the blast was deafening to him and, surely, the mafia shooters as well.

But they'd have far less time to worry about permanent hearing damage. The first shot blasted an oblong spray of buckshot in the man's chest, though the exit wound would be far worse; in Hollywood, that kind of close-range shotgun blast would have sent the target flying backward in slow motion.

Reality was a different story, however, and instead he jolted and stumbled as Worthy swung the Benelli right and fired at the remaining security man before the echo of the first shot subsided. The hasty aiming was sloppier than before, no center-mass hit but instead flying high and left, blowing off the man's trapezius with a few pellets lacing into the side of his neck. One of them must've hit an artery there, because the customary pink mist was accompanied by a spray of searingly bright red blood before he dropped in place, alive but not for long.

By the time Worthy was directing his aim at the commander, the man was simultaneously leveling his Steyr at Jelena and being shot by her. She ripped a half-magazine from her now-drawn Glock, the rapid shots ending when Worthy blew a hole in his midsection, diverted right to re-engage the rightmost man who was currently bleeding out, and then swept his barrel across the carnage for three seconds before determining that no more buckshot was needed. They were all dead, the echo of the blasts fading to the distant shouts of men.

The rescue effort had turned into a sunrise bloodbath, and now it was all Worthy could do to keep himself and Jelena alive until his two teammates arrived.

Reilly was moving almost as fast as he could when he received Worthy's transmission.

"*Three EKIA, we're moving north to take the high ground.*"

The medic diverted left as a result, transmitting as he moved, "Got it, should have eyes-on any second now."

Then he caught his first glimpse of Worthy and Jelena, and the sight brought with it a subtle recognition of the genius in their response—they were heading north all right, and doing so in a straight line to follow the central track of one of the dead Serbians. With enough time, an experienced tracker would be able to determine how many people had crossed that ground and in what direction, but a responding enemy combatant would be left to wonder how many opponents he was facing at the end of that trail. Given that three men had already been slain, he would hopefully conclude he was likely to be outnumbered.

Reilly performed a quick assessment of the terrain in their direction of movement; he'd assumed that Worthy's mention of "high ground" referred to a ridge, and instead saw a very discernable hilltop. It was steep enough to be defensible provided they reached the top, though he questioned the wisdom of remaining in a fixed position for any meaningful period of time.

Apparently the same thought occurred to Cancer, who was trailing him and now faced the unenviable task of determining the team's course of action with the enemy closing in from all sides.

He transmitted, "*Alamo position on the hilltop. They already know we're here, so we're gonna let them come, then thin out their ranks enough to make our next move.*"

Worthy was halfway up the hilltop when he replied, "*What move is that?*"

"*Not sure yet.*"

Sadly, Reilly thought as he charged uphill, it wasn't a statement of ignorance so much as circumstance—depending on where the enemy came from, the team may well have only one direction to go.

But once they escaped the immediate perimeter, what then?

The Janjicari was unquestionably out here for Sidorov's missing bag, though it was unclear if they knew or even suspected that one or more members of the PC-24 shootdown team had never left the area. But if they hadn't entertained the notion before, then Worthy's recent shootout would remove all doubt. Why else would anyone risk coming back to the scene of the crime against such tremendous odds?

Regrettably, that informed the team's actions as much as the mafia's. No snowfall in the forecast today, so any tracks David left in establishing radio contact with the team would become his own death sentence the moment they were discovered. If the team retreated, they'd be leaving David alone amidst an enemy force that would now be searching for the bag *and him*, and finding one would net them both.

Then again, if they continued toward the isolated team leader, they'd be drawing an enemy force along with them, and while the recovery element may be able to outrun pursuit for a time, none of them had a broken leg.

Reilly forced the thoughts from his mind, determined to leave the decision-making to Cancer and instead focus on his task of establishing a defensive position on the hilltop. He was gasping for breath amid the thin mountain air by the time he reached the summit, an L-shaped swath of ground where Worthy was already kneeling, hastily assembling the HK416 from his pack as Jelena surveyed the far side with her Winchester.

Without waiting for guidance, Reilly took up a position overlooking the route both of them had just traversed. He had a 7.62mm weapon, after all, so it made sense for him to cover the most likely avenue of approach; Cancer was packing the same caliber, but he needed the freedom to move and assess the situation as the acting team leader.

Reilly knelt behind a snow-covered slab of rock, bringing his rifle to the high ready and scanning down the rows of tracks that ended in a trio of dead bodies.

He'd barely identified the carnage when a fourth figure appeared, this one jogging into view and scrambling to a stop as he saw the corpses. Then he swung his gaze uphill and almost directly into Reilly's sights.

The medic opened fire then, racking up an easy kill to kick off the engagement and betraying his position in the process. Sure enough, the next two targets he engaged were little more than fleeting shadows, by which time his teammates were shooting as well. Soon thereafter, echoing blasts heralded the first incoming gunfire.

The situation already felt like a sickening repeat of the previous day's defense, once again as a result of David. And while Janjicari had certainly learned how quickly they could fall at the hands of a better trained and equipped, if numerically inferior, team, they had no shortage of human fodder willing to enter the fray.

The next criminal he saw advancing through the trees was moving with a speed and determination equal to any member of a military or terrorist organization Reilly had ever encountered. Money, it seemed, was as powerful a motivator for some as any political or religious ideology.

He took aim at the man and felled the combatant in three shots, then engaged a second and missed entirely before losing his line of sight amid his target's hasty retreat as Cancer transmitted, "*Suicide, can you read me?*"

No response.

The team held a marksmanship and terrain advantage, and could certainly hold this position for a time but not forever. Given the Janjicari had near-full complicity from the state, it was only a matter of time before the opponents surrounding the hilltop were going to be wearing police shields or military uniforms.

A string of bullet impacts whipped up a geyser of snow to his left. Reilly identified a muzzle flash in the shadows of a spruce below and sent a six-shot volley in return. No telling whether he'd hit the offending shooter or merely forced him to displace, and judging from the chuffing of suppressed weapons behind him, barely audible during lulls of gunfire from below, his teammates remained as gainfully employed as he was.

Cancer's next transmission underscored this grim reality with an almost frightening degree of calm.

"*Angel, we are decisively engaged, need guidance now.*"

Ian wondered if this was how it would end, and if by virtue of taking a gunshot four days earlier and thus ending up outside the fight, he'd become his team's lone survivor.

"Copy," he replied to Cancer over the team frequency, "can you get comms with Suicide?"

It was a question he already suspected the answer to. He was sitting in the back of the van in a Bajina Bašta hotel parking lot, facing a pair of open laptops and manning dual radios. Even with the benefit of vehicle-mounted signal amplifiers, he hadn't been able to hear David's brief previous communication, only Worthy's response telling him to make a satellite transmission because the point element had been compromised.

And given the unanswered attempts to make contact since the team had assumed a defensive posture, Ian could only assume they were out of range once more.

"*Negative,*" Cancer confirmed, "*and the spot where Racegun got ahold of him is covered with bad guys.*"

Ian transmitted back, "Suicide is probably trying to get SATCOM signal right now. How long can you hold out at your current location?"

"*You tell me. What's the status of enemy reinforcements?*"

"The last Growler has ninety minutes of station time left, but it's a matter of time before cops are inbound if they're not already. In the meantime, every Janjicari shooter in earshot is going to be closing on your location. I'd say they'll be able to mass another squad-sized element, maybe two, within twenty minutes based on how far they're spread out."

"*If we haven't made it out by then, you'll be talking to a dead radio.*"

Ian felt his lungs constrict. In the span of a few minutes, they'd gone from only David evading capture to potentially having the entire recovery element on the run. There was strength to be had in numbers, but the team was now spread across three locations with no hope of reinforcing each other.

Cancer was in charge, but only Ian had the complete operational picture, or at least as complete as it was going to get. The only question was whether to order his team to hold fast or to flee, with the latter option meaning they'd abandon David in the process. This was the only chance of recovery they were going to have, and if they missed it, the team leader would unquestionably be located by Janjicari who were surely now aware of his presence. In that event, David would be tortured if he didn't kill himself first—would he do such a thing, rather than risk compromising Project Longwing in its entirety?

Would Ian?

"Hold fast," Ian transmitted back, "I'll figure something out."

"*You better.*"

Ian correctly thought that would be the end of the exchange, and yet another voice spoke as soon as Cancer fell silent.

"*Any station this net, any station this net, Suicide Actual.*"

Mayfly responded before Ian could.

"*Suicide Actual, Raptor Nine One—*"

"Break break break," Ian cut her off, now clutching his satellite radio hand mic. "Suicide, this is Angel. Need your location asap."

David complied, transmitting a ten-digit grid as quickly as he could read the numbers off his GPS. Ian was in the process of plotting the point on his computer when the team leader continued, "*You're not going to believe what's in Sidorov's bag.*"

Ian felt a sudden impulse of fury that David could have possibly been so stupid as to open it; then again, any genius he possessed began and ended well within the tactical realm.

But there was no time to address the oversight now, and he transmitted back, "Our team is in the shit right now."

"*I can hear it. If I could move, I'd be there already.*"

The intelligence operative ignored that too; it wasn't that David was speaking out of bravado, but nonetheless the comment was a spectacularly bad idea that the dumb bastard would doubtless have acted on already if both legs were intact. A+ for loyalty, Ian thought, and an F for judgment.

He continued speaking while calculating the azimuth from his team's location to David's. "All I can see on the imagery is trees. But you're making sat comms so you must be on high ground, right?"

"*Check,*" David said.

"Describe the terrain."

"*Looks like I'm on a ridgeline running east to west.*"

"What's the low ground like north of the ridge?"

A pause before David replied, "*Pretty steep descent into a narrow gulley.*"

"Listen carefully," Ian said solemnly, "because this is the only way to save all of you. I'm going to send the team running your way. I need you to set up a shooting position overlooking the gulley, and make FM comms once they're in range. Once you can hear them, vector them into the low ground and right through your kill zone, then into a flanking maneuver up to your location. Meanwhile, you remain in place to pick off any pursuers who follow the tracks. Can you do that?"

David's voice was low with anger as he responded, and for good reason: three of his teammates, along with Jelena, were at grave risk of being killed as a result of his actions the day before.

"*Yeah*," he said, "*yeah, I can do that. Send them. Anyone who follows is fucking dead*."

Keying the FM mic in his opposite hand, Ian transmitted to his besieged teammates.

"Cancer, I need you to bust through the enemy perimeter and move out on a heading of zero-four-five. Make comms with Suicide and he'll explain the rest. I've got to break down here and start moving to the pickup site."

34

Cancer led his team in a run downhill, altering his course slightly at the transmission of the man immediately behind him in the order of movement.

"*Ten degrees right,*" Reilly informed him.

After making the course correction, Cancer keyed his radio and said, "Last man, check in."

Worthy replied, "*Negative contact, but they're right behind us. Maybe thirty seconds back. We need to pick up the pace.*"

"Suicide, can you hear me?"

As with his previous attempts to contact David, there was no response —and, Cancer thought, it was merely the latest in a long list of things that were fucked up at the moment. After all, aside from perhaps Jelena, the sniper was the last person who should've been taking point.

But when breaking contact from a gunfight, the formation evolved however the formation evolved, and once they finished bounding downhill under waves of covering fire, the sniper had found himself leading the retreat. Ideally they'd have time to rearrange the formation to their usual configuration—or at least to the extent possible with a female case officer among them—but time wasn't on their side and neither, it seemed, were radio communications with their still-missing team leader.

To the extent that Cancer could influence the situation, however, his plan had paid off so far. Back at the hilltop, he'd reasoned that if these Serb mafia motherfuckers wanted to come running, then let them; a few minutes of precision fire should have attritted their ranks in short order, and their short stand on the high ground had served to accomplish that task. After all, it was better to make a brief stand from an advantageous position than go running through the woods like chickens with their heads cut off and an army in pursuit.

And yet Ian's guidance had been to do just that, albeit along a specific azimuth that he could only presume led to David's location. If that was intended to be a master plan, Cancer thought, it left much to be desired: sure, they could link up with their missing team leader, but there would be hell to pay in the best of circumstances, much less while trying to carry out a gimp with one working leg.

Cancer complied nonetheless, due more to lack of any feasible alternatives than faith in the process. When every footfall left a track, bailing out hell-mell across channelized terrain surrounded on both sides by high ground wasn't exactly a great survival strategy, though he had to admit it bested running out of ammunition at their previous skirmish.

But that was where his optimism ended. After another ten seconds of running, he made another attempt to raise David with close to zero expectations of a return transmission.

"Suicide, check in."

But the team leader replied at once, sounding as surprised as Cancer felt.

"I've got you—what's your location?"

Cancer vaulted a log and made landfall on the other side, then very nearly lost his balance atop a snow-covered rock on the other side. But he remained upright, stumbling a few more steps before gaining the confidence to resume his run.

"Hauling ass on a heading of zero-four-five. I hope Angel told you more than he told me."

"Yeah," David replied, *"he did. Are you in the low ground?"*

"Fuck no. Just below the military crest."

"You see the gulley? Should be to your right."

He glanced in that direction, finding an undulating descent that bottomed out in a narrow channel with brambles.

"Sure," Cancer replied.

"Go there. Follow it ducks-in-a-row, one set of tracks. I'll call in adjustments once you get closer."

"Closer to what?"

"My kill zone. Once you pass through it, you can buttonhook right and move up to my ambush position."

Cancer tried not to scoff; "ambush position" was a lofty term coming from one fatigued shooter with a broken leg, and at the moment he had half a mind to break the other one rather than comply with the directive.

Instead he cut right, moving down the slope and visually charting a course that would keep his team free from the thicket while transmitting, "You better know what you're doing."

"Do I ever?" David answered without hesitation. *"But Angel sure as shit has this figured out. Hang on, I think I can hear you."*

No surprise there, Cancer thought. Unless there was a particularly loud gust of wind, the enemy could too—three men and a woman crashing through brush as fast as they could made a hell of a lot of noise, particularly when all of them were sucking for air.

David ordered, *"Go left five degrees...that's it...straight ahead, keep coming...a little to the right..."*

Cancer complied with a profound sense of irritation: if there was one person who shouldn't be allowed to give orders ever again, it was the asshole who'd put them in this mess. His anger continued to build, though it abated a moment later when David said, *"Now look up."*

Unwilling to stop, Cancer first verified the terrain ahead, waiting until he'd reached an open expanse of snow extending a few meters to the next tree.

Only then did he cast his gaze up the ridge to his right where, hunkered down in the prone atop a rock outcropping and waving between the brambles surrounding him on either side, he saw the distant figure of David Rivers.

I lowered my hand the moment Cancer looked away and swept out of view behind the trees, then transmitted again.

"*You're out of my kill zone; another fifty meters and you'll see a slope that you can follow to reach my position.*"

By then I could see Reilly slipping past, not bothering to look up at me; he looked like the very effort of continuing to run required his full attention. Jelena, however, possessed sufficient composure not only to visually identify my firing location but to flip me the bird in the process of running through my kill zone. I liked her, I decided, her taste in men notwithstanding.

And, speak of the devil, Worthy appeared and pivoted to perform a momentary scan of their backtrail before flashing out of view with a final transmission.

"*Last man.*"

It was all the clearance I needed. The next person to tread across the open patch of snow in the gulley would pay for it with their life.

After a long night alone I was cold, tired, and severely pissed at myself for placing my team in further danger on my behalf. Some trigger time was just the thing I needed, though to be fair, my motivation to make a successful escape had redoubled in light of what I'd found in Sidorov's bag. Once in CIA custody, the satchel represented the single greatest success my country had achieved so far against Erik Weisz, whose real name, much less that of his organization, remained a mystery.

Now I just had to get the intel out, along with my team.

I'd prepared as well as I could for the engagement ahead, particularly given that any substantial movement involved hobbling around with a walking stick, now abandoned at my side in favor of the HK416 in my hands.

My rifle magazines were laid out before me for hasty reloading. The nearest ones were full, but the most distant mag held the consolidated bullets from my failed attempts to kill Sidorov. I didn't know how many rounds it had left, and that remaining ammo, along with selecting the best possible cover and concealment in the form of a rock ledge flanked by brush, represented my final attempts to overcome a slew of disadvantages. I was, after all, now tasked with making roughly one-hundred-meter shots with a 5.56mm weapon from a suboptimal shooting position while my right leg pulsated in agonizing pain.

I heard the first enemy shooters charging down the gulley to my left, and was somewhat shocked by how closely they'd been following my team. Worthy had cleared the kill zone perhaps twenty seconds earlier, and I took aim through my optic to see the trail of footsteps below.

The first combatant to appear didn't so much as glance in my direction. His attention was resolutely focused on the prints in the snow before him, secure in the knowledge that he was too close to his quarry for them to buttonhook and set up an ambush on their backtrail.

He hadn't accounted for the possibility that one of their number already lay in wait, however, and I let him run directly into my sights before firing a half dozen subsonic rounds.

My opening volley had its intended effect, with a few misses rendered insignificant by the hits. He shrieked and tumbled forward before collapsing altogether. I didn't have time to confirm the kill; a second and third man were scrambling to a halt in an attempt to avoid sharing their pointman's fate. If they'd sprinted past his body instead, they may have had a chance. But they were already bunched up, and their collective skidding stop allowed me to engage them with a minor back-and-forth movement of my barrel as I pumped rounds downhill, wounding if not killing both in the process.

A flash of movement crossed my optic then, and I shifted my aim in time to see a fourth man darting through the kill zone.

Determined to prevent him from reaching my teammates, I overreacted by slinging bullets in a fast and sloppy shifting burst that ended only when my magazine was fully expended.

I performed a reload while observing that I'd hit him at least once, albeit non-fatally—he was on the ground, clutching his leg and looking upward to find me while shouting at his teammates in frantic Serbian.

By the time I took aim and sent a double-tap of finishing shots that silenced him for good, I was fully compromised.

Blasts of enemy gunfire sounded from the low ground to my left, some of which were wildly inaccurate bursts whose bullets peppered the ridge while others were carefully aimed single shots that cracked into the rock ledge I was lying atop. I directed my rifle toward the sounds, struggling to shift my body into a supporting position amidst the eye-watering pain of jostling a fractured tibia and its razor-sharp bone fragments. Under any other circumstances, I would've been reduced to a screaming mess by the movement; but adrenaline overcame all, at least for a time. I began directing my aim first at the visible muzzle flashes and then at any signs of movement, reloading when necessary and maintaining a hellish volume of fire.

What else could I have done?

There was no such thing as breaking contact with a shattered leg, nor would I have been willing to retreat even if I could have—I'd already put my team in enough danger, and I wasn't going to extend those risks any further. They'd have the satchel if nothing else. If I got blown away out here, I decided, so be it.

And once I made my peace with that, the object of the game pivoted from despair to taking as many enemy fighters with me as I possibly could. It was a borderline childish impulse, but it continued to rise within me as I went through successive magazines, progressively shifting my efforts from suppression to precision. Recklessly slinging rounds was all well and good for pinning down the enemy if you had the ammunition to do so, but I was getting down to my final magazines and what I needed more than ever were *hits*. My mind delivered an unsolicited message from my past, a marksmanship saying from the first mercenary team I'd served with: *you're only outgunned as long as you're missing*.

I continued to reload and score hits against all odds, some that I could see in the form of a target dropping out of sight and others that I merely inferred from the steadiness of my reticle on an offending muzzle flash as I pulled off the shot, all while incoming bullets snapped overhead or impacted the ridge with increasing degrees of accuracy. By the time I loaded my second-to-last magazine, I knew there was no way I'd shoot through it without dying; and yet, that's exactly what happened. Despite the near misses, aiming uphill at a partially visible point target was a challenge even for experienced shooters. If none of them managed to hit me by the time I finished reloading, then more would fall.

When my bolt slammed forward, chambering the first bullet of my final, only partially full magazine, I was not only still alive but back in the fight, however briefly.

Time to make it count.

Rather than increase my rate of fire, I became slower and more precise, determined to make every shot accurate while I still could. The approach of death brought with it a graphic level of millisecond-to-millisecond awareness, my actions effortless and occurring amidst an ultra-vivid slow-motion mental processing. I saw a bearded man who would have ripped my arms off in a barfight overexpose himself in an attempt to locate me as he raised his assault rifle, then jolt as a 5.56mm round tore into his shoulder. I blinked once, then watched my sights settling on a kneeling shooter whose barrel flickered as he fired uphill.

There was no conscious aiming involved, nor even pulling the trigger. It was like watching someone else play a video game, my world a muted silence where I could no longer feel the pain from my leg, and barely registered the rock fragments that whipped into my left cheek from a nearby bullet impact. A soft thumping jolt of my buttstock, and a seeming eternity before the kneeling shooter received the round that had left my barrel a fraction of a second earlier. It must have hit him in the gut because he formed a fetal position as he fell; another blink and my reticle was drifting left, sweeping toward a moving silhouette in the trees and blurring slightly as my weapon discharged a bullet at the moment of intersection. My reticle continued to drift, suddenly dropping in response to a new threat marked by a glassy orb that could only be the business end of a high-power scope.

The sniper had finally arrived, and this time I could feel the flesh of my index finger pressed against the finger of my shooting glove, itself pressed against the curved metal of my trigger as I applied pressure with the full knowledge that I was too late. As it turned out, so was my opponent.

We vanished from each other's view as the space between us transformed into a white and gray mist, then billowed with an orange glow—the tremendous concussion of a blast reverberated uphill, followed a moment later by a second explosion. My teammates were behind me, I realized then, hurling fragmentation grenades off the ridge and into the gulley below. They certainly weren't killing anyone, but I'd be damned if the blasts and shrapnel didn't make the enemy force reconsider the feasibility of a frontal assault. More importantly, the clouds of dirt and snow provided a wall of concealment that was temporarily as effective as smoke grenades, which, I reasoned, my team had probably left behind in favor of more lethal options.

The steady march of time went from a trickle to a gush as I was jolted back to reality, returning to the clumsy existence outside the flow state that preceded certain death. Hands grabbed me roughly, dragging me backward with such force that I pulled the trigger, the bullet I'd intended for the sniper sailing harmlessly into the trees.

I flicked my selector lever to safe then, although there was no point in doing so beyond deference to the general principles of firearm safety—my rifle bolt was locked to the rear, magazine empty.

And then the pain hit me like a Mac truck.

Reilly dragged David away from the outcropping, manhandling the team leader who gave a high-pitched yelp before composing himself enough to gasp sentence fragments between hissing intakes of air.

"Ah *fuck*...fucking hurts...fuck? Fuck! You...you *fucker*..."

None of this altered Reilly's actions in the slightest; if David was talking, then he was breathing, and if the medic didn't get him out of the line of fire fast, that simple and unlikely blessing could change at any given moment.

He pulled David up the sloping ridgeline until he was certain they could no longer be spotted from the gulley, where the rest of his team continued firing and throwing grenades until they didn't. Suddenly all that was left were the echoes of gunfire and explosions, punctuated by Worthy's voice.

"They're falling back."

Reilly released David, who let go of his rifle and rolled onto his side, shuddering with unspeakable pain, no longer able to curse or, it appeared, even breathe.

Cancer called out, "That means they're about to come at us from the west. We need to move."

By then Reilly had set down his weapon and unslung his pack, using both hands to recover a roll of high-strength mesh strapped to the outside.

"Nice splint," he said, unfurling the poleless litter and laying it on the ground beside David. The comment wasn't meant to be ironic; David had done a genuinely admirable job of duct-taping sticks to either side of his injury. "I see you paid more attention to my makeshift class than you did in SERE training."

David struggled to remove the satchel strapped across his chest, then writhed his arms out of his assault pack straps as he panted, "At least I didn't roll a snowmobile."

"Neither did I," Reilly objected, "at least, not yesterday."

He smoothed out the mesh until it was as flat as he could make it and extended two sets of web straps that would secure the litter around David's body. "How'd you make it through the night?"

"Disemboweled a tauntaun, climbed inside."

"I figured. Probably had nothing to do with the fact you smell like vodka."

"Probably not."

Cancer appeared on the other side of the casualty, crouching to take hold of David as Reilly did the same and counted, "One, two, three."

They lifted him in unison, shuffling until his body was positioned over the litter and setting him down again. David grunted in pain, which was all Cancer needed to go off.

"Serves you right, you piece of shit. "

Reilly clipped the web straps around David's torso and knees, cinching them in sequence before Cancer had the chance to do what he did next: namely, dropping the team leader's assault pack onto his chest from a height of three feet, then slamming the satchel atop it with the words, "This what all the trouble was for?"

David used one hand to steady his assault pack while the other assumed an iron grip on the satchel.

"The bag is worth it."

"Maybe," Cancer conceded, retrieving the team leader's weapon and handing it to him. "*If* we make it out of here. That's a big 'if,' thanks to you."

This time David had the good sense not to talk back, but that didn't mean he was silent.

"I need ammo," he declared, summoning Worthy to deliver a pair of HK416 magazines before moving out on point, where his usual duties were now complicated by the requirement of determining a route wide enough for the passage of a three-person-wide stretcher team.

Reilly donned his pack, slinging his HK417 and pushing it to his side before routing his non-firing hand through the loop of a carrying handle by David's head and grabbing the material with a wrist wrap. Jelena appeared at the opposite side and did the same, leaving Cancer to take his position at the foot of the litter, where he grabbed two handles and nodded to the medic.

"One, two, three," Reilly said, and then they lifted the casualty in unison, bringing him to waist height before following Worthy, who was already blazing a trail toward their exfil point.

35

Cancer's left arm was killing him.

He was shuffling forward, clasping the twin looped handles at the foot of the litter and painfully aware that more than ten seconds had elapsed since his last rearward scan.

Without slowing his pace, he glanced over his shoulder for incoming fighters—the footprints behind him formed a visual highway in the snow, snaking between trees and out of sight. Despite the visual beacon leading to their current position, however, there was no movement or discernable sound behind him, and he redirected his gaze forward, where Jelena and Reilly carried the litter's front end.

Between them was a very chagrined David Rivers, who had over the previous fifteen minutes or so mastered the art of avoiding eye contact.

Unable to accept that the mafia hordes hadn't yet arrived, Cancer repeated his glance at their backtrail, with identical results.

He was well versed in rear security, and as the team's second-in-command served in the main provider of that capacity more than anyone else.

But it was a far more difficult proposition when carrying the tail end of a fully loaded poleless litter that currently weighed somewhere in the neighborhood of two hundred pounds, most of it consisting of a team leader whose only contribution was keeping his assault pack and satchel from falling off when one or more of the three-person transport team stumbled.

Worthy forged on ahead, free from the usual considerations of monitoring his proximity to the rest of the team beyond a fundamental ability to reinforce them if needed. In stark contrast to a majority of their tactical movements, this was a daylight trek with footprints to follow—there was no risk of anyone wandering off or getting lost, though that single benefit applied doubly so to their pursuers.

The pointman transmitted, "*Be advised, I'm a hundred meters out from the exfil point, slowing the pace. Should have eyes-on in the next minute or so.*"

"Copy," David replied. "Angel, what's your status?"

Ian responded, "*I'm still ten minutes out. Lot of police traffic on the route, but no one's stopped me yet.*"

"We'll get the exfil point secured; plan on a direct approach unless I tell you otherwise."

"*Roger, proceeding.*"

David's gaze fell on Cancer for a brief moment before he looked away, a nonverbal attempt to confirm he wasn't missing something, as if the team leader now realized his judgment required second-guessing. That split second of eye contact was, he thought, probably the wisest thing David had done in the past 24 hours.

But Cancer gave no advice or correction because none was required. There was no chance to retreat, redirect, or alter their plans in any way; at this point, they had to make a beeline for their exfil point, because to do anything else would be to not leave Serbia at all.

As the most experienced man, it fell upon him to monitor the team's collective pulse in terms of fatigue, fear, and confidence or lack thereof. And while that hadn't changed, he ordinarily had a functional team leader to advise—now, however, he bore the full responsibility for both the mundane and the tactical decision-making. David had no idea what the team had gone through to escape the botched aircraft shootdown the previous day, nor what they'd undergone prior to reaching him, which meant that Cancer was running the show.

He looked at Jelena, currently manning the handle on the litter's right side. She had yet to complain but he could tell that her strength was flagging, and Cancer spoke quietly by way of providing a temporary reprieve.

"Switch."

No other guidance was required—they'd pulled this maneuver every few minutes for the duration of the casualty transport.

All three came to a complete stop, lowering David to the ground. While Cancer released his handles at the foot of the litter from his left hand to his right, Reilly and Jelena switched sides to burden their opposite arm, crouching and awaiting his next command.

"One, two, three."

They lifted David once more, and continued following Worthy's tracks.

The team had made remarkable progress toward their exfil point despite their many disadvantages, with their speed no doubt aided by the reality that once the mafia elements in the woods discovered their backtrail atop the ridge, then an enemy element would be inbound at the quickest possible pace.

And the deep sense of fear that Cancer harbored along with that knowledge was compounded exponentially when Worthy transmitted again.

"*Net call, I've got eyes-on our exfil point and it's already occupied by a police checkpoint. There's a squad car down there, two uniformed officers standing around with M4s and sidearms. Doesn't look like they're expecting us.*"

Cancer said, "Hold up."

The formation stopped and lowered David to the ground, after which Reilly and Jelena moved a few steps to either side to pull security. Cancer moved to David's right side and knelt, covering their backtrail as the team leader transmitted, "Angel, be prepared to run a holding pattern until we sort this out."

"*Copy.*"

Cancer whispered, "There's nothing to sort."

But David was unconvinced, objecting quietly, "What if our exfil point is burned?"

"If it was," Cancer continued, "there'd be a hell of a lot more than two cops standing around. They don't have comms, remember? They picked that spot for the same reason we wanted it for exfil: it's a tight turn in the road with concealment in either direction, so no one can see them with time to turn around. We don't have time to wait them out or bump to an alternate location. Bad guys are following our tracks as we speak, and if there's one checkpoint there are going to be others."

"What are you thinking?"

Cancer heaved a sigh, then pointed out the obvious. "Simple. We call in Ian, I smoke the cops, we toss their bodies in the trunk, and Worthy drives the patrol car like it's a police escort for the van. That's a free pass through any remaining checkpoints because none of them have radio traffic telling them otherwise."

"Good plan," David acknowledged, "apart from one detail."

"Which is?"

"Killing them."

Cancer managed to avoid speaking his first thought—namely, *you've got to be fucking kidding me*—and forced himself to present a balanced response. "Don't be an asshole. Mayfly will never be able to tie us to this."

"It's not about that. The state is complicit with the mafia, sure. But it's two beat cops down there. That means they get a chance to surrender, and after that it's on them."

Just when Cancer didn't think he could be any more furious with David, the team leader had found a way to piss him off even more.

"Listen, you little shit—"

"No," David cut him off, "*you* listen. I'm still the team leader, and I've made my decision. The only question is how we skin the cat, and every second you argue with me is another second the Janjicari have to find us. So what's it going to be?"

Cancer keyed his radio and transmitted.

"Racegun, hold fast. Suicide and Doc will pull rear security, I'll move forward to your location to establish overwatch before you move to the road."

Jelena looked over at him and asked, "What about me?"

"Sister," he began, "you're the bait."

36

Worthy descended the slope in near-silence, carefully choosing each footfall to avoid heralding his presence to the two police officers posted fifteen meters away. They continued conversing with one another, a periodic chuckle punctuating their discourse. He could tell they expected their role to begin and end with inspecting vehicle traffic, probably assured that the mafia elements operating in the mountains would take care of any dismounted resistance. Bad situational awareness, he thought, that they'd pay for one way or the other in due time. It was a degree of overconfidence born out of the "big sky, little bullet" theory—with so many forces around them, they simply didn't anticipate they'd actually incur any meaningful degree of risk.

The reality, of course, was far different, and if this was going to turn out badly, the most likely cause would be Worthy betraying his presence too soon.

That role fell to Jelena, who was proceeding toward the cops with considerably less stealth.

He heard her before he saw her, making a noisy approach perpendicular to the road while he paralleled it, their paths converging in an attempt to maintain the best possible fields of fire. By the time Worthy sighted the police officers through the trees ahead, both cops had turned away from him to face Jelena. She was speaking rapidly in her native tongue, effecting the appearance of a hunter-turned-damsel in distress at the sudden gunfire and explosions in the hills behind her.

Worthy wasn't sure how well the gambit would work; these were police officers, after all, and they may or may not be aware that no legal hunter should be in their immediate proximity. While both kept their M4s in hand, neither took aim at the woman who stepped onto the road and approached with her Winchester rifle slung over her shoulder. Worthy, however, raised his HK416 and leveled it at the officers' backsides, both clad in navy snowsuits with sky-blue patches and epaulets. He slowed his march to incremental footfalls, placing one foot and then the other onto the road and closing the final distance for what would be an exceedingly easy pair of target engagements, should he have to take them.

One of the cops barked a response that caused her to halt in her tracks. He took that to be the order for Jelena to stop and put her hands up, and only then did the second officer think to check his backside, looking first up the hill and starting to glance over his shoulder when a cry caused him to look back at the seemingly desperate woman.

She'd bought him an extra two seconds, and Worthy came to a halt with his weapon raised. Jelena spoke a final phrase in Serbian, then pointed directly to Worthy.

Both officers looked at him in unison, their expressions reflecting their shock. And with no time for them to take aim without getting killed in the process, the situation evolved into a pregnant pause where each side waited to see what the other would do, the scene unfolding to the sound of Jelena issuing rapid-fire orders in a commanding tone.

One of the cops looked back at her, then the other, to find that she was now aiming her Winchester directly at them.

And then, almost in perfect unison, they made a move to raise their M4s.

Worthy considered firing a warning shot; at this distance, he'd have time to do so and still gun down both of them if need be.

But before he could squeeze off the shot, two puffs of snow erupted at the side of the road. Cancer had beat him to the punch in a rare show of discretion for the sniper who, Worthy knew all too well, would have far preferred to slay both men by now.

It took a moment for the police officers to process the sight as subsonic bullet impacts, but once they did, one spoke a word to the other and then tossed his M4 down, followed in short order by his partner.

Worthy advanced as Jelena continued issuing orders. The men raised their arms, turned away, and then knelt to be restrained.

37

Ian wheeled the cargo van around the bend in the road, first scanning for any sign of his team and then slamming on the brakes at the sight before him.

The scene was straight out of a bad heist movie more than any discernible paramilitary operation: Worthy and Jelena stuffing two flex-cuffed, blindfolded, and gagged Serbian police officers into the trunk of their own squad car, all while Cancer and Reilly struggled to maintain a two-man carry on a poleless litter bearing David Rivers.

He brought the van to a full stop behind the police car, where Worthy slammed the trunk closed before scrambling for the driver's door as Jelena did the same on the opposite side, both of them clutching M4s and pistols confiscated in the process of apprehending the cops.

Before Ian could linger on the sight, he heard the van's rear doors fly open and looked through the opening in the partition to see David sliding headfirst into the cargo area, his hands steadying an assault pack, rifle, and a checkered satchel.

Reilly and Cancer leapt inside as Ian commented, "Louis Vuitton...nice."

"Good to see you too," David replied.

"What's inside?" Ian began, though that was as far as he could get before Cancer slammed the rear doors closed and shouted, "Drive, asshole!"

Ian directed his gaze forward in time to see the squad car flipping a U-turn and whizzing past with Jelena in the passenger seat.

He pulled forward and mirrored the maneuver with a far worse turning radius, forcing him into a three-point turn that was halfway to completion before Cancer clambered into the seat beside him and grabbed the satellite hand mic.

"Raptor Nine One, this is Cancer, be advised we've recovered Suicide Actual and are proceeding west on exfil. Need you to continue jamming all possible comms, how copy?"

By then Ian was accelerating in pursuit of the commandeered squad car as Mayfly's response rattled through the speaker box.

"*Good copy, what about Sidorov's bag?*"

Cancer sounded incensed as he replied, "Don't worry, we've got it."

Then he ended his transmission and yelled toward the cargo area, "Our dumbass team leader has seen to that."

Rather than object, David asked, "You think this is going to work?"

Ian knew the question was directed at him, but he delayed his response until he'd rounded the next bend. He was, after all, piloting a five-thousand-pound vehicle over a winding road slick with snow and ice.

At last he replied, "If the comms stay jammed, it just might."

He'd barely finished his sentence when Worthy transmitted, "*Police checkpoint ahead.*"

The lightbar atop the point vehicle blazed into a flickering blue glow, and Ian looked beyond it to see an identical squad car parked at the side of the road, with two uniformed officers standing next to it.

It was a bizarre sight, to be sure—normally the team's exfil attempts were conducted with the maximum possible discretion, particularly if they'd been compromised.

Now, they were not only utilizing a public road but announcing their presence outright, all from a position of total vulnerability while transporting a casualty with a broken leg.

But government complicity with organized crime had its benefits, Ian realized, as both officers moved out of the road while looking at the two-vehicle procession with more curiosity than concern. With no radio orders telling them otherwise, the sight was apparently one more in a very long list of seeming paradoxes that they knew well enough by now not to question.

Ian sped past them and transmitted, "Van is clear." Then he returned his focus to the road ahead, where Worthy's squad car led the way west toward the limits of the police perimeter and into relative safety from an intricate web of foes trying to recover the bag that David now held as if it were the only thing in the world that mattered.

38

Worthy guided the squad car around a bend, feeling his blood run cold as he transmitted.

"Another checkpoint coming up—two unarmored vehicles, ten guys. Definitely not police, and I don't think they're mafia either."

"*Then who are they?*" Cancer replied.

Worthy ran through a mental inventory of possible actors seeking to prevent their escape before replying with the only possible conclusion.

"I don't know."

Then, after a final visual assessment, he added, "It's going to be kinetic. Follow my lead."

The two BMW X7 SUVs posted on either side of the road were ringed by men with various new-make assault rifles and, presumably, even more serious hardware packed out of sight. Some were smoking, most were clad in jeans and black leather jackets worn over tactical kit, and all were apparently unfazed by the cold.

One of them stepped into the road and threw up a fist, signaling Worthy to stop—whoever they were, these people weren't naive. They not only understood the extent of government corruption but were active participants in it, operating with the full confidence that a police car would stop at their say-so. Were they national intelligence? Secret police? Worthy wasn't sure, though he knew that while they didn't have radio communications, if he were to speed forward and run over the man flagging them down, he'd soon have two vehicles and a minimum of ten men in pursuit.

So he slowed instead and spoke to Jelena beside him.

"Hand me that Benelli."

She slid the shotgun to him barrel first, and Worthy used his left hand to roll the driver's window down before gripping the steering wheel in a straight arm position that would, in the coming seconds, serve as a shooting rest.

With his right hand, he positioned the semiautomatic shotgun over his left bicep and flicked the safety off as the man approached his left side.

Worthy took a final glance at the vehicles on either side of the road ahead, solidifying his plan before looking out the open window.

The approaching man spoke as he moved, not in Serbian but English, and with a markedly Italian accent.

"Who is in the van—"

With a final reflexive adjustment in the Benelli's barrel orientation, Worthy pulled the trigger to unleash a deafening shotgun blast that echoed in the squad car but projected far worse effects beyond. The man's face vaporized with a single close-range headshot of double-aught buck, and then Worthy floored the accelerator while taking aim at his real target: the front wheel of the BMW to his left. He engaged it with a single shot that sparked off the rim and blasted tiny chunks away from the rubber.

One man down and a vehicle out of the fight, he thought, and he sped past the kill zone as the first incoming bullets thunked into the car and shattered the rear window.

Cancer had one foot atop the passenger seat and the other braced against the floorboard as he angled his HK417 through the window to open fire as Ian floored the accelerator.

He took aim at the men scrambling to cover on the right side of the road, letting loose a wild spray of suppressed shots and adjusting his barrel on a second-by-second basis as the van sped forward. At this point it would be enough to keep his opponents' heads down long enough to disable their vehicle; if Worthy had been successful in taking out a tire of the SUV on the opposite side, and Cancer was sure he had, then the sniper stood a chance of cutting off a new pursuit before it began. Without radio or cell communications, these guys weren't going anywhere if their vehicles were out of the fight.

Worthy's warning that this checkpoint would require a kinetic engagement had given the team members in the van just enough time to lower the windows to prepare: in the back, Reilly was shielding David's body with his own while Ian performed the far more useful function of spraying his assault rifle one-handed out the driver's side.

Cancer had seeded just enough subsonic rounds to clear the bad guys out of the way beside him, and he dropped his point of aim toward the wheels of the BMW to empty the remainder of his magazine. If the X7 had been parked facing the opposite direction, he'd have already lit up the engine block—but blowing a tire was a sufficient consolation prize. He was about to do just that when an enemy fighter appeared behind the bumper, swinging a light machinegun in a low orientation to blast at the van's wheels.

And with that, Cancer was fucked—he was a half-second away from his vehicle and all its occupants becoming stranded well within view of every opponent at the checkpoint, and if he continued on his current plan it wouldn't matter whether he disabled the second enemy vehicle or not.

He chose the lesser of two evils, reflexively aiming at the man and cracking off round after round with all the accuracy he could maintain from the confines of a moving vehicle.

One of his bullets struck the man's arm, causing him to recoil long enough for Cancer to fire three more times in rapid succession. Whether those final rounds were hits or misses, he had no idea, but he didn't hear a burst from the light machinegun amid the mounting roar of wind. Spinning into a reverse firing position, he leaned out the window in the hopes of scoring a hit against the engine block while he still could.

Too late. The van had rounded the bend, and the enemy force was gone from view.

Cancer remained in position nonetheless, conducting a reload from his awkward stance and taking the time to transition into a left-handed grip on his HK417 before the surviving SUV came speeding around the bend.

Worthy transmitted, "*One man and one vehicle down.*"

Cancer replied, "I took out another dude, but they've still got the other truck. I'll try to take them on the move."

But the view behind the van showed him that wouldn't be possible.

At first, he thought the men weren't bothering to pursue at all; then, he caught a glimpse of the X7 rounding the bend behind them.

Before he could so much as adjust his aim, the vehicle promptly braked and disappeared from view.

Cancer slid back into his passenger seat and transmitted, "They're hanging back, trailing us from a distance. I'm assuming all eight of the survivors are packed in the vehicle."

"It's smart," Ian said, keying his radio for the team's benefit as he thought aloud. "Why risk a shootout when they can trail us out of jammer range and call in the cavalry? Racegun, did you get any idea who they were?"

Cancer was in the process of reloading Ian's weapon for him when Worthy replied, "*No idea. Only guy I heard had an Italian accent.*"

"Shit," Ian hissed.

Cancer whipped his head sideways, trying to discern why that would upset an intelligence operative.

Ian explained, "Remember who else has an Italian accent?"

"Yeah," David replied, "because I talked to him over the captured sat phone: Erik Weisz."

"So?" Cancer asked.

Ian went on, "Everything up to now has just been Serbians—mafia searching the hills, police manning the cordon. The guys following us are neither, which means they're a crack team Weisz sent to take possession of Sidorov's bag once it was found, and deliver it to him. Now, all they need to do is flee the jammer bubble or wait a half hour for the EA-18 to go off station. Then they can put out an APB, and that's as good as killing us. We have to find a way to take them down, and that's not going to be easy."

Cancer scanned his mirror for any sign of their pursuers and then pulled out his phone to scrutinize the route ahead and, therefore, their tactical options.

He said, “It’s a few guys in one car. They bleed like anyone else.”

“Don’t underestimate the hired guns,” David called out from the cargo area. “Remember how good we were as mercenaries?”

Ian accelerated to keep Worthy and Jelena’s police car in sight. “I agree. These guys aren’t going to fall for the usual bullshit.”

“Fine,” Cancer shot back, zooming in on his phone’s navigation imagery, “we’ll get fancy. In a few klicks the road makes a hairpin turn that loops around a monastery and back on itself, with two road outlets in between. We set our ambush just south of the loop, before these guys reach a connecting road that takes them out of jammer range. They’ll have to pass through because there’s no other route they can take, and if we don’t see them it means they’ve already turned around. So within two minutes of stopping, we either ambush them or proceed to the next civilization to steal cars and beat the APB. Happy?”

Ian didn’t seem convinced, nor did he second-guess Cancer’s assessment.

“We don’t have a choice,” he said grimly.

Cancer keyed his mic.

“Racegun, pay attention: here’s what we’re going to do.”

39

Ian braked the van to a halt behind the squad car, whose driver and passenger doors flew open as Worthy darted into the strip of woods to the left and Jelena scrambled behind the wheel.

Behind him, a far less graceful debarkation was taking place for the remainder of his team in the van—Cancer and Reilly slid David's litter out of the cargo area amid a soundtrack of grunts and curses from both the transport crew and their human cargo.

Ian accelerated the moment the rear doors slammed shut, pursuing Jelena in the squad car as they drove northward.

He glanced at his side-view mirror, momentarily glimpsing his teammates moving out with David's body suspended in the litter between them, trying to catch up with Worthy as he slipped into the trees to establish an ambush line overlooking the road. The enemy vehicle would be engaged long before its occupants got close enough to identify the tracks; Ian's concern, however, was that his team wouldn't have time to set up for an attack before the enemy vehicle appeared in the first place.

But sure enough, they vanished into the trees while the road behind them remained clear, a testament to the tremendous burst of speed both vehicles had applied in the final straightaway.

Then Ian's focus shifted ahead, where the stolen police cruiser was already slowing for a tight left-hand turn that looped around a series of buildings identified on the map as *Manastir Rača*.

He followed the cruiser uphill past a solid perimeter wall, above which the monastery's structures were partially visible: bright yellow dormitories, a looming stone church flanked by a tower, all set to the backdrop of snow-capped pines rising in mountain peaks all around. Ian negotiated the van through the curve and past two road outlets to his right, circling the monastery completely before the road doubled back on itself. Then he proceeded south on a winding downhill course that very nearly paralleled the route they'd just traversed.

Jelena came to a stop less than a quarter mile later, blocking the road with the squad car as if police business were in progress.

The reality was far different, Ian thought as he killed the engine and exited with his HK416, locking the van as he followed her into the strip of woods to the left.

He dreaded being forced back into physical activity amidst the throbbing pain in his abdomen that had only worsened during the flight through the woods to rescue David, and grunted before transmitting, "We've parked, moving to your location now."

"*Copy*," Cancer replied, and as Ian pursued Jelena through the trees and toward the team's ambush position, he was struck that Cancer had been able to reply at all. They'd outpaced the Italians somewhat, to be sure, but not *that* much. At this point Ian and Jelena were rushing in the hopes they'd make it in time to reinforce a final assault on the crippled X7 before reversing course back to their vehicles. It was simply inconceivable to him that they'd arrive before the ambush commenced.

And yet there were no sounds of gunfire, suppressed or otherwise, by the time he caught sight of his teammates.

Cancer was on the left flank, poised with his HK417 as Reilly did the same on the opposite side of the formation. Between them was David, now in the prone atop his litter with Worthy beside him, both taking aim at a road that still, impossibly, remained empty.

Jelena moved for a gap on the right side, so Ian crouched low and ran beside Cancer, dropping to his stomach and trying to ignore the pain as he angled for a view of the kill zone and awaited the noise from an inbound vehicle.

Nothing.

"*Angel*," David transmitted, "*what the fuck?*"

He sounded as if this unexpected development were a result of Ian's choice instead of the Italians', to which Cancer added, "Maybe they ended their pursuit."

"They didn't," Ian replied, "I can assure you of that."

"Yeah? Then where are they?"

Ian considered the particulars of their situation.

His team was positioned south of the hairpin loop in the road, with a monastery to the north. If their opponents were truly a crack team sent by Weisz—and Ian could explain the presence of Italians no other way—then they weren't about to let a group of Americans escape unopposed with Sidorov's bag. That meant they were still pursuing, which seemed impossible given that their vehicle hadn't arrived.

There was only one possible explanation, and he provided it to his team in the next transmission.

"They anticipated this ambush," he said, "which means we're being hunted. They're already here."

Cancer was on his feet and moving by the time Ian completed his radio message.

"*They're going to hit us from the east, or south.*"

As an intelligence operative, Ian's assessments were typically beyond reproach, but he was no master tactician.

That role fell to Cancer, and he transmitted as he ran northward, "Leave the gimp, everyone else follow me."

He didn't doubt Ian's assessment that the Italians were already outmaneuvering them, but there was no way they'd risk an approach directly into an ambush line. If they knew where that ambush was positioned, the smart move was to dismount south of it, then conduct a flank up the east side of the treeline before circling back on the other side of the road. No way they'd risk a head-on approach from the east, and despite Ian's assumption, they also wouldn't risk wandering into a kill zone by coming from the woods to the south.

Ian transmitted, "*You think they're coming* through *the monastery?*"

"They don't have to worry about cops," Cancer replied, moving quickly now as he identified the edge of the treeline to his front. "We do. If they're really on foot and trying to cut us off, they'd isolate the road outlets to the north and try to flush us back south, toward the police perimeter. Racegun, Doc, you're on the left flank, first maneuver element when I give the word."

Worthy replied, "*You really want to send two against eight?*"

"Everyone else but Suicide will move once you establish a foothold. And there ain't gonna be eight of them for long."

He came to a stop behind a tree and a fallen trunk, using the juncture between the two as a platform to rest his HK417 as he assumed a cross-legged shooting position, quickly settling and then leaning forward into his buttstock.

Then he took a deep inhale to steady his breathing, peering through his optic as he scanned the buildings to his front from right to left. There wasn't much open ground for the enemy to cover, just a scant thirty-meter expanse before the first outbuilding. After that, a pile of stacked logs and three parked vehicles separated him from the next pair of farmhouse-like structures, and behind them were the yellow walls of the monastery dormitories and the stone church beyond. This place was probably infested with tourists during the warmer seasons, but for now it was a snowy, silent expanse occupied only by a group of blackbirds pecking at the snow in the clearing.

The monastery was positioned in the bowl between mountains, providing his opponents with the benefit of a slightly uphill vantage point. If he was right about this, the Italian team hadn't just anticipated how the Americans would react but also composed and executed their response with alarming speed and precision.

And Cancer intended to make them pay for it.

For one thing, it irritated him beyond all measure to have a small group of Italians standing between his team and certain escape after all they'd been through. For another, time wasn't on their side, and the sooner they could be on their way, the better. Cancer was determined to remove this burden from his team with the precision fire he'd mastered over his lengthy combat experience, and he steeled himself with the resolute thought that anyone who crossed his sights would be dead with the first shot.

The blackbirds suddenly took flight, flapping skyward from their pecking grounds.

Cancer turned his barrel toward the flash of movement and, more importantly, the rightmost farmhouse nearest it. Not a second too late, as it turned out—the disturbance had barely come and gone before he identified a human form that he was sorely tempted to engage immediately, restraining himself only out of the solemn reminder that it wouldn't do his karma any good to smoke a monk.

But the man at the end of his reticle revealed himself to be armed a moment later, edging past the building's corner to lift a rifle and sweep the woodline. Cancer had the drop on him, but would nonetheless have preferred to let the pointman proceed past the building and bring his comrades trundling into the clearing before opening fire.

It was, however, not worth the risk.

Whether that enemy fighter had a magnified optic atop his rifle or not, Cancer risked the man spotting either himself or his teammates. He took the slack out of his trigger and broke a clean shot, his 7.62mm round flying true and causing the partially exposed target to fall forward into the snow without a further twitch of movement.

And then—nothing happened.

It was an eerie dissonance to what he'd expected from long years of experience in battle confrontations...men shouting, immediate return fire, and, in the luckiest of circumstances, valorous but tactically idiotic fighters racing into view in an attempt to recover their lost comrade.

But silence ensued instead, and nothing bothered Cancer more. If these guys were as good as they'd proved to be thus far, they hadn't sent that man in alone, nor out of view from the main formation. That meant they knew full well that one of theirs had just died, and conducted the deeply unsettling response of adjusting their approach without fanfare.

He transmitted, "One down, haven't seen anyone else. Seven bad guys remaining."

"*We can't see anyone else,*" Worthy said. "*What do you want to do?*"

It was a good question, and Cancer took a moment to consider his options. A successful counter-assault could end this here and now. Then again, racing forward into a cluster of buildings was a recipe for disaster, as was letting the remaining Italians steal a car only to get back on the team's tail with an unrecognizable vehicle.

The key question was whether the enemy force was fully committed, and Cancer assessed that they were. That was a pointman he'd just slain, and while a daylight charge toward buildings and their many elevated vantage points would ordinarily be lunacy, the Italians had been planning on a hasty dismounted assault south into the woods, which meant they were currently on the ground—and that leveled the playing field considerably. While the Italians were currently somewhere among the monastery structures ahead, they wouldn't be for long, and whatever their response would be to the loss of a man, it wasn't going to bode well for Cancer's team.

His only chance to turn the tables resided in pressing the initiative, in resorting to attack rather than retreat, in the hopes of slaying this final threat to their escape.

"Fuck it," he transmitted, "we're assaulting. Racegun and Doc, flank left—the rest of us will cover you. Go secure a foothold."

Reilly charged out of the woods and into the clearing, desperately trying to keep pace with Worthy, who ran a few meters ahead. But the pointman was a quick bastard, and the vast disparity in their respective body weight worked overwhelmingly in his favor when it came to speed.

They were paralleling the west side of the road that looped around the monastery, making for the leftmost of the two farmhouse outbuildings between them and the yellow buildings ahead. Reilly caught sight of a fallen body in the snow, Cancer's one and only kill on this objective; there were no additional enemy in sight, leaving the medic to wonder if the dead man was some kind of singleton probing element rather than a vanguard for the entire enemy force.

He tried to hurry, fearing that Worthy would arrive at their destination well ahead of him and be faced with possible targets and incoming gunfire alone. Seconds mattered in times like this, particularly when they were the first maneuver element to spill out of the woods. Whatever the vantage point from the building ahead, it would expose countless visual angles that Cancer, Ian, and Jelena wouldn't be able to see. Worthy was about to face that risk alone for as long as it took for Reilly to arrive, and yet when the medic tried to press on with all the speed he could, the pointman continued to extend his lead.

Then fate intervened in spectacular fashion.

Worthy's boot clipped some unseen obstacle beneath the snow—Reilly couldn't tell what, but he saw the pointman go from vertical to horizontal as he flew forward and crashed into the ground.

It was a horrendous and potentially fatal misstep, the kind that never made it into war movies, and Reilly never broke stride. Instead he altered his path just to the left of Worthy, lifting his feet slightly higher to avoid the same end result, and blew past the spot long before the pointman managed to push himself upright.

Now it was Reilly proceeding alone into the fray, closing the final distance with a roof overhang sloping off the left side of the building ahead. The space below was littered with what appeared to be rusty farm equipment, a melee of tripping hazards if ever he'd seen one. He made the split-second judgment that it was a risk worth negotiating in the interests of taking up a firing position from the shadows rather than circling the building completely and, very likely, getting blasted into oblivion as a result.

He decelerated rapidly and slipped beneath the overhang, activating the taclight on his rifle to illuminate a pile of ancient wheels beside a tractor and threading his way along a wall covered by hanging tools: spades, axes, pitchforks, and rakes. Then he dodged a pile of corroded chain on the ground, cutting off his light well before he reached the far edge.

Slowing before the corner, he took aim directly forward and then began sidestepping to clear an arc of visibility ever further beyond the edge.

A low, one-story structure sat directly to his front, and he'd barely panned his aim to its rightmost edge before identifying a similar farmhouse overhang on the building opposite, as well as a flash of movement between them—one of the Italians darting from left to right in some kind of a formation adjustment in progress.

Reilly dropped to a knee and opened fire, chasing the figure with rapid single shots, unable to determine whether he'd scored a hit before the man vanished.

No matter, because the next enemy fighter appeared in short order, this one evidenced by a muzzle flash beneath the overhang of the second farmhouse. This guy, Reilly thought as blasting shots shattered the quiet, had taken up a nearly identical position to himself.

He returned fire with a majority of his remaining magazine, noting from the puffs of bullet impacts that he wasn't the only one returning fire.

Worthy had taken up a position behind him, his shell casings ricocheting off the building and raining down on Reilly as he continued to fire. He heard the clanging pops of incoming bullets striking the tractor behind him before the twinkling muzzle flash finally faded to darkness, and a man's arm was visible writhing in the snow where the shadow met the sun. Reilly used the limb as a reference point for the remainder of the enemy's body, and he continued shooting until his weapon was empty, then conducted an emergency reload as Worthy transmitted.

"Cancer, I think they're flushing east. One more down, and we're in position. You're good to move."

Ian fanned out to Cancer's left, trailing as the sniper advanced on the rightmost farmhouse. He glanced over to see Jelena keeping pace on the opposite side, and beyond her stretched a watermill channel that would limit their ability to push much farther to the east.

No matter, he thought, because all they needed was to skirt the right wall of the building ahead to gain a clear line of sight to the dormitory that stood between them and the church. If the Italians moved west, they'd be in Worthy and Reilly's line of fire; east, and Ian's maneuver element would hopefully be able to gun them down.

That restricted the enemy's options of egress to the north alone, provided they were going to run at all. The team's sudden counter-assault had certainly taken them by surprise, coming as it did just as they were preparing to make for the woods after an audacious flanking maneuver that Ian had been lucky to anticipate. The Italians were a crack team, no doubt, and the numerical odds were damn near equal at this point. More likely than not, the advantage would go to whichever side demonstrated the most audacity in the next minute or two—and given that Cancer was at the helm of his team's response, if they lost now it certainly wouldn't be a result of timidity.

Cancer and Jelena suddenly broke left in unison, clearly having seen something that was denied to Ian by virtue of his position on the flank of the small wedge formation.

Ian heard successive volleys of unsuppressed gunfire a moment later. The Italians were making their stand on the opposite side of the farmhouse ahead, he reasoned, though from the rate they were burning through ammo he wasn't sure how long they could hold that position.

He took cover behind the building's southern wall while Cancer positioned himself at the corner and Jelena instinctively followed—it was a necessary strongpoint, no doubt, because to cede it would be to allow the Italians to get behind them. Given how much suppressive fire the enemy were laying down, that seemed a very real possibility.

But Ian sensed they had another intention, though he couldn't fathom what that was.

He cut left and moved to the corner opposite Cancer, approaching a fallen enemy fighter whose lifeless arm extended beneath the overhang. The sight brought him no small measure of comfort, mostly because it indicated he was proceeding under the watchful eyes of Worthy and Reilly at the other farmhouse; then he saw them break into a run on their way north, causing his sense of reassurance to give way to crushing self-doubt. They must have thought his solo movement meant that the rest of his maneuver element was pinned down, and taken the initiative to bring up the left flank by advancing toward the final one-story building between them and the monastery's vast dormitory. Now his one and only advantage was that adrenaline had almost fully suppressed the soul-crushing pain of his abdominal injury.

No going back now, Ian thought as he pivoted right around the corner, visually clearing the shadows of the overhang before stepping over the dead combatant and proceeding along the wall amid the smell of rust and machine grease. As he threaded his way between piles of scrap metal and rolls of baling wire, he heard the enemy continuing to shoot wildly in unsustainable salvos. They weren't going to maneuver south, he knew, but were instead trying to conceal something that was occurring north of the farmhouse.

Rather than advance he angled his steps left, seeing that the watermill channel ran along the dormitory ahead. The Italians were boxed in at the crook of the water feature, which made their taking a stand at the expense of maneuvering all the more incomprehensible.

The explanation for this seeming disparity occurred with his next footfall as he slipped behind a tractor plow—there was a bridge leading over the channel, and on the other side was an alleyway in the dormitory wall toward which an enemy fighter limped.

Ian took aim, now seeing that it wasn't one but two opponents—one of them must have been wounded by Reilly or Worthy, and the other was helping him to safety. That explained the volume of fire, he reasoned; they weren't preparing to advance but rather covering a retreat, holding their ground until their wounded comrade cleared the dormitory.

A wave of nausea overcame him as he steadied his sights and opened fire, hitting the uninjured fighter in the small of his back and dropping him in place. The wounded Italian he'd been helping along staggered a half-step before falling himself, trying to take aim but in the wrong direction, unsure of where the gunfire had originated until his final moment.

Ian shot him three times, then adjusted his point of aim to the man who'd been trying to help him to safety before firing again with the knowledge that this scene would haunt him for years to come, if not the rest of his life. There was self-defense and there was cold-blooded murder, and his actions just now were identifiable as the former only by the broadest possible definitions.

But he'd barely broken the trigger before a shape appeared around the corner ahead, and Ian reflexively fell backward to exploit the cover of the tractor plow behind which he'd taken his shots.

An automatic burst exploded, the bullets cracking through the air and off the metal plow as Ian pushed himself up to a seated position, taking aim to the side of his cover in anticipation of an opponent coming to finish him off.

Instead the volley ended to the sound of a man shouting in Italian, after which all the other gunfire went silent at almost the same instant.

Ian assumed a crouch and listened for movement before finally rising enough to take aim at the alleyway.

He saw a man dart into it, vanishing before he could take a shot. Ian waited for another enemy to appear before realizing they'd fled already, and he lowered his rifle to see a tall steeple rising over the yellow dormitory wall before transmitting.

"They're moving north. Racegun, Doc, you need to outflank them and set up overwatch on the church before they get away."

Worthy ran forward along the dormitory wall, leading the way for Reilly and thinking that this day was never going to end.

Ian's order for them to keep moving north and set up overwatch on the church had seemed perfectly reasonable, right up until Worthy finally figured out everything working against him.

The main issue was the dormitory building itself. It was a massive L-shaped structure that seemed to have no outlets beyond the passage that the other maneuver element had apparently chased the Italians into. No matter, Worthy had thought, he'd just go through the building; at least, that had been his plan until discovering that each of the tremendous wooden doors was locked, and probably had been from the moment the first gunshots rang out. Nor could he do anything as trite as smashing through a window to climb inside—they were constructed of thick slabs of glass that would take no small amount of time to inflict a crack in with the buttstock of his rifle.

Without breaching equipment, the quickest possible solution was the one he executed now: namely, racing up the west wing of the building all the way to the monastery's northern perimeter.

In tactical terms, they'd transcended the mere foolish and entered a realm of sheer absurdity—he and Reilly were moving even farther from their getaway vehicles, to say nothing of the team leader they'd readily abandoned at the ambush site, all in the hopes of outmaneuvering the enemy fighters driven back by the initial counter-assault. If it worked, the payoff was immeasurable: finishing the fight once and for all, and securing their exfil. And if it didn't, well, the team couldn't afford another casualty. David required a minimum of a two-man carry, and three for anything beyond an extremely short distance. That alone would take the majority of their remaining members, and if even one more in their ranks was immobilized, it would cripple the team in its entirety.

Finally he saw the end of the dormitory wall ahead, slowing with his HK416 raised in case the enemy was about to race out in front of him.

But he arrived at the corner without incident, dropping to a knee and executing a ninety-degree pivot to peer beyond it toward the snow-covered grounds ringing the church. Worthy felt Reilly post up behind him as he took aim toward the only visible movement, the sight through his optic making it clear the remaining Italians hadn't anticipated a bold flank up the dormitory's west side.

Three men were visible, all breaking contact to the north, fleeing past the stone church that provided total cover and concealment from the maneuver element that had sent them bounding back across the monastery—but not from Worthy and Reilly, who opened fire at once.

It was a tragic sight, in a way; minutes ago, Worthy's team had risked getting wiped out, but the instant that balance of power had shifted, the battle became a shooting gallery. Returning fire against opponents who were trying to kill you was one thing, but these men were unquestionably fleeing. No maneuvering to a more advantageous firing position, just a full-blown retreat, and Worthy took no pride in shooting fellow human beings in the back.

But he did so anyway, knowing full well that just as his team had turned the tables seconds earlier, so too could that balance be swung the opposite way with absolute and irreversible finality. The trio was cut down in a hail of 5.56 and 7.62mm fire from Worthy and his team medic, stumbling and falling in quick succession. Nor did this victory mean that the shooting was over—both men continued firing against targets that were now stationary or close to it, one of them rolling onto his side in an attempt to identify his assailants and get a final burst before life escaped him. He never had the chance as Worthy's next round punctured his chest cavity and caused him to go still at last.

Another was already dead or very nearly so, his limbs twitching as he flopped about spasmodically before he too was hit again. The third enemy was a corpse or doing an admirable job of feigning it with stock-stillness, and both teammates lit him up with a final volley of fire that ended in silence as they scanned the courtyard for further threats. It had been an ugly engagement, free of any cause for pride as the gritty matters of battlefield survival often were. But the monastery was quiet, and however many monks lived here in service to God, they'd wisely chosen to remain inside.

"Reloading," Reilly said quietly.

Worthy put his weapon on safe and replied, "Go ahead."

The words had barely escaped his lips when the church door flew open. The pointman took aim and flicked his weapon to semiautomatic in the time it took him to register the lone figure standing there.

He was close to seven feet tall, a scowling, broad-nosed man with bushy black eyebrows and an unkept white beard descending past his sternum. Clad in a formal black robe and matching hat, he looked toward them in disdain and then returned inside, slamming the door behind him.

Reilly murmured, "I'm good," and Worthy conducted a hasty tactical reload with the words, "Looked like Santa Claus after a few years on the homeless trail."

"I was thinking Merlin with a smack problem."

"Good one."

"I know, right?" the medic panted, still trying to catch his breath as he transmitted, "Cancer, we've got three confirmed, no further movement."

The sniper replied, "*Nice work, we're out of here. Start bounding back—*"

But that was as far as he made it before Ian interrupted.

"*Say again, how many EKIA?*"

"Three," Reilly answered.

"Cancer and you each got one, I got two, and you and Racegun just got three —that equals seven confirmed, which means one is still out there."

At this, Cancer hastily transmitted to the team member in the greatest danger from this revelation.

"Suicide, be advised there's one bad guy unaccounted for. He might have fled into the hills, but we're spread too thin to know for sure. He could be headed your way."

I ripped out my earpieces and used my left hand to key the radio three times, indicating both my distress and the fact that he was positively correct. That was the only thing I had time to do while rolling to my side to face the sound of footsteps racing toward me from the north.

If I was lucky he'd race past without seeing me, but the footfalls sounded like they were on a collision course with my position. I wondered if he was following my team's tracks with the knowledge that they represented a surefire path between the forest's obstacles and patches of bramble that he couldn't afford to get tangled up in now.

Or maybe, I thought, he was searching for an opponent to kill.

My sideways roll occurred amid an explosion of pain detonating within my fractured tibia, but I managed to make the most of an extremely suboptimal position, orienting my suppressor toward the incoming noise with barely enough time to take aim in the gap between trees before the man appeared.

I was vulnerable and fully exposed, uncamouflaged and in the prone—but that last detail seemed to be working to my advantage.

His gaze was fixated well above me, scanning the trees ahead and not the ground before him, and by the time he corrected that oversight it was too late to save him. My index finger cycled the trigger with fluid repetition as I lobbed subsonic rounds into the ever-decreasing space between us, first striking him in the thigh, then the lower abdominal, and finally the gut as he crashed to the ground on his back and very nearly skidded into me. That first shot must have struck his femur, I thought, resulting in the supreme irony that now both of us were lying out here with broken legs—

and I hoisted myself to a sitting position before taking aim to finish him off.

The Italian was wearing civilian boots, jeans, and a black leather jacket unzipped over a tactical vest bearing magazines for the Beretta assault rifle that now lay clutched in one hand.

He shifted his grip on the weapon and I took the slack out of my trigger, but before I pulled the shot off, he cast the weapon away, first taking a look at my face, then the extent of his injuries, before finally letting the back of his head rest on the snow with a ragged sigh.

I took in his appearance: a shock of dark hair that was well-combed with product despite the nature of his presence in Serbia, manicured stubble, and deep brown eyes that looked skyward as he spoke in accented English. "I did not think any of you stayed behind."

"I didn't have a choice," I replied. Then, as I saw him using his left hand to reach for a pouch on his vest, I shouted, "Don't even fucking think about it."

He gave a dreamy half-smile, panting for breath as he said, "My cigarettes. You would not deny a dying man one final smoke, would you?"

Before responding, I flicked my rifle's selector lever to fully automatic, an all but useless function in most circumstances outside of point blank range, which this most certainly was.

Then I said, "Only if you let me bum one."

He procured a pack, shaking a cigarette out of it with remarkable aplomb given he was going to bleed out in the snow in the next minute or two, then tossed the pack onto my lap and sparked it with a gold lighter that he flung my way.

I used my left hand to retrieve both items, keeping my weapon trained on him as I lit my own cigarette, then glanced at the lighter. It was engraved with a worn insignia that appeared to be some military unit symbol, far too weathered to have originated with him. An heirloom handed down from a grandfather, I imagined, throwing it toward his side as I took my first drag.

"You're Italian," I said.

He blew a plume of smoke skyward.

"And you are CIA."

"Guilty as charged," I admitted. "You were sent by Erik Weisz. Who is he?"

He lifted his head slightly, just enough for me to see that his expression was one of surprise.

"If you do not know, how should I? We are mercenaries. We hear nothing but whispers and rumors."

I considered his words against my own experience, then decided it checked out. "Yeah, I know a thing or two about that. You're not the only one with a mercenary background, believe me."

I was still on guard, watching the man's hands as he smoked although he made no effort to resist me. Deciding to push my luck, I asked, "What do you know about the death of Kimberly Bannister?"

It was a struggle to recall Duchess's birth name, so ubiquitous was her callsign in Agency channels. And while I didn't expect a straightforward answer, I watched his eyes for recognition. There was none.

Instead he took another drag and said, "This name means nothing to me." Then, his head tilting and gaze falling on Sidorov's bag at my side, he continued, "All I know is that I was sent to find the satchel…and now, I have. Not quite how I expected, I must admit. My team?"

"Dead," I replied. "You're the last."

He swallowed, giving a sad little nod.

"They died with honor, then."

I nodded back. "So will you. I hope I can say the same when my time comes."

"You fight for your country, no?"

"Yes. I didn't always. Can't say I've found much of a difference between the two."

He chuckled, his voice sounding more strained when he replied. The end was drawing near for him, blood continuing to pool in the snow at his sides.

"Then you are a wise man. It matters not who sends us—the team is what matters. That is the only thing that does, in this chaos."

I placed the cigarette in my lips.

"Sounds like you're the wise one, not me."

"And yet it is you who shall survive, and not me."

"For now. Our fates will be no different."

"Indeed," he said weakly, pausing as his left leg twitched once and then went still. "The same end awaits us all."

Then he lifted a hand to the cigarette, plucking it from his lips to flick it up and away. My eyes instinctively followed the burning projectile for a moment, but no more.

By the time my focus returned to him, he was reaching for a pistol beneath his jacket with such speed and fluidity that I feared I wouldn't be able to stop him in time.

But I had a fixed point of aim with a weapon that was already set to full auto, and despite his admirable attempt at distraction, there was no beating the odds. Ultimately, I knew, he just wanted to die as his teammates had, as all warriors secretly do beneath the conscious delusions of retirement: in battle, fighting until the dying breath.

He'd already taken his, and I depressed my trigger to slit him apart from solar plexus to throat to forehead in a single protracted burst.

The action, however, was scarcely complete before another set of running footfalls crunched through the snow. Once more I inflicted the severe and mind-blowing pain required to take aim; too late, as it turned out, because by the time I did so, the incoming threat was already pointing the business end of his rifle toward me—which, a moment later, changed entirely.

Cancer lowered his weapon, taking in the scene with a rueful shake of his head. "Christ, David...smoking with the enemy? I didn't figure you for a traitor."

"Neither did I, brother," I replied, looking for my cigarette, which had fallen in the snow at some point during the brief engagement. "Neither did I."

40

"Heads up," Cancer called from the passenger seat.

Worthy leaned forward in the van's cargo area, looking past Jelena at the wheel to identify the flashing blue light atop an inbound squad car not unlike the one they'd left behind at the monastery. With the jamming effort concluded and word of a shooting at Rača Monastery already hitting the airwaves, it was entirely possible the inbound officers were headed there.

But there was a far more insidious possibility as well, and it served as the reason for Worthy's positioning at the rear cargo door.

He locked eyes with Reilly, seated across from him as the only real backup he'd have. Ian sat beside the medic, but by the time he dismounted as the third man, the engagement would already be over—without loss of life, if at all possible, but nothing was going to stop the van's progress to the cabin safehouse.

Worthy heard the siren now, growing in volume as the two vehicles closed the distance with each other. David adjusted his grip on the HK416 across his chest, and while they'd positioned him with his boots toward the cargo doors so he could cover at least one sector of fire, the truth was that if they had to rely on him to shoot anyone, then the entire situation was totally fucked to begin with.

The siren rose to a deafening volume as Worthy regulated his breathing to offset a quickening pulse—and then the car roared past the driver's side of the van, receding into the distance behind them.

Reilly heaved a long sigh, then leaned back and let his head rest against the side of the van.

Cancer announced, "Fifteen minutes to the safehouse. Still no APB for us."

Well that was something, Worthy thought.

Now that both the mafia and law enforcement were free to communicate over their radio networks, the CIA was relegated to persistent blocking of the local cell towers while passively monitoring various frequencies in an attempt to guide the team's efforts.

Reilly said to no one in particular, "I'm going to need some rakia once we make it back."

"We'll make it back," Ian assured him, "but we're going to have to strip the van and abandon it somewhere. I don't care how many times we change license plates—between the vet clinic and everything that just went down, the make and model alone are too high profile at this point."

Worthy shrugged. "I agree. The real question is how and when we make our move for the border."

David looked up from his litter and protested, "We're forgetting one thing."

"What's that?"

"The Belgrade conspiracy. *Our* conspiracy."

"I don't know what that means."

The team leader explained, "Everyone is going to expect us to flee the country after all this, right? So we've got some room to move in Belgrade."

Reilly objected, "What's left for us there?"

"Gudelj. He shot Ian—no way he's coming out of this without a scratch."

Worthy fired back, "Well we can't exactly ask the Agency for intel as to his whereabouts, now can we?" Then, nodding toward Sidorov's bag on the floor beside David, he added, "And Mayfly's going to want that intel out of Serbia asap. We don't have enough time to run a stakeout."

Ian sucked his teeth and winced.

"We might not have to, though."

"How's that?"

"The Bulgarian hit squad," Ian explained, "that we took out at the liquor store at the start of this whole thing. They had a full packet on him, pattern of life and everything. I've still got a digital copy. Gudelj dealt with the New Zemun threat, so it's reasonable to assume he'll resume at least some facets of his normal routine."

Worthy objected, "All right, I'm not one to back down from a good fight, but let's think this through. This entire op has been a nightmare from start to finish."

"Right," David confirmed.

"We burned our first airfield," the pointman continued, "and were lucky to find out that Sidorov bumped to an alternate site."

"Go on."

"After which we brought down the plane by a miracle shot, to say the least, which would've been great if you hadn't gone rogue to go after that stupid bag—"

"It's a satchel."

"—and break your leg in the process."

"Yeah, yeah," David said dismissively, waving a hand from his litter, "and then you guys rescued me, which I knew you would. Italians showed up, blah blah blah. What's your point?"

Worthy rubbed his jaw, trying to figure out how to word his response when one shouldn't have been required in the first place.

"My point is, maybe we should be grateful we got this far and cut our losses."

Reilly thrust an arm toward him and exploded, "Finally, a voice of reason."

Then Cancer looked over from the passenger seat and said abruptly, "David's right."

"Whoa." Worthy glared at him. "Hold on for just a damn second. You've done nothing but bitch about David since he played Rambo trying to get Sidorov's purse."

"Satchel," the sniper corrected him. "And it doesn't mean he's wrong about this. If we let Gudelj get a free pass after shooting one of ours, what does that say about us?"

Reilly raised his eyebrows. "Oh, I don't know...maybe that we want to live?"

"Wrong answer. Longwing is all about playing hardball, and how you do anything is how you do everything."

The medic looked at him with a thoughtful expression. "You get that from a motivational seminar?"

Cancer shrugged. "Fortune cookie, I think. But if I let standards slip with this, what's next?"

Worthy leaned toward the cab and said, "Jelena, you've been awfully quiet up there. Ian's burned in Belgrade, and so are you. What do you have to say about this bullshit?"

There was a moment of silence before she said, "There's a Serbian proverb about this sort of thing."

"Which is?"

She quoted, "'It is not at the table but in prison that you learn who your true friends are.'"

Reilly turned his head to her, his eyes narrowing. "I can't tell if that means you're for this dumbass plan or against it."

Jelena explained, "I would say we are a lot closer to prison than the table right now, and that you all proved yourselves as true friends when you rescued Ian and me after the uranium meet went bad. I will not repay that by staying behind. If you five are going to Belgrade, then so am I."

Reilly began laughing uproariously, shattering the solemnity of the moment for seemingly no reason whatsoever.

Worthy frowned.

"What's funny?"

"The cops," Reilly said, gasping for air amid his sudden fit of laughter. "I totally forgot those two cops were in the trunk this whole time."

41

Meiling Chen sat at her OPCEN workstation, fingers steepled, considering the reality into which she'd been unwittingly thrust.

The same could've been said for much of her home and workplace ruminations upon finding she was assigned to the Special Activities Center, and more so after learning her destination was a highly compartmentalized targeted killing program chaired by a woman with a reputation she couldn't possibly hope to thrive under, much less surpass.

Before she could process the transition, however, that responsibility had been forced upon her.

Still, she decided, things had gone better than she could have hoped in the interim—though not at first. First, they had gone from bad to worse to hopeless, before the ground team had, for reasons that had very little to do with the best of intentions from her and her newly inherited OPCEN staff, turned everything around in remarkably short order.

Now, the once-disastrous mission to Serbia stood to become the ultimate feather in her cap, provided she could seal the victory in the coming hours. She didn't intend on letting the opportunity pass her by.

Whether that came to pass remained to be seen, and at this point Chen increasingly felt that the determining factors resided well outside her ability to marshal them.

Her introspection was interrupted by the double rap of knuckles on the desk beside her, and Chen looked up to see Wes Jamieson, the bearded former Marine amputee. Duchess had told her in no uncertain terms to regard his advice with extreme caution while listening to and considering every word carefully.

The exact phrase had been more pointed, however, and Chen remembered the dead woman's phrasing now.

We've already got five children to deal with, considering our ground team. Wes is cut from the same cloth so we need to keep a shaker of salt nearby when he opens his mouth—but that doesn't mean he's always wrong.

"Yes?" she asked.

Jamieson said nothing, merely handed her a sheet of paper that, judging by its frayed edge, had been torn from a notepad.

Chen accepted the offering and scrutinized the crude block lettering, straining to decipher its contents and finding them to be a cryptic note that looked like it had been scrawled by a child.

AIR
STAFF SECTIONS IN ORDER
3-PART TRANSFER
INTEL, A.L. TRANSLATION
MED
REMAINING TEAM
HIGHLY ADVISE YOU END W/PEP TALK, GET THEIR SPIRITS UP.
IF THE GROUND TEAM THROWS YOU A CURVEBALL, <u>ROLL WITH IT</u>.

She asked, "What's this?"

Jamieson placed his hands on his hips and explained, "Just some recommendations on the way ahead, ma'am."

Her eyes narrowed.

"So you don't trust me, either. If you want to ask, then ask."

"I'm here to help, not ask about the skeletons in your closet or anyone else's. The fact is, your predecessor had some time in the saddle before being put in the hot seat. You don't."

Now Wes placed both hands on the desk, as if she was missing something obvious, before leaning toward her and speaking in a hushed tone.

"Either way, it's not about your past."

She watched him closely, trying to ferret out any indications of a hidden agenda as he continued, "Our people are in a fragile place after losing Duchess. I get that the Agency investigation is still ongoing, but Gudelj turning against our team is all the evidence anyone needs that her murder was connected to the mission. Hell, only the secondary staff could even attend the memorial service, and they knew her the least out of all of us. So now it's about confidence. You show that to these people—real or convincingly faked, it doesn't much matter so long as they believe it—and they'll be able to do their jobs that much better in the next three hours. That could make all the difference."

Chen turned her gaze to the note in her hand, then back at him.

"You think we'll run into problems with the Croats."

He all but laughed in her face.

"The Croats? Ma'am, I'm talking about Serbian interference and nothing else."

"Meaning?"

He chuckled, then composed himself and asked, "May I speak freely?"

"I'm waiting," she said, a bit more sternly than she intended.

Jamieson swallowed, considering his words. "It's hard to describe how much Croatia hates Serbia, so I'll put it to you like this: our team could have infiltrated through Croatia, gotten rolled up, and once their mission was discovered, the authorities would have driven them to the border *and* donated taxi fare to Belgrade. There's a lot that could go wrong today, all of it on the Serbian side of the border. We're not going to have any trouble from the Croats, mark my words."

He abruptly checked his watch and asked, "Anything else, ma'am?"

"No."

She was silent as he turned to leave, and once that occurred she halted him with a single word.

"Wes."

Jamieson turned to face her, his expression conveying that he anticipated having offended her not because of anything he said, but because he'd encountered that fallout when previously providing his unsolicited feedback to an Agency superior.

Chen met his eyes.

"I took some calculated risks in Pakistan, and three stars are on the wall as a result. It was because of a double agent, not any of my judgment calls. They would've died no matter who was overseeing the operation."

"Yes, ma'am."

He gave her a curt nod and departed then, leaving her to reflect on what was a particularly candid admission given that she'd avoided addressing the topic at every possible juncture. She pondered what had caused her to do so now and, to a lesser extent, whether she believed who was to blame.

Then she took the note in her hand and waited for her staff to go silent in anticipation of the coming time hack. The central OPCEN screen displayed a cover slide for the presentation complete with a date-time group that was about to elapse.

When the final conversations ended thirty seconds ahead of schedule, she announced, "Let's get started."

The slide presentation flipped to a map displaying everything from the Balkans to America's eastern seaboard, with a leapfrogging line denoting a two-part flight path.

Brian Sutherland turned in his seat and began, "Ma'am, the Gulfstream V is wheels-down at Osijek, undergoing refuel and maintenance at this time. Currently no mechanical issues that would preclude the return flight to Ramstein Airbase, Germany, where the team's casualties will be transferred to the military hospital in Landstuhl until the doctors clear them. Everyone else will remain at the airbase during refuel and crew swap, after which they'll make the final leg to Joint Base Andrews in Maryland."

When he went silent, she said, "JI?"

The next slide showed two header titles, *US* and *HOST NATION*, above rows of acronyms and corresponding numbers.

Diane Goldhammer, the OPCEN's personnel officer, narrated the display.

"All mission-essential staff are accounted for at Osijek, currently cross-loading their equipment from the Gulfstream into the Croat vehicles procured by our advance party. That's seven medical staff and five from the Directorate of Analysis, assisted by the eight paramilitary operations officers who arrived yesterday. Total count for US support personnel is twenty, plus 31 Croat primary liaisons: four from the Security and Intelligence Agency, a 22-man contingent from the 4th Special Operations Company, and five Croatian police managing the escort of approximately two dozen officers."

Chen nodded as the slide flipped again. "J2."

Andolin Lucios said, "Ma'am, at this time there are no police APBs on either the makes and models or the license plates for the two vehicles our ground team will use to reach the border. However, investigations continue in the vicinity of Ponikve Airport and the surrounding area, as well as at Rača Monastery. Both provide cause for concern—due to the ongoing canvass of civilian witnesses, it's possible that some detail will emerge that could heighten police recognition of the ground team on the basis of individual descriptions. The risk to force remains high until they reach the border crossing point. We will continue to monitor all police frequencies in support of the exfil, but have extremely limited access to Serbian Security Intelligence Agency channels."

"And the mafia?" she asked.

"There is currently a half-million USD bounty for anyone involved in the PC-24 shootdown and subsequent kinetic activity, but no further details have been provided. However, I assess that any conclusions from the police investigation will proliferate into criminal organizations with close to zero delay."

That was, Chen thought, a rather polite way of pointing out the rampant state corruption. Lucios was nothing if not tactful.

"Next up, J3."

The display screen transitioned to a map showing a route starting at the team's current location, then threading its way north along the border with Bosnia and Herzegovina before completing an eastward semicircle and finally crossing into Croatia.

Jamieson narrated, "From the safehouse in Bajina Bašta, they're looking at a three-and-a-half-hour drive: Route 170 to Valjevo, 27 to Nepričava, then A2 all the way to Jakovo. A2 merging to E-70, and they ride that all the way to Tovarnik."

No surprises there—so long as they weren't stopped by police along the way, the team would have to do little more than blend in with civilian traffic.

She said, "Talk me through procedures at the border crossing."

"Yes, ma'am," Jamieson said, and the slide changed to a satellite view of an oval-shaped swath of pavement where the two lanes turned into seven, each of them passing through a concrete structure. To either side was semi parking, much of it occupied at the time the picture was taken, while a row of three rectangular buildings were lined up end to end and connected by an adjoining road.

He continued, "The border agents will be tracking our arrival updates, their actions informed by two National Intelligence Service members along with three uniformed officers from the Croatian Police for jurisdiction purposes. The remainder of the uniformed police escort will stay behind so they don't escalate the profile of our transfer within eyesight of Serbian soil. Once our two team vehicles arrive, they'll be flagged into a closed inspection lane, then escorted to the headquarters building where our people will be waiting. After that, it's a three-part show."

"So I've heard. Step one, intelligence. Andolin?"

Lucios cleared his throat.

"The lead data analysis officer will take control of Sidorov's bag with all contents, and carry it to the van containing the rest of her team to begin duplication and exploitation immediately. From that point on, intelligence sharing will be..."

He paused, then concluded with a single word.

"...synchronistic."

Now Jamieson's note was starting to make sense, Chen thought, and she asked, "Translation?"

Jamieson responded before Lucios could, cutting off the intelligence officer as he draped an arm over the back of his chair in a half-turn to face her.

"DOA's pound of flesh for their support, ma'am. We will be privy to anything and everything they send as a result, but so will the Directorate of Analysis and any of their regional and transnational groups, plus support units, at their discretion. Basically any and all decision-making on what to do with that intel will fly so far above our span of control that we couldn't spot it with a telescope, right up until the seventh floor needs us to take someone out. Then, we won't be able to react fast enough for their liking."

That too, Chen considered, made a lot of sense given the context.

According to the ground team, Sidorov's bag contained a staggering amount of data storage capacity: forty flash drives totaling eighty terabytes, four cell phones, one satellite phone, and not one but two laptop computers—which, as she'd already been informed, likely meant that one was used for transmitting coded information, while the other had all connectivity disabled and would therefore contain the real "red meat" of anything Sidorov had been running.

"Duly noted," she said to Jamieson, who quickly continued.

"Part two is the medical component. David, Ian, and Reilly will load into the trailer of an 18-wheeler where the medical team will be set up. Reilly is accompanying them because the docs want him present for patient handoff and any questions about their previous treatment, but his medical authority ends the minute they set foot in the trailer."

"As it should. Next."

"Third and final component is equipment and uninjured personnel. Our senior paramilitary operations officer will take over the chain of custody for all serial-numbered equipment, which means a full inventory and a hand receipt signoff between him and Cancer. Once that's complete, Ground Branch will be responsible for driving the team vehicles while Cancer, Worthy, and Jelena load into the Range Rover to begin their debrief process. That brings us to the final leg."

She gave him the nod to proceed, and the next map on the display was highlighted with the team's local route to their destination.

"All told," he said, "it's a 45-minute drive to Osijek broken up into two parts. Each Agency-operated vehicle will move with an unmarked escort containing plainclothes operators from Croatia's 4th Special Operations Company, and the departures will be staggered by five to ten minutes.

Order of movement is the Range Rover with uninjured personnel, then the DOA van, followed by the original team vehicles with the military hardware, and finally the medical truck.

"The uniformed contingent of Croatian police will be standing by in Vinkovci, at which time all vehicles will consolidate into a convoy for a straight shot to Osijek Airport, where they'll use the service road to reach the tarmac. Croat police and operators will form a perimeter while the team and their equipment are loaded onto the Gulfstream, along with the med team and DOA personnel. They'll have priority clearance for takeoff. Our paramilitary officers will remain at the airport to liaise in case the plane has to turn around, then fly commercial out of Zagreb tomorrow morning. Pending your questions, all support elements will be in place well within the next two hours, which means we are all systems go for the ground team to start moving."

His words ended in silence, and it hung heavily over the OPCEN now more than ever.

Over the past six days, there had been a notable shift in the bearings of almost everyone in the staff. A far more bleak outlook pervaded the expressions of everyone present, and she knew beyond any reasonable doubt that it had nothing to do with the many setbacks to the ground team's progress.

She was left to consider the penultimate line in the scrap of paper before her—Jamieson had recommended she end the brief with a "pep talk," and despite the fact that she didn't doubt the benefit of doing so, Chen had no idea what to say.

Maybe that was why Jamieson had delayed his delivery of the note until the seconds before the brief started, she thought—so she wouldn't have time to prepare her words. Whether that was out of a desire for her to come across as genuine or to see what she was really made of, Chen couldn't begin to imagine. She wasn't prone to sentimentality, but perhaps it wasn't required of her at a time like this.

Rising from her desk, she addressed her staff.

"This has been an extremely difficult time for everyone here, with the complications to our mission being the least of it. Regardless of what happens in the coming hours, I want you all to know that I couldn't be more impressed by your conduct and professionalism, particularly in the wake of losing Duchess as suddenly and tragically as we did. I didn't know her for long, but long enough to know that she is and will remain forever irreplaceable."

After a brief pause, she concluded, "I'm greenlighting the team's movement to Croatia. Let's get this across the finish line for her as much as our ground team in harm's way."

There was little in the way of visual response, with the assembled staff holding themselves almost exactly as they had before her brief speech—all but Wes Jamieson, who flashed the most subtle of nods, as if to indicate that nothing more needed to be said.

Taking her seat, Chen eyed the satellite hand mic resting atop her desk. Only one thing remained.

Lifting the mic, she transmitted, "Suicide Actual, Raptor Nine One."

The response was almost instantaneous. "*This is Suicide Actual, send it.*"

"Be advised, all support elements are on the ground and moving to their final positions to receive your team. Plane is standing by, and the Croatian authorities are lending their full support."

Drawing a final breath, she solemnly concluded, "You are cleared to begin movement to the border crossing at Tovarnik."

She exhaled with a grave sense of finality, knowing beyond all doubt that this was the most momentous order she'd given in her Agency career. After all the reversals of fortune, she stood poised to drive home the team's success on the ground by delivering Sidorov's bag to the people who could exploit its full intelligence value and, more importantly, bring all five team members home alive along with the female officer from Affinity Gold who had sacrificed so much to support their efforts in Serbia.

And as if to make light of those incontrovertible facts, David Rivers responded with a tone of lighthearted apology.

"*Copy all,*" he began. "*Be advised, we've hit a bit of a delay here.*"

She blinked quickly, then keyed her mic and said, "Explain."

There was a pause before his next transmission, a message that she strained to comprehend despite its clarity. The possibility of a routine delay seemed almost incomprehensible after several increasingly catastrophic reversals in the team's fortune over the past few days, and it was only then that she recalled the final line of Jamieson's note—he'd warned her of a "curveball," after all, and here it was.

David said, "*You're not going to believe this, but...car troubles, of all things. The minivan caught a nail, and our spare's flat. We're sourcing a replacement tire now, should be on the road within the hour.*"

42

Reilly carried his heavy plastic shopping bag as he moved quickly across the sidewalk, looking left to behold Sava River, its tranquil waters glistening as the sun rose over Belgrade.

The view would have been more enjoyable if it were about twenty degrees warmer out—snow had yet to fall in the lowlands of Serbia, but right now it felt every bit as cold as the western mountains. His coat served to ward off the chill at least somewhat, and if the few staggering drunks he'd passed on the way could handle the temperature, then so could he. Besides, Reilly would soon be too distracted to worry about the cold, and in the best possible way.

He proceeded into a largely empty parking lot at the riverside, identifying a sleek black Mercedes S-Class sedan covered in frost.

Reilly leaned against the car's front quarter panel, setting his bag on the hood and hastily pulling it open before reaching in to retrieve his prize.

There was nothing wrong, he thought, with the American hamburger industry.

He'd come up through the ranks of the classic fast food chains like every other kid, before his teenage years had brought about the deep sense of awakening that life surely held something *more*. After that realization, his culinary journeys had taken him to the dive bars and hole-in-the-wall establishments famed for pushing the envelope of what was possible within the free-wheeling limits of the art. In the process, he uncovered three-quarter-pound patties barely contained by their grease-soaked buns, and a range of toppings unknown to him in his youth: banana peppers, eggs over easy, fried battered onion straws, candied jalapeños, lump crabmeat. Reilly tried them all in the search to find himself.

Like any true seeker, he'd pushed the limits of his former life and been rewarded with subtle cues from the universe. The first time he'd visited a famed establishment to sample "The Thurmanator," he'd barely taken his first bite—which, to his delight, fully justified the hype—when the man on the barstool next to him seized up with a heart attack and fell to the floor.

Reilly had sprung into full medic mode, but it wasn't necessary.

Instead the bartender nonchalantly reached for the phone to dial 911 while the remaining staff calmly and politely ushered excess customers out to whittle their total count to something that more closely approximated the maximum permitted by local fire code. It was quite clear to Reilly that the small matter of a heart attack was not without precedent in that fine establishment, whose employees had, like any true professionals, risen to the occasion with courage and clarity.

He'd found his people.

But the *pljeskavica* that he took into his hands now was another matter altogether—no hamburger, that was for sure, and there remained an air of mystery about the dinner-plate-sized meat patty folded in half and sandwiched between a brioche bun.

Lifting the sandwich to his face, he inhaled the aromas and, not permitting himself to overthink the process, took his first bite.

It had the traditional mayonnaise, mustard, and onions, but so too was it crowned with spicy cream cheese, pickled cabbage, and chili, the entourage effect of their overlapping flavors on par with the best niche burger combinations he'd ever encountered in his travels.

Still, it was the meat itself that elevated this delicacy to the stratosphere of bliss: while the American burger industry considered grass-fed beef progressive, the Balkans had mixed beef, pork, and lamb into one harmoniously spiced patty, and said to hell with whatever the animals ate beforehand.

A cool breeze washed over him and Reilly tittered with delight, swallowing as he eyed the sandwich to strategize the angle of his next bite.

"Hey!" a Serbian voice shouted. "Get the *fuck* off of my car!"

Reilly looked up, at first seeing only the strip club across the street and then, at the crosswalk, three figures fast approaching with one in the lead.

It was, predictably, Branimir Gudelj, moving at an enraged pace as his pair of bodyguards hustled to keep up.

Gudelj had addressed Reilly in English, apparently having assumed him to be a drunk Western tourist wandering the streets after pulling a bender in a city famous for its nightlife. And truth be told, Reilly thought, he *was* drunk—drunk on flavor.

He took another bite of his *pljeskavica*, chewing faster now with the knowledge that his culinary romance was coming to an end.

The second mouthful was even better than the first, and he followed it with a third to stuff his mouth with as much goodness as he could as Gudelj closed the remaining distance. He was screaming like a madman and had every intention of beating Reilly to a pulp while his bodyguards compensated for the very considerable difference in size. The fact that both security men had steel-toe boots made him think they were no strangers to kicking the living shit out of an unarmed opponent, and if that failed, he was looking at getting pistol-whipped or stabbed, perhaps not in that order.

The men were a few meters away now, and the first physical contact was imminent.

Reilly used his remaining seconds to swallow, set his sandwich on the Mercedes' hood, and lick his fingertips.

Then, with blinding speed, he leapt off the car to tackle Gudelj.

The last thing he heard was the metallic whoosh of a minivan door sliding open beside him before his shoulder speared into Gudelj's abdomen and they fell together to the ground. Reilly succeeded in slamming the man into the pavement, the vacuous exhale of the wind being knocked out of his lungs soon eclipsed by the pattering whiffs of subsonic gunfire that ended in the twin thuds of his bodyguards falling dead behind him.

By the time Reilly lifted his head, Worthy and Cancer were already descending on him.

He rolled off Gudelj, letting his teammates take care of flex-cuffing their target with the assistance of a taser as he clambered to his feet, brushing off his jeans and looking around for potential bystanders only to find that there were none—the strip club had closed about twenty minutes ago, and several hours remained before this street was teeming with civilian traffic. Reilly had hoped to have good use for the fake police badge he carried in his pocket, but it appeared that half-measure at proving legitimacy would go unused.

"Let's go," Cancer hissed, and the medic looked left to see him and Worthy shoving a restrained Branimir Gudelj head-first into the passenger seat of an Opel Vivaro.

Reilly made a move to follow, then stopped abruptly and whirled to recover the remainder of his *pljeskavica* from the hood of the car before darting into the minivan and sliding the door shut with his free hand.

Ian pulled the vehicle forward and onto the street, and Reilly permitted himself another bite of the sandwich before setting it in his lap. As he chewed, he retrieved the first of two needle syringes he'd pre-positioned in the seatback pocket before him.

43

Cancer sat atop a bag of team equipment in the back of the minivan, checking his watch impatiently.

The team had only stopped once since leaving Belgrade close to an hour ago, and only to conduct the quick personnel shuffle required to transition from their snatch configuration into one more suited for their border run: Jelena piloting the lead vehicle with Worthy riding shotgun, and everyone else piled into the minivan.

That latter group consisted of five people; however, Cancer thought with relish, the count was going to be lighter by one well before they reached Croatia.

Branimir Gudelj was slumped in the back, his breaths coming shallowly but steadily. Cancer had propped him into a sitting position against the far side, fearful that his lungs could otherwise become obstructed and give him a far more merciful end than he deserved.

Then again, judging by the peaceful expression on the gangster's face, so might the medication.

He yelled up at the passenger seat, "Can you give this motherfucker something to bring him back?"

"Unnecessary," Reilly assured him.

"Yeah?" Cancer asked, checking his watch again. "I think you gave him too much Vitamin K."

"Do I tell you how to smoke?" the medic asked.

"No."

"Then don't lecture me on dosing ketamine. We've still got time. He'll wake up before we get there."

David replied from the middle row, where a single seat back remained upright to support him as he propped up his broken leg.

"If he does," the team leader commented, "it's going to be a rough transition: soaring through the cosmos in a psychedelic lightshow one minute, then staring at Cancer and realizing he's going to die the next."

"Good," Ian called back from the driver's seat, where he remained focused on staying within the speed limit as they traversed the E-70 Highway westward. "Because my stomach is killing me."

Cancer couldn't help himself.

"Sounds like Reilly doesn't know shit about dosing after all."

Reilly shot back, "It's classic drug-seeking behavior. If I gave him any more Percocet, he'd have run us off the road by now."

Gudelj suddenly gasped, his eyelids fluttering open in a vacant expression.

"Hey," Cancer said, "look who's up—just in time."

"Told you," Reilly said.

Gudelj blinked slowly, trying to comprehend why he was tied up in the back of a minivan stuffed with equipment bags, along with a few non-standard items the team had procured on short notice: orange road cones and hardhats, high-visibility safety vests in a startlingly bright neon yellow and lined with reflective strips.

Then he looked at the 45-pound bumper plate beside him before finally meeting Cancer's eyes as the sniper's face creased into a grin.

"How was your last night on earth?"

Gudelj shifted uneasily, but he spoke with total confidence.

"What makes you think it will be my last night?"

"Call it a very strong hunch," Cancer said.

The restrained Serbian all but rolled his eyes, and he shook his head with resigned authority as he replied, "Drop the act, please, and save your breath. If you simply wanted me dead, you would have gunned me down in the parking lot along with my men."

"Is that a fact?"

"It is," Gudelj went on. "Your bosses at the CIA would never permit you to risk a capture operation unless you truly needed me alive."

"You're right about that. If they knew what we were doing right now, we'd be in deep shit. Which is why they have no idea about this little snatch-and-grab, and they never will."

Reilly called out, "Five minutes."

Cancer grabbed a pair of hardhats and safety vests for Ian and Reilly, and handed them to David before passing up the stack of road cones.

Gudelj was undeterred.

"You are trying to frighten me," he began, "into becoming a double agent, but I am man enough to admit when I have been bested. So, well done. I have everything you want: the workings of Janjicari and the New Zemun, the key players in my government who make the machine run smoothly. The only matter to be discussed is wearing a wire, because I can assure you I will be screened before meeting with anyone of consequence. That and, of course, my compensation."

By then Cancer was slipping into the third safety vest, pressing the Velcro attachments together on the front.

He donned a hardhat and replied, "Well, I hate to tell you this, but we don't really give a shit about the mafia or your government."

"I do not believe you."

"Yeah," Cancer conceded. "I figured. Maybe our driver can convince you."

Ian called back, "Mr. Jon Cutler, at your service."

The sound of Ian's voice caused an instantaneous shift in Gudelj's expression, from steadfastness to uncertainty to outright fear.

Then he said, "You—you want to know why we ambushed you...at the uranium exchange—"

"Nope," Cancer cut him off, glancing out the windows to see that the van was now following an onramp that veered into a counterclockwise semicircle to the south. "Not really. You don't even know why, just that

Sidorov gave you the order to do it. So you played along, like the good little soldier you are."

Gudelj swallowed hard.

"The uranium," he blurted, "I can get you the stockpile."

"We're not the repo team. Another office is already running down leads based on the calls you made, so you won't be of much help from here on out."

Gudelj stammered, "Then why did you...why risk exposing yourself to capture me alive?"

After considering the question for a moment, Cancer replied, "That's a tricky one. I suppose you could boil it down to revenge, but it's a bit more complicated than that. You see, our deal is running around the world as a small team, and picking fights with some pretty horrific people. They bring their friends and, well, you get the idea. We're always outnumbered and usually escape certain death by the skin of our teeth."

Gudelj cocked his head, and David preempted the confusion by stating, "Idiom."

"Right," Cancer allowed, bracing himself for the tight turn of a traffic circle ahead as he clarified, "we barely escape, is what I mean. Frankly it's a miracle none of us have gotten schwaked yet."

Gudelj blinked quickly, and Cancer sighed in frustration.

"Killed, okay? At this point a few of us have gotten wounded in the process. But to date no one has ever shot a member of our team and lived to tell about it—until you came along, that is."

Reilly added, "We didn't really have a precedent until our fearless and dumbass leader set one, which was—"

David cut him off.

"You put a bullet into one of ours, and you live long enough to regret it. But no further."

With a mournful shrug, Cancer continued.

"That's where I let him down. He asked me to come up with some particularly gruesome way to kill you, and frankly I felt more than up to the task. Ended up having a few obstacles, though. One, we didn't have time to roll you up without lying our asses off to headquarters. Two, we can't delay any further since we need to make a straight shot out of Serbia whether we want to or not. And torturing you right up until the border has its merits, but bluffing our way through a police checkpoint isn't one of them."

The van pulled to a stop, and Ian initiated the emergency flashers before dismounting along with Reilly.

"So?" Gudelj asked.

"So," Cancer admitted, "I had no choice but to concede defeat. You're not going to be tortured at all."

"No?"

"No. What I have in mind is pretty convenient—just a small detour from the highway that requires only a minute of our time."

"And what is that?"

Gudelj jumped slightly as the rear tailgate opened from the outside, revealing a string of traffic cones blocking the median behind him and two lanes of empty road stretching in a perfectly straight line, with Ian posted on lookout.

Cancer retrieved a length of chain, routing one end under Gudelj's left armpit, around his back and over the opposite shoulder, then around his neck and down before yanking out his legs to pull him flat on his back as he replied.

"A fuckin' bridge."

The Serbian mobster began screaming and thrashing, but it was too late. Reilly held him down as Cancer threaded the ends of the chain through the barbell hole in the 45-pound plate before securing it tight to his chest with an oversized padlock through the links.

Then Cancer and Reilly wrestled him out of the van; with his hands and feet bound, there was little else he could do, no way to overcome the strength of two men working in tandem to drag him toward the side rail that was fast approaching.

He continued to resist his fate nonetheless, twisting violently as they shoved his stomach against the rail and Cancer said, "One, two, *three*."

They flipped him over the side in unison, where he completed the first of two front flips as he pirouetted downward to the Sava River, whose calmly rippling surface erupted with a geyser of water as Branimir Gudelj made impact and, with a torrent of bubbles, began to sink.

Cancer brushed his palms together in recognition of a job well done, glancing both ways down the still-empty bridge before meeting Reilly's eyes.

"Well," he said, "that was easy."

Then, dipping a hand into his pocket to fish out his pack of cigarettes, he completed his statement with four simple words.

"Let's go to Croatia."

LETHAL HORIZON:
SHADOW STRIKE #7

For David Rivers and his team, the mission was supposed to be simple—retrieve a defecting militia leader and deliver him to CIA interrogators.

But nothing is simple in Yemen, where vast swaths of terrain are controlled by Houthi and Al Qaeda fighters. When they locate the asset, the team discovers why he has been deemed critical to their intelligence effort.

The defector has direct knowledge of the team's top target: Erik Weisz, the shadowy figurehead behind the most catastrophic terrorist attacks since 9/11. And as it turns out, Weisz is currently in Yemen, traveling through Houthi territory with heavy security.

As David's crew prepares for a follow-on operation to remove Weisz once and for all, they discover a web of contradictions. A sudden order to stand down leaves the unit questioning the motives of their CIA handler. With suspicious leadership and a deadly conspiracy looming, the team boards a military aircraft to infiltrate the most dangerous corners of a war-torn desert.

David is convinced it will be their bloodiest mission yet—and within hours of being inserted deep into the badlands of Yemen, he and his team realize they are pawns in an exceedingly deadly game of chess.

ABOUT THE AUTHOR

Jason Kasper is the USA Today bestselling author of the Spider Heist, American Mercenary, and Shadow Strike thriller series. Before his writing career he served in the US Army, beginning as a Ranger private and ending as a Green Beret captain. Jason is a West Point graduate and a veteran of the Afghanistan and Iraq wars, and was an avid ultramarathon runner, skydiver, and BASE jumper, all of which inspire his fiction.

Sign up for Jason Kasper's reader list at
severnriverbooks.com/authors/jason-kasper

jasonkasper@severnriverbooks.com